# MASTERMINDS AT WORK

▼

From his coverall pocket Jerry took a crumpled piece of paper and smoothed it out on the tabletop. "What these things are," Jerry said, "is copies of an old statue in South America, from before Columbus. It's called the Dancing Aztec Priest. But here's the thing: The original is made of solid gold, and it has emeralds for eyes, and it's worth a million dollars."

Everybody was taken aback. Frank said, "A million dollars? For a statue taking a crap?"

"That's the story."

"A million dollars," Mel said. "Split four ways."

"A quarter each," Floyd said. He had a far-away look in his eyes. "You know what a quarter of a million dollars is?" he asked them, and answered it himself: "It's a quarter of a million dollars!"

▲

# DANCING AZTECS

# DANCING AZTECS

## DONALD E. WESTLAKE

**THE MYSTERIOUS PRESS**

New York • London • Tokyo • Sweden

MYSTERIOUS PRESS EDITION

This Mysterious Press Edition is published by arrangement
with the author.

Cover illustration by Sonja Lamut and Nenad Jakesevic

Mysterious Press Books are published in association with
Warner Books, Inc.
666 Fifth Avenue
New York, N.Y. 10103

A Warner Communications Company

Printed in the United States of America

First Mysterious Press Printing: August, 1989

10  9  8  7  6  5  4  3  2  1

THIS IS FOR
*Abby, who gave me the harp,*
*Cindy, who gave me the satin lining,*
*Pete, who gave me Flattery,*
*Herb, who gave me the grain of sand,*
*and Aunt Peg, who wanted five books*
HERE THEY ARE

The Hustle is a New York dance.
*The New Yorker,*
*"Talk of the Town,"*
*May 5, 1975*

# THE CAST (most of them) IN ORDER OF APPEARANCE (approximately):

JERRY MANELLI—*city boy, on the move*
HIRAM—*a guard*
MEL BERNSTEIN—*an intellectual, but OK*
ANGELA MANELLI BERNSTEIN—*wife, sister and virago*
MYRNA—*very very*
JOSE CARACHA—*sculptor*
EDWARDO BRAZZO—*functionary, with necktie*
PEDRO NINNI—*patsy*
HECTOR OVELLA—*walk-on*
MRS. MANELLI—*mother and scientist*
FRANK MCCANN—*Irishman*
FLOYD MCCANN—*the Irishman's brother*
TERESA MANELLI MCCANN—*wife and sister*
BOBBI HARWOOD—*ex-wife, on the go*
CHUCK "PROFESSOR CHARLES S." HARWOOD—*pothead*
OSCAR RUSSELL GREEN—*successful activist and unsuccessful drunk*
VICTOR KRASSMEIER—*a la financier*
AUGUST CORELLA—*Jersey thug*
WALLY HINTZLEBEL—*swimming pool salesman and son*
JENNY KENDALL—*a nice girl*
EDDIE ROSS—*her nice boy*
RALPH—*chauffeur*
EARL—*henchman*
RALPHI DURANT—*indispensable receptionist*
ETHELRED MARX—*visitor from another planet*
MRS. HINTZLEBEL—*the world's best Mom*
BUD BEEMISS—*PR man with a heart of gold*
DAVID FAYLEY—*a nice boy*
KENNY SPANG—*his nice boy*

TROOPER LUKE SNELL—*fantasist*
MADGE KRAUSSE—*friend with a sofa*
BARBARA McCANN—*rotten bridge player*
KATHLEEN McCANN PODENSKI—*a fourth*
LEROY PINKHAM—*punk*
MARSHALL "BUHBUH" THUMBLE—*another punk*
F. XAVIER WHITE—*Harlem's Premier mortician*
MALEFICENT WHITE—*fat mama*
JEREMIAH "BAD DEATH" JONESBURG—*The Man*
FELICITY TOWER—*unexploded bomb*
MANDY ADDLEFORD—*the colored lady*
WYLIE CHESHIRE—*mean mother*
MR. MANELLI—*man with a hobby*
LUPE NAZ—*a yam-fed Descalzan beauty*
BEN COHEN—*Sound sailor*
THEODORA NICE—*nice*
HUGH VAN DINAST—*patrician and enthusiast*
MRS. DOROTHY MOORWOOD—*philanthropist*
GINNY DEMERETTA—*cameo appearance*
A HAWK—*innocent bystander*
and
SIXTEEN DANCING AZTEC PRIESTS—*all together now . . .*

# THE
# FIRST PART
# OF THE
# SEARCH

Everybody in New York City is looking for something. Men are looking for women and women are looking for men. Down at the Trucks, men are looking for men, while at Barbara's and at the Lib women are looking for women. Lawyers' wives in front of Lord & Taylor are looking for taxis, and lawyers' wives' husbands down on Pine Street are looking for loopholes. The hookers in front of the Americana Hotel are looking for johns, and the kids opening cab doors in front of the Port Authority bus terminal are looking for tips. So are the riders on the Aqueduct Special. So are the cabbies, the bellboys, the waiters, and the undercover narcs.

Recent graduates are looking for a job. Men in ties are looking for a better position. Men in suede jackets are looking for an opportunity. Women in severe tailoring are looking for an equal opportunity. Men in alligator belts are looking for a gimmick. Men with frayed cuffs are looking for ten bucks till Wednesday. Union men are looking for increased benefits and a nice detached house in New Hyde Park.

Nice boys from Fordham are looking for girls. Rock groups from St. Louis staying at the Chelsea are looking for gash. Male and female junior executives along Third Avenue are looking for a meaningful relationship. Bronx blacks in Washington Square Park are looking for white meat. Short-sleeved beer drinkers in Columbus Avenue bars are looking for trouble.

The Parks Department is looking for trees to cut down and turn into firewood for local politicians. Residents of the neighborhood are looking for politicians who will stop the Parks Department from cutting down all those trees. Fat chance.

Bowery bums with filthy rags in their hands are looking for a windshield to wipe. Cars with Florida plates are looking for the West Side Highway. Cars with MD plates are looking for a parking space. United Parcel trucks are looking for a double-parking space. Junkies are looking for cars with NYP plates because reporters sometimes leave cameras in their glove compartments.

The girls in the massage parlors are looking for a twenty-five dollar swell. The Wednesday afternoon ladies from the suburbs are looking for a nice time at the matinée, followed by cottage cheese on a lettuce leaf. Tourists are looking for a place to sit down, con men are looking for tourists, cops are looking for con men.

Old men on benches along upper Broadway are looking for a little sun. Old ladies in Army boots are looking for God-knows-what in trash cans on Sixth Avenue. Couples strolling hand-in-hand in Central Park are looking for a nature experience. Teen-age gangs from Harlem are in Central Park looking for bicycles.

Picketing welfare mothers on West 55th Street are looking for Rockefeller, but he's never there.

At the UN they're looking for simultaneous translation. On Broadway they're looking for a hit. At Black Rock they're looking for the trend. At Lincoln Center they're looking for a respectable meaning.

Almost everybody in the subway is looking for a fight. Almost everybody on the 5:09 to Speonk is looking for the bar car. Almost everybody on the East Side is looking for status, while almost everybody on the West Side is looking for a diet that really works.

Everybody in New York is looking for something. Every once in a while, somebody finds it.


# IN THE BEGINNING . . .

Jerry Manelli was looking for a box marked *A*.

It was a pleasant sunny Monday afternoon in June, and the big metal birds out at Kennedy Airport roared and soared, while Jerry drove his white Ford Econoline van through the cargo areas toward Southern Air Freight. On the shiny white sides of the van blue letters read *Inter-Air Forwarding*, with an address and phone number in Queens. White letters *I-A* were on his blue baseball cap, and his name in script—*Jerry* —was sewn on the left breast pocket of his white coveralls. He steered the van around mountains of mail sacks, stacks of cartons, cartfuls of luggage, and he whistled as he worked.

Approaching Southern Air Freight's terminal, where the plane from Caracas had just been off-loaded, Jerry saw that a brand new gray-uniformed security guard was on duty here. A stranger. Jerry took one look at him, put on his aviator's sunglasses, and reached for his clipboard. Braking to a stop on the tarmac, he hopped out with the clipboard in his hand and the sunglasses sparkling in the light, and gave the new guard a big cheerful grin, saying, "Hi. You're new around here."

The guard, a tall black man with a bushy mustache and a suspicious manner, said, "They transferred me out from the city. They been too much pilferin' out here."

"Jerry's the name," Jerry said, still grinning, and he jabbed a thumb at the name sewn over his heart.

"Hiram," said the guard. "You work around here, huh?"

"Internal cargo shipment."

The guard nodded as though he understood something. "Ah," he said.

Jerry consulted his clipboard. "Got a pickup here. One wooden box from Caracas, Venezuela."

"We got a whole mountain of wooden boxes," the guard said, "just come in from South America somewheres."

"Lead me to them," Jerry said.

Last night's phone call had come in just after the eleven o'clock news. The voice had been heavily accented, very Spanish sounding: "There weel be five wooden boxes. You want thee one marked with an *A*. You onnerstand?"

"Sure," Jerry had said. "Marked with an *A*."

"You weel make deleevery at midnight, in thee Port Authority bus terminal parking garage, top level, southeast corner. You onnerstand?"

"Port of Authority? You mean in Manhattan?"

"Ees something wrong?"

Jerry had shrugged, saying, "No, that's okay. Port of Authority bus terminal parking garage, top level, southeast corner, midnight."

"Weeth a box marked *A*."

"*A*. Gotcha."

So here he was, the next afternoon, following the new guard Hiram through the piles of cargo to a stack of five wooden crates, each about the size of a case of whiskey, and all addressed to:

> *Bud Beemiss Enterprises*
> *29 West 45th St.*
> *New York, N.Y.*
> *USA*

Each crate was marked with a stenciled letter, *A* through *E*, a different letter on each crate. The one marked *A* was at the bottom of the stack.

"Wouldn't you know it," Jerry said, and kicked the right crate. "That's the one I want."

"Always works that way," the guard agreed.

Jerry put his clipboard on another pile of crates. "Give me a hand, will you, Hiram?"

Hiram gave him a hand, and pretty soon the box marked A—which fortunately wasn't very heavy—was stowed in the back of the van with the sack of registered mail from Northwest Orient (cash, stocks, maybe jewelry) and the package from Seaboard addressed to a dental supply house (possibly gold), and Jerry was saying, "Thanks a lot. See you around, Hiram."

"Have a nice day," Hiram said.

## PRIOR TO WHICH . . .

Until he'd come up with the idea of Inter-Air Forwarding, Jerry Manelli had mostly just lived along from hustle to hustle, starting when he'd dropped out of high school at sixteen and went to work for the numbers people, running their paper. When he saw how profitable that game was, he started carrying some of the action himself. That is, he'd only turn in three quarters of the tickets and cash he'd received, keeping the rest for his own benefit. If any of those players ever hit he'd have to pay their winnings out of his own pocket, but that never happened once. A very nice hustle.

But a little scary, considering who his bosses were. So after a while he quit that and lived on the profits until it was time to hustle again. Then he connected for a while with his brother-in-law Frank McCann's brother Floyd, who was with a construction crew, and the two of them spent a couple evenings a week loading a Hertz truck with concrete blocks or brick from the work site and driving them out to Patchogue on Long Island, where some Irishman friend of Floyd's named Flattery had his own construction company and liked to buy his materials at a discount. But after Floyd nearly got caught one time, Jerry retired again, and when no new hustle came along he went to work in a body shop where the boss was hustling the customers so hard there wasn't any leverage left over.

Shortly after that, Jerry hooked up with an old friend

from high school named Danny Kolabian who had just been fired by a vending machine company, and the two of them put together a very nice hustle, except it only worked a couple weeks. What they did, on Monday morning Jerry and Danny went to the vending machine company's warehouse, using a key the company didn't know Danny had, and they put one of the jukeboxes from the warehouse into a company truck. They crossed the wires to start the truck, and then drove to fourteen different bars that were customers of the vending machine company, and in every bar they said, "We're here to switch the jukeboxes." The Monday bartenders didn't know any different, so at each place Jerry and Danny carried in the machine from the truck, switched it with the jukebox already in the bar, and on the way to the next place they'd rifle the machine's coin box for the weekend's take. They made eleven hundred dollars the first Monday and thirteen fifty the second Monday, but the third Monday four guys were waiting in the vending machine warehouse with autographed baseball bats. Jerry had good legs and good wind so he got away, but Danny was hit twice and recognized once and had to leave town, and was now either somewhere on the West Coast or buried over in New Jersey.

For the next several years life went on like that, from hustle to hustle, until two years ago, when Inter-Air Forwarding had come along, since when Jerry had become almost respectable, a successful private businessman with his own truck and his own route.

The idea had been one of those sudden strokes of genius. Jerry's sister Angela and her husband Mel Bernstein had taken a vacation in Israel, and it was Jerry who'd picked them up at Kennedy on their return to the States. But there was a delay because of a bomb scare—the Arabs again playing the fool—and Jerry had to hang around the airport for an hour and forty-five minutes. Mostly he just sat near the big windows and stared out at the airplanes, until he began to notice all the little trucks. Blue trucks, red trucks, yellow trucks, white trucks, zipping and zapping among the planes, skittering around like ants dressed up for Mardi Gras. Some had airline names on their sides, but others had obscure company names or no name at all. Now and again, one of the trucks would stop near a pile of boxes or canvas mailbags, and the driver would hop out and toss a couple things into his truck, and off he'd go again. Jerry watched that several times, and gradually his boredom changed to interest. "Hmmmmmm," he said, and leaned forward in his seat.

When Mel and Angela finally got off their plane and through Customs—Angela had stashed her new gold bracelet where Customs was very unlikely to find it—Jerry tried to talk to Mel. "Comere," he said. "Take a look at all those trucks."

"I've got a headache, Jerry," Mel said. "I've been on that plane a month."

"Just take a minute," Jerry told him. "Look at those trucks."

Mel said, "You've heard of jet lag?"

Angela said, "Jerry, talk to us tomorrow, okay?"

But Jerry had been sitting there alone a long time. "What if," he said, "what if you had one of those trucks yourself? You go from terminal to terminal, you pick up whatever looks good."

Angela wasn't listening. "Come on, Jerry," she said.

But Mel had listened, even with his jet lag, and now he frowned at Jerry, frowned out at the trucks, thought it over, and then shook his head. "No," he said.

"No? Why not?"

"It isn't that easy," Mel said. "It can't be."

"Why not?"

"*I'm* going home," Angela said.

Jet lag makes people irritable. Mel said, "Forget it, Jerry, will you? They've got security."

"The hell they do," Jerry said, and that ended the conversation for then, because Angela was walking out of the terminal. But that Saturday when they were all having a beer-and-hot-dog picnic in Frank and Teresa McCann's backyard Mel himself brought it up once more, and the result was Inter-Air Forwarding, with all the families chipping in to buy the van. There were Jerry, and his brother-in-law Mel, and his other brother-in-law Frank McCann, and Frank's brother Floyd. As originator of the idea and driver of the truck, Jerry took 50 percent of the profits, with 15 percent to each of the others and an honorary 5 percent for Jerry's parents, who were retired now and trying to live on a fixed income.

It isn't true that airports have no security at all; an honest citizen can hardly get into the men's room without a luggage search and a body frisk. But airport security is meant mostly to impress honest citizens and insurance companies, and secondarily to catch hijackers and other crazies. There is no security against a man with his own truck and his own clip-

15

board, and Inter-Air Forwarding was a safe, reliable financial success from the beginning.

At first the partnership worked only with items picked up from the cargo areas and value rooms out at JFK, but the process of fencing the merchandise put them in contact with customers who had another use for Inter-Air. These were people who would pay to have specific items collected *before* they went through Customs. The occasional anonymous request would come to Jerry by phone, he would make the pickup and delivery, he would collect his fee, and there was never any trouble.

Until the box marked *A*.


## THAT NIGHT . . .

In a place called the Gateway Garden on Queens Boulevard, Jerry was dancing the Hustle with a girl named Myrna. "Tough," Myrna said. "Very tough."

Jerry grinned. He liked to dance, and he liked Myrna. "We're here to satisfy," he said, and spun her left and then right and then out at arm's length.

Back again, torso to torso, with the record of "Love to Love You, Baby" by Donna Summer booming from the speakers, they dipped and weaved through the other dancers, and Myrna spoke close to Jerry's ear: "I got a bottle of Lancer's rosé in the refrigerator. You ever try that?"

"It's pink and it sparkles," Jerry said. "Just like you."

Myrna grinned, not exactly like a little girl. "You wanna drink me, Jerry?"

"You're close," Jerry told her.

"Come on to my place later," Myrna said. "The kid's with her grandmother."

"I got a thing to do in the city," Jerry said. "Maybe after that, like around one o'clock."

"Manhattan? This hour of the night?"

"A guy I got to see." They dipped together, moving with the music, and Jerry grinned at her, saying, "After that, we'll drink a little, eat a little. Have some nice rosé."

"Nice," said Myrna. "Very tough."

Jerry had found himself married one time, seven years ago when he was twenty-two, but the marriage had only

16

lasted four months before he'd realized it was *her* hustle. "I'm not the Welfare Department," he'd told her, and that was that. Now he had the life he wanted. The attic of his parents' house in Bayside had been converted into an apartment for him, with an outside staircase for privacy. He had a good income from Inter-Air Forwarding, he had a nice place to live, he had a good wardrobe, and most nights he was out dancing with girls like Myrna. What more could anybody want?

The record ended. "You have good moves, girl," Jerry said.

"Very very," she said. "There's a guy over there waving at you."

"Yeah?" Jerry looked at Mel, over by the entrance. "Time to go. See you later."

"Who is that guy?"

"My brother-in-law."

"Yeah? He looks Jewish."

Jerry laughed. "What do *I* look?"

"You look terrific," she said. "I'll put a couple glasses in the freezer. It's nice when they get that frosting on them."

"Don't you get any frosting on *you*," Jerry said, and patted her hip, and the next record started: "You Sexy Thing," by Hot Chocolate.

Jerry walked over to Mel, who looked past him, saying, "That's a great-looking girl."

"She thought you looked good, too," Jerry said.

"Yeah?" Mel tugged at his shirt buttons, staring across the room.

Jerry said, "Your wife is my sister."

"I can *look*," Mel said. "Come on."

Mel's station wagon was outside, with the box marked *A* in the back. Mel drove, and Jerry sat there humming Hustle tunes to himself while he looked out at Queens Boulevard, wide and dull, flanked by red-brick boxes. Mel said, "What's her name?"

"Who?"

"The girl you were dancing with."

"Myrna. Stepakowski, something like that."

"Yeah? She didn't look Polish."

"Well, she's half Mexican," Jerry said, making that up for the hell of it.

"That explains it," Mel said, and they took the 59th Street Bridge to Manhattan.

When he was a teen-ager, Jerry had come in to Manhattan all the time on the subway. He and other guys would come in and do a movie, maybe buy records, spend half an hour in a Playland near Times Square. When they got a little older they'd come looking for girls, and drink a lot in the midtown bars, but by the time he was twenty-one, twenty-two, Jerry'd had enough of Manhattan. Who needed it? The beer would make you just as sick right at home in Queens. Now, this was the first time in almost three years that Jerry had crossed the river.

They drove to the Port Authority bus terminal, and up to the top parking level, where they found their contact waiting for them. The contact, a tall, big-shouldered wrestler-type guy in a biege sports jacket and chocolate slacks and white loafers and chocolate wing-collar shirt and white-on-white tie, took one look at the box and said, "What shit is this?"

Jerry frowned at him. "What shit is what?"

"That shit," said the contact. "It's the wrong box."

Jerry switched his frown to the box, sitting there on the tailgate of the station wagon. "The hell it is."

"That box has an *A* on it," the contact said.

Jerry nodded. "That's right."

"You were supposed to get a box with an *E* on it," said the contact.

"The hell I was."

"You were told an *E*," the contact said. He moved his big shoulders around inside his jacket, to show he was getting annoyed.

Jerry stuck his chin out a little, to show he didn't give a damn. "I was told an *A*," he said.

"*E*."

"*A*."

The contact opened his mouth to say something—probably *E*—and then closed it and frowned instead, apparently thinking things over, and when he opened it again he said, "You wait right there."

"I got all the time in the world," Jerry told him.

The contact walked away across the concrete floor, sparsely populated with parked cars, and opened the rear door of a maroon Cadillac Eldorado. He bent down to speak to somebody inside there.

Mel said, "What's happening, Jerry?"

"I think they screwed up somehow."

Mel said, "Are you sure *they're* the ones screwed up?"

Jerry looked at his brother-in-law, ready to lay into him, and then he saw that in fact Mel was scared green. The

18

whites were showing all around his eyes, and his nose was bulging. "Take it easy," Jerry advised. "I'm in the right, Mel."

"I wish that made me feel better," Mel said, and looked over at the Cadillac. "What now?"

Somebody was getting out of the front seat of the Cadillac on the passenger side. He was short and dapper, in an electric-blue jacket of Edwardian cut, black sateen trousers, black patent-leather shoes, a white shirt with lace down the front and an electric-blue string tie. He and the contact walked back over to where Jerry and Mel were waiting, and they could see that this second man was Hispanic; olive-complexioned and brown-eyed, with black sideburns extending in scimitar-design halfway down his jawline and a pencil mustache that could have been used to slice rye bread. He also had a cocky and self-satisfied expression, and he looked Jerry and Mel up and down as though he was a king and they were ill-made beds.

The contact said to Jerry, "This is the fella give you the message on the phone, and *he* says he told you right."

"But of course," said the Hispanic.

Jerry pointed a finger at him. "You told me *A*," he said.

"But of course," said the Hispanic.

"I don't have to take a lotta—" Jerry stopped and frowned at him. "What?"

"But of course," said the Hispanic. Then he stepped forward, while Jerry and the contact both stared at him, and he looked at the writing on the box on the tailgate. "But thot ees wrong," he said, and waggled his finger over it.

"Right," said the contact. He'd been at sea there for a second, but now he was on solid ground again. "It's the wrong box, like I said."

"Thot ees not an *A*," said the Hispanic.

Jerry looked at the contact and spread his hands, as though to say, *You see?*

The contact now was looking at the Hispanic, and not only were his shoulders moving around inside his jacket but there were also muscles moving around under the skin of his forehead. Slowly, softly, dangerously, he said to the Hispanic, "That's not an *A?*"

"But of course not," said the Hispanic. He seemed only politely interested, very slightly puzzled.

The contact pointed at the *A*. "If that's not an *A*," he said, "what is it?"

"Ah," said the Hispanic.

Everybody waited, but the Hispanic had nothing else to say. The contact said, "Well?"

The Hispanic smiled helpfully, ready to be of further assistance. "Yes?"

The contact's finger was still pointing at the *A*, and now it trembled as the contact said, *"What the hell is that goddam letter, you goddam pansy?"*

The Hispanic showed offense by becoming taller and narrower. "As I have told you," he said, "it is the letter *ah*."

"The letter *ah?*" The contact seemed ready to eat concrete. He said "Then what the hell is the letter *A?*"

"Quite simple," said the Hispanic. Withdrawing from his inner jacket pocket the kind of silver pen fancied by untrustworthy attorneys, he quickly sketched on the wooden box the letter:

E

Everybody stared at it. Then, in a voice hushed with awe, Mel said, "He's talking in the Spanish alphabet."

A tiny furrow of doubt formed horizontally above the Hispanic's narrow eyebrows. "Beg pardon?" he said.

Jerry said to him, "You should of been watching *Sesame Street*, you dummy."

The contact said, "The Spanish alphabet? This fruitcake gave you instructions in the Spanish alphabet?"

"Beg pardon?" said the Hispanic.

The contact turned and struck the Hispanic with his fist, and the Hispanic lay down on the cement floor. To Jerry the contact said, "Wait there."

"Sure," said Jerry.

The contact walked away again to the Cadillac. The Hispanic lay quietly on his back, bleeding into both scimitars of his sideburns. Mel said, "Probably you didn't realize it, Jerry, but I was a little worried there for a second."

"A cool guy like you? I would never of guessed."

"In fact," Mel said, "I think I'll go sit in the car. Okay?"

"Sure," said Jerry.

Mel got into the station wagon and the contact came back over from the Cadillac to say, "Okay, no harm done. Tomorrow you pick up the box with the *E* on it, and we meet here tomorrow night, same channel, same time."

"That's two pickups and two deliveries," Jerry said. "I expect two payments."

The contact looked unhappy, but then he gave a quick

nod and said, "Yeah, it wasn't your fault. Okay." Then he extended a small business card, saying, "You got any problems, call this number."

There was nothing on the card but a phone number, handwritten in black ink. "Okay," Jerry said. He pocketed the card and pointed at the wrong box. "What about this thing?"

"Keep it," the contact said.

"Right." Jerry pushed the box into the storage area and shut the tailgate. Then he said, "You want to move your pal, so I can back up?"

"Back over him," said the contact.

# SOME TIME EARLIER . . .

The landlocked South American nation of Descalzo is perched high in the Andes Mountains between Bolivia and Peru. The economy is based on a combination of agriculture (mostly yams and lima beans) and American military aid, and the population is .7 percent white, 1.9 percent Negro, 3.6 percent Amerindian, 92.6 percent other, and 1.2 percent undecided. The government is a parliamentary democracy with a constitution freely adapted from that of the United States; there are two houses in the legislature, with elections every three years, and a president who appointed himself for life back in 1949 after the unfortunate fatal accident that removed his predecessor, who fell out of an airplane. The current president, Pablo y Muñoz Diaz Malagua, who had previously been commander-in-chief of the air force, is a benevolent father to his people, whose standard of living is already above that of Haiti.

Although most North American tourists have not as yet discovered Descalzo, there is much in the nation that could well be appreciated. Apart from the scenic majesty of the mountainous countryside, unspoiled by modern conveniences, there is also the small but vibrant capital city of Quetchyl (pronounced "Clutch"), with its many squares and plazas, each with its magnificent statue of President Malagua, sometimes astride a horse and sometimes not astride a horse. But probably the most stunning attraction in all of Quetchyl, even in all of Descalzo, is the National Museum, with its extensive collection of pre-Columbian artifacts. Pots, knives, bas-reliefs and statuary from the Aztecs, the Olmecs, and the Mayas are displayed as they should be, in unadorned rooms with natural lighting, undistorted by the glare of electric bulbs. Brilliant native artisans manufacture reproductions of many of these pieces for distribution and sale throughout the non-Communist world, providing yet another source of much-appreciated revenue for the nation.

Today, in the Plaza de Libertad, the great square in front of the Presidential Palace, an unusual ceremony is about to be held. Awards in the form of medals will be given to three Heroes of the Republic, three men who recently risked their very lives to save the national treasures for the continued good of the nation. Since President Malagua is to present these medals himself, in person, the Plaza de Libertad is completely ringed by soldiers and airmen carrying machine pistols, while Avenida del Progresos and Boulevard John F. Kennedy are both blocked by Sherman tanks. Clean and attractive members of the populace, provided with small flags bearing the national colors of crimson and orange, have been allowed to enter the plaza and take part in this historic occasion. Film crews from Granada, NBC, and Rediffusion, having paid the necessary fees and emoluments, are on hand to record this tribute for a waiting world.

And now President Malagua, standing in full dress uniform on the portable podium behind the bulletproof clear plastic shield, is about to speak. Wise mothers will keep their children silent.

President Malagua begins:

"Members of the Senate, and of the House of Deputies. Distinguished guests and observers from foreign lands. Members of the Diplomatic Corps. Monsignore Halcon. Lieutenant Colonel Guffey. My fellow Descalzans.

"We are gathered here today to pay tribute to three gallant men, who in their moment of testing proved themselves to be of the very fiber and spirit of Descalzan manhood everywhere. In honoring these three Heroes of the Republic we honor as well ourselves, who are of their blood and their bone and their sinew. And we honor their parents and their teachers and their priests and their good grandparents, whose example and diligence throughout the years have resulted in this moment of triumph and glory forever.

"What was done by these three, by Pedro Ninni and by José Caracha and by Edwardo Brazzo, honors them and honors us in the honoring. For in protecting and saving the world-famous Dancing Aztec Priest, the very pride of our nation, they themselves have become the very pride of our nation, as valuable to us as that which they restored and salvaged in our name. Nay, they are more valuable, they of their flesh and bone and sinew which makes of them ourselves and our own family, blood of one blood, they are more valuable than gold, more valuable than the cunning artifice which fashioned the Dancing Aztec Priest so many millennia before our brief moment here on the stage of human life.

"And so we have gathered here today to express the gratitude of a teeming nation, the heartfelt thanks of mothers of generations unborn for whom the Dancing Aztec Priest has been saved, so that they too might gaze upon it and be enriched, as we have been enriched, you and I, my children, in our many sojourns together in the National Museum.

"Shall it be recorded again what these three did for the grateful nation? How can the story be told too often, a story of such dignity and manliness and courage and patriotism? So the story *shall* be told again, and will resound down the pages of Descalzan history, that when the foreign brigands came by stealth across the border from one of our sister nations—and we lay no blame, we will take no reprisals; our wish for peace with our neighbors remains undiluted by this experience, no matter how severe a trial and test of our national will and our national patience—when the foreign brigands came in their motor vehicle with the four-wheel drive that permits them to travel where only donkeys and mountain goats may feel secure, in the vehicle of the type which our friends in North America have promised us but on which they have not as yet made delivery—though I do not at all hold personally responsible my good friend, Lieutenant Colonel Guffey, the military attaché from our esteemed Free World partner, the United States—when, in fact, for purposes of foul theft and brigandage they arrived at the humble abode of artisan and sculpture José Caracha, who at that very moment by the light of candles he had manufactured himself was preparing reproductions of the Dancing Aztec Priest for export and sale in foreign lands where the fame of the Dancing Aztec Priest of Descalzo has long since spread, little did they realize, these thieves and brigands, the quality and manner of man they would face in Descalzo.

"For José Caracha was not alone that fateful night. No, my children, two others were with him, two other strong arms of the Republic. And one of these was Edwardo Brazzo, Deputy Minister of the Board of International Trade, whose genius and foresight it was which had made possible these sales of reproductions of the Dancing Aztec Priest to foreign lands. And the other of these was Pedro Ninni, a guard at the National Museum, who by the wisdom and foresight of Hector Ovella, Curator of the National Museum, had been sent to the home of José Caracha to guard the world-famous Dancing Aztec Priest during the period when it was not in its accustomed niche of honor within the National Museum.

"And so it was that these three brave men and true were present when the foreign thieves came by stealth and by night to make off with the nation's patrimony. And at what risk to themselves did these three Heroes of the Republic contend with the foe? The proof is that Pedro Ninni shed his own blood in defense of the patrimony of the nation. The proof is that the foreign thieves did *not* get what they came for. The Dancing Aztec Priest reposes once again in the National Museum. The national honor is safe. The national honor has been vindicated. The national honor has been increased by the actions of Pedro Ninni and José Caracha and Edwardo Brazzo.

"And so we shall honor them, with each of the three to receive a brass medal from my own hands as an expression of the gratitude of a thankful nation. And I call upon Pedro Ninni, first, to come forward and receive from my hands this symbol of our gratitude."

And Pedro Ninni, a short and stocky man on crutches, hobbled forward to receive his medal.

## AND SOME TIME BEFORE THAT . . .

"Listen, Pedro," Edwardo Brazzo said in irritation, "do you want to die a poor man?"

"I don't want to die at all," Pedro Ninni said. "Did you hear what they did to Miguel's cousin when they caught him with the donkey? They hanged him by his tongue."

"That's just a rumor," José Caracha said.

"A rumor is good enough for me," Pedro Ninni told him. "Some things I don't *want* to know."

It was nearly midnight, and the three men were huddled together over the bare wood worktable in José Caracha's dirt-floored sod-ceilinged adobe hut. Homemade candles on the table sputtered and stank, casting great leaping shadows on the walls. Jungle noises, anonymous *kreeks* and *kworks*, echoed through the glassless windows, and the men absentmindedly slapped at mosquitoes and chiggers and gnats and fleas as they talked. All around them in the humid night the population of Quetchyl lay sleeping, with their mouths open.

José Caracha said, "Pedro, this isn't somebody's cousin misbehaving with a donkey. This is a serious business proposition, with important people involved. Like Edwardo here."

"That's right," said Brazzo, and he patted the sweat-damp necktie that was his badge of rank. "Think about it, Pedro," he said. "Would I risk my position in the government if I wasn't *sure* of all this? I have a lot more to lose than you do."

"All I have to lose," Pedro said, "is my tongue. And the head I keep it in."

"But nothing can go wrong," José insisted. "The plan is foolproof."

"It is?" Pedro shrugged, and behind him his shadows jumped around on the walls. "I don't even understand the plan," he said. "I don't think there even *is* a plan. We steal the statue, we don't steal the statue, we chase away people that aren't even there, it all makes no sense to me. None."

The other two men sighed, and exchanged glances. Early in the preparation of this scheme they had considered the possibility of shooting Pedro in the head with his own gun, for verisimilitude, but their innate kindliness had made them decide against it. Now they were both having second thoughts.

But no; the plan was set, it was too late to change it. José shook his head, turned back to Pedro, and said, "I'll go over it with you one more time, step by step."

"I'm all ears," Pedro announced.

Edwardo muttered something inaudible, and Pedro gave him a suspicious glare. "What was that?"

"Thinking out loud," Edwardo said. "Go ahead, José."

"Now, listen, Pedro," José said, "with all those ears of yours. Up in the United States there are museums, very very rich museums, and one of those museums in New York City wants our Dancing Aztec Priest."

"Why," said Pedro.

"To put in their museum," said José.

"Why," said Pedro.

In exasperation, Edwardo thumped the table and cried, "What does it *matter* why? They have money, that's all, and they'll give some of it to *us*."

"All right," Pedro said. "Already there are things I don't understand and you can't explain them, but that's all right. Tell me more."

José told him more: "The museum people," he said, "got in touch with some other people, who got in touch with the people who export the marijuana, who got in touch with Edwardo, who got in touch with me, who got in touch with you."

"And I didn't get in touch with anybody," Pedro said.

"You're not listening," José told him. "You're talking, and you're not listening."

"Okay. I'll listen, and no talk."

"Good." José took a deep breath, and went on with his explanation: "I have the original statue of the Dancing Aztec Priest here in my house, on loan from the National Museum, so that I can make a mold from it to make reproductions."

Pedro gestured at the little army of Dancing Aztec Priests on the dirt floor in one corner of the room. "Yes, I see them," he said.

"One of the reproductions," José said, "I did some extra work on, so that it looks exactly like the original." Reaching down beside his chair, he picked up the small statue and placed it on the table, saying, "Here it is."

Pedro frowned at the Dancing Aztec Priest, glittering muted saffron in the candlelight. About eighteen inches high, it was a complicated figure of a man in an unusual pose. Both knees were slightly bent, the left hand was on the left knee, the right foot was raised off the base on which the figure stood, and the right arm was bent up across the chest. The figure was nude, except for rings of feathers around his ankles and a glaring devil mask covering his head. The beady gleaming eyes in the mask were green. "That's very ugly," Pedro said.

"Ugly doesn't matter with antiques," José explained.

Pedro picked up the statue and looked at it more closely in the shifting candlelight. "So this is worth a lot of money," he said.

"Not that one," José said, and picked up another identical statue from the floor. "This one is the original."

"Look out!" Edwardo warned. "He'll mix them up!"

Pedro looked offended, while José said, "No, he won't. I put a red X with a Flair pen on the bottom of the original. See?"

They all looked at the red X. Pedro, putting down the copy, said, "I didn't want to look at that one, anyway. I just want to know what we think we're doing with all of these ugly statues."

"Ah," said José. Putting both statues away, he said, "We've waited for just the right moment, and now at last it's come. Those American archaeologists left this morning in their ATV, and they're certainly across the—"

Pedro said, "ATV?"

"All-Terrain Vehicle," José explained. "Four-wheel drive."

"I don't understand any of that," Pedro said.

Edwardo, speaking through clenched teeth, said, "Pedro, you don't *have* to understand anything except that they traveled through the jungles and across the border and out of Descalzo, and that they left *tracks.*"

Pedro nodded. "Yes. Everybody leaves tracks."

"Good," said Edwardo, and gestured to José. "Back to you," he said.

"Thank you," said José, and he leaned once more toward Pedro. "Tonight, after midnight, the three of us will raise a sudden alarm. We will yell and cry out. You will shoot that pistol of yours."

Pedro said, "At what?"

"Into the air," José said. Being a sculptor, he was a very patient man.

Pedro said, "Why."

"Because we are scaring off thieves," José said.

"But there aren't any thieves," Pedro said. "Except us."

"We will *pretend,*" José told him. "We will pretend that foreign thieves came here to steal the famous Dancing Aztec Priest, and we will pretend that we scared them away."

Pedro said, "Why."

"Because," José said, "everybody will be very happy when the Dancing Aztec Priest is put back in its closet in the National Museum tomorrow, and nobody will notice that it's my copy instead of the real one. And then the real one will be shipped out to New York with all those other copies, and the museum will pay the money, and we will all become rich."

"How rich?"

"Millions of peserinas."

"How much in U.S. dollars?"

"Hundreds," José said. "Maybe even thousands."

Pedro nodded; at last they'd said something he could understand. Then he said, "But why do all this pretending and chasing thieves that don't exist? Why not just put the copy in the museum and send the real one to New York without all this play-acting?"

27

"It's psychological," José said, and frowned doubtfully at Pedro.

Edwardo said, "Maybe I can explain it."

José looked at him in surprise. "Do you really think so?"

"I can but try." Edwardo placed both forearms on the table and looked severely at Pedro. "Pedro," he said.

Pedro sat at attention.

"Next year, or two years from now," Edwardo said, "the museum in New York will announce that they have the Dancing Aztec Priest. If we did not do this pretense tonight, the government would study the imitation in our own museum, would see that it was a fake, and they would ask the question, 'Who has had his hands on the Dancing Aztec Priest?' And they would remember José, and you, and me."

Pedro nodded. "And they would come hang us by our tongues," he said.

"That's one of the possibilities." Edwardo held up his hand like a traffic cop. "But hold," he said. "Tonight, we establish that there are *other* thieves, that we are honest men who have *saved* the Dancing Aztec Priest. Tonight, we prove that someone *else* is stealing the Dancing Aztec Priest."

Pedro's brows lowered so heavily over his eyes that he could barely see. "I don't understand that part," he said. "I never understand that part."

Edwardo said, "Pedro, you must trust us. We are both educated men, José and I, and we *do* understand that part."

José said, "Pedro, all you have to do is tell everybody that a big car like a jeep came here with foreign men in it who shouted that they wanted the Dancing Aztec Priest, and you shot your pistol at them, and they ran away."

"I have never shot my pistol," Pedro said.

"Wouldn't you like to?" José asked him.

For years Pedro had wanted nothing more than to shoot his pistol, but he wasn't about to make such an admission. "They'll make me pay for the bullets," he said.

José and Edwardo both laughed, and Edwardo said, "For saving our famous national statue? Pedro, they'll give you a medal!"

"A medal," Pedro said, grinning scornfully. "Now I *know* you're joking."

Edwardo reached out to pat Pedro's arm. "You listen to me, Pedro," he said. "You're going to be a Hero. You're going to get a medal."

José said, "And the time for us to start is right now."

Becoming immediately businesslike, Edwardo got up from

28

the table, saying, "Yes, you're right. No point waiting any longer."

Pedro blinked at the both of them. "Now? So soon?"

"We'll do it and get it over with," José told him.

Pedro said, "Why don't we have a drink first?" He gestured at José's jug of gluppe, the national drink of Descalzo, fermented from rotting yam skins and lima-bean stalks.

But Edwardo said, "No drinking, not till it's all over. Come on, let's get started."

"I don't think I'm quite ready," Pedro said, trying to sound calm, but Edwardo had already turned toward the window and had suddenly started shouting:

"Hi! Help! Yay, help, thieves! Murderers and assassins!"

"Oh, no," said Pedro.

José was also standing now, also yelling about thieves and murderers while at the same time tugging at Pedro's arm, whispering harshly to him, "Get out there! Get out there and yell! Shoot your pistol!"

"Mother of Mercy," moaned Pedro, and the yelling Edwardo and José together shoved him out the door. "Help help help!" yelled Pedro, meaning every syllable of it, and grabbed his pistol and pulled the trigger. However, in his excitement he forgot to pull the pistol from the holster before shooting it, so that was when he shot his toe off.

# THE NEXT MORNING . . .

Jerry Manelli carried his laundry down the private outside staircase and went into his parents' part of the house through the kitchen door. "Whadaya say, Mom," he said, and dumped the laundry on top of the washing machine.

Mrs. Manelli stood at the stove, left hand on her hip, stirring the spaghetti sauce with a wooden spoon. It was her belief that somewhere there existed a perfect spaghetti sauce, somewhere within the reach of the human mind, and she was determined to find it. She experimented with ingredients, brand names, alternatives. She experimented with pots, with spoons, with higher and lower flame. She tried the same recipe on sunny days and on rainy days and on days with different barometric pressures. She was in her thirty-second year of research, and prepared to go on till the end of time, if necessary.

"You're up early, that's what I say," she told her son, and stirred with the wooden spoon.

"Gotta hustle," Jerry told her amiably, picked up the coffeepot from the back burner, and sniffed at the latest sauce. "Smells good."

"I think it's congealing," she said. "I mean, you're early, considering how late you were out last night."

Myrna and her rosé had helped somewhat to ease his annoyance over the mixup with the box marked *A*. Jerry grinned and repeated, "Gotta hustle," with slightly different emphasis. He put sugar and milk in his coffee, and said, "Where's Pop?"

"Flying a kite," said his mother.

"You're kidding."

"That's the latest. He's over by Alley Pond Park with a kite. He made it himself, it looks like a ravioli."

Jerry's father had retired two years ago from his job in a department store's warehouse out on Long Island, and as soon as he became a senior citizen his name got onto more rotten mailing lists than you could shake your fist at. Everybody wants to hustle the old folks. A running theme in all this junk mail was that retired people ought to have a hobby, take up the slack from no longer having a job. The old man had never *worked* a day in his life—he'd spent most of his laboring years trying to figure a way to slip unnoticed out of the warehouse with a sofa—but he believed this hobby thing as though the Virgin herself had come down on a cloud to give him his instructions. "Man without a hobby shrivels up and dies," he'd say. "A hobby keeps your mind active, your blood circulating, keeps you young. They've done studies, they got statistics, it's a proven thing."

Unfortunately, though, the old man had never had a hobby in his life, didn't really know what the hell a hobby was, and couldn't keep up his interest in any hobby he tried. He'd been through stamp collecting, coin collecting, matchbook collecting. He'd paid good money for a ham radio but he never used it, because, "I don't have anything to say. I don't even know those people." He'd tried making a ship in a bottle, and within half an hour he'd busted the bottle on the radiator and stalked out of the house. He was going to build a St. Patrick's Cathedral out of toothpicks, and got as far as the first step. He figured he'd become an expert on baseball statistics, but the last time he'd looked at baseball there were sixteen teams in the two major leagues and now there were hundreds. He started clipping things out of the newspapers—disaster stories or funny headlines ("Action on Building Bribes Delayed by Lack of Funds," for instance, from *The New York Times*)—and all he managed to do was cut the dining room tablecloth with the scissors, and glue his fingers together.

The old man didn't know it, and nobody would tell him, but it turned out his hobby was looking for hobbies. It was certainly keeping his mind active and his blood circulating, and if he was actually out in the park now with a homemade kite then maybe it was also keeping him young. "Yeah," Jerry said. "Maybe I'll stop over there before lunch." He finished his coffee and put the cup in the sink.

His mother looked at him. "No breakfast?"

"I got a special pickup this morning." He kissed her on the cheek. "See you later."

"If you see your father," she called after him, "tell him dinner at six. Not six-thirty, quarter to seven. *Six.*"

# LATER THAT MORNING . . .

"They look like they're taking a crap," Frank McCann said.

"It's a fart contest," said his brother Floyd. "They're standing around trying to give out with the biggest fart."

Frank and Floyd were in Frank's sunny kitchen, sitting at the white Formica table on which stood four gold-painted green-eyed Dancing Aztec Priests, hopping on their left legs amid a rural scattering of excelsior. The wooden box marked *A* was on the floor beside the table, with its top ripped off.

Frank's wife Teresa, who was also Jerry's sister, looked over at the table from where she was chopping carrots on the drainboard and said, "Maybe they're dancing."

"Yeah, they're dancing," Frank said. "The green apple two-step."

Floyd said, "So what do we do? Throw them out?"

"We'll put 'em in the closet," Frank said. There was a closet in the basement, behind the bar, where they kept things that might be valuable but for which they had not as yet found the right customer. Skis, for instance; there were a lot of skis down there.

Floyd said, "Let's see what else we got today."

So they put the four Dancing Aztec Priests and most of the excelsior back in the wooden box, and then turned to the mail sacks and packages and boxes that were Jerry's regular harvest from the airport. They slit open the canvas mail-bags, punched open the cardboard cartons; crowbarred open the wooden boxes, and quickly separated the wheat from the chaff. All registered letters were opened, and cash was put in one pile, stocks and bonds in another. Small registered packages were likely to carry jewelry, which went onto a third pile. While Teresa went on preparing today's mine-strone the loot heaped up on the kitchen table, with the discarded boxes and bags and envelopes and letters scattered around the floor.

The reason Frank was home during the day was that he was a member of a backstage theatrical union. The union required so-and-so many members be hired for every Broad-way and Off-Broadway production, whether that large a crew was needed for that particular show or not. Frank, a pale-skinned, pot-bellied man of thirty-four, with thinning red hair and a thickening red face, had been with the union twelve years and had pretty good seniority by now, so he generally got himself hired by shows where he was redundant and didn't have to put in an appearance hardly at all.

Floyd McCann, a younger and somewhat thinner version of his brother, was in a construction union and so also had a lot of time off. If they weren't on strike—and they were usually on strike—then something else would happen, like the city running out of money or the contractor failing to get all the right permits. At the moment, blacks were sitting-in at the project where Floyd was supposed to be working, wanting some damn thing, so Floyd was at home again, on full pay, and he'd drifted over to Frank's house for today's opening.

Frank was counting the day's cash and Floyd was separat-ing the "pay to bearer" stocks and bonds from those with names on them, when the kitchen door opened and Jerry came in, wearing his on-duty white coveralls and blue base-ball cap and looking annoyed.

Something had to be wrong. Jerry was *always* at work this time of day, and he *never* wore his coveralls away from the job. Floyd said, "Hey, Jerry," and Frank said, "What's up?"

"We got a problem," Jerry said. "With that goddam box."

"What's wrong?"

"I went to get the right box this morning," Jerry said, "and it was already delivered. Gone from the airport."

Floyd said, "Then that's that."

"No, it isn't." Jerry took off his cap, wiped his forehead with it, and put it back on. "I called that number," he said. "The one the contact gave me last night. The answer was, they still want the box."

"That's tough," Frank said. "Once it's out of the airport, it's *their* problem."

"The way they talked," Jerry said, "I think maybe it's our problem."

"But that isn't right, Jerry."

Slowly, thoughtfully, Jerry said, "I don't think right and wrong is the question here, Frank."

"Oh," said Frank.

"The kind of people we deal with," Jerry said, "I don't think we want any unsatisfied customers."

Frank said, "So what do we do?"

"I'll have to take this other box to the city, to—what is it?" Picking up the box containing the four statues, Jerry read the stenciled address aloud: "Bud Beemiss Enterprises, 29 West 45th Street."

"Sure," said Frank. "You'll make a switch."

Jerry held the box in both arms. "Kicks the hell out of the day," he said.

"Don't worry about it," Floyd told him. "We did terrific yesterday."

"Oh, yeah? What was in that dental supply package?"

"Teeth."

"Oh. Well, you win a few, you lose a few. Hold the door for me, will you, Teresa?"


# BUT . . .

The Goddess of Heaven Chinese restaurant, on Broadway near 97th Street, serves Cantonese *and* Szechuan dishes, and has a menu so large and so long and so intricate in its minute shadings of detail that one time when a Korean philosophy student taking his advanced degree at Columbia stopped by for lunch there, he fell into a cataleptic ecstasy among the varieties of spicy pork and had to be taken away to Bellevue.

Coming to his senses in the waiting room of Emergency was such a seminal experience—particularly after the Goddess of Heaven menu—that he at once gave up philosophy and is today a brakeman on a San Francisco cable car.

In addition to normal facilities for lunch and dinner, and in further addition to its elaborate take-out service, the Goddess of Heaven also provides private rooms for groups from twelve to two hundred. Your wedding reception, office shower, bar mitzvah, or revolutionary call to arms will be given the world-famous Goddess of Heaven treatment of courtesy, graciousness, and fine food: "Your Choice from Our Most Extensive Menu."

Today at twelve-thirty a group of sixteen had taken advantage of this opportunity and was in possession of the Mandarin Room, up a flight of coral-colored stairs from the regular dining rooms. The Mandarin Room, with one green wall, one orange wall, one purple wall, and one glass wall overlooking the traffic down on Broadway, was set up today with connected tables forming a U. The sixteen table settings —heavy plates richly decorated in blue and gold, plus massive silverplate spoons and forks, delicate long red plastic chopsticks, real cloth napkins cunningly folded into the shape of dunce caps, and name cards in the form of tiny parasols—were spaced around the exterior of the U, leaving the center empty.

It would be impossible for the casual observer to guess what common bond had brought these sixteen people together in this room. Young and old, male and female, black and white, straight and gay, they were as disparate as a Gallup Poll cross-section, seeming to share nothing but a general interest in lunch. And yet, throughout the meal they chatted together across lines of class, age, race, and sex with cheerful familiarity.

At the end of the meal, with the ice cream balls and fortune cookies distributed, everybody was smiling and relaxed except for one young woman, Bobbi Harwood, who was *pissed off*. She was pissed off at her husband, Chuck "Professor Charles S." Harwood, who was sitting next to her on her right and blandly assuring her he didn't mind that she'd cuckolded him with yet another black man, by having slept with Oscar Russell Green. "I have *not* slept with Oscar," Bobbi said, through gritted teeth. "I'm telling you for the last time, Harwood." (She never called him by his last name unless they were fighting.)

"But I don't *mind*, sweetheart," Chuck assured her. (He

34

never used terms of endearment unless they were fighting.)

"You stupid, egotistical son of a bitch, you have a mind like a drive-in theater."

"Now, darling," Chuck said. He had an absolutely maddening way of getting calmer and calmer and calmer the more hysterical the people around him became. It was this phlegmatism that had given him, in Bobbi's opinion, his totally inappropriate reputation for intelligence.

Chuck Harwood, a tall angular stooped Lincolnesque figure of thirty-three, was an anthropologist, originally from Chicago and now an assistant professor at Columbia. He had lived all his life either in major cities with adequate mass transit or in utterly backward corners of the world—seven months in Guatemala, fifteen months in Chad—with no transportation at all, and so was one of the few adult white male Americans of the twentieth century who didn't know how to drive a car. Had no interest, in fact, in driving cars.

Which infuriated Bobbi almost as much as his allegedly sophisticated attitude toward her alleged miscegenations. (Chuck never believed she was cuckolding him with white men.) The point wasn't even whether or not she was sleeping with all those black men, the point was whether or not Chuck's avowed nonpossessiveness was hypocritical. *That* was the point, the only point, and it drove Bobbi crimson with rage that he wouldn't admit it.

As for Bobbi, who had begun life as Barbara Ann Callfield in Oak Crest, Maryland, and who was perfectly capable of supporting herself as an independent woman (she was first harpist with the New York City Symphony Orchestra), she had never been either northern enough to feel guilty toward blacks nor southern enough to feel hostile, neither big-city enough to fear them nor rural enough to be bewildered by them. The result was, her unweighted treatment of black men as normal human beings occasionally created misunderstandings. "I like you as a *friend*, Jojo," she would say, one restraining hand on his rippling dark brown arm. While across the room Chuck would suck on his pipe and smile with false indulgence.

As he was doing now, calmly, soberly, judiciously nodding, saying, "You have your own life to live, darling, I've always told you that, and I mean it."

A flower arrangement in a heavy milk glass bowl was within arm's reach. Bobbi reached for it, but before she could complete her intention (whatever that might have been), she and Chuck and everyone else at the table were distracted by

35

the tinkling of a spoon rapped against the side of a teacup. A tall and muscularly built black man had got to his feet at the center of the table, and was calling for quiet.

This was Oscar Russell Green, leader of this group of sixteen and Bobbi's latest alleged lover. With his bushy mustache, modest Afro, and easygoing smile he looked much younger than his forty-three years, and he'd been active in politics and Civil Rights activities for nearly a quarter of a century. He was also no stranger to public speaking, and now he stood in silence, smiling at his audience, until he was sure he had the attention of everyone in the room. Then, with a nod and a grin, he suddenly said, "Well, we did it." And in an abrupt loud voice, fist punching the air, *"We made the system function!"*

And the audience burst into cheers of delight, yelling and clapping their hands and grinning huge grins at one another. Even Bobbi gave off her feud with Chuck, and smiled happily around the table.

Oscar Russell Green nodded and smiled, and when the reaction had tapered off he said, quietly, "They didn't take us seriously, gang. Crazies and weirdos, that's what they thought we were. And they thought we couldn't work together for the common good. White and black, men and women, they thought we'd spend all our time fighting one another and no time at *all* fighting City Hall. Well, they were *wrong!"*

More cheering, more applause.

But now Oscar Russell Green became serious. "I think we can be very proud of ourselves," he said. "And I think we *all* learned and grew and became richer, better human beings as a result of this experience. We learned that we *can* work together. We can make the *system* work—for *us*."

Applause again. Her hands beating together, Bobbi became aware of Chuck's indulgent smile, and she immediately stopped clapping. Then, outraged that he should keep her from joining a general applause by his hypocrisy, she started fiercely clapping again just as everybody else stopped. She yanked her hands down under the table, and began muttering into her throat.

"Well," Oscar Russell Green was saying, "we've had a delicious lunch here today, and I might say we well deserved it. And at the end we got our fortune cookies, and I looked at mine, and it seemed somehow very appropriate, and I'd like to read it to you all." He opened the little twist of paper and read, "He who hesitates is second."

36

The audience laughed at that, nodding and making joking remarks at one another.

(In fact, Oscar Russell Green was not telling the truth. The fortune in his fortune cookie actually read, "He who keeps mouth open sure to catch flies." Last night, however, in preparing today's speech, Green had decided what his fortune cookie fortune would read, and if the real-world fortune cookie of today failed to deliver as specified that was certainly not his fault. And what message was there anyway in, "He who keeps mouth open sure to catch flies"?)

Green went on, "Well, I guess we've all learned that much through this experience, haven't we? Not to hesitate, not to *allow* ourselves to be second. Not *ever*."

Green put the twist of paper down. "Like the Lone Ranger, our work is finished here now, and we can all ride off into the sunset. But we're leaving behind us a tangible reminder of what we have done. Last Monday construction began, and within a year the Stokely Carmichael Memorial Squash Court and Snack Bar will be complete and open and functioning in Morningside Park, bringing the availability of the healthful and upwardly mobile sport of squash to the residents of Harlem of all races."

Which produced a standing ovation. *This* was what these people had in common. Young and old, rich and poor, yin and yang, they came together eight years ago, ignited by the purpose of bringing squash to the disadvantaged. Wealthy matrons, determined political activists, passionate college students, liberally committed advertising men, they were united by a goal, and now that goal had been achieved, they were applauding themselves and their own accomplishment, and why not? They deserved it.

(There was for a while one small point of controversy within the group concerning the name of their accomplishment. A few of the overly educated middle-class types objected to calling it the Stokely Carmichael *Memorial* Squash Court and Snack Bar, on the grounds that Stokely Carmichael wasn't dead, but as Oscar Russell Green finally pointed out at the time, "He doesn't have to be dead for us to *remember* him, does he? Stokely did a lot for the Cause in his moment on the stage of history, and he deserves to be remembered." Which ended *that*, despite some smart-aleck muttering something about Humpty Dumpty.)

But these were more than victors. They were also survivors, the sixteen remaining stalwarts from a pressure group that had once totaled in the hundreds. The activism of the sixties had set them on their path, and in the early days it was easy to maintain a fat membership list for nearly any Civil Rights cause, but it took stamina to remain steadfast halfway through the Sluggish Seventies. They were an anachronism, and they knew it, and more often than not anachronism is its own reward. They could be forgiven if they chose to applaud their own durability.

The standing ovation, like all good things, came at last to an end, and the flushed and happy members of the group reseated themselves, laughing and talking together, until Green raised his voice again, saying, "Ladies and gentlemen, may I have your indulgence for just one minute more?"

He could. He was the one who'd brought them all together in the beginning, who'd led them through the years of fund-raising, public relations, lobbying, and general struggle that had brought them to this moment of triumph, and he could have their indulgence just as long as he wanted it.

"Thank you. I have one more thing to say. Our real reward, our true reward, is being constructed right now up there in Morningside Park, but I thought we all ought to have a little something to take home with us, some little memorial of what we went through together. Like the movie people giving out an Oscar." Grinning, he added, "Well, I'm Oscar, but I can't give you me. I can give you my love, and my gratitude, but I can't give you me."

Bobbi ignored Chuck's smirk.

Green was saying, "So I talked it over with Bud Beemiss and Chuck Harwood, and we decided we all ought to have something like an Oscar, because we all performed magnificently!"

Laughter, applause.

"So here it is!" And up from the floor beside his chair Green lifted a tall package wrapped in brown paper. The paper was ripped off and a Dancing Aztec Priest emerged, glittering, to be placed on the table in front of Green's dish of melting ice cream.

The statue was greeted with a combination of laughter and bewilderment. Smiling at it, Green said, "Now, Chuck found this little fella, and Bud arranged to have him shipped here, and Chuck told me his history, and the fact is, this little man doesn't have one thing to do with squash."

Nobody knew if that was supposed to be a joke or not, so there was a brief hiccup of laughter, soon over, which Green mostly ignored. "This is a copy," he said, "of a very ancient

38

Aztec statue, and it's an Aztec priest doing some sort of dance. At least, that's what he *used* to be. What he is *now* is the *Other Oscar*, our award to ourselves. This is the Rain Dance Oscar, jumping around like we did that day at the Board of Estimate, you all remember that?"

They did. And now they all got it, the similarity between this contorted figure and a photograph that had appeared in the *Daily News*, showing Green hopping around in oratorical frenzy during the group's appearance before the city's Board of Estimate. They saw the resemblance, and they loved it, and they all laughed and applauded and pointed at the statue, and then they redoubled the applause when all at once waiters came in, carrying more golden-skinned green-eyed Dancing Aztec Priests in their arms, distributing them around like after-dinner drinks, one at each and every place.

*How sweet*, Bobbi thought. *How dear Oscar is.* (Not that she'd ever been to bed with him, nor even that he'd ever offered.) But he was just a dear sweet human being, that's all (unlike some she could mention), and this funny crooked yellow statue was just one more example of it. She picked it up, held it in her hands, feeling the cold of it against her fingers, looking at its strained and twisted body, its green eyes throwing off sparks of light in its devil-mask face. She smiled at the statue, loving it, loving Oscar in that moment, and then she became aware again of Chuck watching her, his patronizing smile, his bland eyes, and she turned her head, saying, "Don't spoil this one, Harwood. I mean it."

"My darling, you can do whatever you want. I only hope you'll come back to me when it's all over."

There was no beating him, and no dealing with him. The only way to survive at all was to let him have the last word, try not to let it rankle too much, try to concentrate on other things.

Brandy was brought out then, which helped, in tiny gold-encrusted glasses. The group toasted itself, toasted Oscar Russell Green, toasted the Other Oscars, toasted the Stokely Carmichael Memorial Squash Court and Snack Bar, and then at last it was all over. People got up from the table, moved here and there around the room, shook hands with one another, promised to keep in touch, showed one another their Other Oscars, and finally they began to depart, going down the stairs in groups of two and three, the laughter and good-fellowship continuing down the stairs and out onto the sidewalk, where smaller and smaller groups clustered, separated, regrouped, and finally moved away.

And now, after all these years, Oscar Russell Green actually *did* make a pass! Bobbi couldn't believe it. For years they'd been together, Oscar had been in their apartment, Oscar and Bobbi had been alone together a thousand times, and not once had he ever made a move. But now all at once, on the sidewalk in front of the Goddess of Heaven, he was coming on as though he meant it. "Bobbi, you're holding the wrong Oscar to your breast," he said, gesturing at the statue she held in both arms. And when she merely laughed that one away, he said something else. And then something else. And constantly with a bright-eyed intensity in his smile, standing a bit too close, staring at her in a meaningful way, while Chuck stood next to a nearby fireplug, pipe in gently smiling mouth, expression avuncular and indulgent. Until finally Bobbi had to place her hand on Oscar's forearm, to say, "I want us to go on being *friends,* Oscar."

"*Good* friends, I hope," Oscar said. What was wrong with the man?

And Chuck joined in, saying, "Bobbi, I have to go up to the campus for a few hours. Why don't you and Oscar amuse yourselves?"

Which was the last straw. "And why don't *you,*" Bobbi said, "stick your prick in an electric pencil sharpener? It'll fit."

"See you soon," Oscar said, a big smile on his face, back-pedaling down the block, waving like a song-and-dance man going offstage.

The others all were gone. Bobbi and Chuck were left alone on the sidewalk. "Call a cab, you asshole," Bobbi said. "I've had enough for one day."

Shrugging, amiable, unruffled, Chuck stepped off the curb and hailed a cab. Getting into it, Bobbi barely noticed the little white van that squealed to a halt just to the right, nor the worried-looking young man in white coveralls who hopped out of it and dashed into the restaurant.

# WHICH MEANT THAT . . .

## VICTOR KRASSMEIER * ANNUAL REPORT

*The Current Situation*
While the fluctuations in domestic and international money markets have remained as unpredictable as was forecast in

last year's Annual Report, the general trend has remained down, which was also predicted. To the extent possible this trend has been allowed for in the planning that has taken place within the higher cortical regions of the Victor Krassmeier mind.

*Liquidity*

Unfortunately, the depressed nature of the economy, both domestically and on the international front, has made short-term liquidity measures more than usually difficult to sustain or initiate. Although Victor Krassmeier remains a sound and stable structure, with assets (in property, stocks, partnerships and other interests in various business operations) in the realm of one point six million dollars (see Appendix 1), this problem of short-term liquidity remains a knotty one, and in fact has become increasingly serious.

*Cash Flow*

The cash flow situation is briefly stated. (See Chart 1.) In the fiscal year just ended, cash intake has failed to keep pace with cash outgo ten of the twelve months. This negative cash flow has created a situation in which various recurrent obligations, such as chauffeur's salary and the apartment on West 65th Street with occupant (see Appendix 2), are in very real risk of default before the end of the current calendar year.

*Alternatives*

Quite simply, there are two alternatives open to Victor Krassmeier at this juncture.

(1) He can cut back some of these out-of-pocket expenses.
(2) He can find an additional alternate source of cash income to close the budgetary gap.

The difficulty with (1) is that every suggested economy measure produces great complications in the Victor Krassmeier life-style. (Firing the chauffeur, for instance, would force Victor Krassmeier either to learn to drive at his age, or spend time vying with the masses for taxis.) The difficulty with (2) is that additional alternate sources of cash income don't grow on trees.

*Management Decision*

Having rejected the first option listed above after much soul-

41

searching, Victor Krassmeier has put considerable effort into an exploration of the viability of the second, and has at last emerged with a potentially useful one-time source of income. This has necessitated a brief business relationship—an unofficial partnership, in fact—with a not entirely savory individual named August Corella.

### The New Partner
August Corella is not the usual business partner. He does not, for instance, appear in *Who's Who*. Although he has some sort of administrative post with a bakers' union in New Jersey, his actual interests appear to be much more wide-ranging.

### Previous Relationship
Through his tax-deductible charitable connection with various local museums (see Appendix 3), Victor Krassmeier has become aware of the trade in antique art and artifacts of dubious pedigree. That is to say, items that American museums and the American government see as free trade items that can be bought and sold without question of legality, but items that certain foreign governments, such as Mexico and Italy, see as their own property and therefore "stolen" merchandise. While himself partaking in the negotiations for some of these pieces representing the museum side, Victor Krassmeier first came to have dealings with August Corella, who on occasion appeared as a representative of the seller or dealer or "thief" side.

### The Current Relationship
August Corella initially brought to Victor Krassmeier's attention the potential acquisition by the Museum of the Arts of the Americas of the Dancing Aztec Priest of Descalzo. When Victor Krassmeier conveyed to August Corella the positive early response of the museum officials involved, August Corella proceeded to arrange for the transfer of the object from its present location to the museum. When there arose a question of financing this transfer, Victor Krassmeier suggested an equal partnership, with which August Corella happily agreed.

### Responsibilities of the Partners
Each partner has provided an equal amount of seed money for the project. August Corella's responsibility has been to effect the transfer of the object from its present location to the

museum. Victor Krassmeier's responsibility has been to arrange with the museum the details of the sale.

## Advantage of the Partnership
Since the museum remained unaware that Victor Krassmeier had himself become one of the principals in the sale, he was able in effect to negotiate with himself and thus to push the museum to a far higher figure than had originally been contemplated.

## Anticipated Return
The Dancing Aztec Priest of Descalzo is made entirely of gold, except for its green eyes, which are matched emeralds. In addition to its intrinsic value in terms of precious metal and precious stones, it has an added value as an art object and a pre-Columbian artifact, in that it is unique. Once the statue has been delivered to the museum, therefore, in good condition, and once it has been authenticated by two waiting experts in pre-Columbian art, a check will be turned over to Victor Krassmeier in the amount of one million two hundred forty thousand dollars. After the partnership has been dissolved and all the other expenses of the transaction have been paid, Victor Krassmeier can anticipate a clear profit for himself of between one hundred seventy thousand and two hundred thousand dollars. In cash.

## The Future
Victor Krassmeier's physical plant remains active and capable, with only slight depreciation, except for a continuing problem with the prostate gland, which should not prove to be a serious factor in future business activity. On the national and international economic scene, over the long haul, Victor Krassmeier remains optimistic. The system continues to suffer one of its periodic dislocations and adjustments, but he anticipates—along with most of the rest of the financial community (see Graph 1 and Chart 2)—that the long-awaited upturn will begin to make itself at last evident in the second or third quarter of the next calendar year. His portfolio and other holdings remain basically sound. The "South America matter" should solve the negative cash flow problem, at least until the expected turnaround. Should that turnaround take longer than anticipated to emerge, further partnerships with August Corella or others could certainly

43

be considered. On balance, Victor Krassmeier considers his current posture to be nerve-racking but positive.

---

Victor Krassmeier (senior partner, Winkle, Krassmeier, Stone and Sledge, Members of the New York and American Stock Exchanges; Member of the Board of Directors, Ohio & Indiana Railroad; Trustee, Museum of the Arts of the Americas; Member of the Governing Board, Metropolitan Ballet) gazed bleakly across his desk at August Corella (date unknown), and said, "Another delay? Another?"

"Not exactly a delay," Corella told him. "There's problems."

The office containing these two men was of such hushed opulence that it seemed as though their words were borne to one another on small plush pillows. Krassmeier's desk, of rubbed mahogany with gold fittings, was the kidney-bean shape of in-ground swimming pools, and its smooth glowing surface featured a complex telephone console, an onyx and gold desk set, and a memo pad blank of memos. The semi-abstract cityscape hanging on the side wall over the long low corduroy sofa seemed a fog-drenched reflection of the actual sunny city through the broad windows across the room, but without the stutter of the World Trade Center. Here in this private office on the top floor of the Benchmark Building, surrounded by the symbols and implements of his power, Victor Krassmeier was wont to sit, a big balding man whose meaty shoulders and heavy waist were almost completely disguised by first-rate tailoring, and bask in the pleasant sensations of comfortable self-esteem. He was not at all used to this sudden panicky roiling of the stomach. Blinking sullenly at his crude partner, he said, "Problems? What do you mean, problems?"

August Corella, a blunt-featured man who looked like a cabdriver dressed up for his daughter's graduation, said, "The messenger didn't get it."

"Didn't get it? It's lost?"

"Not exactly," Corella said. "What happened is, our piece got mixed in with fifteen copies, and they all got given away as prizes."

"Prizes?" Krassmeier shook his head, as though to jangle these incomprehensible words out of his ears. "Prizes for *what?*"

"I don't know, Vic." Corella was the only person in the

44

history of the world ever to call Victor Krassmeier "Vic." "And I don't think it matters that much, do you? The point is, sixteen different people got the pieces, and we don't know who got ours."

"But that's awful. We have to get it back."

Corella nodded. "Sure. Somebody has to trace out who those sixteen people are, and then go to all their houses and see which one has the winner. The question is, who's the somebody? You want to do it?"

Krassmeier stared at him. "Me? Personally?"

"Send somebody," Corella suggested.

"Impossible. No one knows I'm involved in this."

Corella had nothing to say. Krassmeier sat looking at him, waiting for something more, but all at once Corella was content to be silent. Krassmeier, feeling himself in a situation he didn't entirely understand, progressed cautiously, saying, "What about the messenger? Isn't it *his* responsibility?"

Corella shook his head. "In the first place, he didn't cause the screw-up. In the second place, he isn't part of the organization, he's an independent operator out at Kennedy. That's all he's ever used for, picking things up at Kennedy."

"Use him anyway."

"I told you, Vic, he's an independent operator. If I let him know that wasn't any ordinary package, he'll go after it for himself, not for you and me. So when he called I cooled him out, I told him it wasn't that important."

"What about the person who *did* cause the mixup?"

"He got punished a little," Corella said. "He isn't in any shape to go look for things."

Krassmeier did not at all want to hear such details. Returning to the main point, he said, "We can't just let this matter go. The statue *has* to be found."

"Right," said Corella. And once again he closed down into that silence.

Krassmeier studied him. Suddenly tentative, he said, *"You* could do it, couldn't you?"

"I got a lot of other stuff on my plate, Vic," Corella said. But he didn't say *no.*

"You have people who could help you."

"Not for free."

All at once, Krassmeier understood where they were and what was coming. Business was business, after all. "Oh," he said.

45

"No matter how you look at it," Corella said, with a little smile, "this is going to cost."

"I see," said Krassmeier.

"I think you and me, Vic, we're going to have to do, whadayacallit? Renegotiate."


# HOWEVER . . .

When Jerry Manelli came out of the library at Grand Army Plaza he felt like he'd been given Novocaine in his whole body, and it was just now wearing off. He kept blinking, and looking around, and when he got behind the wheel of the van he didn't start the engine right away but just sat there, staring across the wide roadway at the Civil War statues all looking so busy and sure of themselves.

Well, now he knew what the story was, and the knowledge was like electric tingles in his brain. It was like the feeling when your car's been totaled in an accident and you walk away from it without a scratch and every part of you is trembling, vibrating like the beginning of an earthquake; hands, knees, elbows, *ears*, all shimmering while you stand there with your new high-pitched voice and you say, "I'm okay, I'm fine, I'm okay." And you're never exactly the same guy after that, ever again.

His new knowledge was like that, some informational absinthe eating into his brain. It had moved him up, out of himself, into something new. The Ultimate Hustle.

No turning back now. How could you spend the rest of your life knowing you'd walked away from the Big One?

What brand-new feelings these were. Jerry had always figured he was one of the sharpest citizens in the sharpest city in the world, and nothing before this had ever fazed him. Driving the van for the first time out past the "Authorized Personnel Only" sign at Kennedy, pulling that jukebox scam, or stealing from the numbers operators, he'd never been playing in a bigger league than he was ready for.

Well what the hell, there *was* no bigger league. He was the same guy he'd always been, in the same town, and he was still ready for anything that came along. Right? Right.

Jerry reached out a faintly trembling hand and started the engine. He was okay, he was fine, he was okay.

# UNFORTUNATELY . . .

"Listen!"

Wally Hintzlebel reared up on his elbows and listened. All he could hear was his own heart pounding. He whispered, "What is it?"

The woman beneath him, a married lady named Angela Bernstein, whispered, "I think it's my husband!"

Wally, a swimming pool salesman whose avocation was afternoon sex, had an absolutely Pavlovian reaction to the word "husband"; he would immediately leap into his pants. That's what he did now, trampolining off Angela, who gave a little *yip* of surprise and pain and fright, and he was already kicking into his loafers and reaching to the nearby chair for his shirt when the dreaded male voice came from downstairs: "Angela? You home?"

Angela too was scrambling out of bed, engaging in a swirling frantic wrestling match with her robe and whispering at Wally, "Hide! Hide!"

"Out the back way!" he whispered. He was nearly dressed.

"Too late!" They could both hear the footsteps on the stairs. "In the closet!"

*"What!?"*

"In! In!" And she kicked and shoved and packed him into the closet and slammed the door in his face.

He would have argued the point, if there'd been time. Never in his career, never, had he been forced to hide inside a house occupied by a husband. If one couldn't get out the door, one could always get out the window. This time, though, it had been impossible to push Angela out of the way, and so here he was in the damn closet, just *knowing* the husband would open this damn door pressed against his nose, and he'd never felt so foolish in his life.

Wally Hintzlebel, a tall stringbean of twenty-four with big round glasses and an engaging smile, lived with his divorced mother in a little house in Valley Stream, just across the city line in Nassau County. Wally had been the man of the house since his parents had separated when he was thirteen, and he just couldn't do enough for his mother. For instance, the swimming pool in the backyard was almost as big as the whole house, and although Wally had gotten a nice discount from his boss at Utopia Pools, it had still cost a pretty penny. But only the best was good enough for Mom.

Wally didn't suppose he'd ever marry. He was perfectly content at home with Mom, who took just as good care of him as he did of her, and as for sex, the world was absolutely full of other men's wives. It was only natural for a swimming pool salesman to say to an attractive prospect, "I bet you look terrific in a bathing suit," and Wally could invariably tell by the quality of the answering smile whether he was going to score or not. In four years of selling swimming pools, he had never for a minute felt deprived.

Nor, until this very minute, had he ever been trapped in a closet with an unexpected husband on the other side of the door. Outside there now, husband and wife were meeting face to face and two simultaneous questions were being asked: "What are you doing in bed?" "What are you doing home this time of day?"

The elbows of wire coat hangers were sticking into the back of Wally's neck, but he was afraid of the jangling should he try to dislodge them. In fact, he was afraid to make any move at all, and so he stood teetered against the door, stuffy clothing crowding him at the back and any number of shoes trickily underfoot, while outside the questions got themselves sorted out and then simultaneously answered:

"I wasn't feeling good, I think I'm coming down with a cold or something."

"I'm supposed to meet Jerry here. He isn't here yet, huh?"

"Jerry? What's *he* up to?"

"It's something about that damn box with the statues in it. Say, what are you wearing under that robe?"

"What about the—Stop that, Mel!"

"Well, look at you. Comere, kid."

"Mel, not now, I—"

"Be good for your cold, baby. Sweat it right out of you."

"Mel, don't. Mel—Mmmmmmmmelllll."

"Let's have a nooner, baby."

"Oh, Mel, I—"

Wally closed his eyes, even though it was already pitch-black in the closet and he couldn't see anything. He sighed, and rested his forehead against the wood of the closet door, and outside the voices had lowered, were murmuring, were accompanied by the squeaking of bedsprings, were getting louder and softer, were carrying on like nobody's business . . .

Could he get away now, sneak out of the bedroom and

out of the house while the husband was otherwise occupied? It was possible, but it wasn't certain, and that element of doubt stayed Wally's hand from the doorknob, because if a cuckolded husband would be angry, a cuckolded naked husband suffering coitus interruptus would be an absolute hydrogen bomb. So Wally stayed where he was, and the team outside drove their wagon right through the pass and into the Promised Land, and then settled down to nuzzlings and cooings of a truly disgusting nature.

Fortunately, the doorbell rang downstairs, bringing that stage of the affair to an end. With a sudden loud twanging of bedsprings, the husband said, "Damn! That must be Jerry."

Angela said, "That's all right, I'll throw on a robe and let him in. You get dressed."

"Tell him I'll be down in a minute."

Wally listened, forehead and cheek both pressed to the door now, but there was no more conversation. Rustlings and shufflings in the bedroom, that was all, and then muffled conversation from far away downstairs.

Then, unexpectedly loud and clear, a new male voice said, "That's okay, I'll wait right here." Only this voice seemed to be coming from directly under Wally's feet.

"You want a cup of coffee, Jerry?" That was Angela's voice. Wally frowned down toward his feet, but the closet remained as dark as ever.

Jerry was saying, "We'll take care of ourselves, Angela. The other guys are coming over, too."

"Who?"

"Frank and Floyd."

*Good Christ*, thought Wally. *It's a convention.*

"I'll tell Mel you're here."

Wally waited. Nothing more was said under his feet, and then a minute or so later Angela's voice sounded in the bedroom again, saying, "Jerry says the other guys are coming over, too."

"I wonder what's up," said the husband.

"Beats me. I'll get dressed and be down in a minute."

"Mmmm. Love ya, baby." And there was the unmistakable *smack* sound of a palm against a bathrobed behind.

Could he get away now? Wally was just fumbling for the doorknob when the door abruptly opened about a foot wide and Angela's hissing voice said, "Stay there!" and his presentation book full of swimming pool photos, which had been left downstairs, was jabbed painfully into his midsection. "Oof," he said, and the door slammed again.

And the husband's voice, beneath his feet, said, "What's up, Jerry?"

"Wait till everybody's here. I only want to tell the story once."

What the dickens was going on? Stooping, trying to shove clothing and hangers out of the way without making too much of a racket, Wally hunkered down in the darkness, shoved his presentation book away somewhere, and started feeling around among the grab bag of shoes. The voices continued just below his fingers, discussing traffic and the weather, and Wally felt a loose corner of carpet. He pulled, and a triangle of light appeared.

This two-story one-family Cape Cod in Hollis, Queens, not far from Belmont, had been built during the housing boom just after the Second World War, and had been altered and adapted and converted by any number of handyman owners since then. Mel and Angela had added the wall-to-wall carpeting in their bedroom, and the floor covering man had thrown in carpet for the closet as well, covering the grill of a hot-air register dating from before a shuffling of upstairs walls had made this space a closet. The equivalent grill high on the wall of the dining room downstairs had been left alone, partly because it wasn't bothering anybody and partly because nobody currently connected with the house knew what it was for. The result was, when Wally put his face and shoulders right down amid the shoes on the closet floor, with his butt stuck up in the air behind him, and when he looked down and at an angle to his right, he could see very clearly through two gridwork grills into almost the entire dining room, where a somewhat chubby man in a white short-sleeved shirt and dark slacks was talking with a younger man in white coveralls.

The doorbell was ringing, and the chubby man was saying, "I'll get it." From his voice, he was the husband. He left the room and the other man—this would be Jerry—paced around the dining room table, looking annoyed but thoughtful.

Now was the time to leave, of course. Even if he couldn't get downstairs with all those men arriving and walking around, he could still go out a second-story window and jump into the backyard. He'd done it before, and so long as you keep your knees bent and land on grass you won't break anything. Your feet will hurt for a little while, but there are worse fates in this life. Lots of them.

So it was time to go, and it was sensible to go, and it was Wally's style to go. And yet, there was something intriguing, something mysterious and interesting, in the manner and conversation of these men. He didn't know why he had this impression; he only knew his instinct told him it would be to his advantage to find out just what was going on in this house.

So he shifted himself among the shoes, trying to find a more comfortable position, and settled down to listen.

## WHEREUPON . . .

Jerry sat at the dining room table and waited until the other two showed up. Mel was hot to know what was going on, but Jerry just said, "Wait. I only want to tell it once." Because it was clear in his mind now, he was calm, he was sure of himself, and none of the trembling showed. He was still vibrating inside, but that was just excitement, adrenalin, the feeling in a toreador the first time he goes out and sees that bull.

Floyd McCann came first, and then his brother Frank. Angela, dressed now in slacks and a halter top, took orders for beer and iced tea and coffee, and at last the four men settled down around the dining room table, with all eyes on Jerry, who started by saying, "We got something here. Something different."

Frank said, "You made the switch?"

"No." Jerry had already decided to give it to them the way it happened, and not pop the finish all at once. "I drove into the city," he said, "and I went to this Bud Beemiss outfit on Forty-fifth Street, and some girl there at a desk said, 'Oh, the other boxes already went to the restaurant.' And I said what restaurant, and she told me this Chinese restaurant uptown. And *then* she told me the idea was, all the statues in those boxes were being given out to people as like prizes. Sixteen different people."

Frank shook his head. "Not good," he said.

"Right. So I quick got back in the truck and headed uptown, and the goddam traffic was *murder*. By the time I got there it was too late; the statues were all gone and the people were gone and it was over. So I called the contact, right from there in the restaurant, and he told me call back in ten minutes, they wanted to think it over. So while I was

51

hanging around I asked the Chink headwaiter there who these people were that got the statues, and he said they're called the Open Sports Committee. So I figure these statues must have been like bowling trophies you see around."

Frank said, "Those statues aren't bowling, they're taking a crap."

Mel said, "Hold it, Frank, let's listen to this. Then what, Jerry?"

"So after ten minutes I called back, and they said it didn't matter, don't worry about it, it wasn't that important. So I said okay, and I left."

Floyd McCann said, "So we're off the hook, right? We don't have to worry about the box any more."

"That's what I figured, too," Jerry said. "At first. But pretty soon it didn't sound right any more. I mean, these people were really hot to get that box, then they think about it for ten minutes and all of a sudden it doesn't matter, think no more about it."

Frank said, "They wrote it off, that's all."

"When they were so hot before?"

Frank said, "They're smuggling something inside the statues. Heroin, something like that. They wrote it off."

"No," Jerry said. "One little shipment of heroin isn't as important as they were acting up till now, and it isn't as *un*important as all of a sudden they're telling me on the phone. See what I mean?"

"No," said Frank.

"I mean, " Jerry said, "they know we wouldn't go after a couple bags of H. If they're trying to make it sound small, it's got to be big."

Mel was looking very interested. "I think you've got something, Jerry," he said. "I think you're onto something there."

"Me, too," Jerry told him. "So I took the Manhattan Bridge down into Brooklyn and I went to the big library down there by Grand Army Plaza. You know the one?"

Mel knew the one, but the others didn't. Frank said, "Get on with it, Jerry."

"So I went in there," Jerry said, "with one of these statues, and I found some girl to help me find out what it was. She went through hell, that girl, she called people in other libraries, she looked in books, and finally she came up with it."

From his coverall pocket Jerry took a crumpled piece of paper and smoothed it out on the tabletop. The librarian's neat small handwriting was a little archipelago in a sea of

52

white. "What these things are," Jerry said, "is copies of an old statue in South America, from before Columbus. It's called the Dancing Aztec Priest. But here's the thing: The original is made of solid gold, and it has emeralds for eyes, and it's worth a million dollars."

Everybody was taken aback. Frank said, "A million dollars? For a statue taking a crap?"

"That's the story."

Floyd said, "But what's the point? What we've got is copies, and *they* aren't worth any million dollars."

"That's right," Jerry said. "But think about this. What if somebody wanted to *steal* that statue down there in South America, and smuggle it into the United States and sell it to some rich guy or something? How's the best way to get it past Customs? *With a whole bunch of copies!*"

"Goddam, Jerry," Mel said, sitting up straight, "I think you're right!"

Frank said, "Jesus, do you think so? A million dollars?"

Jerry said, "That's why they didn't want us looking any more. Not once it's out of the box and mixed with the others. Then they've either got to tell us the truth or unload us."

Mel said, "Jerry. You want to go after it, don't you, Jerry?"

"You know it."

"Wait a minute," Floyd said. "If it really is the original, worth a million dollars, they'll be after it themselves."

"But we've got a leg up on them," Jerry said. "The guy I talked to on the phone, he wanted to know what was the name of the group that had the statues, and I told him I didn't know. But I *did* know. So what we do is get the names of the members of the Open Sports Committee, and then we track down the real statue."

Frank said, "How do we get these names?"

"We'll call the *Daily News*," Jerry told him. "They'll know." He'd been thinking this out all the way from the library.

Floyd said, "If all those statues look the same, how do we know which is which?"

"Gold doesn't break," Jerry said. He had all the answers, he had them all.

"A million dollars," Mel said. "Split four ways."

"A quarter each," Floyd said. He had a faraway look in his eyes. "You know what a quarter of a million dollars is?"

he asked them, and answered it himself: "It's a quarter of a million dollars!"

## SO THAT . . .

The man who jumped out the second-story window into the Bernsteins' backyard had a very thoughtful expression on his face.

## AND THEN . . .

When Jerry finally got off the phone with the *Daily News*— the Sports Department had referred him to the News Department, which had referred him to the Information Service— he wasn't cheerful. "It isn't any kind of sports team at all," he told the others. "It's some kind of black political bunch."

Mel said, "Blacks?"

Floyd said, "Holy gee. We're supposed to go rob a bunch of *niggers*?"

Jerry was slowed, but not stopped. There wasn't any reason it should be easy. What do you want, life on a plate? It was winning the tough ones that mattered. No; it was *going after* the tough ones that mattered. "A million dollars," he said. "It's still a million dollars."

Frank gazed at the wall as though seeing painted on it a panorama of hell. "Four white guys," he said, "crawling around on fire escapes in Harlem."

"Hold on," Mel said. "If it's black politics, there could be whites in it, too. Jerry, did they give you any names or addresses?"

"One name. The leader is somebody called Oscar Russell Green."

"That sounds like a nigger," Floyd said.

Mel said, "We've got to get that membership list."

Then Frank said, "How about Patty Shea?"

While the others looked bewildered—who in hell was Patty Shea?—Floyd said, "Hey, you could be right."

54

Jerry said, "Who the hell is Patty Shea?"

"He's a cousin of ours," Frank told him. "And he's on the police."

Jerry nodded. "I get it. A political bunch, the cops might know them."

Floyd said to Frank, "You call him, you thought of it."

But Frank said to Floyd, "No, you call, you always knew him better than me."

Jerry said, "*Somebody* call."

So Frank did it, while the others watched and listened: "Patty! Is that you? — Yeah, it's Frank. — Frank. — Frank *McCann*, dummy, your own cousin. — Yeah, well, I understand. Listen, Patty, the reason I'm calling, I'm looking for the membership list of a black radical bunch called the Open Sports Committee. — Now, man, you're a police officer, you don't want to know why I'd want a thing like that. — Well, you can draw your conclusions if you want, but the question at the bar is, will you help us? — That's right, the Open Sports Committee." Then he went on and gave Mel's phone number and hung up, saying to the others, "He'll call back, probably within the hour."

Jerry said, "He thinks he can do it?"

"If this bunch ever caused any trouble, the police department will know about them."

"What kind of black radical organization would they be," Mel said, "if they didn't cause trouble?"

Frank spread his hands. "Then we'll have the names within the hour."

Actually, it was closer to two hours before Patty Shea called back. The four men spent the time playing draw poker at the dining room table, with a two-dollar limit. Jerry noticed that Angela seemed kind of nervous and irritable for a while as she served the beer and iced tea and sandwiches, probably because she wasn't used to a bunch of guys underfoot in the middle of the day, but then she went upstairs and changed her clothes again and after that she seemed more cheerful.

Jerry was thirty-seven dollars ahead when the phone finally rang and it was Patty Shea. Frank got on the line with paper and pencil and right away started copying down names and addresses. "Sixteen of them, huh?" he said to Shea, and grinned at the other guys in the room. "A nice round number."

Jerry stood looking over Frank's shoulder as the list grew, trying to figure out which of those people were black and which white. But that was hard to do; blacks have all different kinds of names. Jerry himself knew a black guy out at Kennedy named Murphy.

"Thanks a lot, pal," Frank said at the finish. "Listen, we'll have to get together soon. Have Margaret give Teresa a call, why don't you? — Okay, fine. — [Laughter] No, you won't, don't worry about it." And he hung up.

Jerry said, "What won't he? What was that at the finish?"

"He said he hoped he wouldn't read about us in the papers."

"I'll go along with that," Jerry said.

Mel said, "Okay, now we have the list, what's next?"

Jerry said, "We split up, that way we can cover four of these people at the same time. Remember, those other guys are after the statue, too."

Floyd, who almost always hung around with his brother Frank and never did anything on his own, said, "But what if one guy can't do the job? Maybe it's a place where you got to break in or something and it'll take two guys."

"We'll help each other out," Jerry told him. "Mel, you explain the situation to Angela; she can stay here, and if one of us has trouble he should call in. Or, as soon as one of us finds it, call in. We keep in touch all the time, and then we can help one another out if it's needed."

Mel said, "That's nice, Jerry. Like a regular military operation."

Floyd said, "What do we do? Just everybody grab four names they like?"

"Come on, Floyd," Jerry said. "Let's be organized. Look at these addresses, they're all over the lot. Here's Jersey, here's Connecticut, they're every goddam place. What we'll do, we'll sort them into groups in the same general area, then we won't have to keep running all over the place. Mel, you got any road maps?"

Mel did, and in ten minutes they'd organized the members of the Open Sports Committee into four groups clustered more or less into four different geographical locations. It was Jerry's idea next to number these groups from one to four, place four numbered pieces of paper in a hat, and then each of them would draw a piece of paper to learn his assignment.

All of which worked fine, up to the point where they couldn't find a hat. Jerry's baseball cap was too small and too shallow for the task, nobody else was wearing a hat at the moment, and though Mel was sure he had a hat somewhere around the house, his extensive search for the damn thing produced only his comment, when he'd come back downstairs,

"Boy, that bedroom closet's a mess. We oughta straighten that up, Angela."

"How about a pot?" Angela said. She'd been given a rundown of the scheme, with an introduction to her own role in it—"Taxi dispatcher," she'd commented—and she was sitting on a spare chair in the dining room, smoking cigarettes and restlessly fidgeting her crossed leg.

There was something deflating about getting your assignments out of a pot—the bottom half of a double boiler, as it turned out—but Jerry decided it was worth sacrificing a little dignity to get this show on the road, so the traditional hat was dispensed with, the four hands reached into the aluminum pot, and then nobody liked what they drew.

"Harlem," Floyd said, and either through fright or by contrast with his assignment his face had never looked whiter. "I've never been in Harlem in my life!"

"What about me?" his brother Frank demanded. "I get the South Bronx. That's *worse* than Harlem."

"I can't do it," Floyd said. "That's all, I just can't do it."

"You think *you've* got troubles," Mel said, "look at *my* list. I'm all over the place, I've got Long Island and Connecticut and New Jersey, it'll take me a month."

Then everybody talked at once, until Jerry shut them all up by banging the pot on the dining room table—"Dents!" yelled Angela, but whether about the pot or the table she didn't say—and when the *bong-bongs* had startled everybody into silence Jerry said, "We worked out those four bunches together. Nobody complained ahead of time, so nobody should complain now."

"I can't *go* to Harlem," Floyd explained.

Jerry was unsympathetic. "You want to drop out? If you want, you go home now and you don't get a split, and no questions asked."

Floyd stood there blinking, stuck between the rock and the hard place, and his older brother Frank clapped him on the back, saying, "You can do it, Floyd. Any good Irishman is worth ten niggers."

"There's more than ten niggers in Harlem," Floyd said.

Frank clapped him on the back again, rather forcefully, and told the others, "Don't worry about Floyd. He gets nerved up ahead of time, that's all, but when the ball's in the air he's fine."

Which ended the fuss. Floyd's display of nerves had embarrassed the others out of their own complaints, and everybody got ready to leave. Mel kissed Angela on the ear—he'd

57

tried for her lips, but she'd turned her head, expelling smoke—and she promised a bit irritably that she'd stay by the phone. Also, yes, she'd call Teresa and Barbara, letting them know Frank and Floyd would not be home for dinner.

Jerry called home and said, "Mom, don't count on me for dinner tonight."

"We had some excitement," she said. "Your father was arrested in the park."

"Arrested! For what?"

"He set fire to his kite," she said. "But it's all right now, he's home."

"Good."

"He bought a BB gun."

"That's great," Jerry said.

# AFTER WHICH . . .

Floyd gave Frank the high-sign to stick around, so after Mel and Jerry both drove away the two brothers remained standing together on the sidewalk, where Frank said, "So what is it?"

"We got the short end of the stick, boy," Floyd told him. "You know that, don't you?"

"They didn't cheat," Frank said. "I watched them pretty close, believe me."

"But us micks got it again," Floyd said. "Every damn time. I'll tell you something, Frank. There's times you can get ahead of a guinea, and there may even be times you can get ahead of a sheeny, but there isn't an Irishman born that can get ahead of guineas and sheenies working together."

"A million dollars is still a million dollars," Frank said.

"And the short end of the stick is still the short end of the stick."

"So what do you want to do? Give it up?"

"We'll work together," Floyd said. Being a younger brother, and a union member, and part of a construction crew, Floyd had no experience of individual effort and no desire to gain such experience. At thirty-one he was three years younger than his brother and had deferred to Frank all his life. Frank had cushioned the harder knocks of childhood for Floyd, and was still on tap for those occasional problems of

58

adult life that the union couldn't solve. The dependence relationship between the brothers was so long-standing that neither of them was truly aware of it. They were simply brothers, that's all, and as everybody who knew them said, they were "very close."

But now Frank was showing unusual annoyance, saying, "Work together? How do you suppose we'll do that?"

Floyd said, "Instead of the two of us going our separate ways and getting our throats cut in different alleys, why don't we combine these lists and the both of us go to all eight places."

"That'll take longer," Frank objected. "Jerry's whole idea in splitting up was to get it done faster."

"We won't get it done at all if we're lying in some alley with our throats slit open by some razor."

Frank hesitated, and Floyd knew his brother would come around. After all, how happy could Frank be at the prospect of entering the South Bronx all alone? Pressing his advantage, Floyd said, "The two of us could be *faster*, Frank. In and out of every address that much quicker than one man working alone, looking over his shoulder all the blessed time."

Frank continued to hesitate, frowning, thinking it over, but then abruptly he nodded. "You're right," he said. "All right, we'll do it your way."

A big smile creased Floyd's face. "Good man," he said. "I knew I could count on you."

"There's this couple in Greenwich Village on my list," Frank said. "We'll do them first. Maybe we won't have to go uptown at all."


# ON THE OTHER HAND . . .

Jenny Kendall held up the Other Oscar and smiled at it; funny-looking little thing. So like Oscar to think of a memento like this. "Eddie," she said. "I want to take it along."

Eddie Ross looked over from the plastic storage box he was packing, and gave Jenny a quizzical grin. "That statue? You want to shlep that all over the country?"

"Yes. It'll be our good luck piece. I'll strap it to the handlebars, like Marlon Brando with that trophy in *The Wild One*."

"Fine with me," Eddie said. "I tell you what. I'll bring mine, too."

59

"You will?"

"Sure. They can stand guard over us while we sleep."

"Oh, Eddie," Jenny said, and put the Other Oscar on the bed in order to throw her arms around Eddie's neck and give him a giant squeeze. "That's why I love you!"

It was one of the reasons she loved him. Most of the others she didn't know about. At nineteen, she didn't know yet that minds have underground channels and obscure corners in which much of the main action takes place. It had been terribly difficult to convince her parents that she should be allowed to come away to New York City for her college education, yet it didn't seem to her that there was any connection between that struggle and the boy she'd wound up living with.

Jenny had created a situation in which she could *absolutely not* tell her parents (1) that she was no longer living in the dorm on University Place, (2) that she was sleeping with a boy, (3) that she was going to spend the summer vacation traveling all over the country with that boy on two motorcycles, or (4) that the boy was black. But the fact that her current life was an endless series of secrets kept from her parents had nothing to do with all those quarrels and scenes and struggles during her final year of high school. Not a thing.

As for Eddie, who was also nineteen, it didn't seem to him that he was a complex person, full of ambivalences on the subject of race, nor did it seem to him that Jenny exemplified those ambivalences more than anyone else in his experience. In living with him she denied the racial separation between them, while in hiding him from her parents she emphasized that separation. Eddie was aware of the contradiction, in a vague sort of way, but he knew it didn't mean anything. They were just a couple of kids having a good time, it was as simple as that.

Looking at his watch, Eddie said, "Time we got on the road, girl, if we want to make it to Rhode Island tonight."

"Okay, lover." She kissed him once more, on the nose, and then they rolled their sleeping bags, finished their packing, locked up the apartment for the summer, and departed.

## AT THE SAME TIME . . .

On Manhattan's west side, on 43rd Street, the New York

Public Library maintains a branch devoted to periodicals, newspapers and magazines. Students and researchers of all kinds cluster there, for it isn't true that no one wants yesterday's papers. Some sit at battered wooden tables, turning the pages of large bound volumes, but most have their heads stuck into the maws of microfilm viewers. With their right hands reaching upward to turn the noisy cranks, they watch the machine's metal floor, on which day after day of the world's history flashes by in a gray blur.

The microfilm viewer cranks are the only noise to be heard in the newspaper library, where the general atmosphere is one of timeless calm. The research being done here is surely very serious, but without urgency, and the researchers have the patience, the quiet self-control, the attention to detail usually associated with people who build ships inside bottles. They turn their viewer cranks, they pause, they make a note in the pad at their right elbow, they crank on; but all at a deliberate and reflective pace. Those reading the huge bound volumes of newspapers never flip a page briskly enough to cause a draft; they turn slowly, the page rippling like a leisurely wave over a flat sandbar.

Amid this self-contained calm, Wally Hintzlebel stood out like a black-sheep uncle at a June wedding. He had learned the use of this research tool in high school, and was currently putting his training to good but frantic use, having come here direct from the Bernsteins' bedroom window. From *The New York Times Index* he had copied down every reference to the Open Sports Committee, extending back over a period of three years, and now he was requesting as much microfilm as the librarians would let him have at one time, and was buzzing it all through the viewer with such speed that the machine was actually rocking on the table. (Several other researchers, with the frowns of elephants disturbed at their feeding, had gathered up their own materials and moved to machines farther away.) From time to time Wally would yank the viewer to a halt, would then jump it forward in tiny hops through some particular Monday or Wednesday, and would abruptly stop, stick his head into the opening of the machine, and hungrily read some four-paragraph story. ("Activist Group Disrupts Trustee Meeting," for instance.) Occasionally one of these items would produce a name, which he would scribble at once onto the pad at his right elbow. Less often, an address would emerge and be noted. Then, that article sucked of its juices, forward the viewer would leap once more, with the crank going *urk urk urk.*

This, it must be said, was a changed Wally. The thought of the million-dollar statue had galvanized his brain as nothing before in his life. With his mom at home, and other men's wives outside, he'd always thought of himself as content, but the vision of a million dollars in gold—a million dollars in *anything*—had cut through his contentment like a shaft of sunlight through a vampire, leaving a smoking husk in its wake. He wanted that million. Never had he truly wanted anything at all, but he wanted that million. Oh, how he wanted that million.

How to explain it, this sudden change? From wanting nothing to wanting everything, from utter contentment to raging discontent, from placidity to frenzy. Had these things been inside him all along?

It was strange how content he had always been. Leaving high school, contemplating the prospect of going away to college, somewhere far from Valley Stream, some other world of new faces, a new life, new vistas of possibility, had made him feel nervously expectant, excited, almost giddy, but when Mom had pointed out that there wasn't enough money, and that in any case he couldn't really want to leave her all alone, he hadn't minded a bit. The nervousness, the giddiness, the expectancy, all had simply evaporated, as though they'd never been. "Sure, Mom," he'd said, with his sunny smile. "I won't leave my best girl." And he'd kissed her on the cheek.

Then there'd been the draft. Would his number be a high one? The time neared, everyone in his age group felt the same tense anticipation; will it be a high number, or a low? The nervousness started again, the feeling of bubbles breaking just beneath the skin, the sense of moving through an atmosphere of champagne. Hawaii, Tokyo, Paris, Rome. Visions of uniforms, new faces, the anonymity of the Army, whole worlds of experience and adventure. And then the draft was ended. There wasn't any draft any more. The Army would make do with volunteers. And when Mom pointed out how lucky Wally'd been, he'd smiled, and lifted his calm face to the sunlight, and said, "Boy, I sure am." Calm. Relaxed.

Just last year his boss had told him the swimming pool company was expanding into the Scranton-Wilkes Barre area of Pennsylvania, and if he wanted he could go there as sales manager. That afternoon he'd had the jitters so badly he could hardly drive, and the wife he went to bed with had to tell him twice he was hurting her, but when he got home for dinner with Mom—pot roast, green beans, mashed potatoes—

he looked across the table at her sweet face and it all drained away again, leaving him calm and sure and content. No point even mentioning the opportunity to Mom. As he told the boss the next day, when turning down the offer, "I guess I'm just happy as I am."

Was Wally hustling the boss? No, not at all, he was telling the truth as he saw it. Was he hustling his mom? No, definitely not; she *was* his best girl. How could he ever do anything to hurt her feelings, to make her cry, to make her feel unwanted? That was what his *father* had done. It was Wally's responsibility—it was Wally's joy—to make up for what his father had done to his mother.

(Wally hustles Wally.)

Quiet, now. He doesn't know that. He doesn't know that the college excitement didn't go away, that it went into a Mason jar in his head, tucked away on a high shelf. With the Army excitement next to it. With the sales manager excitement in the same row. With all the other openings, escapes, extravaganzas, possibilities, adventures, freedoms, flights, and potentialities of his life, all in a row on that high dark shelf, all sealed away in Mason jars.

THAT JUST EXPLODED!

Exploded. *Bang-bang-bang-bang-bang-bang-bang.* Blown up, leaving Wally with a brain like a short-circuited pinball machine, containing only one coherent thought: *Gotta hustle. Gotta get that million dollars.*

For what? For coed college dormitories? Army uniforms in Tokyo whorehouses? Scranton housewives?

For the world! The door was open, look at it there, the cage door was open! The door was open and he could *fly!*

But the library was about to close. His expression more and more frantic, his hand at the crank more and more hysterical, Wally zipped through the reels of microfilm, repacked them, brought them back to the counter, ordered more and yet more.

The librarian became dubious. Studying his watch he said, "I doubt you'll have time to—"

"I have time! I have time!" Because, out of the alleged sixteen members of the group, he so far had only eight names and three addresses.

The librarian strolled back with his still dubious expression and his hands full of fresh reels, and Wally yanked them away and fled to the viewer. *Urk urk urk,* went the crank, *urk urk urk.*

"Closing time. Closing time."

*Urk urk urk!*

"Closing time, sir. Everyone else is leaving, sir."

*URK URK URK!*

"Sir, you'll have to stop now."

"Just one more! Just one more!"

*URK URK URK URK URK URK URK!!!*

"*Now,* sir."

Eleven names. Five addresses. No more time. Muttering, Wally staggered away, while the librarian stared huffily at his back.

## ULTIMATELY . . .

Unlike the others, Jerry couldn't immediately start out on the statue hunt. First he had to return the van to the airport, change into his civilian clothes, and pick up his station wagon. So when he left Mel's house it was toward Kennedy that he turned, pushing the van as fast as traffic would allow.

They started working on John F. Kennedy International Airport (originally Idlewild) fifteen minutes after the Wright Brothers' first flight, and they're *still* working on it. Every once in a while there's an official announcement that they'll finish it soon, but don't you believe it. They'll still be working on Kennedy Airport the day the last jumbo jet is dragged off to become landfill in Jamaica Bay.

Because the airport is unfinished, here and there sections of road are blocked off, or curving ramps lead away pointlessly to incomplete buildings, or temporary asphalt roads meander out across weedy fields of unsodded soil. No single person understands everything that is happening or failing to happen at JFK, so it had been easy for Jerry to find a headquarters for himself when Inter-Air Forwarding was first founded.

Between Air Canada and TWA a bit of cement roadway makes a Z-shaped dodge amid tall wooden construction company fences, then ducks down between a terminal wall and a concrete wall supporting some sort of approach ramp up above, then turns right into almost complete darkness, since another wooden fence blocks the exit and support walls flank both sides. On the outermost fence are several signs, one saying *Stop* and one saying *No Admittance* and one saying *Authorized Personnel Only Beyond This Point.*

On finding this cul-de-sac, Jerry had immediately made it his own. With the aid of a flashlight, a brush and a can of white paint, he had marked off two parking spaces on the cement road surface down at the final fence. On the fence itself, with the aid of the same flashlight, a different brush and a can of black paint, he had inscribed over one of the parking spaces *Inter-Air Forwarding* and over the other one *Mr. Spaulding* (his name for himself when at work). At all times, either the van or the station wagon was parked there, and when Jerry was off having lunch both vehicles were there. At the end of each working day, it made a totally secure and private place in which to transfer the day's loot from the van to the station wagon. Unlike most small businessmen, Jerry was perfectly content with his location.

Today, battling his way through the rush-hour traffic, Jerry at last gratefully turned off into the dead end, zigzagged through and down, turned right, and parked next to the wagon. Changing in the back of the van, hanging up his coveralls in there as usual, he hopped out in regular clothing, locked up the van, climbed behind the wheel of the wagon, and looked at his list.

Though he had four prospects, like the others, they were clustered at only two addresses. He had drawn the upper west side of Manhattan, and his list read:

> *Professor and Mrs. Charles S. Harwood*
> *237 West End Avenue*
>
> *David Fayley*
> *154 West 87th Street*
>
> *Kenneth Spang*
> *154 West 87th Street*

Whether Fayley and Spang lived in the same apartment or merely in the same building Jerry did not as yet know. But the married couple were both members of the Open Sports Committee and definitely lived together, meaning that two of the sixteen statues would be found at the same place. Obviously, that was the place to start.

# SUDDENLY . . .

Chuck "Professor Charles S." Harwood ducked, and the Dancing Aztec Priest sailed past his ear to smash itself into smithereens against the marble mantel over the fireplace. Bobbi Harwood, beside herself with rage, reached for the other one, intending to modify her aim.

"Now, Bobbi," Chuck said. He was so *calm*.

"Now, Bobbi, is it?" She reared back with the second Priest.

"You've smashed your own statue," Chuck pointed out reasonably. "Do you really intend to smash mine as well?"

"My own?" Startled, Bobbi lowered the statue and stared at it. The Other Oscar, the Dancing Aztec Priest, the statue Oscar had given her. *Her*. "This one's mine," she announced. "Yours is in the fireplace, you utter revolting bastard."

"Bobbi, dear," Chuck said, as slow and calm and unruffled. as an ocean liner in a windless bay, "you know you *always* get first pick. In restaurants, with our friends, everywhere. You *insist* on being first," Gesturing easily, almost humorously, at the shards in the fireplace, he said, "That was your first choice, so it must be yours."

"*This* is mine." Bobbi clutched the cold nasty ugly sharp-angled little monster to her bosom. "You've ruined my life, Harwood," she said, "but you don't get this. Not this. It's *mine*."

"You're mistaken, sweetheart. The way you can tell which is which, *my* statue is still in one piece. And I hope you won't be silly enough to smash it, the way you did yours."

"This one's mine!"

"Mine."

"*Mine, you teeny prick!*"

"Mine."

So now the argument was about the remaining Dancing Aztec Priest. Before this, it had been about Bobbi's insistence on shopping at Gristede's, which was more expensive, rather than Finast, which was less expensive. Before *that*, back half an hour or so, it had been about his refusal to learn to drive a car, and just before that it had been about whose fault it was they were living in New York. They'd traveled a long corkscrew path from the beginning of the fight, back at the

Open Sports Committee lunch, during the ice cream and Oscar's speech. It was always the same; they *tried* to have an argument about whether or not Chuck minded Bobbi sleeping with a lot of black men, but since they couldn't even agree on the postulates—Bobbi refusing to admit, for instance, that she had *been* to bed with Oscar or any of the others—they could never manage to stick to the point. The fight swelled and roiled within them, unresolved, while they futilely tried to ease the pressure by yelling about other things.

If *only* they could go to California, where people didn't congregate in such heterogeneous (not to say motley) groups. Chuck had been offered several wonderful posts in different elements of the State University dotted like Monopoly hotels through the San Fernando Valley, just north of Los Angeles, but he'd turned them all down. "I can't drive," he always said. "You can't get around Los Angeles if you can't drive."

"Learn!" she would scream. "Learn, you narrow-minded, pig-headed bastard! Learn, you nineteenth-century louse! Learn, you smug asshole!" She was pretty good when she set her mind to it.

But it never had any effect. Chuck, getting calmer and calmer, would do his pipe number and say, "I am learning about man. I'll leave machines to others." Which was enough to make you gnash your teeth for a week.

Or he would turn the whole argument back on her, with some crack about the orchestra. "Would you really be willing to give up music?" She would try to point out that she *wasn't* giving up music, that even in Los Angeles there were orchestras, that all he had to do was tell her *where* they were moving and *when* and she would take care of her own career adjustments. And he would nod, nursing on his pipe, and say, "But I don't believe you've given your notice to the orchestra, have you? Have you?"

Argue with a man like that, go ahead and try.

But she did try, she'd been trying for most of the six years they'd been married, and it was her private belief that the constant wear and tear was beginning to have an effect on her looks. She was only twenty-nine, tall and slender, with ash blonde hair and the kind of long-torsoed body that looks terrific in a bikini, but should she have those crows'-feet about her eyes? Should she have that tense set to her shoulders, should her nose be so thin?

It was the constant battling that was getting to her, she was sure of it. Affecting her looks, even affecting her music; recently she was making the harp sound almost harsh.

And now she was throwing things. This was new, a new development in their war, and Chuck was too stupid and too complacent even to notice. He merely ducked, as though Bobbi had been throwing things at him all along, and then he proceeded calmly to claim as his *her* Dancing Aztec Priest. Standing there with his pipe in his face and both hands in the pockets of his robe—he had showered earlier, in the middle of one of her fury-peaks, to display even further his indifference —he maundered on and didn't even notice that things had changed.

Well, Bobbi noticed. Clutching the Dancing Aztec Priest to her bosom, glaring at his calm face, hearing them both arguing now about ownership of this *statue,* all at once Bobbi knew she couldn't go on with it. Like Russia and the United States, there would always be some other limited war to fight, some other Berlin Airlift or Vietnam War, some dispute about driving or statues rather than the central war that neither side would ever be quite bold enough or crazy enough to undertake.

She looked at the statue, holding it at arm's length. His crazy devil mask and his shriveled little genitalia attracted one's first attention, but now she looked at him, really looked at him, his bent knees, his one raised foot, his off-balance torso, and she decided *he* was ducking, too. Defending himself. Ducking the missiles, ducking the issues, ducking out.

Fighting about a statue? A useless, stupid, plaster-and-paint joke of a statue? She looked from the Priest to her husband. "This is it, Chuck," she said, and all at once she too was calm. "You've heard of the straw that broke the camel's back? Well, this is it, right here." And she gestured with the statue.

The man was incapable of noticing *anything,* not even her sudden calm. "Be careful with my statue," he said, and even smiled slightly.

At which point she understood he *wanted* her to break it; he was goading her to break it just as he'd always goaded her to climb into bed with black men. Yes, he was, he absolutely was. Their marriage was *built* on this eternal argument; resolving the fight wouldn't cure their marriage, it would end it.

And the statue had made her understand. This dumb little creature from South America had shown her, finally, the truth. "Once more," she said, with a calm so steely, so cold, so rigid that Chuck could never hope to match it. "This is the last time, Chuck," she said, "and if you were ever smart or careful in your life this is the time for it. Once more, now. This is my statue."

He shook his head. He had never been smart or careful in his life. "Wrong," he said.

"Okay, Chuck." While he stood there she turned carefully and carried the statue away into the bedroom and locked the door behind her.

It didn't take that long to pack; all she did was jam all her clothing—plus the statue—in two suitcases. What took most of the time was throwing all Chuck's clothing out the window. Shirts, slacks, underwear, socks, jackets, his raincoat and topcoat, all sailing like Daliesque gliders out into the air over West End Avenue. Shoes and hats made a captionless Thurber cartoon as they tumbled down toward the sidewalk. Sweaters, blue jeans, and two bathing suits launched themselves like all the partners in a 1929 stock brokerage, and Bobbi slammed the window behind them.

Next, leaving the suitcases zipped shut atop the bed, she went out to the living room, where Chuck was rolling a joint, their frequent practice at the end of a fight. (End of a *round*.) "Hello, there," he said, looking up from his leather chair. He didn't call her "dear" or "sweetheart," another indication that he considered the fight at an end.

"Give me your robe," she said.

He blinked at her in mild bewilderment. "What?"

"Give me your robe."

"My robe?"

"Give it to me." At last she had as much patience as he.

"Are you going to shower?"

"Give me your robe, Chuck."

Still bewildered, but agreeable, he put down the paper and the plastic bag of grass, got to his feet, untied the belt, removed the robe, and handed it over. He had a bony body, with clearly visible ribs, like the Dancing Aztec Priest. Perhaps she had loved him because he reminded her of a harp.

She took the robe, went back to the bedroom, shut the door, opened the window, and heaved the robe out. It sank with its arms spread wide in horror and despair.

He was sitting naked on the leather chair, like O, lighting the joint, when Bobbi came through again with the suitcase. "Good-by, Chuck," she said.

He looked at her, speechless, holding the match upright.

She opened the apartment door and looked back at him. "You'll burn your finger," she told him, but it was too late.

# NOT TO MENTION . . .

While Ralph the chauffeur piloted the maroon Cadillac Eldorado across the urban and industrial sprawl of Connecticut, August Corella sat in back with his henchman/bodyguard, Earl, thoughtfully puffing a cigar while considering the events of the day. Much had happened since Corella had met this noon with the financier, Victor Krassmeier, and not all of it had been pleasant.

It had begun pleasantly enough. All in all, August Corella would rather deal with a top-level businessman than anybody else in the world. Patsies, pure and simple. In every corporation it was the same; the factory made the stuff, the salesmen sold it, and the executives sat around telling each other how smart *they* were. They were coasting, cushioned by a system they hadn't invented and didn't understand, and they were so sure they were bright and sharp and nobody's fool that they were *everybody's* fool.

The result of today's negotiation with Krassmeier? Another fifty thousand sliced out of his gut, and if it actually cost Corella half that much to reclaim the statues he'd be astonished.

His present plan was simple. Find the person in charge of the group with the statues, go to that person, and buy them all back. Offer three thousand to start, go to a top of ten thousand, and lead the seller to believe two things: first, that there was heroin in at least some of the statues; second, that the Mafia owned the heroin and would kill the seller if he tried anything cute. Neither of those things would be said straight out, but both would be gotten across. And then the *seller* would do the legwork, collecting the statues while Corella dealt with other things.

From Krassmeier's office, Corella had gone directly to the Goddess of Heaven restaurant, where a five-dollar bill had bought him the information that today's luncheon had been paid for by an outfit called Bud Beemiss Enterprises, at 29 West 45th Street. Back in midtown, Ralph and the Cadillac had waited out front while Corella and Earl went up to have a look at this Bud Beemiss Enterprises, which turned out to be a public relations firm with a very snooty receptionist. When

Corella told her he wanted to see Beemiss, she said, "Did you have an appointment?"

"No, I just want to see him."

"I'm terribly sorry, but he isn't in the office this afternoon. There was a special luncheon uptown today—"

"That's what I want to talk to him about."

"Well, he decided not to come back after lunch but to go on home."

"Then I'll talk to him there," Corella said.

"All right," the girl said. "I *am* sorry about the mixup, gentlemen."

Corella said, "What's his address?"

"Oh, I'm sorry," she said. "We don't give out home addresses."

"Then his phone number," Corella said. With the phone number, he could get the address himself.

But the girl said, "I'm sorry, not those either. Would you like to talk to Mr. Beemiss's secretary about making an appointment? He might have some time free tomorrow, I couldn't be certain." Her hand was resting on the complicated telephone console beside her.

"It's today I want to talk to him," Corella said.

"Then I really wish you'd phoned this morning."

Corella stepped back a pace. "Earl," he said. "Explain it to her."

Earl, who was very big and very tough and who had been Jerry Manelli's contact in the Port Authority parking garage, flexed his shoulder muscles inside his jacket. He said, "We think it's important we get Beemiss's address."

The girl smiled at him. She said, "Do you know, when I first moved to New York I was afraid of muggers and rapists and all sorts of things, but for the last two years I've been studying at a women's martial arts center down on Chambers Street, and it's just built up my confidence tremendously. For instance, studying karate and tai chi chuan, I've gotten to the point where just with the edge of my hand I can break a board just about as thick as your head." Picking up the phone receiver, she said, "I'll call Mr. Beemiss's secretary; you can arrange with her for an appointment later in the week."

"Never mind," Corella said, and left the office. Out in the hall Earl said, "Mr. Corella, I could of taken her."

Corella didn't bother to answer. He pushed the elevator button, and said, "Find Beemiss."

"Yes, sir, Mr. Corella."

So then Corella went home to Red Bank, New Jersey, and

waited for Earl to report, which he didn't do until well after five o'clock. He had the address at last, and when Corella and Ralph picked him up on the way through Manhattan, it turned out he had a black eye as well. It made him sullen, having a black eye. Apart from the physical pain, he believed that a black eye detracted from his credibility as a bodyguard and general tough guy.

What had happened, Earl had tried his regular sources of information, looking for Bud Beemiss's home address, but his regular sources of information mostly knew things like the addresses of hit men or where to buy an untraceable gun, so finally he just waited until Bud Beemiss Enterprises closed for the day, then entered the premises and found the address on Beemiss's secretary's Rolodex. He was out of the office and almost to the elevator when who should come down the hall but that damn smart-ass little receptionist. Immediately she was suspicious: "What are *you* doing here?" Irritated in general, and bugged by this girl in particular, Earl didn't try to calm her with some story, but attempted instead to brush on by her. That's when she started doing her nasty karate moves, bouncing him off the corridor walls. And when, plagued beyond good manners, he took a swing at her, she moved in under his roundhouse and poked him a very smart left fist in the eye. Bony goddam hand. If he hadn't fled at last down the stairwell who knows what might have happened?

So now they were heading northeast at last across Connecticut, Ralph the chauffeur annoyed because he'd had a terrific date set up for tonight, Earl annoyed because of his black eye, and Corella beginning to get annoyed it was taking one hell of a long time to get there. They'd traveled on the Merritt Parkway for a while, but now Ralph's road map had dumped them onto a winding blacktop two-lane road in the twilight, surrounded by local traffic that didn't care *when* it got home. Ralph brooded on his lost date. Earl brooded on his throbbing eye, and Corella brooded on all this wasted time. He too had financial pressures these days, though certainly less so than a duffer like Vic Krassmeier, and he wanted that damn statue *found* and *delivered* and *paid for*. But here they were mousing around the boondocks of Connecticut, amid the waving maple trees, following some arthritic station wagon. Annoyance suddenly spilling over, Corella leaned forward and said, "Ralph, you gonna follow that son of a bitch into his garage?"

Ralph hated people to yell in his ear. "Soon as I get a passing zone, Mr. Corella," he said.

Eventually a passing zone did appear, and Ralph angrily yanked the Caddy around the drifting station wagon containing Mel Bernstein, yowling his horn enough to make Mel nearly swerve completely off the road. Then the Caddy tore on northeastward toward 11 Winding Lane, Greenway, Connecticut, the home of Bud Beemiss.

"Goddam it!" Mel hollered, wrestling with the steering wheel. "Goddam road hog!" Then he got the station wagon once more under control, and he too continued northeastward toward 11 Winding Lane.

# IN ADDITION . . .

Mel Bernstein had almost been a lawyer. Until he'd joined his brother-in-law Jerry Manelli's great Statue Hunt, that had been the central fact about him, from which all other facts spiraled out. He had almost been a lawyer, but he was not a lawyer.

The way it had happened—or not happened—was like this. Mel's father, a bus driver with the City of New York, was a compulsive gambler and therefore always broke. Meantime, Mel's mother's brother Phil Ormont (né Goldberg) had a ladies' clothing store in Miami Beach (pronounced "Momma Bitch") and was *not* a compulsive gambler, and he was doing very well, thank you. And he didn't mind caring for his sister's boy Mel on summer vacations, particularly since Mel was bright and personable and could be very useful around the store. So Mel spent his formative summers in Momma Bitch, where the heat and humidity are both ninety-two all the time, day and night, and Uncle Phil kept assuring him his future was made. "Your future is made, kid," Uncle Phil used to say, in the air-conditioned splendor of his store, amid the old ladies fingering the flower-print dresses. "Anything you want, kid, anything you want to be, it's yours."

"I want to be a lawyer," Mel said, more than once.

"It's yours, kid," Phil answered, more than once. "Go help the old lady. Look in her shopping bag, I think she just boosted a package Supphose."

Then, in February of the year that Mel was seventeen and about to graduate from New Utrecht High in Brooklyn, his

Uncle Phil left the air-conditioned splendor of his store, entered the natural environment of Momma Bitch, and promptly dropped dead on the spot. On the sidewalk. Right there in the street. Fat, dead, and moist. Heart; what else?

Mel's mom waited a respectable period of time—three months, until mid-May—before writing to Aunt Rachel, reminding her of poor Phil's oft-repeated promise to put his favorite nephew Melvin through college and law school, and when there wasn't any answer by mid-June she splurged on a long-distance call, and the Ormonts' home phone number was not-in-operation-at-this-time. So she called the store instead and the new owner told her that Rachel had moved either to Las Vegas or Saint Thomas, unless maybe it was someplace in California.

The problem with being somebody who had almost been a lawyer is there's this constant tingle in the fingertips, this feeling that the lifeline has just slipped through your hands. What is the alternate occupation of preference for somebody who thought he was going to be a lawyer?

For Mel it had been lots of jobs, lots of hustles, none of them really satisfying. He'd been a door-to-door salesman, he'd run a mail-order business selling a book called *Danish Marriage Secrets*, he'd even sold Arizona land by phone to Washington Heights housewives. For a while he'd been an insurance expert, testifying in disputed-claims cases, but eventually the number of pending lawsuits against him from losing parties who'd found out he had no qualifications got so numerous and annoying that he quit that hustle, permitted all the lawsuits to catch up with him, declared bankruptcy, thumbed his nose at his ex-creditors, and started again as a used car salesman for an outfit in the Bronx called Big Man Motors. (The television commercial tells the Big Man story: "The Big Man *hates* to say no! *Instant* credit on the late-model used car of your choice! Got no cash for the down payment? That's okay, the Big Man takes anything—your old TV, washing machine, refrigerator, you name it. You come to the Big Man, you gone go way with a *deal!*")

You'd think the main problem with a scam like that would be unhappy customers pushing their dead clunkers back onto the lot, but you'd be wrong. Since the customers, generally speaking, never made *any* of their payments, they weren't in any position to complain. No, the main problem was with the banks that wound up eating all that worthless paper. The way it works, you sell some janitor's assistant a seven-year-old clapped-out Mercury for a sofa down and forty-seven dollars a month, and then you discount the loan to the bank. Two months later the bank repossesses the car, since the janitor's assistant never *will* come up with any forty-seven dollars, and then what does the bank have? A seven-year-old clapped-out Mercury. Meantime, Big Man has converted the sofa to cash through a subsidiary firm called Soul Furniture, the salesman got his commission out of the money the bank paid when it took over the loan, the janitor's assistant got to drive around in a regular automobile for a couple months, and nobody's unhappy except the bank.

Big Man had run through a lot of banks, and was reduced to dealing with some very hard-nosed type alternate sources of financing, and then it turned out these new financers didn't believe in repossessing junk. They believed in breaking heads. A couple of janitor's assistants got their heads broken so bad they wouldn't *ever* need a car any more, and a few others who'd only had secondary bones broken started coming around Big Man looking for the salesman who'd got them into this. It was hard to convince such simple brains that it wasn't the salesman's fault, and Mel decided to try another occupation.

Which was when he found Literature.

## WRITING IS NOT ENOUGH

Of course, you're a writer. *You* know that. But it isn't enough merely to write, you need to be *published* as well. Success in writing is really yours only when you have reached the great Public with your *ideas*.

But how can you "break into" print? Is publishing *really* the closed world that people say? Do you *really* have to "know somebody"? Or, can talent "make it" on its own?

I say you can make it. I've seen others who made it, and I've helped some of them along the way, and I can help *you*, if you have the *talent*, and the *desire*, and if you'll *trust me*.

For a limited time only, the Zachary George Literary Agency is seeking to expand its client list. Send me your short story, your novel, your magazine article, your poem. If it's salable, I'll find the *right* market for it. If it isn't quite "up to snuff," I'll write you a *personal* letter, telling you where I think you went wrong.

Once you're successful, I'll take only the standard 10 per cent commission from my sales of your work.

Until then, of course, it will be necessary to charge an advance against those commissions—fully refundable when you begin to sell—at the following rates:

| | |
|---|---|
| Short story or article | $10. |
| Novelette or TV script | 25. |
| Novel or film script | 50. |

Get in touch with me *today*. Why wait for success any longer?

Mel wrote that ad in a burst of literary inspiration one cool Sunday afternoon in October three and a half years ago, since when it had appeared frequently in the gamier men's magazines, the loonier women's magazines, and the more tolerant writer's magazines. And didn't the stories come in. Short stories combining two or three recent television shows, novels imitating 1960 paperback originals, articles on fluoridation and Reinhard Heydrich, film scripts about people inadvertently taking LSD, poems about sunsets, novelettes about a young girl's first sexual experience ("awakening," in the language of the authors), TV scripts about youth gangs terrorizing subways—oh, the stories came in, right enough. Everybody in America, it seemed, had glared at the TV set and said, "*I* can write better than *that*." It was amazing how many of them were wrong.

As a hustle, and except for the reading involved, the Zachary George Literary Agency was Class A. It still wasn't The Law, but it was nice. Very nice, and very profitable, and actually legal. And the best part was that Mel was now a dignified Professional Man, just like any attorney or doctor or dentist or CPA. He was a Literary Agent.

Within a year, so many hopeful writers had sent in so much hopeless crap that Mel expanded out of his midtown convenience address and his Queens closet full of letterhead stationery into an actual two-room office on Varick Street in Manhattan, with a good-looking secretary-receptionist named Ralphi Durant. If it weren't for all the garbage he had to read, life would be perfect. (He didn't read every word, of course. He'd skip through each submission just enough to get the idea, then send it back with one or another of his stock letters about how your story showed real promise and do send in more of your work. With more of your money.)

But the reading did get grim after a while. It was affecting Mel's digestion, it was making him cranky, it was making him cringe every time the TV was on. It began to look as though progressive brainpoisoning would bring an untimely finish to Zachary George's career. Then, midway through his second year of operation, Mel suddenly found the solution, in the person of Ralphi's boyfriend, a fellow named Ethelred Marx who was a poet, and who was so stoned all the time that his ears steamed, like sewer gratings in the early morning. Ethelred wanted nothing from life but enough cash money to keep himself clothed, sheltered, and bombed while he worked on his projected twelve-million line epic about the American railroads. (He'd been stuck for the last three years trying to find a rhyme for "parallel.") Within Ethelred's gangly corpus, however, lay the remnants of a Rhodes scholar, Guggenheim Fellow, and Ph.D. in American Lit, and it turned out he was the perfect reader for the Zachary George Literary Agency; his zonked mind absorbed all those stories and novels with a Buddha-like receptive wonder, and his letters of response— freely adapting Mel's stock paragraphs—were marvels of erudition, insight, bullshit, and weird linkages.

Not trusting the strange aromas that seemed to hang around Ethelred all the time, Mel signed a lease on a one-room office next to his present two rooms, and that was where Ethelred these days did his reading and his letter-writing and his freaking-out. (Strange noises came from Ethelred, too, sometimes.) Ralphi continued to fend off the amateurs in the outer room of the main office, and Mel spent his days at his desk in the inner room, where he was secretly—even Angela didn't know about this—working on a novel. (One of the early submissions had had an idea in it that Mel kind of liked, so he'd saved a Xerox of the manuscript and was doing his own version of the story. It was about a girl who kidnaps a psychiatrist to get him to cure her nymphomaniac twin sister, and so far as Mel could see it had best seller written all over it.)

Which was why this golden-statue thing was such a godsend. Like most writers, Mel felt everything would be okay if he could just get a little money ahead, so he could sit down and really *write*, without having to worry about anything else. The Literary Agency hustle was doing very well, but it all just seemed to dribble away. The trip to Israel had been expensive, the trip to Rome had been expensive, and in between Angela could always find domestic ways to be expensive. No matter how quickly Mel's income increased, his outgo seemed to increase at the same pace. With a quarter million dollars, though, he could leave Ralphi and Ethelred in charge of the agency, move into a secluded cottage down in Puerto Rico or somewhere, and really *write*.

Driving northeast across Connecticut, in the wake of the road hog in the maroon Cadillac, Mel hunched over the steering wheel and wondered if it was considered ethical for a Literary Agent to peddle his own stuff.


## SIMULTANEOUSLY . . .

Jerry was parking the station wagon next to a fireplug on West End Avenue when a shoe bounced off the hood. "What?" he demanded, and glared all around, like any true New Yorker. His expression became clouded when a gray cardigan sweater with leather patches on the sleeves and a crumpled half-pack of filter Mores in the little pocket on the right-hand side spread itself like a despairing widow over the windshield. "Well, son of a bitch," Jerry said, and, "Wait a damn minute." And he stepped out of the car to a veritable rain of haberdashery.

This was no place for a man without a hard-hat. Skipping through the T-shirts and sweatpants, he trotted across the sidewalk and ducked into the vestibule at number 237. A large gray stone building, it was half a block wide and a dozen stories high, filled with high-ceilinged apartments featuring interesting wall moldings in which the cockroaches bred. There was the usual West Side-style Early Tile Revival décor in the vestibule, in contrasting black black and gray white, with the usual Brass Array addition of rank upon rank of doorbells.

Jerry looked for the name "Harwood" among the doorbells, and finally found it next to the button marked 7K. Fine. He took out his Bankamericard, planning to slide it down between the door and the frame, to force the bolt back and unlock the door, and then he noticed the metal slat screwed into place along the edge of the doorframe, blocking the space he needed to get at.

Well, hell. Now what?

He was still standing there, credit card in hand, when the door was abruptly yanked open and a good-looking but grimly angry girl stalked out, carrying two suitcases. She brushed by Jerry without a glance and marched on out to the street.

Jerry moved fast, and got a hand on the swiftly closing door before it could snick all the way shut. With a glance over his shoulder at the girl—who was kicking her way through drifts of jockey shorts—he entered the building and made his way to the seventh floor.

There was no sound behind the metal door of 7K. Pausing there, Jerry looked up and down the hall, and saw off to his right a door marked *Service*. Service? Going down there, opening that door, he found a grubby gray-painted stairwell, with a landing full of cartons, stacks of newspapers, brooms, and a tricycle missing one wheel. Also the back doors to four apartments: 7J, 7K, 7L, 7M.

"Right." He stepped over several cartons to ring the door-bell at 7K. When nothing happened he rang again, and still nothing happened, so he was already in the process of slipping the Bankamericard in next to the door—no damn metal slat here, anyway—when a male voice called out from inside, "Who is it?"

"Uh." Jerry pulled the card back, slipped it into his shirt pocket, and in a loud confident voice he cried out, "Maint'-nince."

"Is something wrong?" And this time Jerry noticed the voice had a strange hesitant quality to it, a sort of fluttery nervousness.

Jerry's own voice remained loud and confident: "Trouble widda plumbin."

"One minute, please."

Waiting, Jerry looked around at the junk out here, and saw leaning against a stack of newspapers an old red rubber plunger with a wooden handle. Picking it up, he held it over his shoulder like a bindlestiff.

Meantime, several locks and bolts and chains had been rattling and popping on the other side of the door, followed by a brief but bewildering silence. What now? Jerry was about to shout again when the voice, sounding much farther away, called, "Come in!"

Something was screwy here. Holding the plunger in front of himself like a club, Jerry reached out and turned the doorknob and pushed.

The door opened. It eased back in a slow curve, showing more and more of a small cluttered kitchen full of white appliances, off-white paint on wooden cabinets, white tile walls, gray-white vinyl floor and a rectangular kitchen table with green wooden legs and a white metal top. Color was furnished by the many boxes, bottles, cans, plates, cups, pots,

79

bowls, plastic bags, and twisties lying around on all the available flat surfaces.

But the interesting thing about the room was, it was empty. Frowning, peering cautiously into the dead space behind the open door, Jerry advanced pace by pace into the room and it just went on being empty. Now holding the plunger in both hands like a baseball bat, he stopped shy of the table and said, "Hello?"

"Excuse me," said the familiar voice.

It was like Alice in Wonderland. Jerry looked to his right, and a head was peering through an almost closed doorway across the room. Only the head and the fingers of one hand showed, and both were bony. The expression on the head's face seemed uncertain, tentative, unsure of everything including itself; it featured very highly raised eyebrows. It appeared to be male.

Jerry, partly in the character of the maintenance man and partly expressing his own curiosity, said, "What's up, Mac?"

The head said, "Would you like to earn ten dollars?"

People don't throw money away for no reason at all. Doubly suspicious, Jerry advanced across the room toward the doorway and the head, saying, "What's goin' on here? What's with you?"

The fingers abruptly extended into an entire arm, stretched out rigidly toward Jerry with the palm up, like a traffic cop stopping a line of traffic. "Stay right there!" cried the head, and the panic in his voice echoed itself in a great wigwagging of his eyebrows.

Jerry leaned forward, peering. The arm had no sleeves on it. "Say, you," he said. "Are you naked?"

"I want to talk to you about that," said the head.

"So," said Jerry. "Earn ten bucks, huh?" Grasping the plunger near the rubber end, he whacked the handle end into his own palm. "I'll give *you* ten bucks," he promised, and advanced.

"You misunderstand!" wailed the head, and the palm churned back and forth at Jerry as though to erase him from the kitchen. Then, as Jerry continued to advance, head and arm both abruptly disappeared and the door slammed. Or it would have slammed, if it hadn't been a swinging door. Instead of slamming, it coughed, made a faint attempt to open in Jerry's direction, and came to a stop.

Jerry slapped it open again with his own palm, marching through into a long high-ceilinged living room just in time to see a tall, skinny bare-ass guy duck through another doorway and slam *that* door. Which did slam, and which apparently also locked, judging from the *click* that followed.

Alice in Wonderland. Following the White Rabbit. Jerry strode across the room, intending to kick open this next door and see what the Naked Rabbit did after that, but midway two things brought him to a stop. The first was the memory of all that clothing raining down onto West End Avenue, and the second was the smell of marijuana.

Ah? Ah, there it was, the remnant of a joint smoldering in an African-looking ceramic ashtray next to a black leather chair. So Jerry *had* misunderstood. This wasn't some misplaced men's room masher, it was a rich radical-chic bleeding-heart liberal getting smashed on grass and throwing all his clothes out the window.

And the wife? Mr. and *Mrs.* Charles S. Harwood. Was she around here somewhere, too, also stoned out of her mind and out of her clothes? Jerry tried to remember if any of the garments descending from the sky had seemed feminine.

Meantime, Harwood was calling again, through this locked door, explaining at great length what Jerry had just figured out for himself, except that he didn't say he'd thrown his clothes out, he said there'd been an "accident," all his clothing had "fallen" out.

Jerry ignored him, because in glancing around the living room he had suddenly spotted something familiar in the fireplace. Going over there, he went down on one knee and picked up a definite fragment of a Dancing Aztec Priest. The right hand, with a remnant of wrist.

There were more fragments here. Enough for one statue, or two? Jerry rooted in all corners of the fireplace, pulling shreds and pieces out onto the hearth, and when he was finished he was sure it was only one. The Harwoods had received two statues at lunch today, and apparently the husband while smashed had smashed this one. So where was the other?

Harwood's voice had changed by now, becoming more plaintive: "Are you there?"

Jerry didn't bother to answer. Instead, he made a quick search, and when he'd satisfied himself that the living room contained no Dancing Aztec Priest other than the one on the hearth, who would dance no more, he went back to the kitchen and repeated the search there. Still nothing.

He returned to the living room as Harwood was just tentatively creeping out, extending an exploratory naked toe.

Seeing Jerry, he yelped and shot back inside, slamming the door and locking it with another *click*.

But that was the only place left to search, so Jerry went over, lifted one foot, and kicked the door next to the knob with the flat bottom of his shoe. Inside, Harwood yipped like a spaniel.

It took three kicks to pop the lock, and Harwood yipped each time. When the door at last did jerk open, Jerry saw Harwood scooting into a closet, pulling the door shut behind himself.

Good place for him. Jerry took the ordinary skeleton key from the inner keyhole of the door he'd just forced, crossed this cluttered bedroom, and locked Harwood in the closet. Then he searched the bedroom and bathroom, and damn if there still wasn't any sign of the other statue.

Which left nowhere but the closet. Unlocking the door, Jerry opened it and found Harwood brandishing a wooden hanger clutched over his head in his right hand while more or less covering himself with the splayed fingers of his left. He looked like some Dada parody of the Statue of Liberty, and he was truly stoned. He'd gulp-smoked that entire joint in the few minutes after Bobbi left, and the effects had fully caught up with him by now. "A man's home is his castle," he announced.

Jerry ignored him. Gazing around at the completely empty closet—empty except for Harwood and a bunch of hangers—he said, "What the hell is going on around here?"

"I am defending my castle," Harwood explained. "And I'm going to report *you* to the building."

Jerry prodded him on the chest with the plunger end of the plunger. "Where's the statue?"

Harwood blinked at him. The wooden hanger lowered to half-mast. Harwood said, "What?"

"Statue, statue. You got it today at lunch. Two of them. Bust one in the fireplace, where's the other one?"

"Isn't it here?" Harwood, apparently with real surprise, leaned forward against the plunger and gazed over Jerry's shoulder at the bedroom.

"No, it isn't here," Jerry said. Not wanting to carry Harwood's weight on his plunger any more, he pushed till Harwood had his balance back and then put the plunger down at his side. "I can guarantee you it isn't here," he said.

"Then she must have taken it with her." That seemed to give him food for thought.

"Who? Your wife?" Jerry stepped back a pace and considered the situation. He remembered the angry young woman downstairs, with the suitcases. "Oh, is *that* what happened? She walked out on you, and she threw all your stuff out the window."

"I can't understand it," Harwood said.

"And she took the statue with her. Where'd she go?"

"I really don't know," Harwood said.

Jerry turned the plunger around and poked Harwood a little with the wooden end. "Take a guess," he said.

"Ouch," said Harwood. "Don't do that."

"Guess."

"But I don't want to guess."

"No," Jerry said. "You *do* want to guess. What you *don't* want is for me to poke you any more." And he poked again, as demonstration.

"I wish you wouldn't do that," Harwood said. "It makes me lose my equilibrium."

"Look Jack—"

"Chuck," Harwood said.

"I'm losing my patience," Jerry told him.

Harwood looked sympathetic. "Oh, are you a doctor?"

"What?"

Harwood frowned, saying, "What on earth do you want with that statue?" Then, before Jerry could decide what or whether to answer, he became pensive and said, "Do you suppose she'll come back?"

Jerry knifed through to the meat of the conservation: "From where?"

"From out," Harwood said vaguely, and gestured with the hanger like a man trying to point at a flag on a windy day.

"Out *where?*"

"Perhaps I should learn to drive." Forgetting to cover himself, Harwood raised his left hand to pull at his left earlobe, a thing professors do as an aid to thought.

Jerry said, "Does your wife have a boyfriend?"

"Oh, dear," said Harwood. He sighed and leaned against the rear wall of the closet, lost in wistful meditation.

Jerry said, "What's his name and where does he live?"

Harwood slowly focused. "Who?"

"The boyfriend."

"Bobbi's boyfriend?"

So women give themselves men's names; so what? So Jerry was standing talking with a naked man in a closet who'd just said, "Bobbi's boyfriend." So what? "Right," Jerry said.

"Oscar," Harwood told him.

"Oscar?"

"Not the Other Oscar. The *other* Other Oscar."

"Terrific," Jerry said. "Oscar who?"

"Oscar Russell Green." Harwood frowned. "I distrust men with three names."

Oscar Russell Green, a name already on the list. "Fine," Jerry said. "See you later."

Harwood frowned at him. "Were you going to get me a pair of pants?"

"Not that I remember," Jerry said. He closed and locked the door again, and went away.


# EARLIER . . .

Sitting in his Pinto on Eleventh Avenue near the newspaper library, with the back seat full of swimming pool brochures and the windshield decorated by a brand-new parking ticket, Wally Hintzlebel studied his list of Open Sports Committee members, which only included five names with addresses:

> *Oscar Russell Green*
> *291 West 127th St.*
>
> *Professor Charles S. Harwood*
> *237 West End Avenue*
>
> *Wylie Cheshire*
> *58 Ridge Road*
> *Deer Park, Long Island*
>
> *Bud Beemiss*
> *29 West 45th St.*
>
> *Dorothy Moorwood*
> *5 Ronkonkomo Drive*
> *Alpine, New Jersey*

Through Wally's brain and body surged emotions of rage, urgency, greed, frustration, panic, inadequacy, envy, hatred, lust, and despair. He shook in the grip of these feelings, he trembled so much that the car itself vibrated slightly, and a loose screw on the rear license plate chattered a little tune to the gutter.

What to do? What to do? Those four men in Queens, they were surely well on their way by now. *Sixteen* statues, by God, sixteen statues, and he only had five addresses, and the filthy library was closed for the night.

What to do? Break into the library? But he didn't know how, he'd never broken into anything in his life except other men's wives, and then only when the door had already been opened for him.

It might be one of the five. It might be. The million-dollar prize, the true golden statue, it *could* be any one of the sixteen, and so it might be one of these five, the addresses he already had.

A phone booth stood at the corner, glass-sided and unoccupied. Wally, still quivering slightly, got out of the Pinto and trotted to the phone booth, where he called his mother and said, "Mom, I won't be home for dinner."

"Hello? Who is this speaking, if I may ask?"

"Mom?"

"Would you be so kind as to identify yourself, if I may be so bold?"

"It's Wally, Mom."

"Wally?"

"Wally, Mom, it's Wally."

"Wally, you'll be late for dinner. Where are you?"

"I won't be home for dinner, Mom."

"Where?"

"What?"

"Where *are* you, Wally?"

"I'm in Manhattan, Mom. Listen, Mom, I won't be home for dinner."

"Wal-lee? Does Wal-lee have tum a dirl friend?"

"Aw, come on, Mom, you know you're my best girl."

"Does Wal-lee have a heavy date with a sweetsie-sweetsie?"

"Nothin' like that, Mom. Honest."

"Can't you bring her home to your Mommy-Mommy, Wal-lee?"

"Mom, listen, it isn't a date or *anything* like that. I *swear* it isn't. It's business."

"Is Wal-lee extra special positive?"

"Business, Mom. No girls."

"*What* business at this hour, Wally?"

And Wally knew he was beaten. There was no way out of it. "I'll, uh—" He stared through the glass at Eleventh Avenue. "I'll come home," he said. "I'll, uh, I'll explain it to, uh, these business people. I'll be right home."

He hung up on her bubbling appreciation, and raced back to the Pinto. In the car, he kicked the engine into life and yanked the car out among the cabs, turning toward the Midtown Tunnel.

He'd eat fast, that's all. Eat fast, claim he was—claim he was going to a movie, rush back to the city. It could still be done. Blinking through the windshield (the parking ticket, still stuck under the wiper, blinked back, flapping in the breeze), he urged the Pinto toward the tunnel.

# ALSO . . .

Oscar Russell Green was drunk as a skunk. He was drunker than *two* skunkers. Nayamba had taken refuge at her mother's place over in Newark, and Green was letting 'er rip. Letting 'er tear. Letting 'er do anything 'er damn well wanted to do. *Sum*-bitch!

It isn't easy to be a leader of men. Whether you're fronting a crack Marine brigade or a fat-bellied lynch mob, you still have to bring to bear the same leadership qualities of self-reliance, decisiveness, control over others, and unflagging determination. Oscar Russell Green had those leadership qualities in abundance, but unfortunately he also had all the opposite qualities as well, such as self-doubt, indecision, defeatism.

When actively engaged in being a leader, Green had to smother all those qualities in himself that were inappropriate to the Leadership Profile. Which meant that every once in a while, every once in a *great* while and only at moments when the demands of Leadership were temporarily lifted, Green had to let that other side of himself out of its cell and into the exercise yard for a quick walk around. With a bottle in its hand.

It had started today right after lunch at the Goddess of Heaven. The brandy after the presentation of the Other Oscars had tasted *sooo* good, had made him feel *sooo* easy, and had disappeared from the little glass *sooo-oooo* fast, that he had known right away the relinquishing of the reins of Leadership had begun, and he had stopped off in the phone booth near the restaurant's cash register to put his wife Nayamba wise. "Time to visit your mama, girl. The black tornado has just been sighted."

"Have a good time, Oscar," she said, and hung up without another word.

Having finished his Distant Early Warning, Oscar said farewell to his troops on the sidewalk out front, making an abortive pass at Bobbi Harwood *en passant*, which was the first time he'd ever made a play for her. (Aside from the fact that he was always faithful to Nayamba, except while drinking, Oscar had kept away from Bobbi before this because one of the basic qualities of the Leader is that he show no favoritism.) But Bobbi was having none of that, so away went Oscar, homeward bound.

Home was an apartment on West 127th Street, way over near the Hudson River, in one of a group of brick tenement buildings that had been taken over by a neighborhood committee, refurbished inside, and turned into moderate-rental apartments. Having an in with several members of the committee, Oscar had managed to leapfrog over the waiting list, and had a nice three-and-a-half at the top rear, with a narrow view northward and a pretty good view of the Henry Hudson Parkway to the west.

Stopping at the apartment only long enough to leave the Other Oscar atop the bedroom dresser, Oscar had returned to the overworld and had patronized a number of bars and liquor stores before staggering homeward once more, the demands of leadership long forgotten. Trying to drink cheap port wine from the bottle and climb stairs at the same time, he made his way to his door, fumbled with his keys, unlocked his way in, and heard noises from the bedroom.

Hello? Oscar clutched the wine bottle to his chest and staggered with swift purpose to the bedroom, where he found two white men just about to climb out the window onto the fire escape. And one of them had the Other Oscar!

"Hey!" the first Oscar cried.

The two white men stared at him in utter panic. "Oh, no!" one of them cried. "F-f-f-feet," stuttered the other one, "d-d-d-do your stuff." And yet he didn't move, he just stood where he was, blocking the window.

"That's mine!" Oscar shouted, pointing the wine bottle in

surprise and outrage at the Other Oscar. Wine sloshed. "You gimme that!"

The man with the statue abruptly turned, trying to shove his frozen partner out of the way so he could get out the window.

"Oh, no, you don't!" Oscar yelled, and threw the wine bottle. More wine sloshed. The sound of breaking glass was followed by the sight of Oscar's window disintegrating. Both halves; the thieves had raised the bottom half and Oscar's bottle had therefore crashed through both thicknesses of glass.

"Goddam! Goddam! Goddam!" Oscar ran at the burglars, and started wrestling with the one who had the statue, a big red-faced white man, with staring eyes and bad breath.

"Here!" yelled the white man, and tossed the statue over Oscar's head to his partner. "Run, Floyd!"

Floyd ran. Instead of running out the window, though, he ran over the bed, and Oscar caught him before he reached the bedroom door.

After that, the whole thing degenerated into some sort of idiotic schoolyard game, with the two white men tossing the statue back and forth to one another while Oscar played monkey in the middle. And they kept shouting at one another all the time: "Floyd! Floyd!" "Frank! Frank!"

It came to an end at last when Oscar tackled Frank as he was just about to catch Floyd's lateral. The Other Oscar zoomed past them both, whacked into the wall, fell to the floor, and broke its right leg.

Floyd and Frank and Oscar all scrambled for the fumble, and it was Floyd who came up with the main part, while Frank emerged with the Other Oscar's right leg from knee to toe, the statue's uplifted leg, which had snapped off clean.

Oscar, prepared to go on fighting on this front if it took all winter, suddenly found himself with a bunch of guys who didn't want to play any more. Floyd and Frank looked at one another, looked at the broken parts in their hands, and all at once lost interest. "Sorry, fella," Frank said, handing over the snapped-off shin. "Nothing personal," Floyd said, placing in Oscar's other hand the rest of the statue. And, while Oscar stood there gaping, they proceeded rapidly but in an orderly fashion out the broken window and down the fire escape and away.

"Well, I'll be damned," Oscar said. When he closed the window, the rest of the glass fell out, but he locked it anyway. Then he went off to phone the local liquor store that delivered.

# FURTHERMORE . . .

Bud Beemiss was *not* the type August Corella liked to do business with. A soft self-satisfied drone like financier Victor Krassmeier was best, and failing that Corella had no objection to dealing with another tough guy like himself; they could talk the same language, they'd both know where they stood. In a way, Beemiss combined both types, but the result was new, and a lot more difficult.

The house was rambling Colonial-style set amid rolling parkland, and the maid who'd let them in had showed them to a booklined study. "Not bad," Earl said, apparently referring to everything, the maid, the house, the room, even the books.

*Not good either,* Corella thought, but he didn't say it aloud. He waited for Beemiss, already knowing this wouldn't be easy.

Then Beemiss himself bounced into the room, and was even worse than Corella had expected. His pullover shirt, beltless slacks, and rope-soled shoes were the most intimidating kind of casual. He had the neat, tanned, round, fleshless head of a man who takes very good care of himself, and the cheerful blue eyes and wide smile of a man who never gives anything away. He had a glad-hander's version of Krassmeier's board-room toughness, but some stink of the street still clung to him. "Hiya, fellas," he said, flicking the door closed and striding across the room. "What can I do for you?"

The subject of this interview was going to be power; that was plain enough. And Corella was determined to get his own claim for dominance in first. "It isn't what you can do for me, Beemiss," he said, in his toughest style. "It's what I can do for you."

Beemiss' smile turned lopsided, but not with apprehension. He looked merely annoyed that he'd been taken away from whatever he'd been doing—six laps in the pool, maybe, or dyeing his brown hair. "Gentlemen," he said, "I suspect this is a matter to be taken care of at the office."

If you start tough, stay tough. "We'll take care of it here," Corella said. "It's about this Open Sports Committee."

From the sudden glint in Beemiss' eyes, Corella knew the

man had picked up a sudden wrong impression. He probably thought this was political, right-wing tough guys leaning on a liberal. What he started to say confirmed that idea: "Gentlemen, there's no point talking about differences be—"

"You got a statue today," Corella said. He had no time for misunderstandings.

Which stopped Beemiss cold. He frowned at Corella, with nothing to say.

So Corella went on: "Sixteen statues. Shipped to you from down in South America."

Beemiss shook his head. "I confess, gentlemen," he said, "I'm at a loss."

"We know about those statues." Corella let a wintry smile appear on his lips and then fade away. "It's our job to know about them."

"Your job?"

"You weren't supposed to get that shipment."

Beemiss was leaning forward slightly, as though he would understand the words better if he could hear them better. "I wasn't?"

"You were supposed to get a different shipment," Corella told him. "Friends of mine were supposed to get that shipment."

A sudden knowingness altered Beemiss' expression, and he leaned back again, nodding, calculating. "I see."

Good. He'd picked that up fast, much faster than someone like Krassmeier would. Corella said, "My friends want their shipment."

"Yes, I suppose they do." Beemiss was being slow, careful, thinking things over. He still wasn't afraid.

Corella said. "My friends realize it's an inconvenience, so they'll put out cash money, and you people can get something better instead."

"Is that right?"

"Yeah. They'll pay uhh . . ."—and Corella hesitated, Beemiss and the house combining to force him to revise his initial offer upward—". . . four thousand for the statues."

"Four thousand." The pale blue eyes glinted. "Apiece?"

Beemiss mustn't be allowed to get away with jokes. "Four thousand for the whole shipment," Corella said. "And peace of mind."

Beemiss cocked an ear. "What was that?"

"These people, my friends. They're not your ordinary businessmen."

"I was getting that impression."

"If something happened and they didn't get their shipment," Corella said, "their *whole* shipment, you and me, we'd both be in big trouble."

"*We* would?"

"They'd get sore at both of us." Corella gestured at the room. "Now, I see you got a nice house here, a nice family, a nice business in New York, you don't want to—"

"You're not from New York, are you?"

Corella frowned. "What?"

"Jersey, I'd say." Beemiss nodded to himself. "Connected with the docks, maybe, is that where your friends are?"

"You don't want to know my friends," Corella said.

"The question is, do I want your friends to know my friends?"

"I don't get that."

"You want me to give you a list, isn't that it, of all the people who got statues?"

"No way." Corella was offended. "You want me to shlep all over the city? You got a nice office in New York, secretaries; tomorrow morning you put a secretary to work on the phone, call everybody, bring in their statues. Then you turn them over to me."

"I assume you're talking about cash in advance."

"First thing tomorrow morning," Corella said, "you'll have the cash on your desk. What time you get to the office?"

"Usually around ten."

"Ten o'clock, four grand in cash on your desk."

"Four?" Beemiss looked surprised, but Corella was sure the look was fake. "I'm sorry, did I ever agree to four?"

"You want a little more?" Corella shrugged. "My friends won't quibble."

"I should think, for sixteen statues," Beemiss said, "sixteen thousand dollars is a more sensible number."

"On the other hand," Corella said, "my friends won't stand around and get held up either."

Beemiss shrugged. "You know your friends better than I do. At what point does quibbling become holding up?"

"We'll split the difference. Call it eight thousand."

"The way I learned math," Beemis said, "splitting the difference between four and sixteen is ten."

"Half of sixteen is eight. Take eight."

"And on the other hand," Beemiss said, "maybe I don't want the deal at all. Maybe we'd all rather just keep the statues. They do, after all, have a certain sentimental significance."

"Listen to me," Corella said, and now his effort was to combine toughness with fellow feeling. "You and your friends don't want those statues. Please take my word for it. For the sake of your happiness and your health and your well-being you don't want those statues. You want some other statues."

"Twelve," Beemiss said.

Corella shook his head. "No."

Again Beemiss shrugged, this time having nothing to say. Clearly this was not the first negotiating session he'd ever attended.

Corella waited, trying to decide on the right balance of threat and payment, and finally nodded and said, "Take ten, then. And be happy I'm such an easygoing guy."

"Fine," Beemiss said. "I'll accept ten. And replacements."

"Replacements?" Corella spread his hands. "So go get some."

"The *same*. Give us the shipment your friends got by mistake."

A complication; Corella wasn't immediately certain how to deal with it. "I don't think we could do that," he said.

"Then get me another shipment."

"We want our shipment *now*."

"Fine," Beemiss said. "Tomorrow morning you place an order for sixteen more statues, to be delivered to my office in New York, and you send the order slip over with the cash."

Corella was becoming more and more troubled. That clown from Ecuador had arranged the first shipment. Corella had no idea how to go about getting more copies. "You do it," he said. "How much were the damn things?"

"Eighteen apiece, wholesale. That's two hundred eighty-eight dollars for sixteen."

Corella looked, and felt, bitter. "That's a nice profit you're making."

"It wasn't my mistake," Beemiss pointed out.

"All right," Corella said. "In the morning you'll get cash money, ten thousand two hundred eighty-eight dollars. I'll call you in the afternoon."

"I didn't catch your name."

"Mister Kane. And while I'm here, why don't I pick up *your* statue?"

Beemiss raised a slightly surprised eyebrow. "Before the cash is delivered?"

"All right, all right." Turning to Earl, Corella said, "Give him six and a half."

Which meant that Earl, who until now had kept his good profile firmly toward Beemiss, would now have to show himself full-face. Grumbling, looking sullen, he dug out his wallet, peeled off four hundred dollar bills and five fifties, and slapped them into Beemiss' hand. Beemiss, a faint smile on his face as he looked at Earl's black eye, said a quietly ironic, "Thank you."

"The statue," Corella said.

"It's upstairs."

Beemiss left the room, and both Corella and Earl followed. "I'll be right down," Beemiss said.

"That's okay."

So up the stairs they went, all three of them, and along the hall, and into Beemiss' study, where Mel Bernstein (also known as Zachary George) was walking across the carpet toward the open window, the Dancing Aztec Priest clutched in his left hand.


# IN THE MEANTIME . . .

Jerry put his credit card away and walked into the Fayley-Spang residence. David Fayley and Kenneth Spang, both members of the Open Sports Committee, turned out to share this apartment on West 87th Street, in another bulky old apartment building like the one housing the Harwoods. A short hallway flanked by small abstracts and arty black-and-white photographs led to a living room bristling with artifacts. A wooden African fertility goddess with sixteen breasts dominated one corner, near a sleek grouping of black stereo components on dark walnut shelves. A wall-hanging in predominantly red and blue depicted the arrival of a well-hung barbarian at some effete court. Chrome cube end tables flanked the maroon sofa. Spider plants festooned the windows. Some sort of copper implement, suggesting for some reason the Pennsylvania Dutch, stood among more obscure items on a long black wooden table behind the sofa.

It wasn't like the living rooms Jerry knew. The Harwood living room had also been somewhat grander, or artier, than the rooms where Jerry spent his time in Queens, but it had at least maintained the normal pattern, a sofa and two armchairs all grouped to face the television set. A floor lamp at one end of the sofa, a table lamp at the other. The style had been different—flexible chrome floor lamps were not to be found in Teresa's or Angela's living room—but the substance was the same.

Here, though, everything was different. The sofa, squarely in the middle of the room, faced nothing at all, unless that wall of shelves—crowded with books, figurines, small framed pictures, mementoes, curios, forget-me-nots, whatnots, and thingamabobs, artfully arranged—could be thought to take the place of TV. There was, in fact, no television set in the room at all, nor any armchairs. A few wooden chairs tucked into free spots along the walls could presumably be moved forward to make conversational groupings, but the apparent idea of this room was that it would contain two people who would sit together on the sofa and—what? Talk? Read? Stare at the shelves?

The suggestion of a different category of life, an utterly strange approach, was so strong that it briefly stopped Jerry in his tracks. Surely Fayley and Spang were queers, but that wasn't the point; being queer had nothing to do with TVs and sofa placement. Human beings *have* found a variety of ways to live, a fact most people have scant reason to notice. Taken by this idea, surprised and in a way made curious by it, Jerry stood still in the middle of the room, forgetting for a minute the search for the golden statue while he studied the things around him, trying to work out the attitudes, the assumptions, that had led to this other way.

He was distracted from these musings by the sudden appearance in the opposite doorway of a slender, languid young man who strolled into the room as though the presence of strangers in here were simply another part of this different approach to life. As maybe they were.

Jerry's first reaction—startled surprise and apprehension—was smothered by his second reaction—a cultural hostility to homosexuals—which gave way almost immediately to yet a third, different kind of surprise, a kind of comic wonder, when he realized this fellow really did accept Jerry's existence as natural, not at all out of the way. With a little smile, a casual wave of the hand, he nodded at Jerry and said, "Well, hello."

"Hello," Jerry said. Punch him? Make a run for it? Bluff it out? Bluff *what* out?

"I'm David. Kenny's friend."

Jerry pointed at himself. "Jerry."

Rather more than ordinarily casual, David made another

94

of his waving gestures and said, "I assume Kenny's taking care of you?"

"I guess so." It was hard to know what David thought was happening here, and so doubly hard to figure out the right answers to questions. Also, Jerry had just noticed that the calm casual facade of David was marred by very red, very puffy eyes. David had been crying. Was David a nut case?

"Do feel right at home," David was saying, with an almost imperceptible break in his voice. Suggesting, perhaps, that his heart was also breaking?

"Thanks," Jerry said. He was sure by now the statue wasn't in this room, though most other statues from human history were.

"Is Kenny getting you a drink?"

What was the answer to *that* one? Frowning toward the doorway through which David had entered—would the unseen Kenny enter at any second with a gun in his hand?—Jerry hopelessly said, "A drink?"

"You mean he isn't?" David shook his head with a kind of fussy petulance, then offered a long-suffering sigh. "Well, then, I suppose it's up to me to maintain the hospitality of the house. What would you like?"

"To drink?" It was hard to follow this conversation. "Sure, what the hell," Jerry said, and shrugged. "You got a beer?"

"Beer?" Doubt touched David's brow, also perhaps a touch of snobbery. "I'll see," he said, and went away, back through the same doorway.

Jerry was still trying to decide whether or not to follow him, give the rest of the apartment a quick search, when the apartment door opened behind him and another one came in, putting his keys back in his pocket.

Kenny Spang; no doubt of it. A painfully skinny black man with a huge fuzzy Afro, he gave Jerry a look of combined surprise and irony, saying, "And what have we here?"

"You must be Kenny," Jerry said, since he might as well go on behaving as though he belonged here.

"So I must," Kenny said. "And who must you be?"

"Jerry. David's in the kitchen."

"Is he?" A very knowing amusement glittered in Kenny's eyes.

"Getting me a beer."

"How good of David. But then, David is such a good person."

"Sure," Jerry said, and David himself came back, with a tall pilsner glass full of beer.

"Well, well," Kenny said, and watched the glass as David handed it to Jerry.

The truth would have to come out very soon now. Jerry drank beer as quickly as he could.

David gave his roommate a wounded look. "It's good of you to come back," he said, his misery showing through his attempt at unconcern.

"Rather too early, I see."

David showed such serene languor that he looked boneless. "Jerry and I have just been having a chat while waiting for you."

"Waiting for me. That's rich."

If Jerry was going to search the rest of the apartment, he'd better do it now, before these two realized the mistake they were making. Putting the empty glass down, he grinned at them both and said, "Well, you know what they say. You don't buy beer, you just pay rent on it. Where's the head?"

Both of his hosts seemed taken aback by his manner, but it was David who recovered first, pointing at the doorway and saying, "Through the bedroom."

"Fine."

The television set was in the bedroom, at the foot of the double bed. So were the statues, both of them on a high glass shelf over a table with an expensive-looking chess set laid out on it. While scratching the bottoms of both statues with a key, to see if it was plaster or gold beneath the paint, Jerry listened to the conversation continuing in the living room. There was a smirk within Kenny's voice, hurt outrage in David's.

KENNY: "Well, I can't say I care much for your taste."

DAVID: *"My* taste! *You're* one to talk!"

KENNY: "It happens *I* know what I'm looking for, unlike some others I could mention."

DAVID [*Wistfully*]: "I have been looking all my life for a rational love."

KENNY: "You choose unusual places to look."

DAVID: "I'll certainly agree with that."

KENNY: "Well, I couldn't interrupt you two for the world. I'll find *somewhere* to go."

DAVID: "Don't you dare! If you leave here, you'll take him with you."

KENNY: "Losing your nerve, sweetie?"

DAVID: "Well, you'll never lose yours. But if you walk out and leave that creature here I'll never forgive you. I mean that, Kenny, I'm very serious about that."

KENNY: "Giving him to me, are you?" [*Tinkling laughter*] "If you can't stand the heat, stay out of the park."

DAVID: "Oh, you're just vicious. *Vicious!*"

Plaster, and plaster. Putting the statues back, Jerry returned to the living room on the second "vicious," to find the roommates confronting one another like a pair of cats. Jerry gave them his cheerful unaware grin, saying, "Well, listen, fellas. Sounds like you two got a lot to talk about, so I won't keep you. Thanks for the beer. See you around."

"Oh, I'm sure," Kenny said, while David struggled in vain to look unconcerned.

"Well," Jerry said to himself in the elevator going down. "Whadaya think of *that?*"


## AFTER DINNER . . .

Wally Hintzlebel, swimming pool salesman and afternoon adulterer, was one of those people who grow up in the shadow of New York City without ever being a part of it. In the Long Island community where he'd grown up, many of his school friends had had fathers who worked in the city, and during his teens kids he knew would occasionally take the train to Manhattan, but Wally never hung around with that kind of crowd. He hung around with a *local* crowd. He was a small-town boy, surrounded by other small-town youngsters, and the fact of Manhattan upthrust on the horizon meant nothing to him.

In adult life, his swimming pool selling would occasionally bring him over the city line into Queens or Brooklyn, but so far as Manhattan was concerned this was only the third experience of his life. The first, nine years ago when he was fifteen, had been on the occasion of his mother's birthday. Having saved sufficient money, Wally had presented her with tickets to a Broadway musical, plus dinner in a midtown restaurant. Though Mom had kept saying how wonderful it all was, he'd known from the very beginning it was a mistake, and one he'd never repeat. Her strained smile in the grubby noisy train had told him, with no words from her, just how difficult she found this mode of transportation. In the restaurant, her assurances that everything was delicious had alternated with her repeated questionings of the waiter, want-

97

ing to know the ingredients of all the dishes. She kept tasting things and looking far off, as though trying to hear a distant bell, then saying, "What an *unusual* taste." As for the musical, full of nearly naked girls and much boisterous singing, Mom had patted his arm afterward and said, "I'm sure it's a wonderful show."

The second Manhattan experience, five years later, had been during one of Mom's rare absences from home. Aunt Leah, Mom's only sister, was dying in Springfield, Illinois, and Mom had gone out there for a week, four days of bedside waiting, and then the funeral. Wally drove her to LaGuardia Airport for the flight to Springfield, then got back into the car after her departure, suddenly realizing that home was empty, nobody was there; a nervous, expectant tingling had all at once suffused his body, like a sunset blossoming over a western sky. Driving from the airport out to Grand Central Parkway, he came to the point where he could either turn east toward home or west toward the city, and like the trivet on a Ouija board the car suddenly jerked itself westward. What could Wally do but go along?

In its way, this second visit had been even worse than the first. After driving about hopelessly through two hours of late-afternoon traffic jam, knowing no one, having no destination, Wally had settled at last in a hokey tourist bar off Broadway, where he had become very drunk and very sick. Also, the police impounded his car, and he had to spend the night in a hotel room, alternating nightmares with mad dashes to the bathroom. It had cost fifty dollars to get the car back the next day, and Wally had spent the rest of his mother's absence safely in front of the television set in his own living room.

And now he was back for the third time (with a break for dinner), but in this instance Manhattan meant nothing at all. If the trail of the golden statue led to Alaska, to the Congo, to the rings of Saturn, that is where Wally would go. Manhattan was a backdrop only, it had no place in his thoughts.

Which meant he didn't realize until he got to 29 West 45th Street, the Bud Beemiss address, just how unlikely that was to be a private residence. He drove there hurriedly from the Midtown Tunnel, dinner (chicken, peas, baked potato, cherry pie, coffee) roiling in his stomach, and he visualized himself in the Beemiss apartment, clutching the electric coolness of gold, but the instant he saw the building he knew

98

what had happened. Beemiss's office, not his home. And nobody here at this hour.

Blinking, churning, Wally scrabbled in the glove compartment for the list of names and addresses. Beemiss no good, somebody else, somebody else.

Oscar Russell Green, 291 West 127th Street. *That* had to be a home address. Also, Green was supposed to be the leader of the Open Sports Committee, so why wouldn't *he* have a full list of the membership?

Wally lunged the Pinto forward. Oscar Russell Green. Gotta hustle.


# THEREFORE . . .

DOO de doo, de doo, de doo, de-*doot*-de doody doo.

Oscar Russell Green was a rotten dancer, but he didn't care. He had no natural sense of rhythm, he had two left feet, he moved his shoulders wrong, and he had no idea what to do with his hands, but he just didn't give a damn about *any* of that. If he wanted to dance, goddam it, he'd *dance*, that's all. Dance all over the friggin' living room, no matter how much the friggin' furniture got in the way. Hell with the friggin' furniture.

Oscar was dancing the Hustle. He wasn't, actually, but he thought he was, and that's almost the same thing. He was lumbering around the living room, cartwheeling inadvertently from time to time over the larger pieces of furniture, but always picking himself up again and dancing on. Ever on. To the music in his head, or maybe to the music of the spheres. Remembered music.

After the Irish comedy team of Frank and Floyd had departed, Oscar had napped woozily until the doorbell ringing had brought him around to a violent headache. Fortunately, the ringing had heralded the delivery boy from the liquor store, so a lot of quickly gulped hooch had smothered the headache and left Oscar more or less awake and more or less in his wrong mind, his non-Leader mind.

Nevertheless, enough of his right mind had remained for him to fret about the broken Other Oscar and to decide at last to fix the damn thing, right *now*, right this *second*, right this *instant*, where the hell's the Elmer's glue? Kitchen

kitchen kitchen kitchen, ah *hah!* Elmer's glue. Next, he brought the Other Oscar and the Other Oscar's other leg in from the bedroom to the living room, spread a lot of Elmer's glue over the furniture and the lamps and his hands and the floor and various parts of the Other Oscar, and then jammed the leg back on and damn if it didn't stay. Damn if it didn't. He put the Other Oscar on the living room window-sill to dry—he had a hell of a time letting go of the thing, what with all the Elmer's glue all over the damn place—and when he stepped back to view the result (flipping backward over the beanbag chair) it seemed to him the Other Oscar looked as though he was just climbing over the sill, just coming in from the great outdoors. There wasn't any fire escape outside that window, nothing but dark silent air five stories over the street, so this had to be a *real* god to be able to come in through that window. A flying god. "Whadaya hear from the flying nun?" Oscar asked it, and went chuckling away to find his bottle. Then he came chuckling back with the bottle and sat on the Barcalounger—*floop*, it went, and there he was lying on the Barcalounger, all unexpectedlike—and he sat there chuckling for a while and drinking from his bottle, and then he discovered he couldn't put the bottle down.

Good*dam* it. Damn thing, damn goddam sum-bitch dirty filthy goddam—Ah, the hell with it, why put the thing down, anyway? So he just went on holding it and drinking from it, chuckling whenever he looked over at the Other Oscar, and then it occurred to him the Other Oscar looked creepy.

Spooky. Damn if it didn't. Coming in the window that way, all gold and glittery against the darkness of the night sky, green eyes glistening out as if this is a real meat-eater god, hopping on one leg like he's a bad-tempered meat-eater flying god, coming in to lay *waste*, man, gonna waste *some-body* before he's through.

"Sum-bitch," Oscar muttered at the damn thing, and took another swig from the bottle stuck to his hand. If he'd been some sort of superstitious jigaboo, by Jesus, that sum-bitch over there on the windowsill would give him something to superstit about. You get one of your Deep South field niggers, Oscar reflected, that little sum-bitch over there would shake his goddam teeth right out his goddam head. Damn if it wouldn't.

Good thing he himself happened to be an educated city fella. Good thing.

Oscar took another drink, and found the bottle empty. Still stuck to his hand, but empty. And that's a hell of a thing, goddam it. Hell of a thing. Who wants an empty bottle stuck to his hand?

Struggling one-handed out of the Barcalounger—it didn't want to let him go, until the very end, when it flipped upright and bunked him onto the mohair sofa—Oscar weaved his way into the kitchen, and ran boiling water from the tap over his hand until the bottle let go, at which point it finally dawned on him that he'd just turned his fingers into hot dogs. "Ow," he said. "Goddam it, *ow*."

It was one of those pains that built gradually, getting worse and worse long after the cause of it had stopped. Oscar reeled back to the living room with a fresh bottle in his good hand, his bad hand stuck into the opposite armpit, while he hopped on one leg as a curative for the pain of the burn. He was standing there hopping, saying *Ow* from time to time and otherwise cursing and muttering in a general fashion, when he noticed the Other Oscar again, and saw that he and the Other Oscar were both hopping together.

"Hah!" said Oscar, and stopped hopping, and stood there grinning at the Other Oscar, who went on hopping but who didn't seem spooky any more. Not at all spooky.

In fact, in fact, the Other Oscar wasn't hopping, he was *dancing*. That's what he was doing, he was dancing, and so Oscar started dancing with him, and pretty soon Oscar was dancing all over the room, doing his own version of the Hustle, and that's what he was doing when he heard the tinkle in the bedroom.

Tinkle? Glass? Frank and Floyd back? Clutching his half-full—half-empty?—bottle tightly in his good hand, Oscar tippy-toed through the apartment into the bedroom, and there stood *another* white man. Another one.

This one was even weirder. He was a tall skinny bony sort of guy, with limp blond hair. He had on a sports jacket, and his hand was in the pocket, and he was pointing something in that pocket in Oscar's direction. Also, he was wearing a mask over the lower half of his face, like bank robbers in Western movies, only this mask was made of a paper napkin from McDonald's, and the upside-down golden arches right in the middle of the mask made this new loony look bucktoothed, like a beaver.

"Hands up," said the beaver.

Oscar's hands were already occupied, one with holding a bottle and the other with tingling and stinging. "Well, god-*dam* it," Oscar said.

"Back up," said the beaver.

"You guys getting to be a pain," Oscar said, but he backed up. He backed up step by step all the way to the living room, with the beaver following him, pointing that whatchit at him from his jacket pocket and glaring at him with pale, watery blue eyes that made Oscar think, for some reason, of swimming pools. Angry swimming pools.

The two of them entered the living room. Oscar backward, and then Oscar somersaulted backward over the beanbag chair, spraying cheap whiskey in various directions, and when he struggled up to a sitting position this new white man was running across the living room with his hand out at the Other Oscar.

"Hey!" Oscar yelled, but the beaver grabbed the Other Oscar around the torso, turned, and ran the other way.

Except the Other Oscar didn't move. It stayed there on the windowsill—maybe, Oscar reflected, just maybe he'd used a little too much Elmer's glue—and the beaver did a wonderful stunt of running up an invisible wall until he was horizontal with the ground, about five feet up.

At which point the Other Oscar broke. The ankle of the leg standing on the base gave way, and the Other Oscar went off with the beaver, leaving his left foot and his base stuck to the windowsill. The beaver, meantime, clutching the Other Oscar, sailed feet-first into the Barcalounger, which ate him. It just folded up like a Venus fly trap, enclosing most of the beaver except his head and the arm holding the Other Oscar.

"Now," Oscar said, in admiration, "now I never saw *anything* like *that* before."

The beaver thrashed around in the Barcalounger, kicking and squirming, and all at once the Barcalounger up-chucked him again, and the beaver spun around on the floor, leaped to his feet, and was about to dash from the room when he apparently noticed for the first time that the Other Oscar had broken. He halted in midstride, like one of those action photographs that win the Sports Category awards, and he stared at the exposed plaster of the Other Oscar's ankle, and then he said, "Well, shoot." And he tossed the Other Oscar away onto the sofa.

Well, he tried to. Then he tried again. Then he stared at the Other Oscar, stuck to his hand, and at that point Oscar struggled over to him and said, "Lemme help, lemme help."

"Jesus," said the beaver. The paper napkin fluttered every time he spoke.

Oscar peeled the beaver's hand off the Other Oscar, and

the beaver shoved that hand into his pocket, pointed something at Oscar and said, sounding tough, "I want the list."

"You were pointing in the other pocket before," Oscar told him.

"What?" The beaver stared down at himself, as though he'd just been told his fly was open, and then he leaped straight up in the air, turned around in midleap, and landed running in the other direction.

Oscar didn't follow. He listened to the crashing, and then the tinkling, and then the *brong-brong-brong*ing of the guy's retreat down the fire escape. "This is the worst drunk I've *ever* had," Oscar said out loud. Then he put the Other Oscar on the beanbag chair for safekeeping, and turned his attention to the base on the windowsill.

Stuck. Well and truly stuck. Sighing, shaking his head, Oscar went off toward the kitchen to get some hot water.


## ALONG WITH WHICH . . .

*Our Story Till Now:* Earnest, professional MEL BERNSTEIN, while engaged in business activities instigated by his bustling, clever brother-in-law JERRY MANELLI, enters the posh residence of dapper, amiable BUD BEEMISS in search of the ugly, valuable DANCING AZTEC PRIEST. At the same time, unknown to MEL, BUD is in discussion with tough, dishonest AUGUST CORELLA and big, mean EARL in the library, while stocky, disinterested RALPH remains in the new, shiny CADILLAC out front. BUD, AUGUST and EARL, upon entering the room containing the PRIEST, discover MEL in the process of a felony. Everyone is startled. Now go on with the story—

Mel jumped out the window, clutching the golden statue in both hands. Behind him, Corella and Beemiss were both yelling, while Earl was trying to decide whether or not *he* wanted to jump out the window.

Mel landed on his feet. Then he landed on his knees, then on his side, then on his shoulder, then on his head, and then on his back. Then he rolled. At no time, however, did he let go of the statue, nor at any time did any part of the statue break.

Upstairs, Corella and Beemiss were both still yelling. Earl, having decided that jumping out second-story windows was not in his repertoire, was running from the room, headed toward the stairs.

Out on the lawn in the twilight, Mel was staggering to his feet and running in various directions. Having blundered into the side of the house, he oriented himself at last and took off across the rolling lawn, clutching the statue to his chest. The two Beemiss family Great Danes, with whom Mel had become friendly on the way in, romped along at his side, saying, "Woof!"

Corella and Beemiss both finally stopped yelling, and Corella ran out of the room after Earl, while Beemiss stood frowning at the man and dogs gamboling away across the lawn. Bud Beemiss had a quick mind, and it had begun nibbling at the inconsistencies.

Earl didn't have a particularly quick mind, but he had a very quick body, and in no time at all he had bounded down the stairs, leaped across the front hall, flung himself out the doorway, and was rounding the side of the house in Mel's wake. Corella, in less terrific physical shape, was puffing gamely along in the background.

Mel had left the station wagon on a dirt road abutting the Beemiss property, just out of sight of the house, beyond the lawn and some pine trees. Mel and the dogs were just reaching these pine trees when Earl started off across the lawn from the house, and both dogs at once left Mel and turned back to consider this other guy. This one was a stranger to them, *not* an old friend like Mel, and they concluded that his running was a suspicious act. Therefore, they intercepted him and knocked him down.

"Hamlet!" yelled Beemiss. "Ophelia! You stop that! Stop it! Leave that man alone!"

The dogs reluctantly released Earl, just in time to see Corella come around the corner of the house. Ah hah! *This* must be the guy they should defend the house against. The two dogs, smiling happily, loped toward Corella, who made an abrupt U-turn and ran like hell the opposite way.

"Hamlet! Come back! Ophelia! Damn it, come back here!"

The dogs were having too much fun to listen to some old spoilsport. Pretending they couldn't hear their master's voice, they continued after Corella, who scurried around to the front of the house and lunged into the Cadillac, startling Ralph out of a year's growth. The two Great Danes thudding against the side of the car startled him out of a second year's growth. "Jesus!" he yelled, flinging his well-read New York *Post* up in the air. "Jesus *Christ!*"

"Start the car!" Corella yelled at him.

Ralph didn't need to be told twice.

Simultaneously, Mel was starting his own car, while Earl pounded through the pines in his wake, at the same time trying to brush pawprints off his tie. The station wagon was reluctant, but Mel kicked it in the accelerator a lot of times fast and the engine coughed and groaned and started. Mel swung the car around in an even tighter U-turn than Corella had made, and Earl leaped out of the pines. Mel accelerated, Earl grabbed the rear bumper, the car leaped forward, the bumper snapped off, and Earl went sailing back into the pine trees with the bumper in his hand.

"After him! After him!" Corella was yelling.

Ralph was going crazy. "After *who?*" he cried, heedless of grammar.

"Him him him!" Corella screamed, pointing at the station wagon swaying out onto the blacktop road.

Earl came running out of the pines, waving the bumper, and the dogs gave up trying to batter their way into the Cadillac and went galumphing off to play with their other new friend. "No no no!" yelled Earl, and ran back into the pines.

"Hamlet! Ophelia! Come back here!"

Earl ran through the pines and out the dirt road, while Ralph swung the Caddy around the Beemiss circular driveway. The station wagon was bouncing and bucketing away along the blacktop road. Earl and the Caddy intersected where the dirt road met the blacktop, and Ralph slammed on the brakes so Earl could get in. Earl threw the bumper at the dogs, dove headfirst into the Caddy, and Ralph slammed them forward again. Away went the Caddy down the blacktop road after the station wagon, and away went the dogs after the Caddy.

In the first mile, there was no advantage gained or lost between the two cars. The Caddy was bigger and faster, but the road was too curvy and bumpy for Ralph to let it all the way out. In fact, he was having more trouble keeping on the road than Mel was.

But at least they outdistanced the dogs, who finally gave up the chase and turned back, grinning at one another. They'd had a wonderful time. Returning to their territory, Hamlet carried Mel's bumper into the house in his teeth, as a prize of war. He sulked when Beemiss wouldn't let him keep it.

After that first mile, Mel turned onto a somewhat larger and smoother road, in which the Cadillac could use more of its greater speed. However, there was only one passing zone in the first four miles of that road, and Mel used it to pass a car containing a clergyman, a Methodist minister named Actable who liked to go for long leisurely drives while working out the following Sunday's sermon. A curvy road and on-coming traffic kept Ralph bottled up behind the Reverend Actable and his Roadrunner while Mel surged away, until Mel in his turn came upon a Volkswagen Microbus driven by a florist's wife named Muriel Leenk, who had nine children, all of them in the bus with her. She was discussing *Star Trek* with three of the boys.

Another passing zone. Mel zoomed around Mrs. Leenk, and a minute later Ralph zoomed around the Reverend Actable. Then Ralph tailgated Mrs. Leenk for a while, and Mel tailgated a famous economist named Brasspendle, who was driving along having an interior argument with Keynes, in which Keynes just kept making a fool of himself.

Another passing zone! But an ambling diaper service truck filled the on-coming lane while Mel and Brasspendle were in it, so Mel couldn't get around the economist's Saab. Unfortunately, the diaper service truck was no longer in the way when Mrs. Leenk and Ralph got there, and Ralph surged the Cadillac forward as though the thing would actually take off and fly.

Mel, hunched over the wheel, clenching and grimacing and moaning low, saw the Caddy growing huge in his rear-view mirror. Full night hadn't quite settled in, and he could make out the big gleaming menace of the machine behind its four headlights. (Ralph was the kind of son of a bitch who leaves his high beams on when following other cars.) Ahead there was no passing zone. There was nothing, there was nothing, there was—

The Connecticut Turnpike! Not thinking twice, Mel slipped past Brasspendle on the right, swung up the entrance ramp, and shot away eastward on the Turnpike. And right behind him came the Cadillac; doing seventy before it was well away from the ramp.

Mel was doing eighty, eighty-five, eighty-seven, eighty-seven and a half. The Cadillac was doing ninety, ninety-five, a hundred and five.

Mel slammed on the brakes. Mel drove at exactly fifty-five.

"We've got him!" Corella yelled. He was, in his excitement,

pounding the top of the front seat directly behind Ralph's neck, which Ralph hated. "We've got him we've got him we've got him!" *Pound, pound, pound.*

The Cadillac was coming up fast, it was closing the gap. The Cadillac was roaring up on the outside lane. Any second now the Cadillac was going to overtake the station wagon and force it off the road, and then something terrible would happen to Mel Bernstein.

And then Ralph slammed on the brakes, and Corella and Earl both fell on the floor in back. The Cadillac moved at exactly fifty-five.

"What the hell are you doing?" Corella clawed his way up off the floor. "Grab him! Shove him off the road!"

"There's a cop," Ralph said.

"What? Where?"

"Right in front of the wagon. That's why *he* slowed down."

"Jesus," said Corella. "All right. Stay with him."

Earl too had come back up onto the seat, and in an aggrieved way he said, "Damn it, Ralph, take it easy." He was rubbing his other eye, not the one the girl had punched. He'd slammed that part of himself into the seat back on the way down.

Both Ralph and Corella ignored Earl. Both were leaning forward, trying to see the police car beyond the station wagon. Now night was fully settling in, and they had only the station wagon's headlights to show them the other car up ahead, with its bubble light on top of its distinctive police markings. A state trooper. Highway Patrol. "Damn damn damn," said Corella.

In the station wagon Mel was smiling from ear to ear. He wanted to rush up there and kiss that cop. He'd been really terrified when the Cadillac was catching up with him, but now he was safe, at least for the moment. He didn't know what he'd do next, but for right now the people in the Cadillac couldn't get at him.

The state trooper was driving a Fury II. State troopers *love* Fury IIs. State troopers will go on driving Fury IIs until some car company puts out a car called Kill. Then state troopers will drive Kills. State troopers get their self-image from Marvel Comics.

The Fury II and the station wagon and the Cadillac drove in a neat law-abiding row at fifty-five miles an hour, the legal speed limit all across this mighty land (thirty-two hundred miles wide), all three vehicles heading eastward on the Connecticut Turnpike. They drove thirty-three miles in thirty-seven minutes, and then the Fury II switched on its right directional. The state trooper was leaving the Turnpike.

Mel hadn't yet figured out a next move, so he decided he might as well stick with the state trooper. Maybe the people in the Cadillac would go away.

In the Cadillac, Corella thumped Ralph's shoulder, which Ralph *loathed*. "He's taking that exit!" Corella said.

"So's the cop," Ralph said.

"God*dam* it," Corella said.

The Fury II and the station wagon and the Cadillac peeled off like slow-motion dive bombers, curving away down the ramp one after the other, and lining up neatly at the *Stop* sign by the county road. The Fury II turned on its left directional signal. So did the station wagon. So did the Cadillac. The Fury II turned left onto the county road. So did the station wagon. So did the Cadillac. The Fury II drove through the under pass beneath the Turnpike. So did the station wagon. So did the Cadillac. The Fury II turned on its left directional signal. So did the station wagon. So did the Cadillac.

"What the hell?" Corella was clutching the seat back very near Ralph's ear. "What's going *on?*"

"Well, shit," Ralph said. "He's going back up on the Turnpike."

He did. They all did, the three vehicles in a row, back up onto the Turnpike, this time westbound. (*Well*, thought Mel, *at least now we're headed toward New York.*) Once again they lined themselves out in a neatly spaced row and proceeded at fifty-five miles an hour.

"What the hell *is* this?" Corella demanded. "Just what the hell is that son of a bitch *doing?*"

"He's sticking with the cop," Ralph said. "We can't touch him till he gets away from the cop."

"Goddam son of a bitch bastard."

Earl, sitting back in his seat, was pouting, though the other two didn't know it. His good eye was hurting more and more. He did believe he was getting another shiner. *Two* black eyes. It wasn't fair.

The Fury II and the station wagon and the Cadillac traveled forty-one miles in forty-seven minutes.

"He's leaving again," Corella said.

"So's the cop," Ralph said.

The Fury II and the station wagon and the Cadillac left

108

the Turnpike, took the county road through the underpass, and got back on the Turnpike eastbound.

"I can't *stand* this!" Corella yelled. "What kind of chase *is* this! We're on a goddam merry-go-round!"

The state trooper, whose name was Luke Snell, had seen a Clint Eastwood movie on television the night before, and he was spending this tour of duty fantasizing activities for himself based on the plot line and incidents of the movie. Trooper Snell liked to make up stories while driving his Fury II, and often thought he could write stories just as good as that crap they have on TV. In fact, he had put a couple of his story ideas down on paper and sent them off with a reading fee to a big-shot literary agent in New York named Zachary George, and George had written a personal letter saying his material showed promise and giving him some hints on how to whip it into shape better. All of this fantasizing and story-creation took most of his attention, so he remained unaware of some of the things in the real world around him, such as the same set of headlights remaining at all times in his rear-view mirror.

For the next hour and a half, the Fury II and the station wagon and the Cadillac moseyed back and forth on the Connecticut Turnpike at fifty-five miles an hour. Mel and Ralph were both worried about their gas. Earl was worried about his eye. Trooper Snell was elaborating his fantasies. Corella was having apoplexy.

At a little before ten, the three cars left the Turnpike again, but this time when the Fury II reached the *Stop* sign at the county road its *right* directional went on. So did the station wagon's.

"Hey," said Ralph. "Something happening."

"I can't stand this," Corella said. His chin was on the seat back next to Ralph's head, and his breathing was in Ralph's ear, which Ralph didn't care for even a little bit. "I'm going crazy," Corella said.

The Fury II turned right on the county road and drove away from the Turnpike at forty miles an hour. Mel followed in the station wagon, wondering what was going to happen next. Ralph followed, in the Cadillac, wishing Corella would get his damn head out of his ear.

The Fury II traveled four miles on the county road and then signaled for a right again. The Fury II turned in at the trooper barracks.

"Hey hey!" yelled Ralph. "The cop's going off duty!"

"That son of a bitch'll follow him into his garage," Corella said.

But Mel knew he couldn't do that. Getting very worried now, he accelerated hard the instant the Fury II turned off the road, but those Cadillac lights stayed huge and threatening in his rear-view mirror.

Have to keep ahead of them. Straddling the center line so the Cadillac couldn't pass, Mel rocketed down the road as fast as the station wagon, his steering, and the laws of gravity would permit.

Corella, who had sagged into something very like despair over the last two hours, was up and yelling again, pounding the seat top behind Ralph's head, shouting, "We got him! We got him now! *Pass* the son of a bitch, Ralph! Pass him, shove him over, kill him, run him off the goddam road!"

Mel, straddling the center line, came roaring around a tight curve and saw two headlights coming right at him. He thought he was dead. He screamed, and threw his hands up in front of his face, and the headlights passed him, one on either side of the car, and the station wagon raced out of control off the road onto the left and into the woods and ricocheted off several trees.

Ralph was too absorbed in following the station wagon. Also, he too was startled when a pair of motorcycles suddenly flashed by him, one on each side. The result was, he went on following the station wagon longer than he should, off the road and into the woods. Ralph, however, managed to stop the Cadillac with his brakes rather than with the trees.

By one of those coincidences that no novelist would every try to get away with, the two motorcycles were being driven by Jenny Kendall and Eddie Ross, the two NYU students who had been members of the Open Sports Committee. Both Jenny and Eddie lost some control of their machines when they found themselves in a near-collision with two cars in the middle of the road, but they managed to stop without injury, and Eddie yelled at the tail-lights in the woods, "Goddam crazies!"

"Maybe they're hurt!" Jenny cried.

So Eddie and Jenny left their motorcycles by the side of the road, with the Other Oscars strapped to the handlebars, and went back to see if anybody needed help.

As a matter of fact, *everybody* needed help. Earl had hit his nose against the seat this time, and it was bleeding, and he was in an absolute *rage*. Mel, who had leaped from the station wagon with the statue in his hand, and who had run directly into a brier patch, was flailing around like a fly in a bottle. Ralph and Corella, both having leaped from the Cadillac in pursuit of Mel, were getting persistently confused in the darkness and kept capturing each other instead. "Cut it *out!*" Corella yelled, the third time Ralph grabbed him around the waist.

"I can't *see* anything!" Ralph complained, and proved it a minute later when he grabbed Jenny around the waist. Jenny screamed, and Eddie came over and punched Ralph in the nose. Corella came over, attracted by the ruckus, and Eddie punched *him* in the nose. Earl came over, black eyes and bloody nose and all, and punched Eddie in the nose, so Jenny kicked Earl very hard on the kneecap and Earl sat down on the ground and said, "That's it, I quit. I've had it."

Mel, meanwhile, emerging from the brier patch, had run away from the cars and the people and all the activity, and then he came to a pair of motorcycles parked by the side of the road, and to his utter astonishment they both had strapped to their handlebars little Dancing Aztec Priests exactly like the one he was holding in his hand.

"Well, for Pete's sake," Mel said. Then, looking over his shoulder, he saw that the chase had gotten itself organized again, and everybody except Earl was running in this direction.

Were these two Dancing Aztec Priests part of the sixteen Dancing Aztec Priests? How could they be, out here in the wilds of Connecticut, but on the other hand how could they *not* be? Either coincidence was too far-fetched for belief, but the likeliest of the options was that these were part of the sixteen.

Take all three of them? With everybody running in this direction, there wasn't time to untie them both from the handlebars. But then Mel remembered Jerry pointing out that the golden statue wouldn't break, whereas plaster statues *would* break, so he briskly whacked one of the motorcycle statues with the Beemiss statue, and they both broke. Then he whacked the other motorcycle statue with the remains of the Beemiss statue, and that broke too. Then he got on one of the motorcycles, started the engine, accelerated, fell backward off the machine as it leaped forward, and landed on the ground as the riderless motorcycle spurted out onto the road and ran head-on into a gray Fury I, the personal car of Trooper Luke Snell, who was on his way home from work.

# AFTER A WHILE . . .

There was a time in New York City history when "going up to Harlem" was a fashionable thing to do—dancing to Duke Ellington at the Cotton Club, drinking doubtful gin in the uptown speaks—but that time is long since past. Most white New Yorkers these days have *never* been to Harlem, and hardly any of them feel the lack.

Including Jerry. Never before had he visited that Dark Continent above 110th Street, and he headed up Broadway now with a certain tension in his shoulders. But there wasn't much choice; he'd done three of the four statues on his list, leaving only the one in the possession of Harwood's wife, whom the husband had called "Bobbi." According to Harwood, who ought to know, Bobbi had gone off with her boyfriend, the same Oscar Russell Green who was the leader of the Open Sports Committee. He was on somebody else's list, probably Floyd's, but Floyd or whoever would only be looking for one statue in Green's apartment, so it was necessary for Jerry to go up there himself, no matter how much he hated the idea. According to everything he'd ever read on the subject of Harlem, he was about to enter a combat zone.

If you were to come to Harlem without knowing anything of its true history, you might think you were on the site of a once-powerful city that had been abandoned hundreds of years ago by its founders, maybe because of plague, or because the civilization of which it was a part had come to an end, or because creatures from outer space had landed and collected all the inhabitants and carried them away to Alpha Centauri to become goulash. Then, you might think, the empty city was left to rot and weather for several centuries of rain and snow and summer heat, and then some other people arrived—probably by dugout canoe from New Jersey —and moved into the empty hulks, and formed their own primitive society in these relics of the past. Such things have happened in South America, and on the Yucatán Peninsula of Mexico, so why not at the mouth of the Hudson? No reason why not. And in fact, when you come to think about it, that history is pretty close to the truth, isn't it?

When Jerry parked the station wagon on 127th Street, half a block from Oscar Russell Green's address, he gave his hubcaps a lingering fond look before walking away, since he never expected to see them again. Then he moved on down the street to a squarish brick structure that was in rather better shape than most of its near neighbors, and he paused on the sidewalk to remark on the fact that at this very moment there were absolutely no bloodcurdling screams to be heard anywhere in the area. Nor were sirens wailing in the distance, nor were shots being fired. Nor was anybody running down the middle of the street waving a butcher knife. To a reader of the *Daily News* this was, at the least, bewildering. Shouldn't the niggers be throwing each other off rooftops? "It's quiet," Jerry muttered to himself. "Too quiet."

This building turned out to be easy to enter via the credit card method, and the vestibule doorbells revealed that Green's apartment was on the top floor. Jerry went up and listened at the door, to no effect, then looked around for a service door. Finding none, he went up on the roof instead, down the fire escape to what should be the right window, and found it smashed. Both halves had all the glass missing. If Floyd or whoever had already been here, he'd made an awful mess of things.

Inside there was a bedroom, with lights on but nobody in sight. Jerry slid open the window, trying to be as silent as possible, but when he stepped over the sill his foot crunched on broken glass. Tiptoeing, trying to think himself lighter, he made his way across the crackling floor and had almost reached the far doorway when a reeling drunken black man staggered in, shouting angrily and waving a Dancing Aztec Priest over his head. "Here!" he yelled, as Jerry jumped backward, scared out of his wits. "Here's what you want, goddam it! This is the third time tonight, what's the matter with you goddam people? Leave me alone to get *drunk,* for Christ's sake, goddam it!" And he slapped the statue into Jerry's bewildered hand.

Recovering, Jerry looked down at the thing, and saw at once that it had been broken in several places and glued back together, rather sloppily. It was also very sticky. "Well, ńo," he said, and managed on the second try to put the statue down on a handy dresser. "I'm looking for Mrs. Harwood, that's who I'm looking for."

"Mrs. Harwood? Bobbi?" The black man staggered back against the doorpost, blinking around the room as though she just might be here after all. "There ain't no Bobbi here," he decided. "Don't I wish there was. You better believe it, don't I wish there was."

"Where is she?"

"Home." He stuck his thumb in his mouth and did a disgusting parody of pipe-smoking. "With old Chucky-Wucky."

"No, she isn't. She left."

"Yeah? Good girl. Think she'll come here?"

Jerry looked the black man up and down, considering him. "No," he said, "I don't think she will."

"Shit."

"Well, you can't win them all. Any idea where else she might go?"

"Orchestra," the black man said.

Jerry squinted at him. "What?"

The black man reached his arms out in front of himself and made some sort of weird two-handed gesture. "Harp," he said. "She plays the harp. Classical music. Symphony orchestra."

"Do that again," Jerry said.

Now it was the black man's turn to squint. "What say?"

"That thing you did with your hands. Was that supposed to be playing a harp?"

"Sure." The black man did it again, the same weird gesture.

Jerry shook his head. "Doesn't look like playing a harp at all," he said. "Looks like pulling in a pot at poker."

"What, are you crazy? *This* is pulling in a pot." And he did a different weird gesture.

"Now, *that* one," Jerry said, "that's something like playing a harp."

"You don't know shit," the black man told him. "What do you want Bobbi for, anyway?"

"I may not know shit," Jerry said, "but I know the answer to that question, and you don't, and you can go screw yourself."

The black man looked offended. "That isn't fair," he said.

"Then the hell with it," Jerry said. "I'm not going to stay here and be insulted. Where's the front door?"

"I thought you were one a them fire escape types."

"Only coming in." Jerry started past him, on his way to

114

find the front door, then stopped and said, *"Third* time? Did you say I was the third one looking for that statue?"

"There I was wrong," the black man said. "I'll admit it, I was wrong about that. What you are, you're the first one looking for Bobbi Harwood."

"Tell me about these people looking for the statue."

"Why?"

"Why not?"

The black man considered that, then abruptly nodded and said, "You're right. Okay, at first there was the goddam ballplayers."

"Ballplayers?"

"Frank and Floyd. Kept throwin the goddam statue back and forth till they goddam busted it."

"Frank *and* Floyd, huh?"

"That's what they said. Then there was some tall skinny guy from McDonald's."

"From McDonald's?"

"Had the napkin on his face. Looked like a beaver."

Was that the mob guys, the ones that wanted the box marked *E* in the first place? Somehow, the description didn't sound right. Jerry said, "Anybody else with that one?"

"Nope. All by himself. Ran around like a cockroach."

"Huh. Think of that." Maybe the mob, maybe somebody else entirely. But the point right now was Bobbi Harwood. "Be seeing you," Jerry said, and left the bedroom.

The black man reeled after him through the apartment to the front door, where he said, "You sure you didn't come here for that goddam statue?"

"Wouldn't touch it with a ten-foot pole," Jerry assured him. "So long." And he left, trotting down the stairs and out to the street.

There was a lot to think about. Frank and Floyd, for two; what were they doing together? And who was the guy with the McDonald's napkin on his face? And if he wasn't from the mob, where *was* the mob?

But the main point was still Bobbi Harwood. Standing on the sidewalk (he had become so blasé by now that he didn't even notice the prevailing quiet), he looked around almost as though he might see her from here. She was somewhere in this city, right now, with what might be the golden statue. But where?

# AT THAT VERY MOMENT . . .

"I tell you, Madge," Bobbi Harwood said, pouring more of the Almaden Mountain Burgundy from the half-gallon jug into the jelly glass, "I had a revelation tonight. A revelation."

"That's good," Madge said, and yawned discreetly behind her hand.

Bobbi didn't notice. She hadn't noticed much of anything the last few hours, not since she'd stalked out of Chuck's life—that was the way she thought of it now, with a new sense of determination and purpose—and marched away down West End Avenue with the two heavy suitcases hanging from her arms. She'd stamped along, noticing nothing in the world around her, ignoring cabs and catcalls and pedestrians, concentrating exclusively on the activities inside her own head, the new aura of freedom and possibility and movement, the new conviction that she was *out* of it now, well out of it and poised on the brink of a new level of being, and it was only the weight of the suitcases that had dragged her at last back down to earth. Once she had finally noticed that her arms were suffering a great deal of pain, she'd also realized she couldn't simply keep walking down West End Avenue the rest of her life. She would have to have a destination.

Which was when she'd thought of Madge, as she had mentioned to Madge herself several times by now. ("I thought of you right away. Right away.") Madge being a cellist in the same orchestra in which Bobbi plied her harp, and Madge further being Bobbi's best friend in all the world, and Madge even further being someone who was living alone at the moment, it wasn't all that startling that Bobbi had thought of her, but Bobbi herself couldn't seem to get over it.

In any event, she had lugged her luggage another block and a half to a phone booth, where she had called Madge and said, "It's Bobbi and I just left Chuck forever and can I come sleep on your sofa tonight?" Madge had said why-of-course, and Bobbi had taken a cab down here to this pleasant converted brownstone on Waverly Place in the Village, and the two women had been sitting in the front room of Madge's third-floor floor-through apartment ever since, with the traffic going by down below. Madge had produced the then-full-

116

now-nearly-empty half-gallon of red wine, and they had settled down to have a nice dialogue together. Or monologue, really, since the last few hours had seen Bobbi doing most of the talking, her two topics being (A) a specific catalog of Chuck's faults, errors, omissions, and flaws, and (B) a vaguer but equally impassioned catalog of the fresh vistas open to Bobbi now that she had broken out of the trap. Madge's sympathetic smile had become rather more glassy in the last hour or so, but she too had been married at one time, and she knew how terrific it could feel to have a thing like that over and done with, so she was a good sport and let Bobbi run on as long as she wanted.

Which apparently was forever. "A revelation," Bobbi repeated. She swigged half the jelly glass of wine, and said, "I suddenly realized I could be my own person, you know?"

"I know," Madge said, and she really did know. Bobbi had said the exact same thing at least eleven times by now. Quickly, before Bobbi could say anything else that she'd already said, Madge told her, "But I'm sorry, honey, I'm afraid I've had it for today."

Bobbi stared at her, not understanding. "You what?"

"I'm sleepy." Madge got to her feet. "Stay up as long as you want, Bobbi, but I have to go to bed."

"In the morning," Bobbi said. "I'll go see Coalshack." Everett Coalshack was the director of the New York City Symphony Orchestra, where Bobbi and Madge both worked.

"That's right," Madge said.

"He can send me to the right people out on the Coast," Bobbi said. "I know he'll help me."

"I'm sure he will," Madge agreed, not for the first time, and retreated out of the room and out of earshot, while Bobbi went on talking.

"I'll get to California," Bobbi said to the jelly glass and the wine jug and the empty room, "and the *first* thing I'll get is a car. A *car*, goddam it. And a nice little house somewhere near the ocean. And never have to see or hear or speak to that bastard Chuck again."

She went on in that vein for a while, eventually noticing that she was indeed alone, and then she prepared herself for bed, a process that involved emptying both suitcases all over the living room floor. When this exercise unearthed the little gold-painted statue that had started it all, she gave the ugly creature a radiant smile and whispered to it, "You're my good-luck charm. You know that? You made it all possible."

She placed the statue on the windowsill, among the avocado

plants, with the spider plants dangling overhead; a very jungly atmosphere, perfect for the little devil. And when at last she turned out the lamps and stretched herself on the sofa under Madge's other blanket, she saw how the peach-colored glow of the sodium streetlight outside glinted in metallic slivers on all the contorted surfaces of the creature. Coral and gold, with wicked emerald eyes. "Good night, little devil," she whispered to it, and she could almost believe that one of the eyes winked at her.

# SOON . . .

The four women playing bridge in the Bernstein dining room were Angela Manelli Bernstein (north), Teresa Manelli McCann (east), Floyd's wife Barbara Kavetchian McCann (south) and Kathleen McCann Podenski (west). (Kathleen, Frank and Floyd's sister, was married to a Polish gentleman named Howie Podenski who was currently serving three concurrent terms for mail fraud but was expected home soon.) Angela was in four spades, doubled, on the basis of Barbara's promise of strong support, but when Teresa led the jack of clubs and Barbara lay down her dummy hand Angela saw at once that she'd been screwed again. "Barbara," she said, glaring at her sister's sister-in-law, "what in Jesus Christ's holy name made you support spades?"

"Well," Barbara said, blinking in that infuriating way of hers, "you sounded so enthusiastic about it."

"Barbara," Angela said, and in the other room the phone rang. Angela closed her mouth, counted to seven, opened it again, and said, "Barbara, answer the phone. You're *dummy*."

"All right." Barbara went away to answer the phone, and Angela settled down to compare her hand with the dummy's, to see how much could be salvaged.

When Angela had called Frank's and Floyd's wives to tell them their husbands wouldn't be home for dinner, the idea of bringing in Kathleen Podenski for a fourth and settling down to a nice game of bridge had seemed a natural one. And since the Bernstein home was the only one not blessed with children, it had also been natural to hold the game here. (Besides, Angela was on duty for phone messages, of which this one was the first.) The nine children belonging to the other

118

women, ranging in age from Frank and Teresa's eleven-year-old Francine to Floyd and Barbara's four-year-old Ronald, had all been assembled over at Barbara's house with Francine as their baby-sitter and the color television set to keep them out of trouble, so everything was fine.

The only thing wrong, in fact, was what was wrong with the same idea every time they tried it. Floyd's wife Barbara and her partner (they rotated) *invariably* lost every game. Invariably. And Angela, who was a very intense and rather good bridge player, *hated to lose*. Hated it, hated it.

And she was going to lose again, no doubt of it. Down three, at the very least. Jack of clubs led, king X X in dummy (one of Barbara's few honors, as it happened), X X X in Angela's hand. If she played over the jack, surely Kathleen would have the damn ace. If she didn't, Teresa would have the damn ace. Whatever happened, Angela could see herself losing three club tricks in a row. Hell and damnation.

Angela chose to finesse, playing a low club. If Kathleen had the ace but not the queen, she might play high. Except that she didn't, and on the second round Teresa led the queen, and this time Angela played the king over it, and Kathleen had the ace.

Kathleen was leading the ten of clubs, which was now high in that suit, when Barbara came back from the phone to say, "I think it's Mel."

Angela had just about had enough of Barbara. Glaring at her, she said, "You *think* it's Mel?"

"He sounds garbled," Barbara explained.

"In a minute." Angela played that club round through, Kathleen took the trick, and now Angela had to take every last trick after this to make the contract. Fat chance.

Kathleen led another club. Angela was now void both in her hand and in the dummy, but given Barbara's lack of strong cards Angela would prefer to be in her hand, so she played a low trump, and damn if Teresa didn't go over it with a medium-size trump, and now Angela had to decide whether to lose the trick or to use up not only one more trump on this same trick but also to use up one of the few entries to dummy.

"How we doing?" Barbara said.

Angela looked up at her. "We? *We?*" Making a sudden decision, she got to her feet, slapped the cards face-down on the table, and said, "*You* play the hand. I'll go talk on the phone."

Angela left Barbara blinking and went into the living room, where she picked up the phone and snarled, "Hello!"

"Angela? Is that you?" Mel didn't sound garbled, he sounded hysterical.

"What's up?"

"I'm arrested!"

"Arrested? For burglary?"

"Everything but," he said. "Reckless driving, endangerment, grand larceny, assault and battery, attempted murder, willful destruction of property and leaving the scene of an accident. *Attempted* leaving the scene of an accident."

"*You?*" Disdain dripped like honey from her lips. "You don't have the guts for all that."

"The point is," he said, "I'm here in Haddam Neck, Connecticut, and I'm—"

"You're in *what?* Horse's Neck—"

"*Haddam* Neck. Connecticut. And this is the one phone call I'm permitted, and I made the mistake of calling my wife. I'd do better to call Yassir Arafat."

The presence of Barbara back there in the dining room left Angela with no compassion in her heart. "You may be there in Horse's Ass, Connecticut," she said, "but I'm here in Dreadful Gulch, Queens, playing bridge with *Barbara McCann,* and what the hell am I supposed to do about *you?*"

"Jesus, you're a sweetheart. I've been *arrested.*"

"Better late than never."

"Listen, Angela," he said. "I can tell you're in one of your moods, so just listen to what I tell you, and pass it on to Jerry when he calls in. I think they plan to hold me overnight, but I want somebody to get a good Connecticut lawyer up here in the morning. That's *Haddam Neck, Connecticut.*"

"All right, all right. I got it."

"Also tell Jerry, I got to the Beemiss statue and it wasn't the right one."

"Beemiss." Angela was finally starting to jot things down on the notepad beside the phone.

"I didn't get to any of the others," Mel went on, "but I *did* run into two people on somebody else's list. Almost ran into them, anyway. Edward Ross and Jennifer Kendall. I think Frank had them. Their statues weren't any good."

Angela wrote the names on the pad. "Anything else?"

"You're a terrific person, Angela. Your husband is about to spend the night in a jail cell, and *you* say, 'Anything else?'"

Angela made the effort: "Keep well," she said. "Try not to get bugs."

"What a warm human being," Mel said, and hung up.

Angela shrugged. She'd tried, hadn't she? Going back to the dining room, she said to Barbara, "How we doing?"

Barbara was blinking furiously. "Down four," she said.

"It could have been worse," Angela said. She'd expected it to be worse.

"So far," Barbara said, and led a card.


# IN DUE COURSE . . .

Swimming pool salesman Wally Hintzlebel was slowing down. The story of New York is speed, is movement, movement without stopping, on the go all the time, *gotta* hustle, but Wally was slowing down. The nervous energy still crackled and fizzed inside him, it still pushed and poked and prodded, but he wasn't used to the pace, and his brain was slowing down.

That was why it was so good to be in the Professor Charles S. Harwood apartment. Empty, silent, calm. What a place to be, after all he'd gone through. First the library, then the phone call with Mom and the scramble home for dinner and back to the city, then the Beemiss address being not an address, and then the drunken black man with the statue glued to the windowsill. Why would anybody glue a statue to a windowsill?

A bigger question: What sort of person pours boiling water out his window onto the head of somebody in the street below? (All right, technically Wally'd been burglarizing Green's apartment, but he hadn't *taken* anything, had he? Did that deserve boiling water on the head?)

But now, like a safe port after stormy seas, here he was at last in the Harwood apartment, wonderfully empty of crazy people, or indeed of any people at all.

Unfortunately, it was also empty of golden statues, since that pile of fragments in the living room fireplace clearly had once been a plaster copy of the Dancing Aztec Priest. So the million dollars wasn't here. It was necessary to move on.

Out of Manhattan, at last. Of the only two remaining addresses in Wally's possession, one was over in New Jersey and the other was in Deer Park, on Long Island, not far from Wally's own home. Frenzy and lust pushed him to do New

Jersey, but exhaustion and dulled nerves encouraged him to settle for that fellow in Deer Park—Wylie Cheshire, his name was—then go on home and start up again tomorrow morning.

Leave, anyway. He should leave here now, this apartment was useless to him. Still he stood where he was, trembling slightly, his eyes dull but with flickerings deep within as he gazed around at the empty living room. Something was holding him here, something—

Why were the lights on? Every light in the apartment turned on, and the apartment completely empty.

Why was the bedroom stripped? Living room and kitchen looked lived-in—the kitchen, in fact, was one of the messiest rooms he'd ever seen in his life—but in the bedroom the dresser drawers gaped open, empty. What was going on here?

Wondering, frowning, back to the bedroom Wally went and brooded at those empty dresser drawers. And when he turned to the closet he discovered the door was locked. With the key in the keyhole. Puzzled, at sea, Wally reached out a tentative hand, unlocked the door, opened it, and a wild-eyed naked man leaped out at him, babbling, *"Oh, thank God, thank God, I thought I'd starve in there, I was praying somebody would—"*

"I don't want to talk to you," Wally said. He pushed the naked man back into the closet, he locked the door, he went away. To Wylie Cheshire, Deer Park, Long Island. Enough craziness. Enough of Manhattan. Enough.

# ANON . . .

Mel Bernstein's car looked like a hobo's hat after its ricochet romance with the trees of Connecticut, but the damn thing still ran. Mel ran west in it for ten miles before he found a phone booth, next to a closed gas station, where he called Angela once more.

This time she came on herself, and Mel said, "It's me again."

"Listen, Mel," she said. "I'm glad you called back. I was in a very bad mood before."

"I noticed. Anyway, the—"

"We're playing cards here, Teresa and Kathleen and Barbara and me, and you know how Barbara affects me."

"It's water over the bridge," he said. "What I'm—"

"*Under* the bridge."

"What?"

"It's either under the bridge or over the dam," she said. "Water *over* the bridge would be a disaster."

"Exactly," he said. "That's what my entire life is, water over the bridge."

"Poor Mel," she said. "How's your cell?"

"I'm not in a cell. I got out, that's what I'm calling about."

"You *escaped?*"

"They let me go. Listen, I'll tell you the story," Mel promised, and he did, from the time he'd entered the Beemiss residence until the motorcycle had run into the state trooper's car, at which point Angela said, "Come off it, Mel. If you did all that, they'll *never* let you go."

"Well, I had some advantages," Mel told her. "In the first place, the couple on the motorcycles was interracial."

"Oh? Which one was black?"

"The boy."

"Ah hah," said Angela.

"In the second place," Mel said, "the people in the Cadillac turned out to be mobsters of some sort. They kept being evasive with the cops. But the thing that really did it, the trooper that I hit with the motorcycle, he's an amateur writer, he—"

"No," she said.

"Swear to God."

"He's a *customer* of yours?"

"Client," Mel corrected. "He's sent in a couple stories, yeah. He recognized the Zachary George name right away. They wanted my occupation, and I said I was Zachary George's assistant, and this trooper fell over."

"Mel, that's incredible."

"What's so incredible? I get hundreds of pieces of shit in the mail every week."

"But the *trooper.*"

"Angela, to tell you the truth, I think the interracial business and the mobster business would have done it for me, anyway. But the Zachary George connection didn't hurt."

"So they let you go."

"I posted a bond, by check, but it won't come to anything. The mobsters didn't want to press charges or make any waves, and the cops didn't want to listen to the interracial couple, so I'm home free."

"You coming back now?"

"No, it isn't that late, and I've only done one of my four names. Two of them are on Long Island, I'll try them tonight and come home after that."

"Good luck," she said.

"That's what I've got, all right," he agreed, and hung up, and back in the station wagon he studied his list. One of the three remaining names was at an address way over in New Jersey, but the other two were relatively handy to Mel's home:

> Ben Cohen
> 27–15 Robert Moses Drive
> Glen Cove

> Wylie Cheshire
> 58 Ridge Road
> Deer Park

Ben Cohen? No, not first. Mel was ready for a quiet interlude, something safe and easy. Wylie Cheshire, that was the one. There was something comfortingly civilized, sedately English about that name. Deer Park. Wylie Cheshire.


# WHEN ALL AT ONCE . . .

*The Adventures of Frank and Floyd in the Ghetto*
A SERIES OF BLACKOUTS

### 1

From Floyd's list:

> Leroy Pinkham
> 119 West 122nd St.

Leroy, he say, "Buhbuh."
Buhbuh, he say, "Yuh?"
"Lu dah cah."
"Wuh cah?"
"*Dah* cah."

Buhbuh, he look at that car, he see two white men inside there in that car. "Huh," he say.

Leroy, he say, "Dah cah, it been rowndeh block befoah."

Buhbuh, he say, "Yeh?"

Leroy, he say, "Kewbee cops?"

Buhbuh, he say, "Nah."

Buhbuh and Leroy, they sitting on the stoop out front Leroy's house. It after eight o'clock, but not dark yet. Leroy's Mama and Leroy's sister Rose and Leroy's other sister Ruby, they at the church, practicing with the choir. Leroy's other sister Reeny, she to the movies with her boyfriend, and Leroy's big brother Luther, he in the Army. Nobody in Leroy's house. Leroy, he don't like to be in there by himself, so him and his best buddy Buhbuh, what also goes to Liberation High, they out on the stoop talking about the astronauts, until Leroy, he see that car.

Now they don't talk about nothing for a while, and then Leroy, he grin and say, "Man, I *dig* that Chi-neez food." Him and Buhbuh, they ate in a restaurant today for almost the first time ever, and they both of them they really dug it. Chinese restaurant, regular restaurant where you sit down and they's waiters and everything. Him and Buhbuh got to go there cause they helped out with some bunch of people that Miss Tower was working with. Miss Tower, she their favorite teacher at Liberation High, cause they is both got the hots for her. That Miss Tower, she got some beautiful ass, but she don't go for none of that shit at all. She a goddam *virgin.* But pretty to look at.

Liberation High, that something else. It for guys like Leroy and Buhbuh, what dropped out of school and now is like nineteen, twenty, and they ain't getting nowhere. So they can go back to this school, and it ain't like no regular school with bad-ass teachers and dumb subjects and all. It special for older guys what are smart and what *want* to get theyselves an education. Already they been fourteen graduates from Liberation High gone to City College.

So today Leroy and Buhbuh, they got to go to this real Chinese restaurant, with Miss Tower and this whole bunch a people, and they ate up a damn storm. So now Leroy and Buhbuh, they talk about that food at that Chinese restaurant, until Leroy, he say, "Dere it go again."

Buhbuh, he say, "Wuh?"

"Dah cah."

Buhbuh, he look and see that car, and it the same motherfucking car as the last time, with them same two motherfucking white men inside there. Buhbuh, he say, "Muthuh-fuckuh."

"Cops," say Leroy.

"Yuh," say Buhbuh.

They watch that car go down round the corner, and then they talk about a movie they seen on television, with monsters and vampires in it. They talk about that until Leroy, he say, "Lu dah."

Buhbuh, he say, "Wuh?"

"Dem cops."

Buhbuh, he look, and them two white men from the car, they walking on the sidewalk, and they coming this way. Buhbuh, he say to Leroy, "*I* din do nuthin."

"Well, *I* sure as shit din do nuthin."

"So, wuh the fuck?"

So the two white men, who isn't anyway cops but is Frank and Floyd, they comes along and nods at Leroy and Buhbuh with quick nervous little smiles, and then they goes up the stoop and into the building, and Leroy and Buhbuh, they look at one another, and Buhbuh, he say, "Who dey aftuh?"

So they talk about that, all the different people in the building, while Frank and Floyd, they go upstairs and find the Pinkham apartment, and they walk right in 'cause Leroy, he don't never lock the door, 'cause if you lock the door when the place empty the junkies, they gone think you got something in there and they gone bust the door down. So Frank and Floyd, they go in and split up to search the apartment for the golden statue, and when they meet again at the front door they is *both* found it.

Frank, he say, "What the hell is *that*?"

Floyd, he say, "It's the goddam statue. What's *that*?"

And Frank, he say, "Shit. We better take them both."

Meanwhile, Leroy and Buhbuh downstairs, they been thinking and wondering, and they figure what the fuck, it Leroy's house, ain't it? They can go in the goddam house, can't they? They can see what's going on, can't they? So they go in the house and up the stairs and they don't see nothing, and when they going by Leroy's door it open and the cops come out with the two statues Leroy and Buhbuh got today at that restaurant. And Leroy, he say, "Wuh duh *fuck*?"

And the cops, they begin to yell and holler and wave their arms, and one of them accidental hits the statue against the side by the door, and the statue's head, it fall off. And the other one, he yell, "Forget it! That ain't it!" And he hit the

126

other statue against the wall and he head *don't* fall off, and the two white men both stare at the statue with big eyes, and then they push past Leroy and Buhbuh and run downstairs, with the statue that didn't get broken.

And Buhbuh, he yell, "You come back here, my statue!" And he take off down them stairs after them sons bitches.

And Leroy, he run down after Buhbuh.

And all the way down the stairs, them white men, they yelling real loud, "We got it! We got it!"

And down on the sidewalk, Buhbuh, he catch up with them, and he grab the one's arm and he try get the statue back, and they fight this way and that on the widewalk while lots a people on the block, they decide they been outside long enough, maybe they gone amble on inside now, see what's on the TeeVee. And then the white man, he hit Buhbuh across the nose with the statue, and this time the statue's head *do* come off, and the white man yell, real real loud, "Well, *shit!* Here, goddam it!" And he shove the statue in Buhbuh's hand, and him and the other white man, they turn around and they run their asses right outa that block.

And Leroy, he shake his fist and yell after them, "Fuckin cops!" Because in Harlem the cops, they don't got much reputation.

## 2

From Floyd's list:

> *F. Xavier White*
> *211 Riverside Drive*

Maleficent is always in a bad temper when she's dieting, and she's always dieting, so she's always in a bad temper. However, being in a bad temper always makes her break her diet, so besides being on a diet and in a bad temper Maleficent is *also* always gaining weight. As F. Xavier said about her recently, behind her ample back, "Next thing you know, *I'll* have to get that woman license plates."

But even Maleficent, no matter how fat or bad-tempered or hungry she might become, knows there are times to be quiet and permit someone else the center of the stage, and one of those times is right now, so when F. Xavier, with his oily unctuous smile showing every blessed one of his huge capped teeth, makes the introductions, saying, "Mr. Jonesburg, I'd like you to meet my wife, Maleficent; sweetheart, this is

Mr. Jeremiah Jonesburg," Maleficent doesn't respond with any of her usual rude tricks at all. Instead, she smiles sweetly and even does something that might be a curtsy—if is isn't an earthquake—and all she says is, "Pleased, I'm shoo-uh."

Mr. Jeremiah "Bad Death" Jonesburg smiles, with his mouth open, revealing some nightmare version of Ali Baba's cave. Gold and ivory intermixed, with spaces where removals have already taken place, and all guarded by the dragon of his thick, yellow-stained, scabby red tongue. This ugliness smiles, and says, "Hello, fat mama."

Maleficent winces at that one, and so does F. Xavier, because he knows *he'll* pay for it later, but at the moment Maleficent merely goes on smiling, and merely says, "Oh, you. You sure are the one."

Jeremiah "Bad Death" Jonesburg *is* the one, in fact. He's the Man, the Main Man from 96th to 155th, east side *and* west. Them Italians downtown *shake* when they hear the name of Bad Death, because he's the one run them out, run them right out of Harlem and the whole patch. He's the meanest, the baddest, the biggest, the toughest, the coolest *and* the hottest son of a bitch ever to hit the street. Where he walks tombstones grow, and where he sits the sun never shines. His bed is made of politician's bones, and for lunch he eats policemen's orphaned children. He picks his teeth with pool cues, and blows his nose on traffic tickets. He wears Datsuns when he roller-skates, and his toilet seat is lined with pussy fur. His hand can crumble bricks, and his piss cuts through solid steel. He stacks his women three at a time like cordwood, and makes love to them all at once. The Queen of England irons his shirts, and his Cadillac runs on Dago blood. When he's angry bullets melt, and when he smiles trees die. He's so mean he can't look in a mirror, for fear he'll annoy himself. When he speaks transistor radios give up the ghost, and when he farts entire neighborhoods turn into deserts. He is the Man, and nobody forgets it.

And he has come to F. Xavier White, Harlem's Finest Mortician ("Your Every Need Anticipated—Service with a Sympathetic Smile"), to make the final arrangements for a funeral. (There's a rumor that Bad Death also made the initial arrangements for this particular funeral, but that's a rumor no one mentions in Bad Death's presence.)

"Mole Mouth was a friend of mine," Bad Death says, and nobody disagrees with him. "Now, there's a lot of funerals

128

take place in this town in a year, but not many of them is the *best*. What I want for Mole Mouth is the *best*."

"Oh, that's what you'll get," F. Xavier assures him. He smiles a big smile and washes his hands together and says, "You come to the right man, Mr. Jonesburg. I *specialize* in the best."

"Mole Mouth come from down South," Bad Death continues. "Before he come up here and got himself into business he shouldn't of got himself into. Now, a lot of Mole Mouth's family gonna be coming up from Louisiana, Georgia, Arkansas, and I want *them* to see the best. The *best*."

"Yes, *sir*, Mr. Jonesburg."

"And," Bad Death says, "I'll want them to *know* it's the best."

"You'll want a band," F. Xavier says.

"The *best* band."

"I wouldn't inflict on your ear anything *but* the best band."

"That's right," Bad Death says. Then he gazes a moment past the simpering bulk of Maleficent, and he says, "Now, the Dagos, in the old days, when one of their big boys got it, his competitors all got together and gave him a *big* funeral. A special kind of *big* funeral."

"A send-off," F. Xavier agrees. "That's what they call it, a send-off."

"That's what we want for Mole Mouth," Bad Death says. "He was my competitor, and I'm giving him the best funeral, and I want it to be a send-off. Better than *any* send-off them Dagos ever give *anybody*. Better than Capone, better than Charlie Brody, better than anything. I want them to see it, and I want them to know it's the *best*."

"Flowers," F. Xavier says. "Great big horseshoe wreaths of flowers. Lots of black limousines."

"Make 'em white limousines," Bad Death says.

"White limousines," F. Xavier agrees. "And lots of wailing women in black dresses, to throw themselves in the grave. Or, do you want white dresses?"

"White dresses? This ain't a wedding, this's a funeral!"

"Right you are," F. Xavier says, nodding and beaming, while perspiration is running like the Oronoco River down the middle of his back. "Black dresses," he says.

"Then there's something else," Bad Death says. "When a police commissioner or a president or some bastard like that kicks off, they give him a big funeral with uniforms and processions and a lot of bullshit."

"Horse-drawn hearses," F. Xavier says, and tentatively adds, "Black horses?"

"Horses, that's good," Bad Death says. He flashes his smile again, and Maleficent quakes. (She's the only woman on earth who wears form-fitting muumuus, and when she quakes the whole muumuu shimmers, like Jello when the refrigerator door is slammed.) Bad Death says, "But uniforms, too. And big shots."

"Liberation High has a marching band," F. Xavier says. "With uniforms."

"That's not *the* band. Not the band we were talking about before."

"No, no, this is another band. The first band'll be real down home Dixie."

"Two bands. Hmmmm." Bad Death strokes his chin—it makes a raspy noise—and considers that. "I like it," he decides. "Snappy uniforms?"

"Four colors."

"Good. And what about big shots?"

F. Xavier has spent the last half-minute thinking about that, and growing increasingly desperate, because of course most *true* big shots—mayors or baseball players, for instance —wouldn't be caught dead at a funeral like this. But there has to be an answer, and so F. Xavier keeps smiling and keeps thinking, and Bad Death just keeps looking at him.

The fact is, F. Xavier actually does know a lot of big shots of various kinds, a lot of different people in the community. To become director of Harlem's Premier Funeral Parlor, which has always been his dream, he has deemed it advisable to associate himself with all sorts of local organizations and activities. (The Open Sports Committee, for instance.) Over the years, he has come to be on at least nodding terms with everybody from Congressman Rangel himself to Bad Death Jonesburg here, and surely *some* of those contacts could now be made useful.

Congressman Rangel? No. Not a chance.

How about the Open Sports Committee? Oscar Russell Green, Wylie Cheshire . . . those were certainly notable names, even if not exactly big shots. He could call upon their recent sense of camaraderie, remind them if necessary of the automobiles he unstintingly provided during their long struggle. His smile suddenly becoming much more confident, F. Xavier says, "I'll get them for you, Mr. Jonesburg. I can't give you an exact list right this minute, but I assure you you'll be satisfied."

130

"I better be," Bad Death says.

"Then there's the question of a chorus," F. Xavier says, hurrying along.

"Yes," says Bad Death, and one of the dozen men that Bad Death has stationed around the outside of the funeral parlor walks in, raising a hand to catch Bad Death's eye.

"A female chorus," F. Xavier is saying, "in floor-length robes. Black? Or white? Sometimes red can look very——"

"Just a minute," Bad Death says, and asks his man, "What's happening?"

"Two white men."

"Two *white* men? Where?"

"Climbing the fire escape in back."

"Dagos?"

"Irishmen. We looked in their wallets, and they're both named McCann."

"They still alive?"

"Oh, sure. They didn't make no trouble. When we threw the light on them, one of them fainted."

"Bring 'em in here," Bad Death says, and when his man goes away Bad Death shakes his head and says, "Irishmen. Huh."

Frank and Floyd (Floyd is the one who fainted), having been roughed up by a lot of mean-looking black men, and then having been locked away in a room with a stack of coffins, are not feeling very rosy. "I don't know," Floyd says at one point, "maybe a million dollars *isn't* a million dollars."

"If it turns out, after we go through all this," Frank says, "and somebody else found the damn things hours ago, I'm gonna be pissed."

"If I'm even *around* later on to find that out," Floyd says, "I'll be so happy I won't even care. If I ever get back to America, I'll get down on my knees and kiss the ground."

A bunch of the black men come into the room then, and take Frank and Floyd by their various elbows, and walk them away to the room containing Bad Death and F. Xavier and Maleficent. Frank and Floyd don't know it, but F. Xavier and Maleficent are just as scared as they are that some sort of bloodshed is about to take place.

Bad Death, whose leadership role is immediately obvious, looks Frank and Floyd up and down and says, "Irishmen. What in hell is a couple Irishmen doing, sneaking around after *me?*"

Frank and Floyd blink at him. Frank says, *"You?"*

Bad Death gives them his penetrating stare. "What mob you goofs with? You tied up with them Dagos downtown?"

"We're fire escape inspectors," Floyd says, and Frank gives him a disgusted look.

"You come snuffin' around Bad Death," Bad Death tells him, "you in trouble."

Frank, who has figured things out by now, gives Bad Death a crooked grin and says, "Come on, Bad Death, you know we're not with any guinea mob downtown."

Bad Death's eyes narrow. "That's what I know, is it?"

Frank, after all, is a member of a backstage union, and his theatrical background is coming in handy. Grinning at Floyd, and shaking his head, he says, "Well, Steve, looks like our cover's blown."

Floyd has no idea *what* in hell is going on. He says, "Steve?"

"Our cover's blown," Frank repeats, and turns back to Bad Death to say, "You know Irishmen don't work with guinea mobsters. *You* know where Irishmen work."

Bad Death's eyes by now are so narrow he looks like a character in Dick Tracy. He says, on a rising note of doubt and disbelief, "Cops? Cops?"

"Not exactly *cops*," Frank says. He still has the same off-center grin on his face.

Floyd is just as baffled as ever, except he can see that Frank is getting *some* damn message across to this spook, so now Floyd chimes in, saying, "That's right. Not exactly what you'd call *cops*."

Bad Death is leaning forward like a child watching a cake get its icing. In a hushed, delighted whisper he asks, "*Fed*-eral?"

"*You* know what we are, Bad Death," Frank tells him. Taking his pencil flashlight from his jacket pocket he points it at Bad Death and says, "And you know what *this* is, too."

"It's a flashlight," Bad Death says.

"Don't count on it," Frank says. Suddenly stepping backward, he points the unlit pencil flashlight this way and that, saying, "Everybody freeze."

Two of Bad Death's men, who have actually been more or less frozen up to this point, immediately make moves toward bulging pockets, but Bad Death snaps at them, "Cool it! That's one of them disguised guns!"

Bad Death's men are bewildered, and frown at everything and everybody. One of them says, "Boss, that's all bullshit. Those mother-fuckers didn't have no ID or *nothin'*."

132

"That's 'cause they're undercover, you damn fool," Bad Death tells them. Hasn't he, after all, seen all the James Bond movies *and* all the Gravedigger Jones-Coffin Ed Johnson movies *and* all the Fred Williamson movies *and* all the Pam Grier movies? "And that's why they don't carry a regular gun," he says.

"That's right," Frank says, and he suddenly grabs Maleficent, who has been standing to one side paralyzed, like a jelly doughnut turned to stone. Jabbing the end of the pencil flashlight into Maleficent's side, Frank ducks around behind her—there's plenty of room for Floyd back there, too, who immediately joins him—and Frank says, "Gangway! One move out of anybody, and she's dead!"

"Oh!" cries Maleficent. "Oh, Savior!" which is the way she pronounces her husband's name.

"Go ahead and pray, lady," Frank says. "But back up while you're doing it. Slow and steady."

Bad Death and his men look tough and hang tough—and *are* tough, come to that—but they stand there and don't move, while Maleficent backs slowly out of the room, with Frank and Floyd peeking up over her shoulders like a tank crew. F. Xavier, hands outstretched, calls, "Don't worry, honey, they're federal men, they won't hurt you!"

"Though it might be taxing," Floyd says, and chuckles.

Frank, hidden by Maleficent's floor-length muumuu, kicks Floyd in the ankle, and they exit with no more bad jokes, backing all the way through the funeral parlor to the street, where Frank and Floyd immediately split, running like track stars on a bed of coals, while Maleficent shrieks once and falls over on her back.

A little later, several of Bad Death's men will have to go out and heave Maleficent up onto her feet again, but at the moment they and F. Xavier are busy being Bad Death's audience, as Bad Death beams around at everybody and says, "How *about* that? You ready for that? *Fed*-eral, baby, they's fed-eral men and they's got an undercover eye on Bad Death himself! You know you with the *power* when you with Bad Death!" He looks around at the admiring, respecting faces. "Fed-eral," he says. *"Huh!"*

3

From Frank's list:

*Felicity Tower*
*240 St. Paul's Court*
*The Bronx*

In her bedroom, before her full-length mirror, smooth brown flesh gleaming in the lamplight, naked as the day she was born (though considerably altered and improved in size and shape), Felicity Tower is doing the Hustle, all by herself, despite the fact that the Hustle is the first new dance in fifteen years in which people dance while touching one another. *The New York Times*, on August 3, 1975, pointed out that, "The rise of the Hustle provides a socially acceptable way for people to get their hands on members of the opposite sex," which undoubtedly had much to do with the dance's success, even though, as the *Times* also warned, "One must study, practice, and work to achieve success in doing the Hustle."

Felicity Tower had read that item, and believed it without question. She did believe that the Hustle was a socially acceptable way to get her hands on members of the opposite sex (which can be read any way you prefer), and she had no doubt that study, practice, and work eventually bring success not only in the Hustle but everywhere in life.

This belief in work had been drilled into Felicity from infancy, back in Covington, Kentucky, where her upwardly striving parents—a sanitation man and a waitress—had pushed through college each and every one of their seven children (Felicity was fifth) as though they were seven labors of Hercules. The work-and-education ethic permeates Felicity's life. It has led to her current vocation as a teacher at Liberation High, as well as to her activities for such worthy causes as the Open Sports Committee. Unfortunately, it has also indirectly led to her being, at twenty-nine, a beautiful sex-hungry naked brown virgin learning to Hustle alone in front of her bedroom mirror.

If the men who fantasize about Felicity—and there are many of them—could guess the fantasies she has about *them*, alone in her bed on many a sleepless night, they would go off like Roman candles. They would just simply explode in Technicolor. But none of them has ever had the slightest suspicion. Felicity is a volcano, molten and surging within, but never once has she erupted, so that to all men everywhere she remains a volcano impenetrably disguised as an iceberg.

Over the years, Felicity has struggled many ways against her virginity, but nothing has ever worked. Alcohol relaxes her, but in quite the wrong way; she simply passes out, remaining neat and prim the whole time. Analysis proved there was nothing wrong with her attitudes, only with her performance, but failed to suggest any useful ways to improve.

Some drugs made her vomit, some made her paranoid, and some made her pass out, but none released her inhibitions. Group therapy enabled her to talk with other sufferers, but shop-talk alone has never solved anything. Two Caribbean cruises only demonstrated that, though she couldn't tan, she could certainly burn; but even with a peeling nose, which most men consider sexy, she remained an arctic in the tropics.

And now, dancing. Inflamed by the *Times'* lure of getting her hands on members of the opposite sex, Felicity has set herself to learn to Hustle, as at one time she set herself to learn Latin or sew buttonholes. With a record on the stereo ("Ease on Down the Road," by Consumer Rapport), she is practicing the moves before her mirror. Her arms are out in front of her as though holding the hands of an invisible partner, and she is swaying with a sensual grace that would dry the throat of anyone who saw her. Her bare legs are stepping firmly on the 1-2, 1-2, and she is twirling, gliding, shuffling, improvising on the 1-2-3. The hands-out gesture is submissive, the movements of the bare brown hips and shoulders are virtually a definition of sex, and the placid cool beauty of the face would make connoisseurs of us all.

"Ease on dah-own, Ease on down the row-oad." Felicity steps, steps, twirls, sees a startled white face in the mirror, twirls, breaks step, stops, stares at the mirror, sees nothing. She turns, her breasts lifting as she looks over her shoulder at the doorway, and still she sees nothing.

Was it real? Frowning, she stares again at the mirror, as though it might contain a face that didn't exist in the real world, like de Maupassant's Horla. And it does! The face is there, and as she meets the round startled eyes, the face disappears again. Which is to say, it ducks out of sight behind the doorframe.

Felicity's heart is pounding. She had been perspiring lightly from her exertions in front of the mirror, but now that sheen is growing cold and goosebumps are forming all over her body. Blinking, licking her lips, she turns and moves on suddenly unsteady legs toward the doorway.

And in the living room there are two of them, two great hulking white men, massive-shouldered, with great hard hands and tough pitiless faces. "Dear God," Felicity murmurs, knowing she is helpless, falling back against the doorpost, her trembling hand fluttering up to her throat.

One of the men takes a step toward her, his powerful hand reaching out. "Take it easy, lady," he says. (*Ease on dah-own, Ease on down the row-oad.*")

135

"Oh, please," Felicity whispers. She is utterly at their mercy, utterly.

"This won't take long," says the white man.

"Oh!" cries Felicity, and staggers backward along the living room wall until her legs hit the arm of the sofa. She topples onto her back on the sofa, sprawled out, one leg flung across the coffee table atop *Harper's, The New Yorker, The Atlantic, Viva,* and *Penthouse.* She should defend herself, protect herself, but she is weak with terror, boneless with fright. She lies there, unable to move.

The two men are staring at her. Then they stare at one another, and one of them says, in a low awed voice, "Jee-sus!"

"Now, look," the other one says, to Felicity, and lifts up his hand with something in it, "we'll be right out of here."

Something in his hand. Felicity's fear-glazed eyes focus on it, and it's the golden statue, the little naked man, the Other Oscar. And now the white man is holding the Other Oscar carelessly in his hand, and Felicity's mind does wild, improbable imaginings as to what he can possibly intend to do with that thing, until the white man reaches up his other hand and *snaps off a pinky.* A finger from the statue, the pinky of the right hand, raised over the devil-mask head. *Pik,* it sounds, in a sudden silence, because the record has ended in the bedroom.

"Oh!" cries Felicity, as though some bone of her own had been broken.

"Shit!" says the white man, out of some measureless deep of disgust, and he slaps both statue and pinky down onto a table. And then—Felicity stares in shock and disbelief—he and the other white man, without a word, both turn and climb out the living room window to the fire escape and disappear. *Disappear.*

And in the bedroom the record player, which has been engaging in a series of self-involved clicks, now begins to play the next record, which is "The Hustle," by Van McCoy. "Do it! Do it! Do the Hustle!"

"Saved," mutters Felicity aloud. "Saved again." And she bursts into great wailing tears of relief.

4

From Frank's list:

*Amanda  Addleford*
*151 Midwood St.*
*The Bronx*

Because Mandy works late, and because she has to ride the subway every night from midtown Manhattan all the way to the South Bronx, she travels with armament. In her bag, which she holds tight in her left hand, there are a spray can of Mace, a police whistle, a pencil flashlight, and a roll of pennies. If attacked, she can repel the mugger with Mace, whistle for a cop, keep an eye on the criminal with her pencil flashlight, and if all else fails she can put the roll of pennies in her fist and slug him one.

It isn't rape that Mandy fears, though, not at her age. She's sixty-two, she's stout and flat-footed and she walks like a duck, and Valerie in one of her rages once told Mandy she had a face like a potato, a judgment with which Mandy cannot disagree. So her purse, rather than her person, is all she expects evil strangers to be after, but so far—and she's been working for Valerie Woode nearly eleven years now—she has never had to use her arsenal even once. "New York," she commented to Valerie the other night, "just don't live up to its reputation."

Valerie Woode is, of course, the famous Broadway star, currently appearing in a revival of Pinter's *Homecoming,* and Mandy is her dresser and personal maid, even traveling to Los Angeles with her on those rare occasions—five, in all this time—when Valerie consents to appear in a motion picture. (She *never* consents to appear on television, not even a talk show.) With the seven-thirty curtain, most plays break by ten o'clock, but still there's another hour—removing Valerie's makeup and costume, dressing her for whatever after-theater activities, preparing the dressing room for the next day—before Mandy's work is done and she can take the subway home. (Valerie supplies cab fare, which Mandy spends as she pleases, mostly on Loft's candies.)

Tonight, as usual, the subway ride to the Bronx and the two-block walk to the apartment are completely uneventful, but when Mandy finishes unlocking the three locks on her apartment door and steps inside, damn if she doesn't walk smack into two burglars just climbing in from the fire escape through the living room window. (Their own breaking-and-entering noises must have kept them from hearing Mandy's unlocking noises.) "God*dam!*" Mandy yells, exulting in this promise of combat after all these years of preparedness, and paws her hand quick down into her purse.

The burglars—white men, surprisingly enough; the recession must be even worse than the television says—seem both startled and resigned at her presence, but not fearful. Both of them speaking at once—Mandy doesn't even try to listen to what they're saying—they approach her across the room, hands out in meaningless gestures. Mandy grabs the can of Mace, pulls it out of her purse, aims it at the face of one of the burglars, and just as she's about to press the button she realizes it's Frank.

Frank. A stagehand or prop man or something, one of the union men hanging around backstage. Mandy has known him for years, has seen him off and on during the runs of at least four shows. But she has never expected to find him climbing in her living room window.

She lowers the Mace can. "Frank?" she says.

Frank stops talking and stops walking and just gapes at her. The, one with him also gapes at her, then turns and gapes at Frank. He looks a lot like Frank, so Mandy says, "This your brother?"

"I don't believe it," Floyd says.

"I believe it," Frank says. "After tonight I'm gonna believe anything."

Floyd gives it the old college try. "Lady," he says, "you got us all mixed up. You're thinking of some other guys."

"You're Frank," Mandy says, pointing a definite finger at him. "Last time I saw you was during *Lancaster Abbey*."

Frank sighs. "Amanda Addleford," he says. "How'm I supposed to know that's Mandy?"

"Holy Christ," says Floyd. "Isn't there anything we can *do?*"

"It's done," Frank says.

Floyd says, "But she'll call the cops! She'll turn us in! We can't just *leave* her!"

Frank gives him a weary look. "Whadaya wanna do? Kill her?"

Mandy says, "Now, just a damn minute."

"*I* can't kill anybody," Floyd says.

"You can't kill *me*," Mandy informs him. "That's for *damn* sure."

Frank shakes his head and comes to a conclusion. "We'll have to take her with us," he says.

Mandy and Floyd both say, in unison, *"What?"*

"We'll hold onto her until we get the right one," Frank says. "Maybe Jerry or Mel or somebody can figure out what to do with her next."

"You ain't taking *me* anywhere," Mandy announces. Pointing the Mace can at Frank again, this time she does press the button, and a hissing sound happens. As Frank ducks back, a white foam trickles down the side of the can. The hissing fades. Six years in the purse has taken its .toll; the Mace can is dead. "Well, *hell*," Mandy says.

"By God," Frank says, "I never thought I'd see it. Somebody even unluckier than me."

Floyd has moved to a corner of the room, and now he says, "Here's the statue." *Pik.* "Wrong one."

"Naturally," Frank says. He takes Mandy's arm. "Let's go," he says. "It's been a long day, and I want to go home."

# EXCEPT . . .

Wylie Cheshire was mad. He came up out of the game room and yanked at the wall phone in the kitchen in such a manner that his wife Georgia looked over at him and said, "Watch it, there, Wylie, you gone pull the phone out the wall again."

"You shut up, woman," Wylie said, and dialed the sporting goods store with a blunt jabbing fingertip. Then there wasn't any answer because the place was closed this hour of the night, so he broke the connection and dialed the owner's home phone instead, and when the man himself answered Wylie said, "Goddam it, Russ, this here's Wylie."

"Well, hi, there, Wylie. How you doing, old son?"

"*I'll* tell you how I'm doin, Russ. That goddam punchin' bag busted again."

"Busted?"

"Layin' on the floor."

"Well, you hit it too hard, Wylie, I've told you that before."

"It's a punchin' bag, ain't it? Well, I'm *punchin'* it."

"I'll come over first thing in the morning," Russ said. "Nothing I can do about it tonight."

"Goddam it, Russ, I was just showin' my brother-in-law some moves."

"You don't know your own strength, Wylie."

"The hell I don't," Wylie said. "I'll see *you* in the morning." And he slapped the receiver onto its hook, glared at Georgia and her sister Faith, who were cleaning up the dinner dishes, and went back down to the game room, where Faith's no-good husband, Deke Finburdy, was admiring the Other Oscar in the trophy cabinet. "Can't get it fixed till tomorrow," Wylie said, and drop-kicked the punching bag into the far corner of the room, near the dartboard.

"This yere's new, ain't it?" Deke was gesturing at the Other Oscar.

"Yeah, it's new," Wylie said. He was still angry, and in no mood to talk, so he just grabbed himself another beer out of the refrigerator, dropped onto the sofa, and sulked. Damn punchin' bag.

The truth was, it was his no-good brother-in-law Deke Finburdy that Wylie really wanted to punch. A stumblebum and a ne'er-do-well, Deke had married Wylie's wife's sister on *purpose*. Just to get on the gravy train, that's all, live on Wylie Cheshire like some kind of flea. No wonder Wylie hit that punching bag too hard, with Deke around.

Now, Wylie sat drinking beer and glowering while Deke occupied himself admiring once again all Wylie's mementoes, the framed photographs and awards, the trophy case full of prizes, the signed footballs. It was all there, Wylie's four years of varsity ball down at Grambling College, his three years with the New York Giants, his six years with the Kansas City Chiefs, his two years in the Canadian Football League, and his triumphant last three years with the Cincinnati Bengals. Defensive guard all the way, one of the biggest, meanest, roughest, smartest, and all-around best linemen in pro ball.

And here were the mementoes to prove it, everything from the football he'd carried for his only touchdown (wrenching it out of Sonny Jurgensen's hands and lumbering eleven yards to the end zone with it) to the photograph of his round black unsmiling face next to the round white smiling face of Howard Cosell, the time Wylie had been guest announcer on *Monday Night Football,* four years ago, just after he'd made public his retirement.

Wylie had started brooding over the possibility that he might shoot himself a little darts—the bull's-eye *did* look something like Deke's nose—when one of the kids came down and said, "Daddy?"

Wylie gave the kid one eye. "What *you* doin outa bed?"

"There's a white man creepin around the house, lookin' in the windows."

Wylie gave the kid both eyes. "A white man?"

"Lookin' in the windows," the kid said.

Wylie had lived in this mostly white neighborhood for seven years without any trouble—face it, Wylie Cheshire never had any trouble *anywhere*—but since his retirement from pro ball he'd devoted himself to any number of black causes (a man has to do *something* with himself, not just lay around the house all day), and the stories he'd heard from his less muscular brothers had made him just itch to get his hands on one of them bigots. Was this to be his chance? "Which side the house?" he asked the kid.

"Back by the bedrooms."

A peeping tom, instead of a bigot? That would be disappointing, but on the other hand any action was better than just sitting here, watching Deke paw the mementoes, so Wylie got to his feet and said, "Deke. Comere."

Deke, an eager and obedient mutt, trotted over and said, "Yeah, Wylie?'

"Kid here says we got a peepin' tom outside."

"Yeah?"

"What we gone do," Wylie said, "is flank him. We treat him like an end-around, and we make him turn and run up the middle. You got that?"

"Sure, Wylie," Deke said. He was willing, but that was about the best you could say for him.

"Okay," Wylie said. "You go out the front door and around the left side of the house. *That* side." He pointed, with one of those big hands. "Got it?"

"Sure, Wylie."

"And *I'll* go out the back door and come around the other way. Let's go."

The kid said, "Kin I come along? Kin I? Kin I?"

"You go with Deke," Wylie told him.

"Gee, thanks!"

So upstairs they went, and off their separate ways. Wylie went out the back door without letting the screen slam, went on the balls of his feet across the patio, skipped over Georgia's rose bed, and went softly to the corner of the house, where he peeked around and in the light-spill from various windows beheld the white man jumping up and down, trying to look in the bathroom window, which was higher than the others.

So, just a peeping tom, after all. Then, as Wylie continued to watch, Deke and the kid came around the front corner of the house and trotted in the direction of the white man, who saw them, spun around twice, and ran directly toward Wylie. Though he didn't know it yet.

Wylie clued him in. As the white man neared the corner, Wylie jumped out, in defensive guard stance, feet planted wide, elbows up high and to the sides, forearms ready to smash, shoulders hunched forward and head hunched down. And stood there.

The white man came to a screeching halt. He threw one

panic-stricken stare over his shoulder at Deke and the kid, and then tried to run around Wylie to the left. Wylie moved just enough, gave him a forearm tap, and the white man tried to run around him to the right. So Wylie moved to his right and gave out with another forearm tap.

This wasn't a white man who gave up easy. This time he feinted to the left and tried the right again, and got Wylie's forehead bonking off his nose. He gave a little nasal cry at that, fell back a step, and then devoted himself full-time to feinting; left, right, left, right, never quite going anywhere. While Deke and the kid stood some distance behind him, watching the fun.

Finally, Wylie decided they'd played enough. Straightening out of the lineman stance, lowering his arms to his sides, he said, "Boy, if Alex Karras couldn't get through me, what chance you think *you* got?"

A slow learner, this white man. One last feint to the left, and he tried to go to the right again. So Wylie stuck out his arm and clotheslined him, and the white man went *wham* on his back on the lawn, and lay there for a while trying to breathe.

Deke and the kid came up then, and the kid stared fascinated into the white man's reddening face. "What is he, Daddy? Is he Ku Klux Klan?"

"We'll ask him," Wylie said. "Soon's he catches his breath."

Deke was frowning down at the white man, and now he said, "By golly, I do believe that's the fella sold Willy the Willys," referring to his brother Willy, who was an even bigger good-for-nothing than Deke himself. Looking across the body at Wylie, Deke said, "*You* remember, Wylie. I went with Willy when he bought that car, that red Willys that never *did* run worth a damn, and a couple months after he bought it some fellas come around from the finance company and broke both his arms."

"'Cause he didn't make his payments," Wylie said, remembering the incident well. His part in it had been to refuse to loan Deke's brother any money.

"He *give* 'em a whole washing machine," Deke said. "Anyway," he said, looking down at the white man, whose face by now was *very* red, "I'm pretty sure that's the fella sold him the car."

Wylie looked down at the red white man. "That right, fella?"

The man on the ground shook his head violently back and forth, while at the same time gargling. Apparently he was having trouble starting up his breathing machinery again. As a humanitarian gesture, Wylie tromped on his stomach a bit, to help him get started, and then the fella began to gasp and breathe and pant and flop around and generally behave like a landed trout. Wylie waited until that phase had ended, and the fellow's complexion had come pretty much down near white again, and then he reached down, grabbed a lot of shirtfront, and stood the white man on his feet. Still holding the bunched shirt, Wylie said, "You a car salesman, fella?"

"NO!"

Deke was squinting almost in the fellow's face. "I'm sure it is," he said.

Wylie said, "You come around here to sell me a car?"

"I— I— I—"

Wylie shook him a little, to get him unstuck. "You what, fella?"

"I—I—I—heard the house was for sale!"

"You did, huh? Where'd you hear that?"

"At the gas station! Over by the Southern State!"

Wylie shook him again, out of irritation. "That's the dumbest lie I heard," he said, "since I stopped talkin' to owners."

Deke said, "Wylie, lemme call Willy, he can come right out and look for himself. *He'll* know if this is the fella."

"Good idea," Wylie said. "Come on, car salesman, let's go inside."

"I have to leave now!"

Wylie released the shirt-front and closed his hand around the fellow's upper arm. "Let me help you change your mind," he said.

# SEQUENTIALLY . . .

Angela and her sister Teresa were partners now, and Teresa was dummy when the phone rang. She went off to answer it, returning a minute later to say, "It's Mel."

Angela was trying to make a particularly tricky no-trump bid, and barely looked up. "Again?"

"He sounds *weird.*"

"What's he want this time?"

"I think you better talk to him, Angela. I'll play the hand."

Angela tried a finesse from dummy in diamonds, but

143

Barbara was too stupid to be finessed. Down came her ace. "Shit," Angela said, got to her feet, and handed the cards to Teresa. "Sorry, partner, we're down one."

"We'll do what we can," Teresa said.

Angela went into the living room and spoke into the phone. "Now what?"

*"What took you so long?"* The shrill rapid whisper was only barely recognizable as Mel's voice.

Angela was in no mood for a lot of crap. "What's the matter, Mel?"

*"I'm captured!"*

"Where? Back in Haddam's Ear?"

*"On Long Island. Some huge black football player's got me!"*

"Mel, I don't know what to do with you tonight."

*"Send the guys out to Wylie Cheshire's house, 58 Ridge Road, Deer Park! Hurry!"*

"There's no guys here. You're the only one ever calls."

*"Listen, Angela, this is a phone in the bathroom! They won't let me stay in here much longer! They're waiting for a guy I sold a car to, years ago! Once he gets here and identifies me, I don't know WHAT they'll do!"*

"I'll come out myself," Angela decided. Anything was better than more of that bridge game. "Give me the address again."

*"These are big mean guys, honey!"*

"I'm a big mean girl. What's the address?"

*"Wylie Cheshire, 58 Ridge Road, Deer Park!"*

"Be right there," Angela said.

# BEFORE LONG . . .

Greater New York is in some ways like a house. Manhattan is the living room, with the TV and the stereo and the good furniture, where guests are entertained. Brooklyn and Queens are the bedrooms where the family sleeps, and the Bronx is the attic, full of inflammable crap that nobody has any use for. Staten Island is the backyard, and Long Island is the detached garage, so filled up with paint cans, workbenches, and a motorboat that you can't get the car in it any more. Hudson County over in New Jersey is the basement, with the furnace and the freezer and the stacks of old newspapers, and the Jersey swamps are the toilet. Westchester is the den, with paneling and a fake kerosene lamp, and Connecticut is the guest room, with starched curtains and landscape prints. The kitchen is way up in Albany, which means the food is always cold by the time it gets to the table, and the formal dining room was torn down by William Zeckendorf and friends back in the early fifties.

Jerry Manelli had spent most of his life in just one corner of this house, and he was only now beginning to realize it. The last twenty-four hours had been frustrating, but they'd also been interesting, catching his attention as nothing had done for years. While he'd been moving in the small circle of the family and Inter-Air Forwarding and a succession of Myrnas, the world all around him had been full of strange neighborhoods and even stranger citizens, and if they weren't people you'd want to be around every day of your life, so what? They were new experiences, and it had been a long while since Jerry had had any new experiences.

The problem was Inter-Air Forwarding. The damn thing was *too* successful. It had started out to be a hustle, and bit by bit it had turned into a job. A job. He could get arrested for it, but that didn't make it anything different; it was still a job.

Thirty years from now he could steal himself a gold watch, and retire with the old man, looking for hobbies.

It had been the faggots' incomprehensible living room that had set him off, for some damn reason, that and the comedy scene they'd played out, each of them believing the other one had brought Jerry home. That would make a good story, except the living room put a twist on it that confused things. And you had to see them in *that* living room to get the point. Jerry could maybe tell the story to the other guys so they'd laugh, but they wouldn't actually get it, because they wouldn't understand about the living room. Not even Mel, who was the family intellectual. (Jews couldn't help themselves that way. Your Jew was the only kind of guy that could be an egghead—read books, listen to classical music on the car radio —and still be an all right guy.)

But other things had added to Jerry's present weird mood, his new view of himself as someone who'd suddenly found he was in a six-foot-deep rut when all along he'd thought of himself as sailing. There was Harlem, and the drunken black man. There was the stoned naked man in the closet; in some sort of oddball way, he'd been fun to talk to.

But the capper was the missing wife, Bobbi Harwood. What an exit! Throw all his shit out the window, pack your bags, and *gone*. Gone where? Into the billion corners and crevices of New York City, out into a world of such endless possibility that the mind couldn't even grasp it. It seemed to Jerry that Bobbi Harwood must also have found herself in that six-foot-deep rut, and she'd done the only sensible thing there was to do: *leap!* Get out of that rut, and go someplace else.

But where? Thinking about Bobbi Harwood, trying to figure out where and how to find her, had made Jerry more and more aware of just how easy *he* was to find.

How can you tell the Tuesdays from the Thursdays? You can't.

Thinking things over, Jerry drove down from Harlem almost all the way to the Midtown Tunnel before he stopped at a phone booth to call the Bernstein house. But then it wasn't his sister Angela who answered but his brother-in-law Frank's sister-in-law Barbara, who said, "Nobody's here but me."

"Where's Angela?"

"Mel called and said he was in some kind of trouble somewhere, so Angela and Teresa and Kathleen went out to rescue him."

"Angela and Teresa and Kathleen? Where's the *guys?*"

"Frank just called about ten minutes ago. He sounded really upset about something, and he said he was on the way back, and he asked me if anybody else had found the right statue, and when I told him no he used curse words."

"What about Floyd?"

"He's coming with Frank."

"Well, I'm on my way back, too," Jerry told her. "I got three of my four statues, but none of them were any good. I'll have to look for the fourth one tomorrow."

"Will you want a cup of coffee?"

"I'll want a beer," Jerry said. "Lots of beer."

"That's funny," Barbara said. "Frank said the exact same thing."

# LATER . . .

Angela Bernstein, Teresa McCann, and Kathleen Podenski got out of the station wagon in front of Wylie Cheshire's house, where Mel was being imprisoned. Angela said, "You two go in there and distract them."

The two women looked blank. Kathleen said, "Distract them?"

"Tell them you're Avon Ladies."

"We don't have any display things."

"Tell them you're Avon Lady Avon Ladies, you're here recruiting new Avon Ladies."

Both women look doubtful. Teresa said, "I'm not sure I—"

"Oh, for God's sake," Angela said, "use your imagination! Start a Tupperware party, be Welcome Wagon girls, be their local Muscular Dystrophy volunteer, be taking up collections for PONY. Do *something!*"

"Well, all right," Teresa said, but she still looked doubtful. So did Kathleen, but at any rate both women finally started up the neat slate walk through the clipped green lawn toward the brick ranch-style house where Mel was a prisoner.

And Angela went around to the side of the house. This was an expensive Long Island neighborhood, with large house lots, so the nearest neighbors were far away beyond privacy screens of shrubbery. Angela, waiting till Teresa and Kathleen had done their Avon Lady ding-dong at the front door, began to move down the side of the house, looking in windows. In the living room, greeting Teresa and Kathleen, were two black couples; the women were young and personable, one of the men was kind of lanky and loose-jointed, and the other man was a *monster*. "Good Lord," Angela murmured, "I wouldn't want to go to bed with *that*." And she moved along.

In one bedroom were any number of black children asleep in bunk beds. In another were two black girls asleep in matching youth beds; lace frills skirted *everything* in the room, including the wastepaper basket.

Finally the rear of the house. The back door was unlocked and inside was an extremely neat kitchen. The lady of this house ran a very tight ship, from the look of things.

But where was Mel? Cautiously Angela crossed the kitchen and moved through an empty dining room. Ahead she could hear the murmur of conversation; Teresa's voice, Kathleen's voice, other voices. Angela couldn't make out exactly what was being said, but the tone seemed generally calm and civilized, so she remained unworried.

But where in *hell* was Mel? Not in the master bedroom, and not in the excessively masculine little den, and that was it for the house, except for the basement, so back to the kitchen Angela went, and down the stairs to a family room so cluttered with sports equipment and trophies it looked like Abercrombie & Fitch's window after a bombing.

Mel was in the utility room with the furnace and water heater and washing machine and drier, and he looked just as white as they did. "You made it!" he said, in a shrill whisper, and tried to clutch Angela to him.

"Later," Angela said, disengaging herself. "Come on, let's get out of here before something goes wrong upstairs."

Upstairs, things weren't precisely going wrong, but they were going just a bit agley. Teresa and Kathleen had entered the house without discussing what exact cover story they would use, and so Teresa had gotten herself rather thoroughly entwined in a presentation of herself as a spokesperson for the League of Women Voters before she realized that Kathleen appeared to be collecting for cystic fibrosis. The glaze slowly spreading over the eyes of Wylie Cheshire, Georgia Cheshire, Deke Finburdy, and Faith Finburdy was not diminished when both women simultaneously switched horses in midstream. Were these women asking them to *vote* for cystic fibrosis?

Meantime, Angela was trying to hurry Mel upstairs, but Mel was whispering, "Wait a minute, will you? Let's get what we came after."

"Well, *hurry*."

Mel hurried. He crossed the family room, plucked the Dancing Aztec Priest from its place amid the trophies, and finally joined the jittering Angela on the stairs. Up they went, and out the back door, and around to the front of the house, where a wiry black man who'd just clambered out of a thoroughly disreputable old Buick took one look at Mel and shouted at the top of his voice, *"You!* You *are* the son bitch sold me that car! *Hey, Wyyy-lieee!"*

"Oh, no," said Mel.

"You shut up," Angela said to the black man. "Just shut up, that's all."

And at that instant Wally Hintzlebel leaped out of nowhere, grabbed the Dancing Aztec Priest out of Mel's astonished hand, spun away, and ran pell-mell into Angela, so that the two of them went sprawling together onto the lawn.

"The statue!" Mel shouted, and the aggrieved black man punched him in the eye. "Ow," said Mel, and punched him back. The house door opened, and a *lot* of people came running out.

Angela and Wally sat up and stared at one another. "You!" said Angela. "What the hell are *you* doing here?"

148

"Grab the statue!" Mel shouted at his wife. He was scuffling with the black man, who had grabbed him around the waist and was trying to give him a bear hug.

Wylie Cheshire came chugging across the lawn, plucked Mel and the wiry black man apart, and said to Mel, "Who let *you* out, goddam it?"

"Wylie!" yelled the black man. "That's him, that *is* him!"

"Shut up, Willy," said Wylie. He shook Mel a little. "Who let you out, huh? Just tell me that much."

Mel, however, was paying insufficient attention to Wylie, since he was watching instead the byplay on the lawn between Angela and Wally. Angela and Wally were sitting facing one another, and Angela was saying, "You listened in that closet, didn't you? You *dirty* bastard."

"I got just as much right as any of *you* people," Wally said.

"*Give* me that statue," Angela snapped, and tried to grab it out of Wally's hand. The two of them rolled on the lawn.

Meanwhile, Willy was shouting, "Wylie, he sold me that Willys!"

"Shut *up*, Willy, like I told you before! You listen to me, you! How'd you get outa that—"

"Oh, leave me alone," Mel said, and pushed Wylie away as though he were a flea. Wylie gaped at him in utter amazement, and Mel went over to say to Angela, "And what's all *this?*"

Angela, having kneed Wally a good one, was struggling to her feet with the statue in her possession. "Come on," she said.

"You better answer me, Angela," Mel said. (In the background, Willy was now explaining to Deke Finburdy that it was indeed Mel who had long ago sold him that Willys, while Georgia Cheshire was asking Teresa for more information about the League of Women Voters, and both Faith Finburdy and Kathleen were standing around with their mouths open.) And Mel repeated, "You better answer me."

"Oh, don't be stupid," Angela said, and made as if to march away.

Wylie Cheshire stopped her by standing in front of her and saying, "That's *my* statue, lady."

"Oh, it is, is it? Then *here*." And, in total exasperation, Angela whammed him over the head with it.

Fortunately for Wylie, it wasn't the right one. It broke, and Wylie staggered back, and Angela gave everybody the same disgusted glare—Mel and Wylie and Wally and Willy and

Deke and Kathleen and Teresa and Faith and Georgia—and marched away to the station wagon. Enough was enough.

## AT WHICH MOMENT . . .

"I don't understand this scheme," said Pedro Ninni.

"You *never* understand, Pedro," Edwardo Brazzo said. His tie was even limper and more sweat-soaked than usual, and his small original store of patience was completely used up. "Why don't you, Pedro," he said, "just accept the fact that you are a *dumb useless stupid creature,* and do what we tell you to do without *arguing* all the time?"

"No," said Pedro.

"No?" Edwardo stared at him. "No what?"

"No everything," said Pedro.

José Caracha, with his sculptor's patience, entered the conversation then, trying to smooth things over. "It's a hot night, Edwardo," he said. "Let's not get excited."

"Not get *excited?* When all this idiot does is question and argue and complain and say no, no, no *everything?*"

"He doesn't understand, that's all," José said. Turning to Pedro, he said, "Let me try to explain."

"I am not a dumb useless stupid creature," said Pedro.

"Of course not," José agreed. "Edwardo is just a little nervous, that's all."

"Nervous," echoed Edwardo. "Our *lives* are at stake."

"Easy, easy," José told him. Turning back to Pedro, he said, "Pedro, you know that something seems to have gone wrong up in the United States, and we don't have our money."

"I never believed in it, anyway," Pedro said.

"Be that as it may. You also know that Hector Ovella, the curator of the museum, is a member of our little group, and is just as annoyed as we are that he hasn't been paid his money."

"I'm not annoyed," Pedro said. "I never *did* believe we'd get any money."

"You *see* what we have to put up with," Edwardo said.

"Gently, gently. Pedro, the point is, Hector very unfairly blames *us,* we three, and he says if he doesn't get his money by the end of the week he will turn us all in to the authorities."

"And they will hang us by our tongues," Pedro said, "as I expected all along."

"Which is why," José said, "we have to leave the country."

"Santa Rosita Rosaria isn't out of the country," Pedro said. "Santa Rosita Rosaria is a city *in* this country."

"That's right," José said. "We know that already, Pedro, we've lived here all our lives."

"So why do you want to go to Rosie?" Pedro said, giving the common slang nickname for the town of Santa Rosita Rosaria.

"Because," José said, while in the background Edwardo made fists and ground his teeth, "because no one will let us board a plane that is leaving the country. But they will let us board the plane to Rosie, and then we will hijack the plane and force it to take us to New York."

"Here comes the bad part," Pedro said.

"Not at all bad," José assured him. "It simply makes sense that it doesn't take three men to hijack an airplane. So *one* of us will hijack the airplane, and when the airplane reaches New York the other two will simply drift away while the hijacker gives himself up to the authorities and resquests asylum as a political refugee. Then the other two can go to the people in New York who owe us the money, and collect the money, and use some of it to hire a lawyer in New York to get the hijacker out on bail, and then all three of us will go somewhere completely different and live on the rest of the money."

"In *New York* they'll hang me by my tongue," Pedro said.

"They don't do things like that in New York," José promised him. "They're very civilized, very nice in New York."

"You can't explain anything to a dunce like that," Edwardo said.

"Yes, he can," Pedro said. "Thank you, José, you explained that like an intelligent person and I understood it completely."

"Fine," said José. "I knew you would. And now, we draw straws to find out which one of us will be the hijacker."

"Hmmmm," said Pedro.

# AND AFTER THAT . . .

When Jerry got back to the Bernsteins' house there were a lot of people there. Mel and Angela were in the kitchen, arguing

151

about something. Teresa and Kathleen and Barbara were in the dining room, arguing about bridge. And Frank and Floyd were in the living room with an old fat colored woman, arguing with her about whether or not they should have kidnapped her.

"What's going on here?" Jerry said.

Neither Mel nor Angela would answer him, none of the card-playing women would give him an answer he cared about, and Frank and Floyd kept both talking at once. Jerry pointed at the colored woman and said, "What the hell'd you bring *her* back for? *She* ain't no Dancing Aztec Priest."

"I don't dance for *nobody*," the colored woman said.

Frank finally got sufficient silence around him so he could answer the question, and then he said, "Jerry, I had to do it. She recognized me."

"Recognized you? What do you mean, recognized you?"

"I mean recognized me as in recognized me. As in, 'Hello, Frank.' That's how."

"You *know* her?" The social combinations necessary to such a thing boggled Jerry's mind.

"She works at the theater," Frank said. "She's a maid, she's seen me around backstage. Her name's Mandy, that's all I ever knew. How'm I supposed to know she's somebody called Amanda Addleford?"

"Well, you're *all* in trouble," Mandy announced, "unless you let me go right this minute."

Jerry told her, "We're in trouble no matter what we do, lady."

Frank said, "We couldn't kill her, could we? No. And we couldn't leave her there to call the cops. So we brought her with us."

"You can't keep her," Jerry said. "She's out of season."

"Ever since the Emancipation Proclamation," Mandy said.

Frank said, "Jerry, I was hoping you'd come up with something."

"You were, huh?"

Floyd said, "We did pretty good otherwise, Jerry. We got the—"

Jerry said, "Not in front of the prisoner here, okay? I mean, she knows too much already; let's start cooling it."

Frank said, "So what do we do with her?"

"You let me go," Mandy said. "Right this second."

Jerry said, "We'll stash her while we think it over. Just a minute." And he went out to the kitchen, where Mel and Angela were still arguing, and said, "Listen, do you have a closet upstairs where we can stash this old woman Frank and Floyd brought back?"

"Closet!" yelled Mel, and for some reason that made the argument even worse than it was before. Mel screamed at Angela, and Angela screamed right back at Mel, and Jerry couldn't make any sense out of it at all. So Jerry went back to the living room and told Frank and Floyd, "Screw it. Come on, bring her along upstairs, we'll find someplace to stash her."

"You're making a big mistake," Mandy said.

"It wouldn't be my first today," Jerry told her.

In the kitchen, Mel was yelling the phrase "in the closet" in various ways: "In the closet!" "In the *closet?*" "*In* the closet!" Jerry and Frank and Floyd and Mandy went upstairs in search of a closet. They looked around and finally settled on the closet in the master bedroom, which could be locked from the outside. But just as they were about to shove Mandy in there Mel came bounding up the stairs, shouting, "Not in *that* closet!"

"Now what?" Jerry said.

Mel flung himself into the closet as though gold had just been discovered on the inside. He tossed out shoes, hangers, and assorted flotsam, backward between his legs like a dog digging for a bone, and then he yanked back the corner of carpet and yelled, "Look at this! You can hear every goddam thing in the dining room!"

So you could. The women were arguing about bridge in the dining room.

"Okay," Jerry said. "Okay, Mel, no need to get excited." Frank said, "But where do we put Mandy?"

"On the next bus," Mandy said.

Mel said, "Put her in the bathroom."

Jerry said, "What if somebody has to take a leak?"

"We got that half-bath downstairs." Mel came out of the closet, viciously slammed its door behind him, and suddenly bellowed downward through the floor, *"Jezebel!"*

Faintly from the kitchen came the response: *"Asshole!"*

Mel ran out of the bedroom, yelling.

"Everybody's gone bugfuck," Jerry told himself. "Come on, let's put your friend in the bathroom."

So they put Mandy in the bathroom, regardless of her alternate suggestions, and went downstairs to the living room.

Jerry sat on the sofa. "I think somebody better offer me a beer," he said.

"I'll get it," Floyd said. "Frank?"

"Certainly," Frank said, and Floyd went away, and Frank sat down. "What a night," he said.

Jerry said, "How come you and Floyd were together?"

"We combined our lists. Don't get upset, Jerry, it worked out. We went to every address. We got two of Floyd's statues, and two of mine."

"That leaves four," Jerry pointed out.

"One of them on Floyd's list," Frank said, "was an undertaker in Harlem called F. Xavier White, and when we got there some black gangsters were talking about a funeral with him. They put the arm on us, and we're lucky it wasn't *our* funeral. No way to look for statues in the middle of all that."

"Okay."

"Floyd's other one," Frank said, "was somebody called Marshall Thumble, also in Harlem. We found the address, but there wasn't anybody home and we couldn't find the statue. But we *did* find an extra one at Leroy Pinkham's place."

"An *extra* one?"

"It's been that kind of day," Frank said. "Maybe that one's Thumble's. Maybe it's somebody else's. Maybe it wasn't one of our sixteen at all. Anyway, they both broke, so neither of them was gold."

"What about the two on your list?"

"Edward Ross and Jennifer Kendall, down in Greenwich Village. We went there first, but there was nobody home and no statues. It looked like they'd cleared out. We didn't waste any time, Jerry, we covered both lists."

"And brought back second prize."

"You mean Mandy?" Frank's face twisted into a combination of apology and straining thought. "I didn't know what the hell to do about that, Jerry."

Floyd came back with the beer, and with Mel, who was red-faced and breathing hard. Beyond them, Jerry saw Angela hurtle out of the house, raging mad. Her car was heard to start, to roar, and to spin away with a great squealing of tires. Jerry drank beer and said, "Mel, we're going to figure out where we stand here. Can you give it your attention a minute?"

Mel glared at the front windows. "Why not?" he snarled.

"Sit down, Mel," Jerry suggested.

Mel frowned, looking around, seemed about to say several dozen angry things, and then abruptly dropped onto the sofa at the other end from Jerry. "I got two of mine," he said, glaring now at the coffee table. "And two of somebody else's."

Jerry said, *"More* extras?"

"Extras?" Mel's brows came down as though he was trying

to burn a hole through the coffee table just with his stare. "Edward Ross and Jennifer Kendall," he said. "They're on——"

Delighted, Frank said, "They're mine! How do you like that!" Then he looked bewildered and said, "How'd *you* get them?"

"They were in Connecticut."

Jerry, with a list of the sixteen Open Sports Committee members on his lap, had started checking them off, and now he said, "You got Beemiss?"

"Yes," Mel said. "And Cheshire." His glower increased. *"Cheshire."*

"Fine," Jerry said. "And I got three of mine. That means we got eleven for sure, and maybe twelve, depending on that extra one Frank and Floyd found."

Floyd said, *"I* think that's Marshall Thumble's."

"You'll find out for sure tomorrow," Jerry told him. "You and Frank. Also go back to the undertaker. There's only four, maybe five statues left, and it has to be one of them. Mel, what about you?"

Mel turned and brooded at Jerry, as though deciding whether or not to kill him with an ax. "What about me?"

"You feel up to doing some more tomorrow?"

"I'll do my other two," Mel said. He leaned across the sofa toward Jerry. "Why *wouldn't* I do my other two?"

"That's fine," Jerry said. "And I'll look for Bobbi Harwood. It has to be one of this last bunch, remember, and we're still ahead of the mob because they spent all their time futzing around with Mel in Connecticut."

"They'll be back tomorrow," Floyd said.

"We'll worry about it then." Jerry finished his beer. "That's it for tonight. Time for everybody to catch their breath."

Frank said, "What about Mandy?"

"Your buddy in the bathroom? She can stay there tonight. We'll work something out in the morning."

Mel sighed, and seemed to relax. "I'll give her a blanket and pillow," he said. "She can sleep in the tub."

"And I can sleep in my bed." Jerry got to his feet and stretched. "Good night," he said.


# AT LAST . . .

Everybody has been running very hard, but the time has come

to slow down. Jerry Manelli is having a final beer at home, in front of the television set, unwinding by watching *Bringing Up Baby* on Channel 5. Frank and Teresa McCann are lying in their separate twin beds, watching *The Tonight Show* on Channel 4. Floyd and Barbara McCann are making love, but because of the thin walls of their house and the nearness of their children they are being very careful not to have a very good time.

Angela Bernstein has come home, and she and Mel are sitting at the kitchen table discussing their marital problems with Mandy Addleford, who is sympathetic but practical, like Ann Landers.

Wally Hintzlebel is sitting at his kitchen table playing canasta with his mother and telling her lies about those scratches on his face that he got from Angela Bernstein. Oscar Russell Green is asleep face down on his living room floor, with the television set showing *Bringing Up Baby* to the top of his head. Felicity Tower is wide awake in her bed, glowing like the filament in a light bulb.

Far away to the south, Pedro Ninni and Edwardo Brazzo and José Caracha are asleep in Quetchyl, with their mouths open. Somewhere in the New York area the *real* Dancing Aztec Priest glitters in the dark; no switches were made in Descalzo, the real statue *is* one of the remaining four.

Financier Victor Krassmeier, suffering from constipation, is sitting on his toilet, reading *Barron's*. Mobster August Corella is having a Rob Roy in his living room, watching *The Tonight Show* and sulking about his day. Earl is in bed with a steak, placing it alternately over each eye and watching *The Tonight Show* with the other. Ralph is dreaming that he is driving a car down a mountainside with no brakes.

Wylie Cheshire, with a white X of bandage on his forehead where Angela Bernstein crowned him with the Dancing Aztec Priest, is watching *The Crimson Pirate* on Channel 9 and feeling sulky and mulish; beneath the X, the bump is still growing. Luke Snell, with his own white X of bandage on his upper lip from where he hit the steering wheel and knocked out three teeth when the motorcycle rammed him, is also watching *The Crimson Pirate*, but isn't enjoying it as much as he'd expected.

Bud Beemiss is sitting in his study with a very dry Tanqueray martini on the rocks, brooding at the space where his Dancing Aztec Priest used to stand, and thinking things over. Downstairs in his house, Hamlet and Ophelia are asleep with smiles on their faces.

David Fayley and Kenny Spang, each terribly hurt with the other for having brought Jerry Manelli into the house, are lying side by side in bed, wide awake, not speaking and not touching. Jenny Kendall and Eddie Ross are in one sleeping bag together in the woods in Rhode Island, making love; they'll do just fine with one motorcycle and one sleeping bag and each other.

Leroy Pinkham is lying on the floor in his living room with his sister Ruby and his sister Renny, watching *Bringing Up Baby*. Buhbuh is lying on his own living room floor a few blocks away, watching *The Crimson Pirate*.

F. Xavier White is sitting up in bed, listening to Maleficent tell him everything he did wrong today, which was everything. Jeremiah "Bad Death" Jonesburg is sleeping happily, dreaming of funerals.

Chuck Harwood is curled up on his closet floor, snoring in his sleep; he's going to be *very* stiff tomorrow. Bobbi, her mind full of confusing dream fragments, is sozzily asleep on Madge's sofa.

In their homes, in their beds, Ben Cohen and Mrs. Dorothy Moorwood are peacefully asleep, neither of them guessing what's coming their way on the morrow.

Everybody is settling down now. Everybody is going to sleep. You, too.

# THE
# SECOND PART
# OF THE
# SEARCH

Everybody in New York City wants to get somewhere. At Christmas everybody wants to get to Macy's, and in the summer everybody wants to get to the beach. At five o'clock everybody wants to get through the tunnels. On Saturday night everybody wants to get to the newsstands for Sunday's paper. Everybody uptown wants to get to Zabar's and everybody downtown wants to get to Balducci's. Everybody all the time wants to get into the next elevator, the next subway, and the next-door neighbor's pants.

White-collar workers want to get to the executive washroom. Executives want to get to Palm Springs or Palm Beach. First-class passengers at Kennedy want to get to the VIP Lounge. Cabbies want to get across town. Children want to get to Radio City Music Hall, grownups want to get to an X-rated movie, and 1 per cent of the population wants to get to a Broadway show. Door-to-door salesmen want to get a free trip to Puerto Rico for writing a million dollars in sales.

McDonald's wants to get into the Village. Men in last year's bow ties want to get back into the swim. Executive assistants want to get into a corner office. Over at ABC, they want to get into the running.

Shoppers want to get into an air-conditioned cab. Seducers, male and female, want to get into something a little more comfortable. On weekdays, people with a cause want to get into City Hall Park, but on Sundays they want to get into Central Park.

People on the A train want to get to Harlem.

Messengers want to get to the seventeenth floor. Ex-alcoholics want to get to the church basement. Burglars want to get on the fire escape and pigeon breeders want to get on the roof.

Gotta hustle.

Almost everybody wants to get on television. People on local television want to get on network television. People on network television want to get to Palm Springs or Palm Beach.

Retired people on the upper west side want to sit in the sun on the benches in the middle of Broadway. When they get there, they want to be in Miami.

Men want to get next to women. Women want to get equal with men. Girls want to get in the Little League and boys want to get in the big leagues. Smart children want to get into the High School of Music & Art and dumb children want to get out of high school.

People in tenements want to get into high-rises. People in projects want to get back into tenements. Actors in NY want to get to LA. People at the top of the Guggenheim Museum want to get to the bottom. So do ass-pinchers, river-dredgers, and investigative reporters.

Everybody in New York City wants to get somewhere. Every once in a while, somebody gets there.

## AT THE CENTER . . .

Jerry Manelli wanted to get moving, but his mother wouldn't let him out of the house two mornings in a row with no breakfast. "You can take five minutes to eat an egg," she said.

"The way I figure it," Jerry said, "the mob's already *had* an egg by this time."

"So they'll have indigestion and you won't."

"Okay, okay," Jerry said, and used the time to call around and make sure the other guys were on the move. Frank was waiting for Floyd, who had just left the house. When Jerry called Mel, a burry female voice said, *"Bern*-stein res-dince."

"Hey," Jerry said. "What the hell *you* doing out?"

"I'm on parole," Mandy told him. "I gave my word I wouldn't run away. You want anybody? These pancakes are burning here."

"Where's Mel?"

"Up with Miz Bernstein, getting dressed."

"Don't let him hang around all day."

"What about *me?*" Mandy wanted to know. "I don't wanna hang around all day neither."

"We'll figure something out this afternoon," Jerry told her. "When this other stuff is done."

"Huh," said Mandy, expressing the deepest doubt, and broke the connection.

Jerry stepped out to the backyard, where his father was shooting at a stamp-collecting album with his new BB gun.

The old man was skinny, and he didn't like to wear his teeth. "How's it going?" Jerry said.

"I think the barrel's bent."

Scrambled eggs were ready, with spaghetti sauce on top, and Jerry sat down to shovel them in. His mother, watching, said, "Take it easy, take it easy."

"Some other time, Mom. I gotta hustle."

"That's all you care about, hustle, hustle, hustle."

Jerry gulped down coffee. "So? What else is there?"

"I guess you'll find out now, won't you?"

Jerry wiped his mouth on the paper napkin and got to his feet. "Meaning what?"

"You'll find this golden statue, won't you? Your share's a quarter of a million dollars, isn't it?"

"So?"

"So then you'll have it," his mother said. "Everything you've hustled for. And what then?"

"Are you kidding?" He stared at her. "Mom, I could blow that in a month. You kidding? Two hundred fifty grand? Blow it in a month. I wouldn't even have to leave New York."

She frowned at him. "Then what's the point?"

"The point? Hustling's the point. See you later, Mom," he said, and got moving out of there.


# ON THE SOFA . . .

Bobbi and Madge had breakfast together companionably in Madge's living room, sunlight filtered dappling through the spider plants and avocados. Bobbi was on the sofa, with her breakfast spread before her on the coffee table, while Madge had the chair over by the television set, with her plate on a hassock. "Mmm," Bobbi said. She ate scrambled egg. She chewed some bacon. She swallowed coffee and munched toast and went back for more scrambled egg. Madge, watching her with interested doubt, said, "How can you *eat* all that? Why don't you have a *hangover*?"

"Because today," Bobbi said, "I am a new woman. A totally new woman." She drank more coffee, bit off another chunk of toast, and suddenly grinned. She giggled, with her mouth closed.

Madge made a quizzical grin. "What's so funny?"

Bobbi chewed, chewed, chewed, swallowed, washed it all down with coffee, and laughed aloud. "I threw all Chuck's clothes out the window!"

"So you told me last night. Several times."

Suddenly serious, intense, Bobbi stared across the room at her friend. "I left him, Madge, I left him for good!"

"You mentioned that, too."

Bobbi frowned. "You think he'll be all right? What if he's stuck in there forever, without any clothes?"

"He's fine," Madge said. "I phoned there this morning, and there wasn't any answer, so he's up and out. *With* his clothes on."

"And looking for me."

"Wouldn't doubt it for a second."

"Mm." Absent-mindedly chewing, Bobbi looked around the room, organizing her thoughts, and then spied the Dancing Aztec Priest, the Other Oscar, standing on the windowsill amid Madge's jungle, and she smiled. The Other Oscar; he had made it all possible, he had made it happen. He danced in there among the greenery, his golden skin glistening with sunlight, his green eyes vivid with intelligence, his very posture a command to *do* and *be* and *move* and *become*.

"What are you smiling at?"

"My future," Bobbi said.

"You know what you're going to do?"

"Absolutely. I'm going to California."

"So you really are, huh? No morning-after second thoughts?"

"This isn't the morning after," Bobbie told her. "This is the morning before. The morning before my life *begins*."

Madge grimaced. "Send that to the *Reader's Digest*," she said.

"I'm really going to do it, Madge."

"Well, bully for you. Got your schedule worked out?"

"As soon as I get dressed I'll go see Everett Coalshack at the orchestra. He can give me references and letters of introduction to people on the West Coast. And then I'll pick up my harp and I'm off. Today." Suddenly both ravenous and impatient, she stuffed her mouth with food and asked Madge if she had the Yellow Pages.

Madge said, "What?"

"Fumfumfumf," Bobbi said again, then chewed quickly, slugged down some coffee to clear the way, and said, "Do you have a Yellow Pages?"

"Sure." Getting it from the shelf under the TV, bringing it across the room, Madge said, "What's the idea?"

"I have practically no money," Bobbie explained. "I'll go to the bank this morning and take out a couple hundred, but there isn't much more than that *in* there, and I'm not going to Chuck for *anything.* Not that he has anything."

"If you find money in the Yellow Pages," Madge said, "show me the listing."

"Not money," Bobbi told her. "A way to California."

"Fascinating." Madge sat on the sofa next to Bobbi to see how it was done.

Very simply. Bobbi turned to the Automobile listings and under the heading Automobile Transporters & Drive-Away Companies there were about twenty-five companies offering to ship your car to or from anywhere. "Right," Bobbi said, and reached for the phone.

Madge said, "Ship a car? You don't *have* a car."

Bobbi said, "Where do you think they get their drivers?" And she made her first call, saying to the person who answered, "Hello. I'd like to drive a car to California."

As it turned out, there were only two problems. In the first place, she wanted a car to drive *today,* and that was a bit too precipitous for most companies, though they could provide her with a car next Monday or Tuesday. And, in the second place, she didn't call the companies in alphabetical order but by some intuitive sequence of her own, so that it wasn't until the eighth call that she reached Beacon Auto Transport, where a harried-sounding young woman said, "Girlie, you're on. We had a guy didn't show up this morning. If you've got the seventy-five-dollar damage deposit and valid references we can check on the phone and you can be out of town this afternoon."

"I'll be there in two hours," Bobbi said.


# IN THE EXECUTIVE SUITE . . .

August Corella and Victor Krassmeier sat moodily together in Victor Krassmeier's private office, waiting for the arrival of Bud Beemiss. Corella hadn't liked coming back to Vic this way, and he *certainly* hadn't liked calling in Bud Beemiss, but what choice did he have?

The truth is, August Corella was not a member of the Mafia. He had a few nice hustles going, that's all, principally a sweetheart union in the bakery business, and it helped most of the time to give the impression he was a card-carrying mobster, but in fact he was not now nor had he ever been a member of the mob. Any mob.

And because of that, because he was not a bona fide mobster, there'd been nothing he could do about it when both Earl and Ralph refused to come to work today. Ralph claimed he had the flu this morning, and coughed a few times unconvincingly into the telephone. Earl, more straightforward, said he had two black eyes and a very prominent cut on the tip of his nose and he was not, repeat *not*, leaving his apartment until everything, repeat *everything*, had healed up. And maybe not then.

A mafioso, of course, wouldn't put up with such shit. A mafioso would smile and say, "Nobody quits, Earl. *You* know that." But if Corella tried such a threat, Earl would hang up and go to work for some other union thug.

So Corella, alone, had driven his Cadillac across the river this morning, and he had called Vic, and he had called Bud Beemiss, the PR man whose house in Connecticut had been the scene of last night's foolishness, and he had set up this appointment because what August Corella needed now was a new gang and a new plan.

And to keep that goddam statue out of the hands of those goddam Inter-Air Forwarding punks.

Vic Krassmeier broke the brooding silence at last, saying, "Whatever happened to the fellow who caused all this trouble? The one who didn't know the alphabet."

"Oh. He's out of it. Earl punished him a little and put him on a plane home to Ecuador."

"May it have crashed," Krassmeier said devoutly, and his intercom buzzed. "Yes?"

"Mr. Beemiss is here," said the metallic female voice. "Send him in."

When Beemiss came in a minute later, bouncing and smiling in his suede jacket, he looked like a man who was pretty damn pleased with himself. If only it were possible to have Earl punish this one and put him on a plane somewhere. Antarctica maybe.

"Ah, good morning," Beemiss said, approaching Corella, a mocking smile on his lips. "Mister Kane, isn't it?"

"Corella."

"Corella? Much more realistic." And Beemiss insisted on shaking hands.

Corella introduced him next to Krassmeier, who sat behind his desk and refused to stand, to shake hands, to smile, to speak or to do anything other than grunt. Beemiss seemed amused by that, and when he sat down he turned his amused expression back to Corella, saying, "I must admit that bit of vaudeville last night made me curious."

It was time for the truth. Corella said, "One of the statues you people got is the original. We smuggled it in from South America."

"Ah," said Beemiss. "I was wondering if that might be it."

"There was a screw-up," Corella told him, "and you got the wrong box. Before we could straighten it out, this other bunch found out about it. That was one of them got your statue last night."

"Which I assume was the wrong one."

"Right."

"I also assume you have a buyer for the right one."

"Sure," said Corella.

Beemiss waited, amiably curious, and then said, "Who?"

Corella looked over at Krassmeier, who brooded briefly and then shrugged. Apparently, he believed all hope was lost, anyway. So Corella told Beemiss, "The Museum of the Arts of the Americas."

"Ah." Beemiss turned his smile on Krassmeier. "You're a trustee there, aren't you?"

Grumbling, Krassmeier said, "Yes."

"You negotiated for the museum?"

"Yes."

"And how high did you permit yourself to be pushed?"

Once again Krassmeier and Corella exchanged glances, and this time it was Corella who shrugged. Krassmeier said, "Slightly more than a million."

"Slightly? Is there a number figure for that slightly?"

"Two hundred forty thousand."

"That's some slightly," Beemiss said.

Corella said, "There've been a lot of expenses. At the South American end, for instance."

Beemiss chuckled. "Yes, I can imagine the South American end could be terribly expensive."

Krassmeier, leaning forward over his desk, said, "The point is, we'd like you to assist us."

"Yes, I see you would," Beemiss said. "If these other people don't already have the statue."

"We can only hope they don't."

"I'll do that," Beemiss assured him. "And if they don't have it, you want me to get it and sell it to you."

"*Sell* it to us?" Krassmeier sounded truly shocked.

Beemiss did his annoying chuckle again. "You aren't asking me to *give* it away."

"We'll share in the profits," Krassmeier said.

"I'm always happier with a dollar figure," Beemiss told him. "I tell you what, I'll take that slightly."

"You'll do what?"

"I'll take the two hundred forty thousand."

"Two hundred forty thousand *dollars?*"

"Leaving you a million between you," Beemiss pointed out.

"There isn't that much left," Krassmeier protested.

Beemiss shrugged, smiled, and said nothing.

Krassmeier said, "You may have the best access to the statue, but *we* are the only access to a market."

"I don't necessarily have to play at all," Beemiss said.

Corella had been watching in silence, but he could see now that Krassmeier wasn't going to get anywhere. Some negotiator. Quietly, Corella said, "All right."

Beemiss nodded. "Thank you."

Krassmeier stared at Corella. "All right? But you know yourself there isn't that much left. The expenses—"

Corella gave Krassmeier his blandest look. "We can make adjustments, Vic," he said.

It was fascinating to watch the expressions move across Krassmeier's face, as he gradually realized how totally Corella had been making a fool of him. Heavy expenses, Krassmeier's share constantly shrinking— It was a pity to have to discard that whole con, but Corella was a realist, and the time had come to slice the pie a different way.

Krassmeier's face was moving toward purple, and he might actually have started yelling accusations even with Bud Beemiss in the room, but Beemiss himself broke the spell, saying, "That's fine, then. We'll want to put something on paper right now, vague about the job to be done but specific about the emolument. Then I'll start phoning my fellow committeemen, rounding up the statues. May I use a phone here?"

Krassmeier wasn't yet capable of ordinary speech, so Corella answered for him: "Sure," he said. "Vic won't mind."

Krassmeier growled.

# WAY DOWN SOUTH . . .

Since the nation of Descalzo is draped like a saddle over the spine of the Andes, it is generally very difficult to travel between Quetchyl, near the eastern border of the nation, and Santa Rosita Rosaria (commonly known as Rosie), far in the west. To facilitate this trip for government functionaries and the better class of businessman, an ancient DC-3 travels regularly from Quetchyl to Rosie on Mondays, Wednesdays, and Fridays, and from Rosie to Quetchyl on Tuesdays, Thursdays, and Saturdays. (On Sundays, while the pilot offers *very* sincere prayers at Mass, the two mechanics work feverishly from dawn to dusk to make the plane at least possible for one more week.)

Today, a Wednesday, the plane is to leave Quetchyl for Rosie at ten A.M., and among its passengers are Pedro Ninni, José Caracha, and Edwardo Brazzo, the tickets having been bought by Brazzo with most of his savings. Pedro, like the others, is in civilian clothing today, but his official museum guard pistol is concealed in the depths of the brown paper bag containing his goat-thigh sandwich and his bottle of gluppe. (This is one adventure, regardless of what José and Edwardo think, that Pedro will *not* go through sober.)

Pedro had known from the beginning, of course, that he would be the one to draw the short straw. The short end of the stick was his by right, by birth and by fate. What he didn't know for sure was whether or not he would actually go ahead and hijack this airplane. A great big airplane full of people; it didn't even *sound* right. Maybe he'd just take the ride to Rosie and then kill himself. Or, permit Edwardo and José to kill him. Or, perhaps he would flee the country on foot, although Peru and Bolivia both had an inclination to return Descalzan nationals wanted by the authorities back home. (Governments prefer to stay on good relations with neighboring governments.)

Could a man *walk* to New York? It sounded no more difficult than stealing a plane to New York.

How many armed guards there are at Quetchyl International Airport! Brown-uniformed men with automatic machine pistols, blue-uniformed men with rifles, gray-uniformed men with holstered revolvers. And every last one of them gives Pedro a suspicious glare.

Edward and José are sticking very close to Pedro, giving him no opportunity either to run away or to gulp down a lot of gluppe. While waiting for the announcement to board their plane, the three of them sit close together in the muggy airless waiting room along with the other eleven passengers for this flight, who are five government officials, two priests, an American doctor on a malnutrition survey for the United Nations, his Canadian assistant-mistress, a lima bean merchant, and a French journalist looking for examples of undemocratic behavior. These fourteen people sit crammed together in the small room surrounded by armed guards, and when ten o'clock becomes ten-thirty, becomes ten forty-five, Pedro begins tentatively to allow himself hope. Perhaps the flight won't take off. Perhaps the plane has died. Perhaps someone hijacked it yesterday, on its way here from Rosie. Perhaps the pilot has come to his senses. Perhaps—

*"All aboard for Descalzo International World Airways Flight six-seventeen, Quetchyl to Santa Rosita Rosaria, boarding at gate twenty-seven. All aboard, please. Final call."*

Final call? It's the *first* call. But that isn't the point; the point is that the blessed airplane apparently is going to take off after all. Cursing his fate and clutching his paper bag full of gun, goat, and gluppe, Pedro reluctantly passes with the others through the airport's only gate and crosses the tarmac to the plane, which sags in the hot humid sunlight like a molting member of an endangered species. Painted in the national colors of crimson and orange, but in a random pattern similar to World War II camouflage stripes, the plane looks as though it is suffering from a rare but horrible dermatological disease.

Pedro stumbles on the steps. As he is suddenly realizing, not only is this the first time he has ever hijacked a plane, it is also the first time he has ever *flown* in a plane. Is this monstrosity actually going to leave the ground? "Santa Maria," whispers Pedro. "Santa Teresa, Santa Clara—"

"No, señor," says the stewardess. "Santa Rosita Rosaria." A yamfed Descalzan beauty, well over four feet tall and with her ample form squeezed into a mini-skirted uniform of orange with crimson polka dots, this stewardess is named Lupe Naz and she is a four-year veteran of these flights. One look tells her that Pedro is going to be one of those problem passengers. He'll be terrified on takeoff, he'll probably throw up, and there's undoubtedly something alcoholic in that disgusting paper bag. Giving him a professionally sympathetic smile, she adds, "Enjoy your flight, señor."

Pedro groans, and boards the plane.

Since this plane doesn't make international flights, it need not conform to any rules or laws other than those of the Descalzan government that owns it. It is, therefore, the only DC-3 in the world with seats five across. Edging sideways along the aisle after José and with Edwardo herding him from the back, Pedro despairingly permits himself to be placed in a middle seat on the three-seat side, with José by the window to his right and Edwardo by the aisle to his left.

An engine starts! "Ai!" cries Pedro, and stares out the mingy little window as the filthy machine out there pops and whines and roars and chokes and smokes and whizzes and rattles and finally settles down to a sound midway between a tractor and an avalanche.

And the *other* one starts up! Pedro stares in horror past Edwardo's grim visage, and sees the wing on the far side of the plane shaking like a palm frond. "The plane is dying," Pedro mumbles to himself, and then louder, "The plane is dying!" And then, yet louder, *"The plane is blowing up!"*

Since the passengers are well scattered amid all the narrow empty seats, only a few of them hear Pedro's cry above the tubercular spasms of the engines, and of these few the priests merely cross themselves and the French journalist merely smiles patronizingly, while one of the five government officials, the Assistant Deputy to the Associate Director of the Ministry of Involuntary Farm Labor, leaps to his feet in panic and runs off the airplane and straight home, an act he will regret bitterly later on, when he learns what a treat he has missed.

One other pair of ears has also picked up Pedro's squeal; those of stewardess Lupe Naz, who has been dawdling in Pedro's general neighborhood in full expectation that he would be causing trouble soon. She rushes forward, her orange-with-crimson-polka-dot mini-skirt riding high over her generous buttocks encased in purple panty-hose, and speaking *very* firmly, she says, "You will sit down at once! This airplane is not going to blow up. This airplane has *never* blown up!"

Pedro stares at her, his panic abating only slightly. Then he squints, rearing his head back; he has trouble looking at her, the crimson polka dots seeming to swim and fuzz on the orange background. "What?" he says.

"Sit down," Lupe tells him, "or I will be forced to call the guards."

Edwardo and José each grab an elbow, and Pedro finds himself seated. "Ung," he says.

"And stay there," Lupe tells him. Smiling at Edwardo, who is nearest her, she says, "This must be your friend's first flight."

"Friend?" says Edwardo, with a big innocent smile on his face. "We're not together. We're all strangers to one another."

Lupe looks at the three of them crowded together in this one row, then glances around at all the acres of empty seats. "Ah," She says, and walks away, and looks back to see the strangers whispering furiously among themselves.

Pedro is whispering, "She's a crazy woman! This plane has never blown up? What does *that* mean? Things can only blow up once!"

Edwardo, throughout all this, is whispering, "Shut up! Shut up! Shut up!"

And José, simultaneously, is whispering, "She'll suspect we're together! We have to split up!"

But then the plane jolts, and they are all stunned into silence. (This is also José's first flight, and Edwardo's third.) They look out the windows, and the airport is moving! "Aiiiiii!" moans Pedro.

"Calm *down!*" cries Edwardo, pounding the seat arm with his fist.

The airport is moving faster, rushing backward toward safety. A terrible jouncing has overtaken Pedro's seat. His ears are full of sea water. A crimson haze full of orange polka dots pulsates before his eyes. *"Nnnnnnnnnnnnnnnnnnn!"* cries Pedro, and as the DC-3 struggles upward off the patched and bumpy runway Pedro lunges his head forward and throws up into his paper bag, all over his gluppe, and his goat, and his gun.


# ON THE WEST SIDE . . .

Jerry was looking for a parking space on West End Avenue when he saw two faces he knew: Oscar Russell Green and Professor Charles S. Harwood, both squinting in the morning sunlight as they walked north toward 72nd Street. Green was talking, steadily and emphatically, with many hand gestures, and the professor was nodding in a professorial way, the while puffing on a black or dark-brown pipe. The professor was dressed now, in rather rumpled and dirty shirt and slacks, and on closer examination his shoes didn't match.

The hell with a parking space. Jerry pulled in at the nearest hydrant, took his parking sign out of the glove compartment —a hastily scrawled *Broke Down Gone For Help* on the back of an envelope—left it prominently atop the dashboard, and went off on the trail of Green and Harwood.

Who were just reaching 72nd Street and turning east, Green still expostulating and Harwood still ruminating. Jerry, wishing he could get close enough to hear what these two had to discuss, followed them half a block along 72nd Street, until they entered a small restaurant of the sort that features bare wooden tables, many hanging plants, and jumboburgers on rye bread. They'd be sharing breakfast, apparently, meaning the professor's wife hadn't yet come home.

Briefly, Jerry considered following them into the restaurant and having a meal at the next table, but both of those fellows had seen his face last night. Also, this would be a fine time to look over Harwood's apartment again, in search of clues to the whereabouts of the little woman.

So off he went, back to West End Avenue—a cop lacking *any* milk of human kindness was writing a ticket on the station wagon—and this time there was no trouble at all entering the building, since a sullen skinny black man in green work clothes had the door propped open and was sloshing the vestibule with soapy water. He gave a dirty look when Jerry walked on his wet floor, but Jerry gave him a dirty look back, took the elevator upstairs, and credit-carded himself into the Harwood apartment.

Very little had changed in here, except there was no longer anybody living in the closet. Also, a small mound of filthy wrinkled clothing lay on the bed; a scant percentage of last night's clothing rainfall.

A quick look through the apartment convinced Jerry that the only place that might at all be useful was the rolltop desk in the living room, messily crammed with papers. On close examination most of these turned out to be bills, but among the Second Notices and Third Notices (and a few Final Notices) were some letters, old grocery lists, notes about meetings ("Madge, Russian Tea Room, 1:30"), and an address book. This last was a little *too* helpful; it appeared to contain everybody in the Western Hemisphere. That there were as many as four addresses beneath some names, three of them crossed out, showed this to be an old address book only

172

sporadically updated. Certainly many of the people in here hadn't seen or heard from the Harwoods in years.

Okay. Back to the reminder-type notes. Jerry went quickly through these again, keeping track of the frequency with which people's names appeared, and at the finish there were three names that recurred the most in the neat small handwriting he'd decided belonged to Bobbi Harwood. (The other handwriting, large and messy and hard to read, seemed suitable to the professor.) These three were Madge, Bill, and Eleanor. The address book produced one each of Madge and Eleanor (Madge Krausse, 18 Waverly Place, and Eleanor Bonheur, 298 East 81st Street), but seven Bills.

Oh, well. A cute telephone stood on the rolltop desk, a modern re-creation of the tall phone reporters used to use in thirites movies, and Jerry now drew this close and began calling Bills.

1) "Hello?"
   "Hello. Is Bobbi there?"
   "Who?"
   "'Bobbi.'"
   "Bobby who? Do you have the right number?"
   "No."

2) "Hello?"
   "Hello. Is Bobbi there?"
   "Hold on."
   (Pause)
   "Huw-wo?"

3) "Hello?"
   "Hello. Is Bobbi there?"
   "*My* name is Billy."
   "Hi ya, Billy. Is Bobbi there?"
   "Well, there *was* somebody here named Brucey, but he went home. Could a Billy help?"
   "No."

4) Eleven rings. No answer.

5) "Hello?"
   "Hello. Is Bobbi there?"
   "Not right now. Do you want his L.A. number?"
   "No."

6) "Hello?"

"Hello. Is Bobbi there?"

"Knock-knock."

"What?"

"Come on, come on. Knock-knock."

"Okay. Who's there?"

"Bobby."

"Bobby who?"

"Bobby pin! Hyar hyar hyar hyar hyar hyar hyar!"

"Terrific. How about Bobbi Harwood?"

"I don't get it."

7) "Hello?"

"Hello. Is Bobbi there?"

"Listen. Do you mind if I tell you something?"

"What?"

"Nobody calls me any more. Listen, I know why, I
don't blame anybody, there's nobody to blame but
myself. I come on too strong, that's the problem, I
scare people away. But it's just I'm so lonely, so
damnably *lonely*, this feeling of depression, this
grayness, this— I haven't shaved in three days, do
you know that? I'm afraid to go near the razor. And
the window. I was just walking toward the window
when the phone rang. Nobody wants me, that's what
I thought, nobody cares, nobody will even know
I'm gone. But then the phone rang, and I thought,
*maybe.* Maybe somebody *does* care, maybe, maybe
it matters, after all; maybe there's one small spark
of hope left!"

"Sorry. Wrong number."

So much for the Bills, except number four, who could be
tried again later. And that left Madge and Eleanor, and for
no particular reason Jerry called Madge first.

"Hello?"

"Hello, Madge?"

"Yes?"

"Is Bobbi there?"

"No, she left. Chuck?"

"Yeah. Where'd she go?"

"I think you might catch her at the orchestra office. And
Chuck?"

"Uh-huh?"

"I think she really means it, you know. If you want her back, you'll have to work at it."

"Oh, I want her all right," Jerry said.

# ON CLOUD NINE . . .

"Good luck, darling."

*"You're* my good luck, sweetheart."

"And hurry home, darling," Angela said.

"Oh, I will," Mel promised, and they kissed once more, long and lingering, before he at last left the house and trotted out to his battered station wagon, its sides still streaked with bark from the trees of Connecticut.

What a wonderful new world this was! The sun was shining, the air was clean and clear, and Mel's heart was overflowing with the tenderness of love. What had happened in the past, with Angela and—that fellow—had turned out to be for the best after all. For the best. They'd seen that, he and Angela; they'd both finally seen it last night, during the long hours of talk with Mandy at the kitchen table. And later last night, in the wonderful warmth of their bed together, they had exchanged new vows, sincere heartfelt vows, and this morning there was a kind of soft glow surrounding the both of them, like overripe cheese. Their marriage, on the very brink of disaster, had been saved.

Luck was with him now, Mel was sure of it. *He* would find that golden statue today, because this was Mel Bernstein's day. Hear that, world? Today is *Mel Bernstein Day!*

Meaning that the golden statue presently had to be in the possession of either Ben Cohen or Mrs. Dorothy Moorwood, the two Open Sports Committee members left for Mel to check out. Had to be, had to be. One of those two had the statue, and Mel would find it, because *this* was his day.

"For Angela," he whispered, and started the engine, and drove away from there, heading first toward the nearest of the two:

> *Ben Cohen*
> *27-15 Robert Moses Drive*
> *Glen Cove, Long Island*

# ON THE SOUND . . .

If you're a Jewish retail merchant in Harlem, your smart move is to take an interest in the community, which was why Ben Cohen, whose liquor store was on Lenox Avenue not far north of 125th Street, devoted so much of his time and effort and money to causes like the Open Sports Committee. But on his own time Ben Cohen was a member of an entirely different community; he was a boat person on Long Island Sound.

New York City is amid more water than any other major city in the world, and pays it less attention. Paris has some little brook called the Seine, and they run another bridge over it every fifteen feet. The way London carries on about the Thames you'd think it was a big deal, including lining it with all their classiest buildings, such as Parliament. San Francisco, the wind-up toy of cities, *never* gets over its Bay, and Venice is so much in love with *its* Bay that it's sinking into it.

New York is full of water, and neither looks it nor acts it. Of the five boroughs of the city, only one—the Bronx—is on the mainland of the United States, and yet you can spend months in New York without seeing any water except what comes out of the faucet. Manhattan Island alone is surrounded by three rivers (the Hudson, the Harlem, and the East), one creek (Spuyten Duyvil), and a kill (Bronx). The island is fourteen miles long and less than two miles wide, and of the six ways off the southern half four are tunnels. People who travel to and from Manhattan Island every working day of their lives never see a shoreline until they go to the beach for summer vacation.

For those people called by water, therefore, the only thing to do is leave town, and for most of those people the place to go is Long Island, which for much of its hundred-mile length is flanked by two protected bodies of water, Long Island Sound to the north and the Great South Bay to the south. In the summertime the boat people are as numerous off the two coasts of Long Island as pigeons in the park. And one of them, every chance he gets, is Ben Cohen.

Today was one of his chances. He'd have to go to the

store this evening, but most of the daylight hours he could have to himself, so here he was alone on the Sound, getting the *Bobbing Cork II* ready for summer.

Hell of a boat, the *Bobbing Cork II*, a gleaming white Chriscraft with the wheel on an upper deck over a compartment that could sleep four. His twin seventy-horsepower black Mercury engines gleamed at the stern, where two white and pale-green director's chairs stood on the pale-green indoor-outdoor carpeting. The white plastic bucket filled with water (for people with sandy bare feet) stood next to the white rubber welcome mat with *Bobbing Cork II* inscribed on it in pale-green italics. The hibachi, spotlessly clean, stood on its own low white Formica shelf in a corner.

Inside, pale-green and white continued to dominate, on the vinyl cushions of the two settees (the trundle beds slid out from underneath) and on the Formica-topped table and the Formica-faced cabinets and shelves. The curtains, white with green dots, were plastic, and so was the white cabinet of the television set. The interior of the head was white plastic with green toilet paper.

But up top, up by the wheel, *that* was Ben Cohen's territory. Captain of his ship, with his Budweiser hat at a jaunty tilt, under a canvas top and flanked by a pair of long fish teasers looking like a set of whip antennae, when Ben Cohen was at the wheel of the *Bobbing Cork II* Ben Cohen was at *home*.

This space was to Cohen what a den is to many men. Pictures of the family and the store, in weatherproof frames, were mounted all about the dashboard, along with other memorabilia, including most recently the Other Oscar, which he had taped to the top of the dash between the statue of the pregnant mermaid and the statue of the monkey sitting on the book marked "Darwin" and studying a human skull. And the white director's chair at the wheel had written on it, in pale-green script, *Cap' Cohen*.

Cohen was up here now, polishing the brightwork with a diaper (to own a boat is never to lack for something that needs to be cleaned or painted), when a voice on the dock suddenly called out, "Hello?"

Which is no way, Cohen knew, to talk to a boat. The proper hail is, "Ahoy, there!" Knowing, then, that this was a landlubber. Cohen went ahead and gave the proper response anyway: "Ahoy yourself!"

"Is Mister Ben Cohen here?"

Ashore, Ben Cohen was *Mister*, but afloat the term *Mister*

177

meant a mate or other junior officer, and afloat Ben Cohen was *Captain,* but what did a landlubber know? "Right here," Cohen said, and came down the ladder to see an ingratiating smile on the face of an under-forty man in a rumpled light-tone jacket and tie. He was standing on the dock in the sunlight, leaning slightly in Cohen's direction. There was nothing of the boat person about this fellow, and Cohen did not warm to him. "What can I do for you?" he said.

"I stopped by your house," the stranger said, "and your wife told me I might find you here."

"Oh, she did, did she?"

"My name's, uh, Mel George, and I'm—Uh. Could I come in for a minute?"

"In? You mean aboard?"

The stranger gave an affable laugh. "I guess that's what I mean. I don't know that much about boats."

"I can see you don't," Cohen said. "Come aboard, if you want."

"Thank you." Mel George stepped carefully over the side and directly into the bucket of water. "Ak!" he said.

Cohen shook his head. "Mostly people don't do that unless they're barefoot," he said.

"*Goddam* it!" said Mel George, and in pulling his shoe-clad foot out of the bucket he tipped it over, sloshing water all over the carpet.

"Take it easy!" Cohen said.

"I'm really very sorry," Mel George said. He had his wet foot up in the air, like a dog taking a leak, and was shaking it. Then the boat moved slightly, and Mel George lurched and kicked the hibachi off its stand.

"Take it *easy!*"

"Sorry. Sorry." Mel George leaned over, bumping into a director's chair, and picked up the hibachi. The director's chair bumped into the other director's chair, and they *both* fell over.

"Holy *shit!*" said Cohen.

A fairly large boat had just gone by, and that little movement of the boat a few seconds earlier had been the first wavelet of that passing boat's wake. Now a larger roll of wake tipped the *Bobbing Cork II* left, then right, and Mel George dropped the hibachi into the Sound. "Oh, my gosh!" said Mel George.

"What in hell are you *doing?*" cried Cohen.

Mel George clutched at various parts of the boat, getting oily fingerprints all over the brightwork. The wake passed be-

178

neath the boat in several successive rolls, and Mel George stood there wide-eyed, holding on like a sleep walker waking to find himself on a building ledge. Cohen took the opportunity to right the director's chairs and place one of them handy to Mel George, "Sit *down*, goddam it."

Mel George sat down. "I'm terribly sorry about that, uh, thing," he said. "I'll pay for it, of course."

"You'll tell me your business with me," Cohen told him, "and then you'll go away and leave me to clean things up around here."

"Yes, of course. I really am sorry, it was a very unfortunate way to begin, particularly because, well, in fact, I'm from UJA."

"I gave at the office," Cohen said. Which wasn't the truth. But he had decided some time ago that he couldn't give financial support both to black causes *and* Jewish causes, and his choice for various reasons had been to stick with the black causes and let the Jewish causes struggle along without him. Including the United Jewish Appeal.

Mel George, unfortunately, was not to be so easily dissauded. "This isn't precisely a contribution I'm asking for," he said.

"I don't have any spare time," said the master of the *Bobbing Cork II*.

"Oh, we know you're a busy man," Mel George said. "We wouldn't want to take up any of your time."

"Not money and not time? What is it, then?"

"Well as you know," Mel George said, "the project of planting trees in Israel has been wonderfully successful for many years." And he went on from there to a long rambling account of most of the Jewish philanthropies of the twentieth century, whether connected with Israel or not. B'nai B'rith was mentioned, rather confusingly, and the kibbutzim, and the annual Chanukah Festival in Madison Square Garden. All of the words formed rational sentences, and all of the subjects were familiar to Cohen, and yet he had the feeling nothing was making any sense. What, after all, was this fellow talking *about*? He tried to find out a few times, asking direct questions, but the answer tended to be even foggier than the phrase that had prompted the question, so after a while Cohen just sat back in the other director's chair and waited for this squall to wear itself out.

Then Mel George coughed and said, "I'm sorry, I'm a little hoarse."

"I shouldn't wonder," said Cohen.

"Could I have—would you have some water?"

"Water? Of course." Rising, Cohen said, "Would you prefer seltzer?"

"No, thank you, just plain water would be fine."

"Ice cubes?"

"Why, yes, thank you. Thank you very much."

So Cohen went inside to the galley and got a glass of water with ice cubes, and when he came outside Mel George was gone.

No, he wasn't. There he was up by the wheel, smiling around in that infuriating ingratiating way of his. God alone knew what damage he could cause up there. "George!" cried Cohen. "Come down from there!" And then, in somewhat less harsh tones, "I have your water."

"Thank you, thank you!" Coming down the ladder, he smiled and said, "I was just enjoying the view from up there. Beautiful, beautiful. You have a beautiful boat, Mr. Cohen."

*It was until you got here.* But Cohen didn't say that aloud. Instead, he said, "Here's your water."

Mel George thanked him again, drank the water, and then said, "Well, I don't want to keep you. But you will bear us in mind for when we call again, won't you?"

"Bear you in mind for *what?*"

But Mel George was returning the glass, smiling, saying a lot of fuzzy things, and preparing to leave the boat. Off he went, his left arm held oddly down at his side as though he'd hurt himself on the ladder—wouldn't that be nice—and while Cohen watched in bewilderment the man stepped ashore, waved his nonstiff hand, and turned to walk back down the long wooden dock to the land.

Had the fool hurt himself by breaking something up by the wheel? Cohen hurried up the ladder and saw at once what was missing; the Other Oscar. The bastard had stolen it! The stiff left arm, concealing the statue beneath his coat!

Turning from the wheel, Cohen saw Mel George still walking away along the dock. And then, providentially, a young man appeared on the shore, coming this way. Grabbing up his pale-green megaphone, Cohen yelled at him, "STOP, THIEF! STOP HIM!"

The young man, a tall and skinny fellow in pullover shirt and gray slacks, apparently understood at once, because he suddenly ran forward to block the end of the dock. Mel George, seeing him there, stopped and pointed at him and seemed to be saying something. Some lie, no doubt.

Cohen hurried down the ladder, off the boat, and along the

180

dock, running as fast as his sure-grip sneakers and his middle-aged spread would permit. Mel George, looking over his shoulder, saw him coming and dithered a bit, like a base-runner caught between the second baseman and the short-stop. Then, making the only decision he could, he suddenly jumped forward, trying to run either through or around the younger man.

Who wouldn't permit it. He and Mel George feinted one way, then the other, and as Cohen came panting up the young man punched Mel George in the nose and Mel George sat down hard on the wooden dock. The statue of the Other Oscar dropped out from under his jacket onto his lap.

"Thank you," gasped Cohen. "Thank you." Stooping, he picked up the statue out of the thief's lap and turned to smile pantingly at the young man. Who then punched *Cohen* in the nose, grabbed the statue, and ran away.


# IN THE SOUND . . .

Wally Hintzlebel's day had begun with an argument with his mom. That *never* happened, trouble with his mom, but it did this morning. and it ended with Wally screaming God-knows-what at his mother and running out of the house. (He couldn't remember what he'd screamed at her, and he certainly hoped she couldn't remember either.)

He blamed the bad dreams. He'd slept fitfully, waking up and waking up to hear his heart beating like running foot-steps, then dropping back into dream worlds of chains and monsters, running and running and more running. Great glaring crevices in the vaulting ceiling of the cave, through which sunlight spat, charring everything it touched. Drown-ing in green-gray murky seas, with the slithering tentacles streaming off him. His foot and ankle imprisoned inside a boulder, with the great black night rolling down the mountain-side. Laughter and cawing, and the Dancing Aztec Priest hop-ping on one leg, mocking him, flying backward up into the trees with brown fur on the leaves. Then up again gasping into his own bedroom, sweat enameling his body, his mind full of what he hadn't done. The statue, the statue! Did they have it already? Was it too late, was it already too late? Did *they* sleep?

No wonder he'd fought with mom over breakfast, when she'd started in again about those scratches on his face, her terrible teasing about girl friends. He'd screamed, he'd thrown things, he'd run from the house, he'd started running, and he was *still* running.

To the library in Mineola first, driving his car faster than he'd ever done, where forty frantic minutes of research (*urk, urk, urk*) increased his list by four more names and six more addresses. Then out of the library and directly to the nearest known address, one Ben Cohen, 27-15 Robert Moses Drive, Glen Cove.

Where Mrs. Cohen told (a) that her husband was probably on his boat in the marina near Bayville, and (b) that another gentleman had been asking for Ben not half an hour ago.

Drive! Run! Don't let them get ahead! On to the New Wally, on, on, on to the marina, where suddenly someone was shouting through a megaphone, "Stop, thief! Stop him!" And there, coming along the dock, was the husband. The self-same husband. The infuriating bad-penny intrusive pain-in-the-ass *husband*.

Not this time. Running to the land end of the dock, Wally blocked the way, crying, "You stop that! You give me that!"

The husband pointed at him. "Stay out of this," he had the gall to say. "This is none of your affair."

Wally was trembling all over, from rage. "You give me that statue," he said. "It's *mine*."

"You dirty eavesdropping son of a bitch, go mind your own business!"

Some fat man in a Budweiser hat—probably Ben Cohen—was pelting this way along the dock. The husband glanced back at him, ducked this way and that in an effort to get around Wally, and then Wally boiled over, *boiled over,* and punched the bastard in the nose!

The husband sat down. The golden statue appeared in his lap. Wally would have taken it then, but the fat man arrived and picked it up, babbling his thanks until Wally punched *him* in the nose. Wally was transformed into a new continuum of existence, a new way of being. Wally now was a person who would punch *anybody* in the nose.

He had the statue. He'd grabbed it out of the fat man's hand, and now he turned away and *ran,* taking off toward the parking lot where he'd left the car.

But he didn't get there. The damn husband was after him again, and damn if he wasn't a fast runner. He headed Wally off, and Wally had to veer to the right around a big open-

182

fronted structure full of boats on trailers. The heavy crunch of the husband's feet on gravel sounded close behind him, closer and closer, and he veered away again, through a space in a chain link fence and out over a blacktop parking lot—not the one with his car, damn it—and off to the right again when the husband's grasping hand slid off his shoulder.

It was like one of the bad dreams, running and running and getting nowhere, with doom smashing and thundering behind. Out through a gate, across more gravel, around a small white clapboard building, across a wooden pier. Veering again, crying out, gasping for breath, staring desperately at the sky, dashing out along a network of docks with boats moored all around, running across the back of a boat whose startled occupants all looked up gaping from *The Price Is Right*, down along another dock with the pounding feet still close behind, and—

The end of the dock. Far out there the weathered gray boards came to an abrupt end. There were no boats tied up that far out, nothing but Long Island Sound and Connecticut far, far away. "No no no!" screamed Wally, still running. "It's mine! It's mine!" Clutching the golden statue to his chest, he ran full-tilt off the end of the dock and into the Sound. And the pursuing footsteps splashed right after.

# IN THE CITY . . .

Almost nobody lives in New York, and that's especially true of those born there. They live in *neighborhoods,* the way small-town people live in small towns, and they very rarely leave their own districts. The average citizen of Ozone Park, say, in Queens, has probably never in his life been to the Midwood section of Brooklyn, and why should he? It's just another neighborhood, exactly like his own, with churches and stores and movies and schools, and with nothing in particular to attract the interest of outsiders. And though most citizens of both Ozone Park and Midwood are likely to have been to Manhattan—because they work there, or they've had an occasional special night out—they don't really think of Manhattan as being part of *their* hometown. "I'm going to the city," say the people in the outer boroughs.

For Jerry, therefore, although he was a New Yorker born

and bred, and although he considered himself a total New Yorker, and although the pace and flavor of New York were immutably a part of his character, this sudden crash course in Manhattan was a true eye-opener. The only difference between Jerry and the average out-of-towner tourist was that Jerry was already used to the nervous rhythms of the city, the pace, the hustle, movement without stopping. But the look of it, the variety of it, they were things he had never known, or had learned too early and had forgotten.

The main object was still the statue, of course, but Jerry was beginning to enjoy this search for its own sake. Moving around the city, seeing it at different times of day, seeing the people in it, he was feeling that tug of belonging, of connection, that some people get when they stand by the great salt sea. The sea, or the city, it's all the same, it calls to the blood, a restless endless pulse calling home all those who recognize the deep linkages. Jerry recognized them. *This* was the home of the hustle, in more ways than one, and hustle was Jerry's middle name.

Driving down Broadway from the Harwood apartment toward the orchestra office in midtown, Jerry smiled around at the jagged gray verticals of Manhattan. When this was over, maybe he'd come stay in the city for a while. Be a nice place to spend a million dollars.

## UP IN THE AIR . . .

The goat-thigh sandwich was ruined, but the gluppe bottle had been tightly corked and once the outside had been thoroughly rinsed—and aired a while, perhaps—it would be just as drinkable as it had ever been.

The gun, however, was a more complicated proposition, and that was why Edwardo was crammed into the tiny lavatory with Pedro, his nose wrinkled in disgust against the stink. The contents of Pedro's stomach had to be removed from the gun without causing any harm to the gun's mechanism, because it would be perhaps too chancy a matter to hijack an airplane with the aid of a gun that has been rendered inoperable by a combination of vomit and water. Not trusting Pedro to clean the gun as carefully as necessary, Edwardo had swallowed his pride—and his bile—and joined him in the john, in a space so small that some normal lavatory operation were not possible in here for full-grown adults at all. (These Quetchyl-Rosie flights tended to finish with a wholesale dash by the passengers for any available bathroom, hedge, or concealing wall. It is advisable to walk *very* carefully when visiting the airports at either Quetchyl or Rosie.)

"There," Edwardo said at last, patting the gun with a lot of paper towels, an operation that couldn't be done without repeatedly elbowing Pedro in the ear, "I think it's all right now."

"Should we test it?"

Edwardo gazed at Pedro speculatively, almost yearningly, but then he shook his head. "No, Pedro," he said. "We should not test it. What we *should* do is put it to use."

"Use," echoed Pedro. And his face, particularly his eyes, immediately got that thick blunt dead-pig look that overcame his features whenever anything had been said that he didn't want to understand.

"It's time to take over the airplane," Edwardo said, and pressed the gun into Pedro's unwilling palm. "Don't shoot anything unless you intend to," Edwardo suggested.

"Shoot? Why would I intend to shoot?"

"Because you're going to hijack the plane now."

"*Now?* I haven't even had lunch!"

That word "lunch" in this tiny foul-smelling closet almost did Edwardo in completely, but he closed his eyes and his throat and his sphincter, and in a few seconds the spasm passed, and he could open his eyes and say, slowly and softly and with utter conviction, "You are going to hijack this airplane now, Pedro, or I am going to throw you out of it. Personally."

Pedro looked at Edwardo, and he saw eyes glittering with such fury that he could almost have read a comic book by their light. There is a time to be stupid and a time to be smart, and Pedro was smart enough to know the difference. "Yes, Edwardo," he said.

"Yes, Pedro," said Edwardo. "I will leave here first, to allay suspicion. You will count to fifty, and then you will leave there and walk directly to the pilot's cabin and show him your gun and say, 'Take me to New York.'"

"Yes, Edwardo."

"Yes, Pedro."

The process of cleaning the gun had spattered water on Edwardo's clothing, particularly the front of his trousers, so now he pulled off a handful of toilet paper—they'd used up all the paper towels—and tried to pat himself dry. But it couldn't be done in this tight space, so he gave Pedro one last warning glitter and left the lavatory.

Stewardess Lupe Naz, having reason to keep an eye on that vomiting passenger in the first place, had been interested to see him enter the lavatory some time ago with another man. Not at all usual, though honeymooning couples had been known to do such things on these flights, not very successfully. At any rate, here came one of the men—not the up-chucker, the other one—back out of the lavatory, dabbing at wet spots on the front of his trousers with a lot of toilet paper. Lupe wrinkled her nose in disgust, which meant she was already wearing the right expression when he passed her and she caught a whiff of him. Holy Mother! What had they been *doing* in there?

Pedro, alone in the lavatory, was counting fifty swallows of gluppe. His bruised and terrified stomach was reacting like a pit of snakes when a flaming torch is thrown in, but he didn't care. All right, he'd agreed to hijack this terrible airplane, and he *would* hijack this terrible airplane, but there was nothing in the agreement that said he had to be conscious while he was doing it. If you're going to hijack a plane at all, it might just as well be during an alcoholic blackout.

Fohty-eight, fohty-nine, fifty—

Not much left in the bottle. No point carrying the damn thing around, not with, *um-ung, ung, ung, ung, ung, ung*—only six swallows left in it. Pedro belched fire and smoke, wiped his mouth on his sleeve, ignored his raging stomach, left the bottle of gluppe in the toilet, and at last went out of the lavatory. Passing the stewardess without noticing her dirty look—nor her surprised look, nor her revolted look—he made his lurching way down the aisle and tried to climb over Edwardo back to his seat in the middle. And Edwardo kicked him *very* hard in the shin.

"Ow!" said Pedro. "Wha'd you do *that* for?"

It isn't possible for a human being to hiss a sentence with no *ess* sounds in it, But Edwardo did the impossible. *"Get up to the pilot, you idiot!"* he hissed.

"Oh," said Pedro, and then became aware of the gun, which he had tucked into the front of his trousers, under his flapping shirt-tail, which he never tucked into his trousers. "Sorry," Pedro said. "Forgot." And he burped at Edwardo and José—both flinched—and staggered off toward the front of the plane.

Stomach and head were both buzzing now. A field of orange

with crimson polka dots was all around the periphery of his vision; or was that the stewardess? No, it was a field of orange with crimson polka dots all around the periphery of his vision, and steadily closing in, like the shutting of an iris.

He was at a door. Knobs never had been his strong point. He stood there fumbling for a while, until the stewardess officiously arrived, clutching at his elbow and saying, "Sir! Sir!"

"S'okay," Pedro assured her. "I got it." And he did, because at that instant the doorknob turned and he and the stewardess both lurched into the pilot's quarters, the door slamming again behind them.

Edwardo and José, both of whom had been watching proceedings with slitted eyes, now looked at one another. "Well," said José, "it's in the hands of God now."

"If only it were," Edwardo said. "In truth, it's in the hands of Pedro."

In truth, the stewardess was in the hands of Pedro. Given her height and weight and general build, she seemed to consist almost entirely of primary sexual attributes, and try as he might Pedro couldn't seem to get his hands off them. The two of them lurched back and forth off-balance in the tiny pilot's cabin, behind the bewildered pilot and co-pilot, and it was only when Lupe Naz reared back and slapped Pedro's face that he woke up enough to catch his balance and remember what he was here for. And also to realize that his stomach's protests against gluppe and lurching in combination were getting much more imperative.

Meanwhile, everybody else was talking at once. "What's going on here?" the co-pilot was saying, while the pilot was saying, "Get him away from the controls!" and the stewardess was saying, "Rapist! Pervert! Degenerate!"

First things first; the stomach would have to wait. Lugging the gun out from under his shirt, Pedro said, "Take me to New York," and threw up on the pilot.


# UPTOWN . . .

Leroy, he say, "Lu dah."
   Buhbuh, he said, "Wuh?"
   Leroy, he say, "*Dah*."
   It the funeral. Aloysius 'Mole Mouth' Dundershaft, he

187

going to Queens, get *him*self buried next the Long·Island Expressway.

Man, it some funeral. It start with horses, four black horses and four white horses. Only the police, they say the horses, they can't walk cross no Hundred Twenty-Fifth Street blocking traffic all the time, so F. Xavier White, he put them horses up on flatbed trucks. Two trucks, with four black horses on the first truck and four white horses on the second truck. And each one them horses, they got a fella in a black suit and a white shirt and a black tie standing up there with him, by he head. And the cab them trucks, they been spray-painted black just before the funeral, and the drivers them trucks, they in black suits and white shirts and black ties just like the fellas with the horses. And the horses, they lifting their tails and shitting on the trucks.

Then after the horses come flower cars. Four flower cars, all piled up with wreaths and sprays and bunches and horse-shoes a flowers. They white flowers and yellow flowers and red flowers and orange flowers and blue flowers and purple flowers and pink flowers. They carnations and gladioluses and roses and lilies and delphiniums and sweet Williams and irises and peonies and daisies and chrysanthemums and baby's-breath and gillyflowers and phlox. And they a bunch other flowers, too, and green from ferns and rhododendron leaves. And some, they got satin ribbons on them with words on them, like SYMPATHY and GOOD LUCK and TO A PAL. But if you look real close, some others got satin ribbons on them what say like CONGRATULATIONS and MAZEL TOV and BON VOYAGE, which is only right in a certain way of looking at things, and the answer is, F. Xavier, he made a deal with a wholesale florist down on Sixth Avenue below Macy's, what his flower cars would deliver all the wholesale florist's flowers what was going to Queens, if F. Xavier, if he could use them first at the funeral. So Mole Mouth, he got all the flowers in the *world*, and they a lot a weddings in Queens, they gone be *late*.

Then after the flower cars come the hearse, and after the hearse come *another* hearse. Two hearses. Mole Mouth, he getting a send-off to beat *all*.

The first hearse, that a Cadillac Fleetwood hearse, black and shiny as a brand new bowling ball. It have maroon upholstery inside, and it have a lectric slab that swivel out the side door to put the casket on and then swivel back in, so nobody, they got to break their back bending over. And they got on the side windows black lacy curtains like the kind

188

undies for women they sell in the men's magazines what women don't read. And the casket, it so pretty it a *shame* to bury it. Make a nice stereo cabinet. Great wood, resonate like crazy, put the woofers right *in* the son bitch. Dark rich wood, stained the color ox-blood shoe polish. Chrome handles, chrome hinges, shine like fenders. Nice shape, lots a turned wood, plenty beveled edges, look nice in the dining room.

Inside, where nobody can see it, they so much padded pink satin it look like a fat lady at a wedding turned inside out. And Mole Mouth, he in there too, lying on his back, his left hand on the family jewels and his right hand on his left hand. He dressed up something *fierce*, in three-tone platform shoes, and pleated green-and-black check pants and an amber turtle-neck shirt and a two-tone green Edwardian jacket and a green beret. And he got his earring on, and *four* sets a beads, and three rings, and the digital electric watch (it keeping perfect time, right this second), and the chrome ID bracelet (a gift from a lady) what say on it MISTER RIGHT-ON. He look terrific, except around the face a little and except for some seepage down around the base a the spine. Pity nobody thought to take a picture.

Then the second hearse, that another Cadillac Fleetwood hearse, the same as the first one except it got gray upholstery instead a maroon. And the casket in the second hearse, it *almost* as terrific as the casket in the first hearse. In fact, it look like the same casket but it can't be, on account it cost a hundred twenty-seven dollars less. But it sure look pretty. And inside is all Mole Mouth's favorite threads, and all his favorite tapes, and his favorite transistor, and his copy a *Penthouse* what showed up too late for him to read it, and his address book, and his two net bathing suits, and a live dove as a symbol that now there's peace between Mole Mouth and Bad Death Jonesburg. And that dove, he making a *mess*.

And after the two hearses come the band. The *first* band. It up on a flatbed truck, too, like the horses, and it a sextet, everybody dressed up in black and looking real solemn. They a piano player, a fat fella with a big wide mouth and a bowler hat, and a skinny little clarinet player with a black string tie and *long* long fingers with maybe six big bony knuckles on ever blessed finger, and a long-armed bass player with a bushy mustache and a bald spot on top he head, and a chubby little trumpet player with sweat drops all over he forehead and great big pop eyes that roll when he play, and a long sad-looking trombone player with gold-frame glasses falling off the end he nose, and a nervous little drummer shape like a spider

189

sitting up top a whole big set snare drums with a picture a palm tree on the bass.

Now, this band playing, and what they playing, it funeral music. *Jazz* funeral music. Very slow, but syncopated. Lots a looooonnnng loooowwww trombone notes, full a growl. Lots a piano left hand. The clarinet, it tootle. and teetle, but it don't make no fuss about it, and even when the trumpet, it stride, it stride *soft*. Same like the bass, it walk slow and stately, it go *bum* dum *bum* dum *bum*, like a fat man carrying a crown on a little red pillow.

(Later on, coming *back* from the cemetery, this band gone *wail*. Then you gone *hear* something. You gone hear that trombone waa-do-du-deedle-du-do, and that trumpet climb up la-*bat*-da-badda-bah, and that clarinet skeetlee-dee-titty-dee, and them drums fa-*bot*-ba-ba-boo-budeh-bah, and that bass go *thun*-thun-tha-thun-thun, and that piano triple-skipple-dipple-whipple-fipple-ripple-*roo*. You gone see that piano player *smile* under that bowler hat, and that trumpet man's eyes, they gone pop right out he *head*, and that trombone man's glasses, they gone steam up like in a Turkish bath. Because this the idea, on the way the cemetery you got to think about him what dead, so you play the long slow music with the heavy walking beat. But on the way back from the cemetery, it time to think about the living, it time to come *up* out your sadness, come *up* to happiness again. At least, that's what them handkerchief-heads from Down South, them Dundershaft relatives, that what *they* think.)

Now, after the band come eleven black Cadillac convertibles, on account Cadillac the only kind convertible made in the United States any more—don't complain, *you* didn't buy no convertibles neither—and these eleven convertibles, they has they tops down so the general public, it can see the celebrities.

About them celebrities. F. Xavier, he had a lot a trouble about them celebrities. First he try calling them almost-celebrities from the Open Sports Committee, and that don't get him nowhere at *all*. Nobody home, everybody busy, everybody mad about this thing or that thing, don't nobody remember no solidarity worth a damn.

So after that he try some other people what might be celebrities, but don't nobody want to go to no funeral, and don't nobody *double* want to go to no Mole Mouth Dundershaft funeral. And F. Xavier, he figure he got to get some celebrities to *this* funeral or pretty soon they gone be another

190

funeral. Because Bad Death, he calling up all the time, he saying, "You got them celebrities yet?"

"Working on the list, Bad Death."

"You fuckin' better."

So F. Xavier, he think about things, and when Maleficent, she start bad-mouthing him he turn around quick and whup her with a floor lamp, which nobody ever done before, and she go lock herself in her bedroom and call the Dunkin Donuts and tell them send over a whole *lot* a stuff. And F. Xavier, he give himself a shock when he plug the floor lamp in again, and it just like a light bulb over a character's head in a comic book because all a sudden he *know* what to do about celebrities. And he make a whole bunch a phone calls, and everybody he call say yes, and when Bad Death, he call the next time, F. Xavier, he say, "I got em, Bad Death."

"Oh, yeah? Who you got?"

"I got Sammy Davis, Jr. And I got Muhammad Ali. And I got—"

"You shittin me?"

"*Me,* Bad Death?"

"You really got all them people? Who else you got?"

"I got Diana Ross, and I got Flip Wilson, and I got Bob Teague, and I got Pam Grier, and I—"

"Pam Grier!"

"Sure, Bad Death."

"What she doin after the funeral?"

"Uh. Well, listen, Bad Death, these people, you know, they all want to come on account this gone be the social event of the *year*, but they don't want no trouble in their lives, so in case the police is watching this funeral—"

"Well, shit, *sure* they gone be watchin the funeral. You kiddin me?"

"Well, these celebrities," F. Xavier explained, "they gotta pretend they don't know you, see what I mean? They'll just ride in the cars, but they won't talk to nobody or nothing."

"Oh, sure," Bad Death said. "I get it. You got anybody else?"

"Let's see my list here. I told you about Pam Grier."

"You sure did."

"So then I got Redd Foxx and Diahann Carroll and Shirley Chisholm and Jim Brown."

"Who was that one?"

"Jim Brown."

"No, the one before that."

"Shirley Chisholm?"

"Who dat?"

"Congresswoman from Brooklyn. Very important woman, Bad Death. Big-time celebrity."

"Well, okay. The only politicians I knows is precinct captains."

So that took care the celebrities. So now the celebrities, they in five convertibles in the funeral procession, two celebrities per convertible. Only not the front two convertibles, cause in the front two convertibles is Mole Mouth's immediate family, a bunch of wooly-head niggers from Down South someplace, staring around at everything and eating Kentucky Fried Chicken outa plastic buckets on the floor the convertibles and generally making fools a theyselves. But starting with the third convertible, here come the celebrities.

Leroy, he say, "Buhbuh."

Buhbuh, he say, "Whu?"

Leroy, he say, "Lu dah."

Buhbuh, he say, "Lu *wuh?*"

Leroy, he say, *"Dah!* Ain dah Sammy Davis Junyuh?"

Buhbuh, he look, he say, "Nah."

Buhbuh, he right. That ain't no Sammy Davis, Jr. That F. Xavier's cousin Jim Haye from South Ozone Park, what *look* a little like Sammy Davis, Jr., special when he got that black eyepatch on what the real Sammy Davis, Jr., don't wear no more. (When F. Xavier, back at the funeral parlor, when he point to Jim Haye and say Bad Death, "There Sammy Davis, Jr.," and Bad Death, he say, "How come he wearin that eyepatch? He don't wear that no more," F. Xavier, he say, "He lost the glass eye." And Bad Death, he say, "Playin what?")

So now Leroy, he say, "Well, ain' dah Muhammad Ali?"

Buhbuh, he look, he frown, and he say, "Nah."

Buhbuh, he right again. That ain't no Muhammad Ali, that F. Xavier's nephew Lucius White from New Rochelle, sitting in there next to Jim Haye with his jacket shoulders all full a paper towels and his arms up in a boxer's handshake with himself.

So that the first car celebrities. Jim Haye with a eyepatch on and Lucius White wearing paper towels, both a them nodding and waving to the multitude, what stare back. And that F. Xavier, he had to be pretty smart *and* pretty dumb, try to pull a stunt like this.

So now the next Cadillac convertible come along, and Leroy, he say, "Gah dammit, Buhbuh, ain' dah Diana Ross?"

"Nah," say Buhbuh.

"How bow Flip Wilson?"

"No way," say Buhbuh.

That Buhbuh, he batting a thousand. That ain't Flip Wilson, that a casket salesman from Detroit name a Happy Charlie Lincoln, who *do* look like Flip Wilson. He look like Flip Wilson so much that people say it all the time; they say, "Man, *you* look like Flip Wilson." And right away they sorry they say that, 'cause right away Happy Charlie Lincoln, he do fifteen minutes a Geraldine. It *awful.*

And nor ain't that Diana Ross. Who that is, that Maleficent's little nephew Alexander Sternfeather. When F. Xavier, he call him and ask him help out in a matter a life and death, that Alexander, he say, "*I* ain' gone dress up like any girl." And F. Xavier, he say, "This ain't dressin' up like *any* girl, Alexander. This dressin' up like Diana Ross. This dressin' up like a *star.*" So he talk Alexander into it, and they give Alexander some really heavy threads, and they give Alexander a wig almost tall as he is, a scale model a Versailles made outa yak hair. And now Alexander, he getting such a big kick outa being a star, he singing "Stop in the Name of Love" while waving at them multitudes. Good thing they can't hear him.

So now Leroy, he getting mad, he getting pissed *off,* he stand up from the curb where him and Buhbuh, where they been sitting, and he point, and he say, "Now. You tell me dat ain't no Bob Teague."

Now, ain't nobody perfect. Buhbuh, he don't watch no Channel 4 news, he don't know Bob Teague from McTeague, he say, "Beat me, man. Mebbe so."

"Hokay," Leroy say. "An you tell me, what dat in dere with Bob Teague?"

Buhbuh, he look, he say, "Dunno."

"It Pam *Grier,* you dum-dum!"

Buhbuh, he say, "Poo."

Buhbuh, he back on the beam. Pam Grier, poo. *That* ain't no Pam Grier, sitting there in brown leather pants and brown leather jacket and snakeskin shirt. That F. Xavier's cosmetician in the funeral parlor, name a Theodora Nice, who put out all the time for the drivers on the cosmetology table. She don't even *look* all that much like Pam Grier, though she been fixed up more in that direction at the moment, but they something about the expression in her eyes that make a lotta men, they see her, among the things they think, they think, "Pam Grier."

As for that Bob Teague, he ain't no Bob Teague neither. Maleficent, she come out a the bedroom after she cool off, she full a contrition and Dunkin Donuts, and when F. Xavier,

193

he tell her what he scheming, she say she gone help out, on account her no-good sister's no-good husband, Roosevelt Jackson, he look like that fella on the TV, that Bob Teague. So Leroy, he wrong again.

He gone be wrong twice more in another minute, when he say, "Lu *dah*. Redd Foxx *an* Diahann Carroll!"

"Wrong *an* wrong," say Buhbuh.

Leroy, he say, "Buhbuh, you a pain in the ass."

That may be, but Buhbuh, he a *right* pain in the ass. Redd Foxx, *huh*. Who that is, that Maleficent's diet doctor, Doctor Erasmus Cornflower, a nasty goddam charlatan and quack, what F. Xavier had to point a pistol at this morning before he'd sit still and let Maleficent dye his hair red. He ain't at all happy in that convertible, which is okay, on 'count when he frown like that he look almost *exactly* like Redd Foxx on television when he mad at he family.

And you know who dat Diahann Carroll is? She made up a lot, and her hair different from usual, but Leroy, he should a *known* who that is. Buhbuh, *he* know. "Leroy," he say, "you got your eyes up you asshole. Tha Miss *Tower*."

Leroy, he say, "Huh?" And he stare. "You fulla shit," he say. But then he stare again, and if that convertible, if it hadn't gone on by already by then, he would of maybe run right over to it and look *close*, because damn if maybe it wasn't Miss Tower, after all.

It is. Felicity Tower was almost the only Open Sports Committee member what F. Xavier could get in touch with this morning, and she come down when he say he need help, but they ain't no high school teacher in the *world* a big star celebrity except maybe Sam Levenson, and he the wrong ethnic. So Maleficent and Theodora Nice and F. Xavier, they all work on Felicity, and when they done she still one a the most beautiful women ever, but she don't look like no block a ice no more, what she look like is Diahann Carroll. O-*kay*.

So Leroy, he shake he head at that convertible, 'cause he don't know *who* that is no more, but then he look at the next convertible, and he frown, and he say, "Buhbuh."

And Buhbuh, he say, "Wuh?"

And Leroy, he say, "Who dah in dere wih Jim Brown?"

And Buhbuh, he say, "*Whut* Jim Brown?"

"Well, *hell!*" Leroy say.

Well, that ain't no Jim Brown in there, but who that is in there with him is Alexander Sternfeather's mother Lois. It used to be everybody told Lois she look exactly like Nat King Cole, but these days everybody tell her she look exactly like

194

Shirley Chisholm, so that who she supposed to be, but Leroy and Buhbuh, they ain't up on current events. Not *that* kind current events.

About that Jim Brown. The funny thing about him, his name really *is* Jim Brown, and he used to play football one time, and then he was a sparring partner for a while, and then he busted safes until he went up to Attica for a while, and now he drive one a F. Xavier's hearses (except today), and if ever a fella from a protection racket or something like that come around pester F. Xavier, F. Xavier, he send the fella talk to Jim Brown, and that take care a that. So all that was done with this Jim Brown, make him look like the other Jim Brown, is give him a mustache cut out from the back part of Alexander Sternfeather's Diana Ross wig.

So now Buhbuh, he say, "Okay, Leroy, who *dah?*"

He mean the fellas in the next convertible, which is the eighth convertible, and which has in it Bad Death Jonesburg his own self, and three a his close associates. And Leroy, he look, he say, "It beat the shit outa *me.*"

"You doan think tha no Wallace Beery or nothin', huh?"

And Leroy, he grumpy, he don't answer.

So now three more convertibles go on by, full a evil and dissolute men, and then Leroy, he get happy and excited again, he say, "Buhbuh!"

And Buhbuh, he say, "Wuh?"

That Leroy, he say, "Lu dah! Dat our *band!*" Then he turn, he give Buhbuh a cold-fish look, he say, "Or you gone say tha *not* our band?"

"Oh, it our band, all right," Buhbuh say.

You can count on Buhbuh. It the Liberation High School band, marching. Only they up on a flatbed truck like the first band and the horses, so the kind a marching they doing is back-and-forth marching. They going in and out with each other, they doing all their tricky moves for the band competitions, only they doing everything *small*, on account they don't want nobody fall off the truck. So they spelling out HELLO and TEAM and USA and all like that, steady marching back and forth and in and out and up and down on the flatbed truck, on account most a them, they don't know how to play standing still.

They a colorful band. They got a red uniform, with silver buttons and white piping and a gold stripe down the pants leg. All their brass instruments real bright and shiny in the sun, and when they marching around up there they look like a *Mad Magazine* idea of a Norman Rockwell cover for

*The Saturday Evening Post*. They playing John Philip Sousa's "Thunderbird," and many the people on the sidewalks watching, they give them a toast in the same.

Meanwhile, up ahead, Felicity, she smiling and nodding and waving at the multitude, she being Diahann Carroll to beat *all*, when just on a sudden she see, standing right there on the sidewalk, them two cruel white men what broke into her apartment last night but got scared off before they could complete their evil designs. And the smile and the nod and the wave all falter, and it Felicity Tower looking out at them two men, not any Diahann Carroll at all.

And the two men on the sidewalk look back at her, and one of the men, Frank, he say, "Hey, look. That ain't Diahann Carroll, that's that broad from last night!"

And a minute later the convertible with Bad Death in it go by, and Bad Death, he poke his associates with his elbows, he say, "There's them feds. They got they eye on me."

The associates is very impressed.

Meantime, the funeral procession, it still going on. After the Liberation High band come three black Checker Marathons filled with professional mourners what F. Xavier, he got from a fellow mortician name of Israel Yid way down on Second Avenue. And these professional mourners, they got the Marathon windows rolled down and they got their heads sticking out and they moaning, "Oy!" and "Vey iz mere!" and similar sentiments, to regret the passing a Mole Mouth Dundershaft. And Leroy and Buhbuh, they don't know *what* to say about that. They just look at it, with they mouth open.

Then after the three Checker Marathons come one last flatbed truck, it containing three massed choruses a gospel singers, all female and all wearing floor-length robes and all singing at the top they voices. They singing hymns, and these hymns is made up mostly a two words. One a the words is, "Wah-ya-*yow*-ow-ow-wu," and the other word is, "Jesus."

And Leroy, he say, "Lu dah!"

And Buhbuh, he say. "Wuh you see now, Sidney Poh-tee-yay?"

And Leroy, he say, "I see my mama!"

Now this time, this time Leroy right. That is his mama up there, and his sister Rose and his sister Ruby, and they all got they mouths open wide, and they all got they hymn books out in front a them, and they all *singing for glory*.

"Hey, Mama!" Leroy yell, but ain't nobody can hear nothing when they in the middle three massed choruses a gospel singers, so Leroy's mama, she don't look up from her hymn book at all. And the truck go on by.

With the jazz band and the marching band and the professional mourners and the massed choruses, this a funeral you can *hear*. This a funeral attract *attention*.

Now after the massed choruses come a dozen more cars, only these is not your regular-type funeral cars. One a them is a pink Cadillac with a white bearskin interior and mandalas painted on the hubcaps. And one a them is a silver Lincoln Continental with lemon suede interior and black metal eyelashes over the headlights. They is all different—the only thing they all got the same is the little automobile TV antenna curling up over the roof on every one—but they is all got the same general name for them. They is pimpmobiles, and for those that think the Holiday Inn sign is pretty these here pimpmobiles is the last word in beauty. And they is being driven by they owners, who is business associates of either Bad Death or Mole Mouth, and who wanted to come to be a part a this special occasion, but who didn't want to be in no car they themselves wasn't driving, on account everybody got enemies so why take chances? And, anyway, they make a colorful part a the funeral procession, particularly since some a them got very attractive-looking girls in the passenger seats, girls that wouldn't somehow have fitted in with the massed choruses a gospel singers.

And finally at the end is a sleek black Cadillac Eldorado, with F. Xavier smiling and sweating and happy in the back seat. (Maleficent, she too fat to go out the house, she stay home all the time.) F. Xavier, he done it now and he know it. He The Funeral Man from here on out. This a funeral they gone be talking about for *years*. Walter B. Cooke, he don't understand *nothing*.

Leroy and Buhbuh, they trail along after the funeral a little ways, and then Leroy, he say, "Lu dah."

Buhbuh, he say, "Wuh?"

Leroy, he say, "Dere dem cops."

This time, Leroy, he right *and* wrong. It them cops, sure enough, but them cops is no more cops than that Jim Brown they seen was Jim Brown. Them cops is Frank and Floyd, and now the funeral it out they way they crossing the street, off to get Marshall Thumble's golden statue.

Buhbuh, he say, "Where they goin, them bastids?"

Leroy, he say, "Less follow em."

So they follow them cops, and damn if them cops, if they

don't go to Bubbuh's house and go on inside. Buhbuh, he say, "Wuh the fuck?"

So Buhbuh and Leroy, they stay outside and wait, while the sounds a the funeral, they fade away in the distance. 'Cause the funeral, it gone over a Hundred Twenty-Fifth Street to the Triborough Bridge. Then it gone over the Triborough Bridge and down the Brooklyn-Queens Expressway to the Long Island Expressway, and out the Long Island Expressway to the cemetery, at fifty-five mile an hour, with the jazz band playing and the Liberation High band marching around and spelling ATIO (which is all from Liberation High they can spell without a whole mess a trumpets and tubas falling off the truck), and the professional mourners yelling out the windows, and the massed choruses hollering about Jesus, and all the girls in the pimpmobiles watching "Let's Make a Deal."

And Frank and Floyd, they can't get inside the Thumble apartment, so they go back out the building and they see that kid Leroy Pinkham again, and they see the other kid with him, and Frank, he go over to Buhbuh and he say, "Are you Marshall Thumble?"

And Buhbuh, he say, "What of it?"

And Frank, he say, "Why didn't you say so before?" And him and Floyd, they walk away, and Buhbuh and Leroy, they don't say *nothing*.


# ON THE PHONE . . .

By the time they'd finished breakfast and returned to the apartment, Oscar had convinced Chuck that something was going on, and Chuck was beginning to convince Oscar what that something was. "The *only* explanation I can think of," Chuck said, "is that the original somehow got mixed in with all our copies."

"I just don't see how," Oscar said. His forehead was deeply ridged with bewilderment.

It was being quite a morning for Oscar. First, he'd awakened with the granddaddy of all hangovers, some big mean hairy dog scratching and biting inside his head, and then he'd seen where somebody had busted his Other Oscar into a lot of pieces and then badly glued them back together again. Memory had followed, confused and sporadic, and when he'd remembered that one of last night's visitors had been asking for Bobbi Harwood he went to the phone to call Chuck, and there wasn't any answer.

Which was all wrong. Over the last three years, Oscar and Chuck had worked more closely together than any other two members of the Open Sports Committee—they even had keys to one another's apartments—so that Oscar knew Chuck's teaching schedule, and at nine-thirty on a Wednesday morning Chuck had no class and should certainly be home. Most likely asleep, in fact. As for Bobbi, she was *never* out of the house before noon.

So down to the Harwood apartment he'd gone, walking through the apparently empty rooms. Shattered statue in the fireplace; poor bastard in even worse shape than Oscar's. Usual mess in the kitchen. Every stitch of clothing out of the gaping dresser drawers in the bedroom. And Chuck himself, naked in the closet. "Good Christ!" said Oscar.

"Oscar," said Chuck, painfully straightening, "you might not believe this . . ."

Oscar listened to part of the story, then went downstairs to rescue what he could of Chuck's clothing, and then the two of them had a sorting-out conversation during breakfast in a nearby restaurant. Back in the apartment, Chuck brought up the idea of the original Dancing Aztec Priest having gotten mixed in with their copies. "I'm not saying it was total accident," he explained. "More likely there was chicanery afoot, and it misfired."

"Run that one through again."

So Chuck told him about the flourishing museum trade in stolen artifacts, and the estimated million-dollar price tag on the original Dancing Aztec Priest, and the fact that the Priest was famous enough in art circles to be worth acquiring but not so famous (like the Pietà, for instance) that a museum would be unable to show it, and then he went on to suggest that the original might have been stolen in South America and sent north with a shipment of copies. "But the smugglers," he finished, "took the wrong one at this end. They got a copy instead of the original."

"You know," Oscar said, "I think that makes sense."

"And the *next* thing to do," Chuck said, "is make some phone calls and see if any of the other statues were attacked last night."

"Right," Oscar said. "But what about Bobbi? Don't you want to know where *she* is?"

Shrugging, Chuck said, "She'll be back. Let's concentrate on these statues."

"If you say so."

They alternated the phone calls. First Oscar called Wylie, and was given a *very* excited account of the smashing of Wylie's statue on Wylie's forehead. Then Chuck called Bud Beemiss, who was out of the office; Chuck left a message. Then Oscar called Amanda Addlefor, but there wasn't any answer. And then Chuck called David Fayley and Kenny Sprang:

"Hello?"

"Hello, David? Chuck Harwood here."

"Oh, hello, Chuck."

"You got a cold? You sound all stuffy."

"No, I've just been sort of upset, that's all."

"That's too bad. Listen, I'm calling about that little statue Oscar gave everybody yesterday."

"Oh, Bud already told me."

"What?"

"About how we have to give them back to that museum in Rochester. So I put them both right away in the closet. Bud said he'd come around this afternoon and pick them up."

"Oh, he did, huh?"

"So everything's all right, Chuck."

"I'm glad to hear that, David."

After which, Chuck and Oscar had a hurried tense conversation bristling with surmise, interrupted by the phone ringing. Chuck answered:

"Hello?"

"Hello, is this Chuck?"

"Bud?"

"Chuck?"

"Is this Bud Beemiss?"

"Sure. How are you, Chuck?"

"We were just talking about you, Bud. Oscar and I."

"You were? Is Oscar there? I wanted to get in touch with both of you."

"About the statues."

"Beg pardon?"

"You wanted to talk to us about the statues, Bud."

"As a matter of fact, I did, yes."

"That's a funny thing. *We* wanted to talk to *you* about the statues. I left a message at your office."

"I haven't been— You wanted to talk to *me*? About the *statues*?"

"Do you think maybe we ought to put our cards on the table, Bud?"

"I really doubt that, Chuck."

"Think about it, Bud. Would it be better for us to compete or cooperate?"

(Pause)

"Bud?"

"I'm thinking. I'll tell you what, Chuck, let me get back to you."

"How soon, Bud?"

"Just a few minutes."

"Three minutes, Bud. After that the line will be busy."

## AT THE CURB . . .

Jerry found the office address of the New York City Symphony Orchestra, in a building on 47th Street between Madison and Fifth. Of course, there's no parking within *miles* of an address like that, but what choice did Jerry have? Since he didn't know if Bobbi Harwood had already been here and gone, he'd have to leave the car and go up to the orchestra office and find out. He'd present himself as a friend of the husband, who had become so despondent he'd unsuccessfully tried to kill himself last night, blah, blah, blah. But the thing was, he'd have to leave the car alone and unattended in midtown Manhattan.

Although Manhattan, like all the rest of America, is entirely dependent on automobiles, it has made less provision for them than any place else in the country. The streets are too narrow and not decently maintained, through traffic and local traffic have to share the same routes, there are too few ways on and off the island, and there are far too few parking spaces. Midtown parking garages are almost always full by eleven in the morning, and no spaces become available again until around four in the afternoon. In the theater district they fill up again by seven-thirty in the evening. No department store in Manhattan offers parking space for its customers, and no office building in Manhattan offers parking space for its customers, and no office building in Manhattan offers parking space for more than a tiny fraction of its tenants. In the other boroughs you can at least park by the curb like a normal human being, but in all of Manhattan that matters you can't park by the curb at *all*. And if you do the Police Department will come along with big dirty dark-green tow trucks and tow your car away to a rotting pier shed over by the Hudson River and charge you fifty dollars or so to get it back.

Maybe it would be better for mid-Manhattan to become car-free, with shuttle buses from great parking areas on the fringes, like Norman Mailer wanted. Or, maybe it would be better to slam seven or eight elevated superhighways across the island, knocking down everything in the way, like Robert Moses wanted. But if any breed of politician in the world truly understands the word "compromise" it is a New York City politician, so what Manhattan has is the worst of both philosophies; they fill the city with cars every day, and then pretend they haven't.

So here was Jerry in midtown in a car, and he had to get into that building over there. Oh, well. A bunch of trucks were parked along here—another element in the Manhattan madness being that trucks can do any damn thing they please —and Jerry tucked the station wagon in among them. He dashed into the building, and was still studying the directory when out of the corner of his eye he saw Bobbi Harwood emerge from one of the elevators, pushing ahead of herself some huge black triangle on wheels.

What the hell was *that?* It was black leather, like a suitcase, but it was huge, taller than the girl pushing it, and it was an elongated triangle in shape. Could it possibly contain the statue? And if it did, how in hell was Jerry going to get it away from her?

Watching her cross the lobby, the truth suddenly hit him. Orchestra. The damn thing was a harp!

Walking around with a harp. You're supposed to have a statue, lady, not a harp.

Jerry followed the girl back out to the street, where a Police Department tow truck was *already* attaching itself to the front of the station wagon. "Well, crap," Jerry said.

Bobbi Harwood had turned left, toward Fifth Avenue, pushing the wheeled harp without too much apparent difficulty across the uneven sidewalk. Her head was up, her shoulders were back, her arm was firm as she guided the harp, and she moved along like a person with a purpose.

Argue with a bunch of cops over a twelve-hundred-dollar station wagon? Or keep an eye on a girl with maybe a million-dollar statue in her possession? Pausing only to say to the stolid policemen, "Keep up the good work, guys. We got to clear all these cars out of the way so the cars can get through," he hurried along in Bobbi Harwood's wake.

# IN MOURNING . . .

Maleficent White was in mourning. She mourned her last youth, and she mourned the lost sylphlike slenderness of her girlish figure. (Actually, she never did have a sylphlike girlish figure, although for one brief period in her late adolescence she'd been blessed with a rather attractive luxuriance; what people farther downtown call "zoftik." But a traditional part of mourning is overstatement of the virtues of the mournee, so what the hell.)

Beyond the above, Maleficent mourned also the failure of so many of her good intentions. She mourned all those Dunkin' Donuts she'd engorged today. But most of all and above everything else, she mourned the death of her marriage with F. Xavier.

Dead. It must be dead, utterly dead, after all these years. And she was its murderess. Fat had made her bad-tempered, and bad temper had made her fatter, and the combination of fat and bad temper had driven her husband away.

Into the arms of Theodora Nice. Yes, that's right, Theodora Nice, the undertaker's cosmetician who regularly put out for the drivers on the cosmetology table and who was reproducing Pam Grier in today's spectacular. Maleficent had never read a Simenon novel, yet the logic of the progression was obvious to her. F. Xavier was the successful merchant, she was the unappreciative wife, Theodora Nice the attractive young employee. Was it life that imitated art, or art that imitated life? Whatever the answer, there was no question in Maleficent's mind as to what had happened in her own life. She was seeing everything clearly now, after years of selfish blindness, and she *knew*.

It had started with F. Xavier whupped her with that floor lamp. When she'd got over her rage, and had come out of her room again with Dunkin' Donut sugar all over her cheeks, she had for the first time in years seen F. Xavier as the agile, clever, admirable go-getter he really was. And had she ever appreciated him? She had not. She had nagged at him, complained at him, dragged him down every chance she got, and he had never once argued back, never once defended himself, never once raised a hand against her. It wasn't until he was at the riskiest moment of his life, not until he was walking in the shadow of Bad Death Jonesburg, that he had been driven even beyond *his* endurance and had turned on her, popping her one time with the floor lamp.

Popping sense into her head, too late. F. Xavier was out in the world right now, going through either the greatest triumph of his career or its final disaster, and where was Maleficent? Here in the mortuary,' alone. Fat had her body, and Theodora Nice had her husband, what was left?

Suicide, that's all. Leave F. Xavier to rest in peace with Theodora. Put this big fat body away forever.

Suicide, yes. But how? One look at the fleshy folds of her wrists told her she's never'be able to saw down through those things to the veins. The F. Xavier White Funeral Home was four stories tall, and a jump from its roof would surely do *anybody* in, but it had been years and years since Maleficent could climb that many stairs. She'd drop dead before she reached the third floor.

Poison. That was the answer. Eating and drinking had been her abiding vice, now let them bring her abiding peace. The embalming rooms in the basement contained a sufficient variety of deadly liquids for any taste, so that was where Maleficent headed, step by heavy step down the wide stairs —wide to permit the passage of caskets—to the chemical-smelling white-walled room where the last remains were prepared for that final transformation.

The cosmetology table leered at her. Mirrors reflected her. In the cold storage room two customers patiently waited their turns. The smells down here were sharp and acid, but they were also clear and clean. Soon it would all be over.

What Maleficent didn't know was that Frank and Floyd McCann, having gained access to the alley behind the building and having climbed the fire escape past a series of locked windows, had just forced the lock on the door to the roof and were starting down the stairs toward the top floor.

Maleficent, far below in the basement, having selected the liquid with which she would dispatch herself, poured it into a beaker. A clear watery liquid, vaguely blue in color, it was one of the few things Maleficent had ever seen that did *not* look appetizing. But that at last wasn't the point, was it?

Frank and Floyd, believing the funeral home to be empty

because everyone had gone off with the funeral, made a quick search of the top floor without finding the golden statue.

Maleficent, about to drink, stopped with the sudden realization that she had best write a note, or else the police would surely believe F. Xavier had murdered her so he could get together with his paramour, Theodora Nice. (Amazing that she had never read a Simenon novel.) A note, a note. Carrying the beaker of evil fluid, she looked around the bare antiseptic rooms, but could find neither pen nor paper. She would have to go upstairs, a long and difficult process, involving a pause for breath at every second step.

Frank and Floyd, not having found the golden statue, moved down to the third floor.

Maleficent reached the tenth step, and paused to catch her breath.

"Gotta hustle," said Frank. "Christ knows *when* they'll come back."

"Right, right," said Floyd, and the two of them started their search of the third floor.

During her pause at the twelfth step, three from the top, Maleficent sniffed a bit at the nasty blue fluid in the beaker. It smelled *awful*. It smelled like ammonia, mothballs, and Days-Ease all mixed together in a rusty pot. Probably gonna taste like that, too.

Well, what did it matter what the stuff tasted like? She was *done* with taste, wasn't she? Too many sweet things altogether; time for a little something sour. Time and past time.

Hustling, Frank and Floyd continued to ransack the rooms of the third floor.

During her pause at the fourteenth step, one from the top, Maleficent began to wonder if maybe there just might could possibly be some small tiny scant reason for hope after all. What if—just what if, now—what if she *really* went on a diet? What if she gave up that quack and charlatan, Dr. Erasmus Cornflower, and simply *stopped eating* for a while? And what if she was kindly and friendly with F. Xavier from here on? What if she turned over a new leaf and became a changed woman? A *better* woman. Would there still be hope?

No golden statue on the third floor. Frank and Floyd hustled down to the second floor. Neither of them was in any hurry to meet Bad Death Jonesburg again.

Reaching the top of the stairs, Maleficent paused for a final time, looked at the beaker of poison, and realized she was

205

just fooling herself. She was just hoping against hope, when there wasn't any hope. The damage had been done. F. Xavier would be happier without her, happier with Theodora Nice. He *deserved* Theodora Nice.

"A sign," she murmured, and lifted as many chins as she could in order to gaze heavenward. If there was hope, if she should stay alive and go on a *real* diet and treat F. Xavier nice from now on, then let Heaven give her a sign. Something, anything, to let her know she could go on hoping.

She waited, watching and listening.

Was that a muffled thump, from the direction of Heaven? Apparently not.

With a sigh, Maleficent gazed into the beaker again, saw that the fluid had not miraculously changed color nor disappeared, and realized there was nothing for it. She had to go through with it now. Write the note, drink the poison, die.

Pen and paper would be in F. Xavier's office, beyond the room in which casket models were displayed. Sad, sighing, Maleficent made her slow way in that direction.

Frank and Floyd finished on the second floor, and hustled down the stairs to the first floor, the business part of the mortuary. "You go that way," Frank said, "and I'll go this way, and we'll meet back here at the stairs."

"Right," said Floyd.

Floyd's path took him to the casket display room. Entering, he saw through an open doorway on the far side what appeared to be an office; the corner of a desk, a leatherette chair with wooden arms, a tall filing cabinet. And what was that on top of the filing cabinet? Wasn't it a Dancing Aztec Priest?

The room Floyd was in was long and fairly narrow, lined on both long sides with casket models, some open and some closed. A dark brown strip of carpet ran down the middle to the open office door, and Floyd was moving quickly along this when he heard the sound behind him.

Someone was coming.

Bad Death Jonesburg, that's all Floyd could think of. It had to be Bad Death without Frank. *"Damn damn damn!"* Floyd whispered, and looking around he knew he'd have to hide. Furthermore, you and I and Floyd all know *where* he had to hide. So into an open casket he went, lickety-split, a waist-high one on a metal stand, and yanked the lid down over himself as the door at the far end of the room opened and Maleficent waddled in, muttering to Heaven under her breath.

A word about subjective time. One minute is sixty seconds (a thousand one, a thousand two, a thousand three, and so on), as everyone knows, but those sixty seconds can expand or contract something wild, depending on what's happening. For instance, to a couple on the first night of their honeymoon, sixty seconds can go by in one delicious shiver, but on their return home, when their flight is stacked up over Kennedy Airport for two hours, sixty seconds can outlast a marriage.

Maleficent, at the best of times, was not a fast walker, and this was not the best of times. Probably nobody ever jogs toward the room where they will write their suicide note, and poor Maleficent wouldn't have been able to jog if her underwear was on fire. It would take Maleficent, in other words, much longer than sixty seconds to traverse the entire distance of that room, along the brown carpet aisle between the rows of caskets. *Much* longer.

For Floyd, on the other hand, who hadn't discovered until he'd closed the lid that the satin lining in this coffin wasn't attached, and who was now being smothered by the lid lining, which had fallen down onto his face and body, sixty seconds had lost *all* meaning, since he didn't believe he could stand this for *one* second. In pitchblackness, in a *casket*, believing someone named Bad Death Jonesburg to be in the near vicinity, and at the same time to be smothered by heavy clinging satin, is one of the least pleasurable experiences available in this world of ours, and Floyd didn't like it *one bit*. He didn't want it. He didn't want that awful clingy slickness against his face, he didn't want his nose and mouth clogged with it every time he tried to draw a bit of air into his lungs, and he didn't in any way at all want to be lying on his back in darkness inside a casket. No!

Surely sixty seconds had passed by now, and with them the other person, Bad Death or whoever it was. Surely he or she had gone on by now to some other room. Surely it was safe to get out of here now, because surely surely *surely* it was NECESSARY.

Which tells us again about subjective time. It had been exactly forty-two seconds since Maleficent had entered this room and started across it when all at once the lid was flung off the casket just to her right and some great gleaming pink *creature* sailed up out of it, beating its great gleaming pink wings and moaning like the souls of all the damned hooked up together.

And, *"Yow!"* said Maleficent, throwing her hands up in the air. (The beaker, with its noxious contents, arced across the room and utterly spoiled an expensive set of draperies on the side wall.)

*"Yow!"* echoed Floyd, who could neither see nor breathe nor get this goddam stinking rotten filthy *satin* off his head, and who in his thrashing dislodged the casket on its rickety stand, and over went everything, Floyd, satin, casket, stand

. . .

. . . and Maleficent, who simply gave herself up for dead and swooned on the spot. Over on her back she went, out like a light, rocking gently.

When Frank, who had heard the ruckus, dashed into the room, he found Floyd struggling his way out of a mélange of splintered wood (casket), bent metal (stand), and torn cloth (lining), while a dead woman lay on the floor with her arms spread out. "Jesus Christ!" Frank said. "You didn't have to *kill* anybody!"

"I didn't," Floyd said savagely, kicking the last of the satin off his ankle. "But I'd like to kill the son of a bitch that didn't sew that lining in."

Frank was having trouble catching up. "What?"

"Never mind," Floyd said. "Besides, she isn't dead. It's that same fat woman from last night. She just fainted again."

"Oh," said Frank.

"And there's the statue," Floyd said, pointing.

"At last," said Frank.

But it wasn't the right one. Frank hit its head against the filing cabinet and it broke right off. "Shit," said Floyd.

"Right you are," said Frank. "Let's get out of here."

But before leaving, out of some obscure need for revenge, Floyd placed the headless statue at the feet of Maleficent White. Then he and Frank departed, and when Maleficent regained consciousness a few minutes later she'd had all the signs from Heaven a body could want. Great pink ghosts flapping around, a headless golden statue dancing at her feet; the message might not be clear, but it was loud.

"All right," Maleficent said aloud, sitting there on the floor. "I'll stay alive. And I'll lose weight. And I'll be good to Savior."

All good resolutions. And as to the diet, as she was becoming uncomfortably aware, she'd made a good start, having already lost fourteen ounces.

# EN ROUTE . . .

"But you don't understand," said the pilot. (He didn't look so much like a pilot now, in his Hawaiian shirt and Bermuda shorts and Japanese shower clogs borrowed from the luggage of cooperative passengers. His own clothing had not survived Pedro's arrival, and had been jettisoned over the unsuspecting Andes after the pilot's visit to the disgusting lavatory.) "You just don't understand," he repeated.

"People a been tellin me that all my life," Pedro said. (He was into the best drunk of his career, high and sailing. His incessant throwing up was leaving him with plenty of alcohol in his system, but none of those side effects of headache and diarrhea and general discomfort well-known to the habitual gluppe drinker.) "People a been tellin me that all my life, but here I am. I'm dune fine. Jus fine."

The pilot might have pointed out that a person who, while drunk, hijacks an airplane in the sovereign state of Descalzo, *belonging* to the sovereign state of Descalzo, cannot really be said to be doing "fine," but the pilot's attention was on a different aspect of the problem. "This airplane," the pilot said, "only has a range of seven hundred miles. We'll run out of gas before we ever leave South America."

"Then we land," Pedro said, "and get more gas."

"Refuel? You don't understand!"

"There you go again," Pedro told him.

"New York is five thousand miles from here! To get to New York we'll have to land and refuel *seven* times!" (It was only six, actually; the pilot was making a common error.)

"Then that's what we'll do," Pedro said. "Land and refuel seven times." And he swigged gluppe, a fresh bottle found in the co-pilot's briefcase.

"But you don't understand!" wailed the pilot.

"That's okay, too," Pedro said.

"Our top speed," the pilot said, "is three hundred fifty miles an hour. It will take *fifteen hours* to get there!"

"That's okay," Pedro said. "I ain' in no rush."

"Then take the damn train," said the co-pilot. He was bitter about his gluppe.

Both Pedro and the pilot ignored the interruption, since

the pilot was saying, yet again, "But you don't understand, you just don't understand the situation."

"Sounds okay to me," Pedro said. "What time we get into New York?"

"Around three in the morning," said the co-pilot. (Despite his bitterness over the loss of his gluppe, he was in fact looking forward to New York. He'd always wanted to go there.)

The pilot was determined to explain the situation. "This is a very old airplane," he said. "We have trouble making it go all the way from Quetchyl to Rosie. I'm not sure it can *make* five thousand miles."

"Oh, sure it can," Pedro said. "You'll take care of it. We'll be jus fine. Jus fine."


# AT ODDS . . .

"I don't even *agree* with this," Mel Bernstein said. "I don't understand how it happened, I don't like it, and I absolutely do not agree with it. I think it's wrong. I think, when you come right down to it, when you come to the bottom line, I think what I ought to do is stop the car and take you off behind a wall someplace and kill you."

"You wouldn't do a thing like that," Wally Hintzlebel said.

Which was unfortunately true. Regretting the fact that he wasn't a killer—and that it was so obvious he wasn't—Mel hunched over the steering wheel, glowering, and took the on-ramp for the Throgs Neck Bridge. "You can pay the goddam toll," he said. And to think he'd thought this was Mel Bernstein Day!

After Mel had chased this son of a bitch into Long Island Sound, they had grappled a bit in the water before finally making their way back to the dock and clambering up on it, both of them exhausted. Mel, who had gained possession of Ben Cohen's statue by that time, had rubbed the base of it against the wooden boards of the dock, once he got some strength back, and after a while a certain amount of gold paint had rubbed off, revealing hints of dirty white plaster beneath. "Fine," Mel had said, and dropped the damn thing in Wally's lap. "It's yours." Then Mel, sopping wet, had splashed back to his car, in the nearby parking lot.

But after he'd paid the parking fee at the little shack by the entrance, and just as he was about to drive away toward his next and last prospect, Mrs. Dorothy Moorwood of Alpine, New Jersey (which must be at least fifty miles from here), damn if this bastard Wally hadn't come trotting along, equally wet, waving his arms and yelling that he wanted to talk, hold up a minute, hold up, let's talk.

What Mel should have done, of course, was run the bastard down and be done with it. What he *did* do, however, was stop the car and let Wally in and listen.

And what Wally had wanted to talk about was *joining* them. He wanted to team up with *Mel*, wanted to go into partnership with him.

Mel, of course, had been outraged. "Why, you son of a bitch!" he'd shouted. "First you go to bed with my wife, and then you try to steal my statue, and now you want to be my *partner?* Get out of the car!"

"That's all the past. Let's forget about all that."

"*Not* to mention the punch in the nose! I'm not likely to forget *that!*" And Mel, caught up in the whirlwind of his own rage, had punched Wally very hard on the nose.

Which Wally had taken with no argument at all, as though it had simply been another element in the discussion. "I know the way you feel," he'd merely said, pressing two fingers and a thumb to his reddening nose. "And I don't blame you. But this is better for you, too. I won't stop looking for the right statue, and if I'm on my own and I find it, you won't get *any* of it."

"You won't find it!"

"I might. I know just as much as you do."

"Oh, yeah? What's Mrs. Dorothy Moorwood's address?"

Promptly Wally had responded: "Five Ronkonkomo Drive, Alpine, New Jersey."

Which meant that Wally *did* know just as much as Mel; or in any event, he knew too much simply to be sent away. Much as he disliked the idea, Mel had realized it would be necessary to join with Wally, after all, at least until he could get together with Jerry and Frank and Floyd, who would undoubtedly deal with the problem briskly and definitely. In the interim, though, "All right," Mel had told him.

"Half and half," Wally had said.

"Half of what I get," Mel had agreed, congratulating himself on his slyness.

Not sly enough. Wally had given him a penetrating look: "You have to split with your friends?"

No point lying. "Yes."

But Wally had merely shrugged. "Okay. We're in it for halfs." Meaning he must have some nefarious plan of his own in mind.

Then there'd been a delay, because Wally had to get his bag from his car. "I keep extra clothes in the car, in case I'm away, um, away for some reason of, um . . ." And, blushing while Mel glowered at him, he'd trotted away and then trotted back again with his canvas overnight bag. Finally, then, Mel had turned the car in the direction of Alpine, New Jersey, with Wally at first in the back seat changing into dry clothes, but more recently up front, looking bright and alert and prepared to become fast friends.

It was the *look* that Mel couldn't stand. The look, and the fact that his own clothing remained sopping wet. (Without Wally, he might have gone home first to change his clothes, but he was not *about* to bring Wally home.) And, finally, the whole infuriating goddam thing. Everywhere he went, there was that son of a bitch Wally. He didn't *want* Wally; why did he have to *have* Wally all the goddam time?

Which was why he'd made his remark about killing Wally behind a handy wall. Instead of which, all that happened was that Wally paid the toll on the Throgs Neck Bridge.

Damn it.


# IN TRANSIT . . .

Hustle. Gotta hustle. Everybody walking the midtown streets was moving fast, in a hurry, staring out straight ahead, walking against the DON'T WALK signs, pushing along, getting there, moving on, moving fast. And among them Bobbi Harwood, pushing her harp, with Jerry striding half a block back. Some people looked startled when they saw the good-looking girl pushing the six-foot-tall triangle along the sidewalk, and some people smiled, but most people ignored it.

From the orchestra office, Bobbi first led him down Fifth Avenue to a branch of Capitalists' & Immigrants' Trust at 44th Street, where she cashed a check while he read a pamphlet on auto loans. From there, she went down to 42nd Street, turned right, and pushed the harp along the broad sidewalk past the library and Bryant Park and the little

212

stone comfort station there. The day was sunny and bright —Manhattan in June can be a beautiful place—and the park was full of people, feeding themselves, feeding the pigeons, reading, chatting, or just lifting their faces to the sun.

None of that for Bobbi Harwood; she led Jerry briskly across Sixth Avenue and on as far as Times Square, where they turned left down Broadway. At 39th Street they turned right, and Bobbi entered an office building in the middle of that mini-block between Broadway and Seventh.

She went into the elevator first, with Jerry at her heels. They were the only two aboard, plus the looming black presence of the harp, and he saw that the button marked 7 was lit, so he pushed 15. Up they rode together, not looking directly at one another, and at 7 he held the door open while she off-loaded the harp. (The little wheels wanted to get stuck in the crack, but she'd obviously traveled with this thing before and had it under control.) He held the doors an instant longer than necessary, and watched her turn left as they slid shut.

Quickly now he pushed the button for eight. Up one floor, and out to take a quick look at the floor diagram posted next to the elevators. YOUR ARE HERE. And Stairway B was just to the left.

Bang, bang, bang, down the metal stairs and through the door to the seventh floor hall. One of the offices to the left.

Six of them. A dentist. An accountant. An auto transport company. Something called Nebula Musical Attractions. Something called Those Wonderful Folks, Inc. And a photographer studio.

Jerry started opening doors, leaning his head inside. The dentist's waiting room contained two glum-looking people, neither of them Bobbi Harwood, and no harp. The accountant's outer office contained a brassy-looking receptionist with Chinese red hair, who gave Jerry a jaundiced look and said, "Yeah?"

"Bobbi Harwood come in yet?"

"Who?"

The auto transport company was a large office with two rows of desks, at one of which Bobbi Harwood was talking with a stocky young woman who was simultaneously nodding, chewing gum, writing something on a form, and dialing a telephone. Bobbi seemed to be showing some kind of identification.

Christ on a crutch. Was she taking a *car* some place? Back down in the elevator Jerry went, and out to the street, where he found a phone booth down at the corner of Broadway. He dialed Angela's number and waited, tapping his foot. Two rings. Three rings.

"Hello?" Angela's voice.

"Listen," Jerry said. "I don't have much time."

"Jerry! Oh, I wanted to tell you, what an absolute *jewel* you found us with Mandy!"

"Yeah, we'll have to work something out there. We can't keep her forever."

"Oh, but we can!"

"Say again?"

"You know she's been working for that actress, Valerie Woode. Well, apparently the famous Miss Woode is also famous for her terrible tantrums, and when Mandy called to say she might be late this evening dear Miss Woode just *screamed* at her. I could hear it in the next room, coming over the phone."

"Angela, I don't have much time."

"Well, the *point* is," Angela said, "the point is, Mandy is *staying!*"

"She what?"

"She's working for *us*, now, for Mel and me! She never did like those late hours with Valerie"—Angela was a name dropper—"and she didn't like living up in that nasty neighborhood in the Bronx, so she's moving right in here, in the spare room, and she'll work for *us!*"

Jerry stood there in the phone booth, nodding slowly.

"Jerry? Are you still there?"

"Yeah," Jerry said. "Frank and Floyd kidnap her, and you're *keeping* her."

"I'm *hiring* her, Jerry."

Jerry brought himself with an effort back to the issue at hand. "Listen, Angela. Before I forget what's going on at this end, copy down an address."

"All right. I have paper and pencil right here."

"Terrific. Broadway and 39th Street, in Manhattan. There's a phone booth on the northwest corner. That's where I am right now."

"All right."

"I don't have my car any more, and I'm going to need wheels. I'm following the girl with the statue, and it's getting tricky."

"You want a car brought to you there?"

"I want the car brought here," Jerry told her, "but I

214

probably won't be here when it shows up. So the next time I land, I'll call this phone booth and say where the car should be brought. Got it?"

"Got it."

"Maybe Teresa can bring it."

"She has kids," Angela said. "I'll bring you my wagon."

"You gotta stay on the phone there."

"Mandy can take care of any calls that come in."

"Mandy!"

"You can't believe how reliable she is, Jerry."

"I can't believe any of it," Jerry said. And then, looking up, he saw Bobbi Harwood emerging from the building, coming this way, pushing her harp. "Here she comes! Get here as quick as you can!" And he hung up.

He waited in the booth till she'd pushed the harp on by, then set off in her wake. She walked half a block down Broadway, then abruptly turned, stepped off the curb, and flagged an immediate cab. Jerry, on the hop, ran frantically out into the street, and there wasn't a bit of yellow anywhere to be seen. Damn! Hell! Crap! Corruption!

Fortunately, it isn't that easy to get a harp in to a cab, so Jerry had more time than he might have. With the help of her cabbie, Bobbi Harwood finally loaded the thing in back, and then she sat up front with the driver, and off they went.

By which time, another cab had turned the corner a block away and stopped next to the wildly semaphoring Jerry. Leaping into it, he yelled, "Follow that cab!"

It was a fleet taxi ("V.S. Goth Corp," it said on the door), so a thick Plexiglas partition was between Jerry and the driver, with a small grillwork at one corner to permit speech and a small movable trough in the middle to permit payment. This system protects drivers from being mugged, but it also means none of them can ever hear anything the first time. Therefore, "What?" yelled the driver.

The girl's cab was moving away. The light would change and Jerry would be stuck here, with this idiot. *"Follow that cab!"*

The driver, a short squat man with a mouth made for cigars, turned to give Jerry an appreciative grin through the Plexiglas. "Yeah, yeah, that's a good one," he said. "Where you wanna go?"

"Straight," Jerry told him. "Straight down Broadway."

"Fine," said the cabbie. He threw the meter, and headed straight down Broadway.

Unfortunately, Jerry's cabbie was more of a hustler than

Bobbi's cabbie, and down around Herald Square Jerry suddenly found himself in the lead. "Hey!" he yelled, through the little grill. "Take it easy, will ya?"

"We're doing fine, we're doing fine," the cabbie assured him.

"*Slow down!*" Jerry yelled. Casting a quick look back, he saw they had now gained half a block on their quarry.

"I tell you what, Mac," the cabbie was saying, in the necessary loud voice, "I drive my cab, and you do what you do."

"*Slow down! I got a heart condition!*"

The cabbie took his hands off the wheel in order to lift them in a gesture of despair; everything happens to *me*. Fortunately, he also took his foot off the gas, and they slowed down. Also fortunately, Bobbi's cab didn't make any turns for the next few blocks, and by 29th Street was out front again, where it belonged.

*Un*fortunately, Jerry's cabbie did nothing in moderation, and they were now moving so slowly that pedestrians were surging ahead. They were coming dangerously near the end of the traffic-light cycle—the one-way avenues have staggered traffic lights, set for a steady speed of approximately twenty-five miles an hour—and if they got stuck at a light while Bobbi's cab continued with the greens, he'd lose her forever. "*Not* THAT *slow!*" Jerry yelled.

The cabbie gave him a very dirty look, through the Plexiglas. "You know you're a pain in the ass," he said. "You know that, don't you?"

"Don't get a red light," Jerry warned him.

They went through the 27th Street light on the yellow, but after that the cabbie put on a little more speed, and they kept Bobbi's cab in view, and then Jerry saw it make the illegal left-right at 23rd Street.

Here's the situation. The avenues run parallel, north and south, but Broadway comes down at an angle from northwest to southeast, and where it crosses the avenues it make the big squares and circles of Manhattan; Columbus Circle at Eighth Avenue, Times Square at Seventh Avenue, Herald Square at Sixth Avenue, Union Square where Fourth Avenue turns into Park Avenue South. Below Columbus Circle Broadway is one-way southbound, and so is Fifth Avenue, so at Madison Square, where Broadway crosses Fifth, the Fifth Avenue traffic is given the choice of staying on Fifth or switching to Broadway. But the Broadway traffic is forced to switch over to Fifth, and the only way a driver can stay on Broadway is to make a quick left-right jog at 23rd Street, which is illegal because no left turn is permitted at 23rd Street. However, every cabbie in Manhattan makes that illegal turn at least once a week, because time is money and nobody wants to lose the cycle of green lights. Therefore, Bobbi's cab did the 23rd Street jog.

"Stay on Broadway!" Jerry yelled.

"Yeah yeah," the cabbie said. But he didn't keep to the left.

"At Twenty-third! At Twenty-third!"

"It's against the law," said the cabbie, as another cab made the illegal turn in front of them. This bastard, because he was sore at Jerry, was planning to drive down to 22nd Street, make the left *there*, wait at the red light, then make the right, go one goddam block to another red light, waste two full minutes, and get them onto the *next* green light cycle, two minutes behind Bobbi and hopelessly lost.

No way. *"Do it!"* screamed Jerry, pounding on the Plexiglas with his fists. *"Do it, you son of a bitch!"*

New York cabdrivers are argumentative, but they aren't crazy. One look at Jerry's face through the Plexiglas, and this cabbie hunched his head down into his shoulders and made the left-right jog.

And so they proceeded, down to Union Square, where Bobbi's cab kept to the right and Jerry's cabbie, following Jerry's screamed orders, did likewise. Down past 14th Street, now on a two-way street called University Place, and then a right turn on 9th Street, and Bobbi's cab stopped at one of the big postwar apartment buildings where the northern part of Greenwich Village used to be, before NYU bought up all the land and turned it into Indianapolis.

"Stop at the corner!" Jerry yelled.

"Gladly," said the cabbie.

When they stopped at the corner, Jerry stuck a five-dollar bill in the pay trough, and looked behind him while waiting for his change. Bobbi was pushing the harp into the apartment building.

The cabbie, making change, took the opportunity to point at the intersection in front of them and shout, "That's Fifth Avenue there! Remember all that stink about stay on Broadway? That's *Fifth Avenue!*"

Of course. And Bobbi's cabbie had come down Broadway because 9th Street is one-way and he had to be at the other end of the block to get to the address Bobbi wanted. Which was too complicated an explanation to give this cabbie even

217

if he deserved it, which he didn't, so Jerry told him, "You drive your cab, and I'll do what I do."

The cabbie shoved the change in the pay trough and gave Jerry an angry smile. "You're an asshole," he said. "You know that, don't you?"

Jerry took his change, and ostentatiously dropped a nickel tip in the trough. "Here," he said. "Go get your head examined."


# IN PARTNERSHIP . . .

### PARTNERSHIP AGREEMENT

1. The purpose of this document is the formation of a limited partnership to be known as The Statue Company. The purpose of The Statue Company is the furtherance of educational and charitable projects in the Western Hemisphere.

2. There are three partners in The Statue Company. These are:
   1) Victor Krassmeier
   2) August Corella
   3) The Open Sports Committee
      A) Though the membership of the Open Sports Committee numbers sixteen, for the purposes of this document it is limited to three individuals, who share one-third the voting power of the partnership. These individuals are:
         i) Oscar Russell Green
         ii) Robert Beemiss
         iii) Professor Charles S. Harwood

3. The Statue Company does not anticipate revenues.

4. Should The Statue Company, despite anticipation, obtain revenues, these will be distributed as follows:
   A) The first three hundred thousand dollars to the Open Sports Committee, for equal disbursement among its members.
   B) A fourth hundred thousand to be set aside for payments to other non-named members of the Open Sports Committee, should these become necessary.

C) All remaining revenues, after reasonable expenses, to be divided between the remaining partners.

5. Pursuant to Section 4, Sub B, if the Open Sports Committee does not require the fourth hundred thousand for payments to other non-named members, such money shall be returned to the assets of the partnership and distributed in accordance with Section 4, Sub C.

6. Further pursuant to Section 4, Sub B, the Open Sports Committee, speaking for both present and absent members, holds its fellow partners in The Statue Company harmless from any and all demands over and above the fourth hundred thousand.

7. There is no general partner.

8. There have been no investments made in The Statue Company, nor does the partnership own or control anything of value, nor has the partnership any assets, nor does The Statue Company intend to engage in any business or activity controlled, licensed, or regulated by the City of New York, the State of New York, or the United States of America.

9. The laws of the State of New York shall apply to this partnership.

10. This partnership may be terminated, either orally or in writing, by any partner at any time.

"We aren't getting anywhere," Beemiss said.

"That has been obvious," Krassmeier told him, "for some time."

Once the squabbling had resolved itself at last into agreement, if not into mutual admiration, the partners had repaired to this neat but anonymous spare office at Winkle, Krassmeier, Stone & Sledge, containing two desks with telephones. Chuck Harwood sat interminably at one of these, trying to find his wife, who had one of the statues but who was, for some reason, not immediately available. (Chuck was reticent and bad-tempered on that topic.) So Chuck was calling everybody he knew, starting with the black males and going on to the white males and finishing with the white females, while Bud and Oscar alternated at the other phone, trying to find out what was doing with the rest of the statues.

There were sixteen to be accounted for. The four held by Chuck, Oscar, Bud, and Wylie Cheshire had already been eliminated, while those held by David Fayley and Kenny Spang were apparently still in the running and were now safe from the Manelli gang. (Krassmeier had already arranged for a messenger to pick them up, and Bud had phoned the weeping David to let him know the messenger would be coming by. As with all messengers, this one was now late.)

Which left ten statues to deal with, only ten. Confidently expecting the inventory to take almost no time at all, Oscar and Bud settled themselves at the desk and started phoning. Then Mandy Addleford failed to answer her phone. So did Dorothy Moorwood. So did Felicity Tower and Jenny Kendall and Eddie Ross. Ben Cohen, Leroy Pinkham, and Marshall Thumble were also not at home, but at least with those three it was possible to leave a message with a relative: "Please tell him to call just as *soon* as he gets in."

As for F. Xavier White, Oscar called that number and the conversation went like this:

"Savior White's Fu-*ner*-eal Home, Mrs. White speaking."

"Hello, Fissy?" (Oscar was one of the few people on earth, not including F. Xavier himself, who could get away with calling Maleficent by that nickname.)

"Who's there?"

"It's Oscar, Fissy. Oscar Russell Green."

"Oh, Oscar! Oscar, I've just undergone a miracle!"

"You have?"

"I'm reborn, Oscar!"

"In a funeral parlor?"

"I've received a sign, Oscar!"

"That's wonderful, Fissy."

"I'm a new woman now! Everything's gone be different!"

"Fissy, uh, about that statue—"

"How'd *you* know?"

"Huh?"

"You're part of the sign! My God, my God, I *do* believe! Oh, I *will* diet, I *will* be good to my man, I will *not* remain in the coils and toils of Doctor Eramus Cornflower. I will *not* permit any Theodora Nice to—"

"Fissy? That statue I gave—"

"Praise the Lord!"

"Do you still have it, Fissy?"

"I'll treasure that statue all my born days!"

"You've still got it. And it's in good shape?"

"Wonderful. 'Cept for the head, naturally."

"The head?"

"It's gone! Oscar, the head is *gone!* Isn't that wonderful?"

"Wonderful," Oscar agreed, and hung up, and told the others, "The wrong one."

220

After that, while Chuck went on with his morose telephoning and Bud and Oscar went back to dialing numbers that didn't answer, Krassmeier sat on the leather sofa to one side, sneering contemptuously at everybody like some road-show Sidney Greenstreet, and Corella with his stinking cigar marched back and forth like an expectant father who isn't entirely sure he *is* the father. Until, during a pause in the calling, the phone rang and it was Leroy Pinkham for Oscar. Him and Buhbuh, they just got back from the baddest funeral in the history of the *world*. Leroy wanted to talk about the funeral, but Oscar finally dragged him around to the subject of statues, and Leroy told him a couple of plainclothes cops had come around and taken his and Buhbuh's both, and busted them. Two more down.

And another two fell when Bud called his office to say he wouldn't be back this afternoon, and his secretary told him somebody named Eddie Ross had called collect from Rhode Island to ask if he and somebody named Jenny could get two new statues because some crazy person had smashed theirs.

"Okay, okay, okay," Corella said, when he heard that part. Rubbing his hands together, he said, "We're finally getting somewhere."

(Meanwhile, Chuck was in conversation with a black faculty member who lived on a houseboat at the 79th Street Boat Basin and who was sympathetically suggesting other black faculty members—as well as two Jewish faculty members and a Czechoslovak faculty member—with whom Bobbi might have taken up.)

Next, Krassmeier himself got on the phone, calling the messenger service, which told him the messenger was on his way. Krassmeier threw his weight around, insisted on speaking with the manager, and the manager told him the messenger was on his way. Krassmeier stooped to heavy sarcasm, and the manager hung up on him.

More useless telephoning followed, interrupted at last by a call from Ben Cohen. And when Bud mentioned the statue, Ben Cohen went through the roof. It had been stolen by a filthy sacrilegious probably-not-even-Jewish son of a bitch who'd claimed—could you credit this one?—to be from the UJA! And *then* it was stolen from *that* son of a bitch by some *other* son of a bitch, and the two of them ran off somewhere, who the *hell* knows where? And after he himself last night had regilded a spot on the statue's tuckus where the paint had scraped off and the white plaster showed through.

When Bud got off the phone at last and reported all this to the others Corella said, "So they don't have it yet."

Oscar said, "But who's this *other* one? I remember distinctly there were three sets of them came around last night."

"Some *other* breach of security, no doubt," Krassmeier said, glowering at Corella.

"Not from me," Corella told him. He was beginning to get a little pissed off at Krassmeier.

At that point the messenger finally arrived with the statues from David Fayley and Kenny Spang, in a brown paper bag. While Krassmeier submitted him to a lot of heavy irony and innuendo, Corella removed the statues from the paper bag and twisted their heads off. "Wrong ones," he said.

Four to go.

# DOWNTOWN . . .

His name was Hugh Van Dinast, and his family went back to the Patroons. They had lived in New York, near Washington Square, since the only people one knew were fellow parishioners at Grace Church. One of his great-grandmothers was portrayed, unflatteringly, in Edith Wharton's *The Age Of Innocence*. His family had been in shipping in New York when shipping was the thing to be in. They had also been in the Street, and several branches of the clan still were. Others, inevitably, were in banking, and most of the younger sons for the last five or six generations had taken up Law (corporation, of course, not criminal), though increasingly the less combative males went into education or the arts; currently, the Van Dinasts could boast two extremely academic painters, a daily book critic on *The New York Times*, a distinguished professor of economics at Columbia, the world's foremost authority on Colley Cibber (currently at Stanford), and Hugh Van Dinast himself, Associate Professor of Political Science at New York University. A liberal conservative (he favored food stamps, opposed busing, spoke out against Vietnam a full three months before Hubert Humphrey did), he was about to take his sabbatical year in California, studying that state's volatile and unique political progression for a planned massive volume tentatively titled *Tomorrow the World*.

Six feet four inches tall, Hugh Van Dinast was at forty-three utterly the patrician New York type in appearance. His hair was thin and sandy, his eyes mild and blue and somewhat watery, his nose unobtrusive, his mouth broad and made for easy smiling, his chin slightly recessive, his body built for the uniform of a palace guard. His accent seemed British to most Americans, but other New Yorkers recognized it at once and bridled at it. One assumed he would spend his evenings swapping condescending remarks with William F. Buckley and George Plimpton, although in fact his acquaintanceship with those two gentlemen was slight, and he much preferred the books of Gore Vidal. (Seeing him with Jimmy Breslin, as one on occasion might have done, they being in approximately the same vocation, was to undergo a strangely Kiplingesque echo; for if that wasn't the Colonel with his loyal Master Sergeant, there is no such thing.)

Twice married and twice divorced, Van Dinast was engaged in no serious sexual affairs at the moment, but was looking forward to something tanned and exciting occurring out in sunny California. (Which was one of the reasons he was basing himself in Los Angeles rather than the state's capital, Sacramento.) Unlike most of the Van Dinasts of the last eleven generations, who had married tall self-controlled blonde ladies but who had reserved their true passions for fourteen-year-old Polynesians of either sex, Hugh Van Dinast's passion was for tall self-controlled blonde ladies. Neither of his wives had had the faintest idea what to do with a passionate Van Dinast, and in the collision of his passion and their alarm both marriages had foundered. It had seemed to him, in recent years, that perhaps for one of his temperament marriage was not, in any event, the ideal, nor even a possible, life-style. Perhaps, not to put too fine a point on it, there was just too much of Henry James in his character, not to mention his upbringing and heritage, for him, no matter the intensity of his desires, to find happiness in either a marriage within his own class and social set or in a crosscultural alliance, of even the unlikeliest sort.

It was while he was pondering this problem yet again, in the study of his seventeenth-floor apartment in The Ambassador, that Ingrid, his black maid, entered to say that the driver was here for the car, and was waiting in the parlor. "I'll be right along," Van Dinast promised.

He would be living fourteen months out there, in faraway California, and did not wish to spend that long driving some rented green Impala. On the other hand, he had neither the time nor the patience to drive his own silver-gray Jaguar

223

XJ12 across America. He was, in other words, the ideal customer for Beacon Auto Transport, and like most of such companies' customers he was under the mistaken impression that his car would be driven by a professional transporter, an employee of the company.

Imagine his surprise, then, when he entered the green-and-gold parlor with its view south toward The Mark Twain, the next nearest high-rise apartment building, to discover the driver to be a *very* personable young woman, tall and blonde and quite obviously self-controlled. "Well, my dear," he said, with a smile at once charming and friendly, "you're hardly what I expected."

The girl's expression combined disinterest with distraction. "I'm not?"

On the surface, Van Dinast remained calm, friendly, even affable, but underneath his emotions had begun to roil. In the first place, the pay could not be particularly lavish for an occupation such as auto transporter, and in the second place, he recalled Beacon's having made a point of its drivers having all been bonded, which meant that, in addition to being tall, blonde, and utterly self-controlled, this young woman was evidently *poor but honest*. The combination, for Hugh Van Dinast, could not possibly be resisted, and he can be forgiven for the scene that followed.

To begin with: "I hadn't expected anyone so attractive," he said.

"Thank you," she said, but without the slightest trace of warmth or response in her voice. Most men would have understood the depth of the girl's indifference by then, but Van Dinast had *never* heard the slightest trace of warmth or response in a woman's voice, and so had no idea whether he was progressing famously or not at all.

And so he trembled at the brink of his third marriage. The prospect of finding his kind of woman outside his own class was overpowering. A tall, self-controlled, blonde woman who was *not* sized like muslin; was it possible? "I trust you'll enjoy my—my car," he said, and the boldness of his hesitation frightened him and yet thrilled him; already this girl was bringing him out of himself.

"Just so it gets me there," she said.

"You'll be staying in California?" Instant fantasies, instant scenarios, formed in his brain.

"Forever," she said.

"My own stay won't be quite that long, unfortunately," he

224

said, while reminding himself that he would have reached California by the time she got there, and that she would be delivering the car directly to him. "I'll only be a bit over a year," he said. "I'm going for my sabbatical." And yet, at the same time, a part of him despised him for trying to impress this creature; "sabbatical," indeed. Dropping that word into the conversation, knowing she wouldn't understand it, anticipating the inevitable question.

Which did not, for some reason, ensue. "That's nice," she merely said, and nothing more.

Van Dinast continued his pursuit. "And you? Are you going out for any specific reason?"

"To get away from my cocksucker of a husband," she said.

Van Dinast recoiled. Passion, yes; vulgarity, never. "Well, well," he said. "Shall we go down and look at the car?"

"Yes," she said.

In the front hall was some monstrous black piece of luggage, or something; it reminded Van Dinast of monks in Bergman films. "My harp," the girl said, and wheeled it out to the hall.

Riding down in the elevator toward the garage, alone with the girl (and her harp) in this small chrome box, Van Dinast found his interest growing again as the immediacy of the girl's vulgarity waned. And wasn't vulgarity, in the larger scene, merely indicative of life? "I've always been fond of music," he said, smiling at the black-encased harp.

The girl shrugged. "It's okay," she said.

They left the elevator at the parking garage in the basement, where the XJ12 slouched in its accustomed slot. A great silver-gray beast of a car, it was Jaguar's four-door sedan combined with the Jaguar sports car's V-12 engine, a big roomy powerful machine, an elegant monster. A beauty.

Even the girl was impressed. "Very nice," she said. *"Very* nice."

"Get behind the wheel," he suggested. "The seat is *infinitely* adjustable."

But first she had forms to deal with, a great sheaf of them out of her purse. The car had to be gone over for dents and scratches and tears. They both had to sign, here and here. And then, finally, she got behind the wheel. Van Dinast, after democratically closing the door behind her, trotted around and slid in on the passenger side.

Although the car was English, it was the export model, with the steering wheel on the left. The girl was devoting her attention to adjusting the seat, studying the controls, fiddling with the rear-view mirror. Van Dinast, smiling in utter infatuation at her clean profile, said, "It is a beauty, isn't it?"

"Yes, it is," she said, without interruption of her tasks.

"I care a great deal about beautiful things," Van Dinast said, and put his hand on her near knee.

She gave him a cold and dangerous look. "Watch it," she said.

He didn't watch it. God help him, he couldn't watch it. He was as helpless as his grandfather had been, when the fourteen-year-old Polynesians had climbed over the rail of the ship. "Bring me *that* one," the old bastard had said. "To my cabin." And the same blood flowed through the hand that now tightened its clutch on the girl's knee. "My dear," Van Dinast said, his voice suddenly husky, "I hope you don't think I'm some cheap masher. From the instant I saw you—"

She rabbit-punched his wrist. "Get *out* of there!"

He felt nothing; his hand remained clamped where it was. "Give me an opportunity," he begged. "Get to know me. We'll have lunch!"

She dug nails into the back of his hand. "Goddam it, *stop!*"

The Polynesians had also been squirmers. Van Dinast's other hand shot forward, cupping the back of her dear head, the soft straight blonde hair, the curve of the skull; that small fragile bowl full of thought and memory, emotion and desire.

And a mind of its own. *How* she squirmed, muttering fresh vulgarities, as inexorably he brought her forward, her beautiful face toward his adoring lips. His trembling right hand slid up her cool round thigh, his determined left hand brought her closer, closer—

And she bit his nose.

"Nga!" he said, which is the way a person says *Ow* while his nose is being bitten. Both hands left her utterly desirable person and flew protectively toward his face. His eyes had watered, a stinging sensation was spreading raylike through his cheeks.

But the girl, rather than press her advantage by continuing her physical assault, made the mistake of turning away, searching for the door latch in this unfamiliar car. Van Dinast, still smarting and blinking but in no way deterred, laid both hands on her again, and brought her back.

This was not the sequence he'd had in mind, but the strength of her opposition had escalated his approach from compliments and lunch offers almost immediately into the realm of physical dominance. Clutching at her with both hands, roiling her blouse and skirt, parrying her blows with elbows and forearms, he was panting like a miler and gasping withal, "Just have *lunch!* Give me a *chance!* Get to *know* me!" And meanwhile his hand, getting to know her, was inside her blouse, clamped to her braless breast.

"I'll scream!" she screamed, and then did so. Her nails tried for his face, but had to be content with his arms.

He felt nothing, he was dissuaded by nothing. Hadn't he had this same scene with both his wives, more than once?

There *are* class differences. Neither of his wives, with all their opportunities, had ever abruptly grabbed his genitals and twisted. "YYYYYYYYYYY!!!" he said, and when next he could sit up straight she was outside the car, adjusting her clothing and looking *very* angry.

In small and rheumatic movements he left the car. She watched him, glaring, across the silver-gray hood. "You keep your distance, you son of a bitch," she said.

"No, no," he assured her, trying for a smile through his grimace. "You're right, you're absolutely right. That was shocking behavior on my part. Shocking."

"You're goddam right." Her bag was on the hood. Continuing to watch him, she was withdrawing from it materials of restoration; a crumpled Kleenex, a comb, a Wipe 'n Dri.

"I'm a very lonely man, Miss Harwood," he said, having seen her name on the form he signed. "Usually, I'm really a very civilized man. Please believe that."

"You're another faculty masher," she told him, and ran the comb through her hair.

The phrase, such an obvious class contradiction, startled him, so that he repeated it. "Faculty masher? Where on earth did you pick up an idea like that?"

"You aren't the first one I've seen," she said, "but you're the worst. Usually they have to get drunk at a party first, and tell you how the head of the department doesn't understand them."

"Good God!" he said. "Are you a *faculty wife?*"

"Not any more," she said.

Terror trembled the hands he rested on the hood of the car. "At what school?" (*Not,* he prayed to Henry VIII's God, *let it not be NYU.*)

"Columbia," she said.

"Columbia." And he was thinking, Harwood, Harwood. "Oh dear. I believe I may have met your husband."

"You act like you trained with him."

"Oh, I *am* sorry. Mrs. Harwood, I—"

"Mizz," she said.

"Yes, of course. Mizz Harwood, I hope you'll believe me when I say I lost control for just a moment, and I will *not* lose control again."

"Not around me, you won't," she said.

"I hope, Mizz Harwood, I hope you'll still take the car, and—well, and just behave as though none of this had ever happened."

He could see her thinking it over. In fact, she told him her thoughts. "What I'd really like to do," she said, "is go straight to the nearest cop, and spread you all over page three of the *Daily News*."

"Oh, Mizz Harwood." One hand fluttered in air, asking for sympathy.

"*But,*" she said, "I'm determined to get out of town *today*, and this is the only way I can do it."

"Oh, Mizz Harwood!"

"But *you,*" she said, and pointed a finger at him. "You get out of here. Go away, back into that elevator."

"Are you sure you understand all the controls? Have you driven this sort—"

"Go," she said.

"I give you my word of honor, I would nev—"

"Either you go or I go."

"I'll go," he said. "But I do hope you can believe this was only an aberration, that it could *never* be repeated."

"Fine, fine," she said. "Go."

"Yes. I'm going." He backed away a few paces. "Um— have a—have a pleasant trip."

She merely glowered.

So at last he did depart. And, riding up in the elevator, he was thinking about their next scheduled meeting, in California. Surely she would be over her mad by then. He would be civilized, restrained. (After all, he now did have a more accurate picture of her, as a faculty wife, someone toward whom one's behavior should be less earthy than toward an ordinary woman chauffeur.) They would have a common topic of conversation by then—his car—and surely she would accept a drink.

With a sleeping pill in it.

Make it two.

# ACROSS TOWN . . .

When Madge came out, in response to Bobbi's honking, Bobbi could see the expression of awe that came over her face. And why not; it was really an incredible car, even with the back seat full of harp, jutting up like a black iceberg.

Sliding in on the passenger side, Madge said, "Holy cow, what a car!"

"Travel in style, that's what *I* always say."

"Man or woman?"

"Man."

"You shouldn't have taken the car," Madge said. "You should have stayed there and married him."

"Not that one," Bobbi said, and as they proceeded across Waverly Place toward Seventh Avenue she told Madge all about the attempted rape. And she remained unaware of the gasping man running along the sidewalk in her wake.

After Hugh Van Dinast had finally retired, she had spent a few minutes familiarizing herself with the Jaguar, and had then loaded the harp, and driven it out to the street. (She had been baffled at first by the closed garage door at the top of the ramp, until she noticed the box-with-button over her head, attached to the driver's sun visor. One push of that button, and the door had obediently slid up out of the way.)

Ninth Street being one-way, she'd had no choice but to turn west; but that was the direction she wanted, anyway. Driving to the corner, she waited for the light to change, while behind her a man she didn't notice searched frantically and vainly for a cab. Then the light did change and she turned left, traveling one block to the red light at Eighth Street. (The unobserved man trotted after her, spinning in circles in search of a cab.)

The Eighth Street light turned green, and Bobbi drove south the last remaining block of Fifth Avenue to Washington Square, where she turned right (that light was green) and went the long block with Washington Square Park on her left until she/came to the red light at MacDougal Street. (The unnoticed man pelted along behind her like Jack running for his beanstalk.)

The light turned green. Bobbi steered the Jaguar forward

half a block (how the following man ran!), then pulled to the curb in front of Madge's building and honked the horn three times fast, the prearranged signal. (How the following man sprawled across a parked car, gasping!) And now Bobbi and Madge were heading for Buffalo Roadhouse for lunch.

First to Sixth Avenue, where the light was red. (The following man walked after them, conserving his strength and still looking for an empty cab.) Bobbi's recital of her encounter reached the basement, and then the light turned green and she continued west, across Sixth Avenue and along the next block of Waverly Place, which was just as narrow as the preceding block but which was for some reason two-way. Dodging on-coming fenders, Bobbi continued with her story and continued not to see the head bobbing at a corner of her rear-view mirror.

Waverly Place veers north before joining the spaghetti-plate of intersections making up Sheridan Square, where Seventh Avenue is crossed by Christopher Street, Grove Street, Washington Street, and West Fourth Street. In veering, Waverly Place bisects briefly, so that one of the more unusual intersections in Manhattan is that between Waverly Place and Waverly Place.

At that intersection, Bobbi and her pursuer both took the left fork, and from there turned onto Grove Street, made tangential contact with Sheridan Square, and turned left on Seventh Avenue. Since there was only a stop sign at Grove and Seventh, the following man had to put on a *real* burst of speed in order to keep the Jaguar in sight. And still there were no empty cabs.

"That's *terrible!*" Madge was saying.

There are parking meters on this part of Seventh Avenue. Sometimes, there are even open parking spaces. Bobbi drove slowly, looking for one.

It wasn't the following man's idea of slowly. Panting, running, swaying from side to side like the wounded cavalry-man bringing news of the Indian attack, he reeled southward on Seventh Avenue, desperate for an empty cab.

And there it was! Coming down in the left lane, his side of the street, an empty cab, its vacancy light glittering in the sunshine, an empty cab, by *God*, an empty cab! The following man lurched out into the street, frantically waving his arms, and the cab eased to a stop.

About to enter the cab, the following man glanced after the Jaguar, and half a block ahead the thing had come to a

230

stop. It was parking? It was parking, backing into a space. The cabbie's window was open. The cabbie was saying, "Well?"

"Never mind," said the following man, still panting, and shut the cab door.

"*You* again!" yelled the cabbie, for indeed it was he again, a thing that never happens.

The following man, gasping for breath and holding his side, made his way back to the sidewalk. The women were getting out of the Jaguar, on their way to lunch, after which Bobbi would drive Madge back to her place and pick up her luggage.

"The next time I see you I'm gonna run you down!" screamed the cabbie. "You know that, don't you?"

The following man sat down on the curb and breathed. He didn't say a word.

# IN THE LURCH . . .

> (*Caption to photo*) Mrs. Dorothy Moorwood, local socialite whose charitable interests are well-known throughout the area, greets friends at Hill House, her lavish estate near Palisades Park. Mrs. Moorwood, who has been staying in New York City recently, involved with a charitable concern that she describes as "very close to my heart," will entertain "a few close friends" at Hill House for the duration of this month, before summering at Cap d'Antibes.

Acid rock drifted over the greensward, and a naked fat man slept under a tree, an unlit toke stuck in his navel. "Jeepers," said Wally. "What kind of place is this, anyway?"

Mel and Wally had left the car out by the public road and had walked through a bit of mosquito-infested woods, and now the house was visible—and audible—across a broad sloping expanse of neatly barbered lawn. Although it was barely five o'clock, every light in the house seemed to be on, and people in all manner of dress and undress could be seen moving about the interior. Others cavorted on a large patio and swimming pool area to the right, and on tennis courts to the left, and also here and there on the lawn. A party was not only in progress, but had obviously been under way for some time, possibly for years.

Wally had insisted on bringing along the canvas bag, to carry the statue in once they found it, if it turned out to be the real one, and now he held it up for Mel to see, saying, "We can pretend we're guests, just arriving."

It was Mel's intention to ditch Wally here, whether or not the Moorwood statue turned out to be the right one. They had come here in *Mel's* car, and Mel had the keys to that car in his pocket, and by the time Wally managed to get himself back to New York the rest of the search should have been completed. Then Wally could go take a flying leap for himself.

The first step in Mel's plan was to separate. Then, if he was the one who found the statue, he could simply leave, whereas if Wally found the statue he'd have no choice but to bring it to Mel. Therefore, as they neared the house Mel said, "You take the second floor, I'll take the first floor."

Wally looked dubious. "Shouldn't we stick together?"

"In the first place," Mel said, "shut up. And in the second place, we'll get done quicker if we separate. There's *other* people looking for these statues, you know."

"Okay," Wally said. "Whatever you say."

By now they had reached the house, which contained hundreds and hundreds of people, several of them famous, many of them attractive, and some of them personally known to their hostess, who was upstairs at this moment, performing an alternative sex act with a Fender bassist. People seemed to be dressed according to the time of day when they'd joined the party, their apparel ranging from floor-length gowns and formal dinner jackets to bathing suits and denim overalls.

Parties of this sort never used to exist in the real world, but in the middle sixties trendy movie directors started putting such parties in their movies—it started with trendy *English* movie directors, actually—and trendy people with money to spend saw these movies and realized they'd been doing everything wrong. No more bridge, no more horseback riding, no more chamber quartets. *Certainly* no more croquet, no more tennis, no more picnics, no more daytime swimming, no more standing around chatting with a drink in one's hand. Live rock music, flashing lights (strobes, if possible), people in funny clothes, lots of marijuana, girls with sparkly eye make-up; *that's* the ticket.

232

Mel and Wally didn't so much blend into this scene as disappear in it. Since both were obviously unfamous, unsexy, unuseful, and uninteresting, nobody saw them. They walked around the patio side of the house, entered through the open french doors, and *nobody saw them.*

Inside, a five-man rock group was getting along famously without its fifth man, the Fender bassist moaning in ecstasy upstairs. They were getting along *so* famously, in fact, that it was impossible for people to hear one another talk, so Mel merely rapped Wally on the side of the head with a knuckle and pointed toward a staircase visible beyond the next doorway. Wally nodded and went away, rubbing the side of his head.

The statue wasn't downstairs. Mel moved through the throng, taking a puff on a stick here and a stick there, munching a fried chicken leg out of a big silver tureen—the trendy movie directors had never exactly made it clear how the guests were to be fed—and looking everywhere for the statue, but it just wasn't to be seen. After twenty minutes, Mel found himself at the other end of the house, and he stepped outside to clear his head for a minute, get some relief from the rock music, and gaze thoughtfully at the people playing an imaginary game of tennis on the tennis court. (Some imagination; if they were going to be cutesy, the imaginary game to play on a tennis court should obviously be golf.)

"Here's the statue."

The voice, which was Wally's, had come from over Mel's head. Looking up, he saw at first only the clear blue sky of late afternoon, but when he turned a bit he saw Wally himself, standing at an open second-story window with his canvas overnight bag in his hand. "You wouldn't believe what they're doing up here," he said.

"You got the statue?"

"Here," Wally said, and tossed the bag out the window.

It never occurred to Mel to catch it until the thing had already thudded onto the slate walk at his feet. Then he looked down at it, looked up at Wally, and said, "What'd you do that for?"

"I thought you wanted it."

Mel went down on one knee and opened the bag's zipper. Wally called, "Is it the right one?"

Mel withdrew from the bag a broken-off dancing leg. "No," he said, dropped the leg, and ran like hell.

# IN TEXAS . . .

Dallas-Fort Worth; now *there's* an airport. The Descalzans gaping out the tiny windows at all those expanses of gray concrete couldn't believe their eyes. It was as though all the pillboxes from World War II had been gathered together in the same place. No Descalzan eye had ever been able to gaze over such incredible distance without seeing one tree, one dog, one piece of shit. No Descalzan had ever seen such flatness, such smooth regularity. The movie theater in Quetchyl, which had so often showed them the tall buildings of New York and the tall hills of Los Angeles, had never prepared them for such a thing. It was like some early saint's vision of the City of the Dead, full of da Vincian perspective.

The FBI men in bathing suits, pretending to be fuel company employees as they ineptly refueled the plane, seemed so proper to this setting, so clean and gray and nonhuman, that the Descalzans were reduced to nervous laughter at the sight of them. Pointing and giggling, they succeeded only in making the FBI men even more annoyed.

Reporters and photographers and TV news teams had been kept inside one of the squat broad buildings, where they could gaze out at the scene through the huge tinted-glass windows. The Descalzan plane, with its unknown hijacker on his incomprehensible pilgrimage—why would a Quetchylian want so earnestly to go to New York?—was becoming a news sensation. The plane's first three stops, in Central America and Mexico, had fueled both the aircraft and the interest of newsmen everywhere. It was too late now for the network news programs (seven to seven-thirty P.M. Eastern Daylight Time), but blurred footage of the plane being fed gas, lit by the lowering sun, was being transmitted live anyway to television stations all across the country.

In the control tower, FBI men were recording the conversation between the controller and the Descalzan pilot. A part of the conversation went as follows:

"Tower?"

"Yes?"

"We need some clothing here."

"Clothing? Okay. For the hijacker?"

"Well no. For me and the co-pilot and Miss Naz."

"Say again?"

"Miss Naz. Our stewardess."

"Clothing for your stewardess?"

"And the co-pilot and me."

"Why?"

"Well— The fact is, it turns out that landing makes this fellow throw up." The pilot sounded very sad.

# IN AMERICA . . .

Traveling by road from New York to Los Angeles, one enters America somewhere in Pennsylvania and leaves it in northern Utah. The two coasts, which are very similar to one another, are *not* America, nor is Utah, nor is Nevada. In America, for instance, the only place you can be sure of a sensible drink and a decent meal and an inoffensive room for the night is the Holiday Inn, which is not at all true on either coast, nor in Nevada, where there are better places, nor in Utah, where there isn't any place at all. Another difference is that Americans are gregarious friendly smiling people wearing pastels, whereas Coastals are nervous paranoid in-group people wearing either loud colors or black. Yet another difference is that the fifty-five mile speed limit for the most part doesn't exist in America, but Coast people take it *very seriously*. And yet a further difference is that Americans chill their red wine.

Bobbi Harwood entered America, at the wheel of Hugh Van Dinast's Jaguar XJ12, at eleven minutes before ten P.M., and Jerry Manelli, driving his sister Angela's Ford station wagon, entered America seven seconds later. Neither of them noticed.

Bobbi was mostly noticing the Jag. What a terrific car! *Years* of her life wasted on a man who refused to learn how to drive or own a car, while all the time cars like this were being manufactured and sold and operated and parked and traded-in and stolen and fixed and loaned and borrowed all over the world. If she'd needed any more confirmation that she'd made the right move in leaving Chuck, this silver-gray beauty was it.

Jerry too was mostly noticing the Jag, but with more complicated emotions. He'd finally picked up the station wagon from Angela several hours ago, down on Seventh Avenue, while the two women were having lunch. He'd also picked up a sandwich and a cup of coffee to munch on in the car while waiting, and it's just as well he did, since those two women were in the Buffalo Roadhouse *forever*. Jerry, parked across the street in front of the Tamawa Social Club, which happens to be the very seat and substance of Tammany Hall, became bored enough to lie on the ground and howl by the time Bobbi and Madge, full of hamburgers and Bloody Marys, came back to the Jaguar and drove it away on the complicated route—because of one-way streets—required to bring it once again to a stop in front of Madge's apartment. With Bobbi waiting at the wheel, and Jerry waiting at the other wheel half a block behind her, Madge went into the building and came out a few minutes later with the two suitcases.

Jerry gazed at those two suitcases with covetous eyes. Somewhere within one of those bags was the Dancing Aztec Priest, wrapped in a sweater or skirt, surrounded by hair curlers and scarves, Most of the sixteen statues had already been checked out, and the odds were steadily increasing that this was the one, the big one, the million-dollar baby. Jerry could almost see it in there, golden and gleaming, dancing away, green eyes glinting with the knowledge of its secret.

The bags were put in the trunk, and the women had an extended farewell scene on the sidewalk. Embracing, kissing, talking, nodding, more embracing, crying, more talking, more kissing, more crying, more embracing— What were they, a pair of dikes?

All right, already; it was over. Into the Jag went Bobbi, and at last they got moving. Over to Sixth Avenue, up to 31st Street, and a left turn directly into the Lincoln Tunnel traffic jam, backed up halfway across Manhattan Island. What with all the screwing around, Bobbi hadn't managed to get under way until quarter after five, and she and Jerry were stuck in the middle of the rush hour.

They crept through the tunnel, two cars between them, and got to New Jersey fifteen minutes later. A not too painful run across routes 3 and 46, and then at last they were on Interstate 80, and Bobbi immediately put the Jag's ears back and let 'er rip.

Directly into the Vascar trap. "Eighty-three point six in a fifty-five mile zone, miss. License and registration, please."

Jerry, who'd had both feet pressing the accelerator to the floor while the Jag was rapidly dwindling in the distance, had fortunately noticed the anonymous little blue van parked on the side of the road and brought himself back down to sixty-two before the Smokies got a reading. At a demure fifty-five he passed the parked Jag, traveled another four miles, and stopped on the shoulder for ten minutes until she came by again, doing sixty-three and a half.

Neatly and discreetly across New Jersey, over the Delaware River into Pennsylvania at the Water Gap, and by then it was nearly seven and Jerry was getting hungry. Bobbi, however, was still grooving on the car, and once away from Stroudsburg she let it out once more. Jerry, pounding the steering wheel annd kicking the accelerator, strained after her, but over a rise she went and when he topped the rise in his turn she was *gone*.

Son of a bitch, son of a bitch, son of a bitch. He didn't know her ultimate destination, he didn't know where or when she would stop to eat or sleep, and he couldn't count on the Highway Patrol to handicap her for him every damn time.

Maybe she'd slow down after a while. The Ford would run at over ninety, it's just that it couldn't get up there as soon as the Jag. Once she tired of testing the Jag's limits, maybe he could catch up with her.

Unless she left the highway, stopping for a meal or for the night.

Twenty miles, thirty miles, forty miles. No sign of her. Unconsciously he was slowing down a little, thinking things over. Okay, what's the worst that could happen? She could leave the road, and he wouldn't know where. But she'd get *back* on the road, wouldn't she? This thing has to be a long-haul proposition, she isn't taking a car to some place like Erie, Pennsylvania; people don't do that sort of thing, hire an auto transport outfit for some minor little hop. It's to Chicago at the very least, more likely even farther, maybe out to the Coast somewhere.

Okay, fine. He eased even farther off the accelerator, coming down to just over sixty. He could drive through the night, that's all. It would mean a night without sleep, but at a steady sixty he could do it, and *somewhere* along the line he would of necessity pass the place where she had socked in for the night. Then, at six or seven in the morning, he would stop by the side of the road and wait, and sooner or later she would pass him by. It was hell of a way to do things, but it was the only solution he could come up with.

And if she *didn't* pass him tomorrow morning? Well, Madge had to know the final destination, so Jerry could call Angela around eleven in the morning and tell her to have Frank and Floyd go *lean* on Madge and find out where Bobbi Harwood plans to come to earth. So while the situation was completely rotten, it wasn't quite hopeless.

He had just about reached that conclusion when he saw the headlights nearing in the rear-view mirror. Coming fast; a state trooper? Wouldn't *that* be a bitch, after he'd already slowed down. Slowing even more, he watched the headlights grow, watched them rapidly overtake him, and then they swung out and passed on his left, and it was *her!* The Jag's interior light was on, and she was in there eating a sandwich, a plastic coffee cup atop the dashboard. The way she was nodding her head, she had the radio on and was listening to rock music.

Son of a bitch; *she* gets to stop and eat. Jerry accelerated in her wake, and found that now she was doing a steady eighty. Fine. Keep that up, lady, and we'll get along just great.

A few minutes later, her interior light went off. And a few minutes after that, *zip, zip,* they entered America.


# IN LINE . . .

The neat spare office at Winkle, Krassmeier, Stone & Sledge was neat no longer. Meals had been eaten here, cigars and pipes and cigarettes had been smoked here, arguments had raged here, ashtrays and half-full coffee containers and punches had been thrown here, ties and shoes and jackets had been flung off in exhaustion or fury here, and inoffensive plaster statues had been torn to pieces here. The place looked, in short, like a rented summer cottage on September 15.

After the decapitation of the Fayley-Spang statues, there had been only four Dancing Aztec Priests unaccounted for, all held by women: Bobbi Harwood, Felicity Tower, Mrs. Dorothy Moorwood, and Mandy Addleford. Then Mrs.

Dorothy Moorwood finally surfaced, via phone from her estate in New Jersey, sounding all bubbly and gurgly. Oh, there was such a *party* going on, no one could hear the phone at *all!* Oh, the poor Other Oscar, someone dropped it out the window and it just smashed all to *bits!*

Three to go. Then Oscar dialed Felicity Tower's number yet again and damn if this time she wasn't home. (She'd hung around after the funeral for a while, because certainly Bad Death and his associates would be too boorish and blind to know they should treat her like a lady, but all she'd gotten was one nine-year-old boy wanting her to autograph a baseball. "All the best, Tom Seaver," she'd written, and had gone weeping home in a taxi.) Oscar asked his question about the statue, heard about the two sex-crazed white men who had broken it, and finally managed to hang up. "Not Felicity's," he told the others.

But Mandy just refused to be home, so finally Oscar and Bud went up to the Bronx together in search of her, leaving Chuck morosely on the phone, still tracking down his missing wife, while Corella paced the floor with a cigar in his teeth and Krassmeier brooded like an evil walrus on the sofa. These three were still at the same occupations when Oscar and Bud came back two hours later, with more negative news. "Mandy's place was empty," Oscar said. "We broke in, and her statue was there, with a finger missing."

Krassmeier made another notation on the master list. He paused, frowned at the list, counted, counted again, looked around at everyone and said, "Fifteen."

Corella stopped pacing. "Fifteen? One to go?"

"Bobbi," said Oscar. "Bobbi Harwood."

Oscar and Bud and Corella and Krassmeier all turned to look at Chuck Harwood, who was talking on the phone. "Thanks, Madge," he was saying. "Bye." Then he hung up and looked at the four men looking at him and said, "That was a friend of Bobbi's. Some guy she thought was me called for Bobbi there this morning after Bobbi left. Bobbi spent last night there, and she just left in a car for California."

# IN THE MOOD . . .

After dinner, Bobbi sat over a final cup of coffee and

239

watched the old folks dance. "How MUCH Is That Doggie in the Window?" asked the accordion, while the guitar and drums went *chop-chop-chop*, and the fellow holding the clarinet smiled under his long nose at the folks having a good time. (When he smiled, his face was an upside-down T.)

Bobbi had arrived at this Holiday Inn, not very far from Oil City, Pennsylvania, a little after eleven. She had wanted to make it as far as Ohio tonight, but the quick sandwich in her car just hadn't quelled her hunger pangs, and in any event she'd felt herself tiring, so upon seeing this joint's sign she'd come right in, saying to the desk clerk, "Can I still get something to eat?"

"Usually," he'd said, "our kitchen is closed by now, but we're having a high school reunion tonight. If you hurry, you should still have time for dinner."

She'd hurried, and she'd had time for dinner, but her first view of the high school reunion had given her pause. It was a *fiftieth* reunion, a couple of dozen seventy-year-olds chortling and hollering around a bunch of tables connected in a big U next to the dance floor. The waitress, a stocky charmer who'd had a local beauty parlor do its level best to make her natural hair look like a cheap wig, had been smiling and cheerful and gregarious, humanized and sentimentalized by all those beaming survivors. Bobbi had ordered a Gibson on the rocks, Roquefort dressing on the salad, shrimp scampi, neither the baked *nor* the french-fried potatoes, a half-bottle of Blue Nun liebfraumilch, a cup of coffee, and a sambucca. No sambucca? Okay, anisette. (The waitress hadn't been sure about the anisette, but after an extended conference with the bartender back she had come with the clear liquid in a proper little glass.) And now she was sitting and watching the high-school crowd (most of whom had finished their meal with some variation on apricot brandy) table-hop and dance and laugh and wave and tell stories and generally goof around.

Bobbi was not the only nongrad present, three other tables also being occupied. In a corner were a fiftyish couple in pastels and blued hair, who were eating steaks and pointedly not talking to one another; they did their silent quarrel so well that it testified to years of practice. At another table near them was a stout rumpled salesman eating Yankee pot roast and reading a newspaper that seemed to be called the *Meadville Register & Sun-Democrat*. And beyond the celebrators was a youngish man of about Bobbi's own age, eating surf and turf and drinking Heineken's beer and giving the reunion crowd little squints and frowns, as though he didn't quite get it.

Well, in fact, Bobbi didn't quite get it either. It seemed somehow as though that group had some sort of specific reference to herself and her departure from Chuck, but what? Studying them, sipping her coffee and her anisette, she felt herself giving the group the same little squints and frowns as the young man across the way.

Well, what was the story with these oldsters? They were locals, obviously, who had stayed local. Most of them looked reasonably prosperous. The men tended to be dressed in styles rather too young for them, and the women were dressed as though for church. Some of the men seemed to have heard of alcohol before, but every last one of the women was made giggly at the very thought of liquor in a glass.

And were they *all* old grads? No; obviously a few of them were husbands or wives of old grads, though the majority were widows and widowers. Having outlasted their sexually active lives, they were cheerfully returning to the pointless raillery and flirtations of fifty years before, picking up the same jokes and the same playful relationships that had been dropped for grown-up life half a century earlier.

Should I stay with Chuck? Are these people suggesting it doesn't matter, none of it matters, I shouldn't struggle, because all the decisions finally come down to the same place, anyway?

"In Dreams I Kiss Your HAND, Madame" . . . One couple moved alone on the tiny Holiday Inn dance floor, he in powder-blue sports jacket, white shirt, red and black bow tie, pale gray slacks, highly polished black shoes, she in gold slippers and a pink and gold floral design gown like anteroom wallpaper, with a loosely fitting bodice and a tubular skirt. They were doing ballroom dancing together, and they'd *been* doing ballroom dancing together for forty years. They had danced like that to Ray Noble, and now they were dancing the same way to everything the clarinetist could remember about Benny Goodman, which wasn't very much. His hair was dyed black, and her blue-gray hair had been placed in the control of the same Junker beauty operator who had plasticized the waitress, but it didn't matter. They were graceful, smooth, comfortable, and accomplished, and they smiled continuously together. The last time either of them had made a mistake—

241

or surprised the other, for good or for ill—was in 1942.

Their dance was a mating ritual, and much more obviously so than more recent dances. His moves were authoritative, masculine, in command; smooth, capable, easy, and reliable. Her moves were graceful, complementary, feminine, in agreement; not subservient but still auxiliary, necessary but deferential. They were a smoothly functioning team, but not a team of equals.

No, not quite that. They *were* equal, in their importance to the dance, in the scope of movement given each partner, in the relationships between their movements, in the amount of spotlight that each received. But the team nevertheless consisted of a leader and a follower.

The other old grads were watching with great smiles on their faces, laughing out loud at particularly felicitous spins and turns. They weren't so much watching the dance as sharing in it; if a part of their group was capable of this, *all* were capable of it. How many divorces, unhappy marriages, unfaithful husbands and wives, lost loves, missed opportunities were represented at that U-shaped table? Yet, none of them mattered. The couple that had honed its movements, its partnership, its unity for forty years represented them all.

I was right to quit Chuck. Because if it doesn't matter at the end, so what? It's *during* the life that it matters. If Chuck and I were here, with thirty more years together, we wouldn't be the couple on the dance floor, we'd be among the also-rans at the tables, pretending the dancers represented our own lives.

The number ended, and everyone applauded; the old people, Bobbi, the musicians, even the quarreling fifty-year-olds, who were both looking misty-eyed now and who, after the applause, held one another's hands over the dirty dishes. Saved from truth once more.

"If we can prove we're old enough, you think they'll let us dance?"

Bobbi looked up in surprise, and it was the young man from across the room, the Heineken's drinker. Glenn Miller's "In the Mood" was being run through the accordion and clarinet like steak through a meat grinder. The young man had a rather tough-looking face, relieved by a kind of quizzically amused grin and clear level eyes.

*It's a new world,* Bobbi thought. "I'm not as good as *they* are," she said.

"We'll plead youth and inexperience." And he held out his hand for her.

242

She took it.

A good half of the old people were dancing to "In the Mood"; chins rested on shoulders all over the place. The ballroom couple had toned down their movements, but were still the most graceful and charming sight in the county; elsewhere, a certain stiffness harked back yet again to high school dances, except that fifty years ago it had been shyness and now it was sciatica.

Bobbi and the young man stepped onto the floor, and he grinned at her again, saying, "Do you Hustle?"

"To this?"

"It's perfect," he said. "Trust me. Have I ever lied to you?"

He took her hands. *La*-da-da, de-dada, la-da-*da*-de-da Da. Their shoulders, flat and level and set back from their bodies, moved in unison as though operated by a marionettist from above. Their hips had an undulating underslung motion; understated sex. Their feet slid left and right, just above the floor.

"Nice," Bobbi said. She was smiling, and he was smiling. Their hands were warm together. Other dancers, catching their eye, smiled and nodded at them. Everybody was happy. In the corner, the fiftyish couple paid their bill and left, arm in arm. The salesman went away with a newspaper under his arm. The male half of the ballroom dancers caught Bobbi's eye and winked; she laughed, and winked back.

*La*-de-da, de-dada, la-da-*da*-de-da Da.

The next number was "Ease on Down the Road." Bobbi and the young man looked at the musicians in pleased surprise, and the clarinetist nodded at them, smiling his inverted T while doobing through his clarinet.

Ease on dow-own. The ballroom dancers did their best; they frugged or something, without touching. The spear carriers retired. Bobbi and the young man held each other's elbows, and spun around the floor. "My name is Jerry," he said, "and I'm from New York."

"Of course," she said.


# ON THE TRAIL . . .

Jerry said, "Where you heading?"

"Los Angeles," Bobbi said.

The old folks had gone, laughing and shouting into the night. The musicians had packed up their axes, lit up their Trues, and decamped. The waitress, much of her sentimentalism draining away, had requested payment of her checks and had walked from the kitchen to the exit wearing a black-and-red hunting jacket over her white uniform. The bartender had rinsed a hundred glasses, had played the bells on his cash register for ten minutes, and had finally turned off a lot of lights and gone away. And Jerry and Bobbi sat alone in the Holiday Inn dining room, nursing a pair of anisettes and having a conversation.

"Los Angeles?" Jerry shook his head. "Why?"

"Why not?" she said.

Which wasn't an answer, but what the hell. Jerry played it her way: "Because it isn't New York," he said.

"Maybe that's the reason."

Jerry frowned at her in disbelief. "You don't like New York?"

"Well, I'm not a real New Yorker. I only lived there seven years."

"Lady, I was born in Queens," Jerry told her, "and let me tell you something. *Nobody's* a real New Yorker. You get closer, and you get closer, but nobody gets *inside*. You know?"

"No," she said. "*You're* a New Yorker."

He shook his head. "Up till a couple days ago, I hadn't been in Manhattan in four, five years. I used it up when I was in high school, you know? I got to be seventeen, eighteen, I thought I knew about Manhattan, I thought it was a bore, you know what I mean? But all the Manhattan I ever used up was just some dumb kid's *idea* of it. The last couple days, I been in the city, moving around, looking around, and I don't know that place at all. You ever been in Vegas?"

"Where?"

"Las Vegas."

"No. Have you?"

"Sure." Jerry held up a finger. "It's one neighborhood," he said. "That's what every place is, except New York. One neighborhood. You could be in Vegas six days, there wouldn't be anything left you didn't know. I'd like to visit New York sometime, you know? Pretend like my place is a hotel, go out every day, see the city."

She laughed, looking at him with interested eyes. "That's a very funny idea."

"Why not? The first week, do all the tourist stuff: Radio

244

City Music Hall, Statue of Liberty, Empire State Building, Staten Island Ferry, UN Building, all of that. Second week, the stuff that only some of the tourists know, like the Cloisters up at Fort Tryon Park, and the Circle Line, and the Brooklyn Botanic Gardens, and like that. Third week, the nut stuff, things I'd just like to do. Like ride all the subway lines on the same token; you know you can do that? Some kid did it about twenty years ago, took him twenty-four hours. Or how about the Staten Island Rapid Transit; ever hear of that?"

"Never," she said. "What is it?"

"The Toonerville Trolley, that's what it is. You ever go watch the Stock Exchange?"

"No, I never did."

"Neither did I," Jerry said, "and I lived in New York all my life. You can go there and watch them down on the floor. How many places got a Stock Exchange?"

"Very few," she said.

He glanced at her, and then away. Every time he looked across the table at her she was smiling at him as though it was Christmas time and she'd found him under her tree. He'd never had a girl look at him like that before, and especially not a girl he was figuring to rob a little later tonight. It was confusing, and unsettling, and he didn't know what to do about it, so he covered himself by a steady stream of talk. Christ knows what he was talking about.

New York. The girl said, "You know, I never did any of those things. Except the Statue of Liberty, we went there once. But that's all."

"Then you're a New Yorker," he told her. "You gotta be a tourist to see the place. Ever eat in Chinatown?"

"I didn't know where the good places are."

"They're *all* good places, and they all look like crap. I went a few times when I was in high school, I'd like to go back there again. And Rockefeller Center. I used to know a guy in school, he was a nut, he liked to sneak around where people couldn't see him, he fell in love with Rockefeller Center. You know there's a whole other level down underneath, with stores and wide walkways and everything?"

"Oh, sure," she said. "I've gone down there to get out of the rain sometimes. You can go two or three blocks underground."

"You can go all *over* underground," Jerry told her. "This guy claimed he could get out of the subway at Grand Central and walk underground as far as 51st Street and Eighth Avenue. I'd like to find out if that's the truth."

"Oh, I know one!" She was getting caught up in it now. "The escalators at Lincoln Center!"

"Escalators?"

"All the buildings there have huge windows," she explained. "And escalators. A girl I know in the orchestra says it's a *terrific* kick to ride up and down the escalators and look out the windows at the same time. You go up and you start with just the fountain, really, and then there's Ninth Avenue and Broadway, and the traffic, and the other buildings, and it just keeps changing. I've always wanted to do that."

He was dubious, but he said, "Maybe so. And all the museums, that's something else. I went to a couple of them on class trips when I was a kid, but whadaya get out of something like that? Nothing. Who knows, maybe today I'd get a kick out of it."

"Like the Fire Department Museum," she said. "You'd *have* to love that one."

"Fire Department? Where's that?"

"Way downtown, near City Hall. It's full of terrific old fire engines. A friend of mine took me there one time. You *have* to see it."

"Okay," Jerry said. "As soon as I get back. Or, should I wait for you, and you'll take me?"

"I'm not going back," she said, but she didn't sound happy about it. Positive, yes. Defiant, yes. But not happy.

"You're not going back? Never?"

"I've left my husband," she said, "and it's for real, and I'm never going back."

"To him, or to New York?"

"Neither."

"How come? Is he the mayor?"

"What?" She looked blank for a second, and then she laughed. "It's all connected in my mind," she said. "It's a journey into independence. Or does that sound stupid?"

"No, I can see that," he said. "If you're making a big move, you want to make a *move*."

"Right," she said. "If I'm leaving, I'm *leaving*."

"Sure," he agreed. "If you're throwing out the bath water, you might as well throw out the baby."

She frowned at him. "Somehow that doesn't sound the same."

"Why would anybody want to live anywhere except New

246

York?" he asked her. "You're quits with your husband, so you punish yourself by living in some tank town somewhere."

"Los Angeles isn't a tank town."

"The hell it isn't. Los Angeles is three Long Islands next to each other. But no Midtown Tunnel."

Laughing, she said, "If you're so crazy about New York, what are you doing way out here in the provinces?"

"Business," he said. "I'm coming out to get something, and then I'm going right back."

"All right," she said. "But what if everybody felt the way you do? What if everybody wanted to live in New York?"

"They do. That's why they all hate New York so much—it's envy. But you know who the big guy is in the social set in Indianapolis? The one that just got back from a trip to New York. He could go to Chicago or St. Louis or any damn place, and all people say is, 'How was the trip?' New York is the only place in this country he could go, when he gets back people say, 'Tell me all about it.' "

She laughed again, and said, "Maybe *you're* the mayor."

"I'm not so dumb," he said, and a fellow in a yellow blazer came over to apologize, and to say they wanted to close up the dining room now for the night. "Sure thing," Jerry said, and the two of them walked out to the semidark lobby.

The original idea in Jerry's head had been that he would scratch up an acquaintance with Bobbi Harwood, hustle her into bed—in *her* room—and grab the statue once she was asleep. He could be on his way back to the city before sun-up, he could be in Mel's living room—either with the golden statue, or with proof that this wasn't the right one—before noon. That had been the original idea, but something had gone wrong somewhere, and now he didn't know what the hell to do.

The problem was, she liked him. The other problem was, he liked her. Who could expect a thing like that from some ditzy broad that throws her husband's clothes out the window and takes off like an asshole for California? Who could expect that she *wouldn't* be a ditzy broad after all—except for maybe that Lincoln Center escalator idea—or that she would have such a nice friendly smile, or that she would act like a real human being instead of a bar pickup?

But without the original idea Jerry didn't have any idea at all, so it was with some variant on Plan A still in mind that he

247

now said, "I'd ask you up to my room for a nightcap, but I don't have anything to drink. But I'd like to go on talking."

"So would I," she said, smiling. "I wish I could. This has been a lot of fun, Jerry. You make me think I might want to visit New York someday."

"It's a rotten place to visit," he told her. "Do you want me to tell you why?"

"Yes," she said, "but don't do it. I'd love to talk with you till morning, but I put in a seven-thirty call, and I've got a lot of driving to do tomorrow." She held out her hand; the friendly brushoff. "I really did enjoy meeting you, Jerry."

He took her hand, but didn't immediately release it. "Any reason you have to get up that early?"

"Several," she said. "But the one that counts right now is that I'm not going to be a runaway wife shacking up with a strange guy her first night on the road."

He released her hand and stepped back, a pained smile on his face. "All of a sudden, I run out of arguments."

"I did enjoy meeting you, Jerry," she said, and they exchanged a few more words in the same vein, and then she went away to her room and he went away to a phone booth and put in a call to Mel.

Who answered in person: "Yeah?"

"Mel?"

"Jerry! By God, what happened to you?"

"I'm out in the middle of nowhere. What's happening back there?"

"She's got it, Jerry!"

"What? Who?"

"Bobbi Harwood!" Mel's voice was running up and down its range, full of excitement, and behind him several other voices could be heard whooping and shouting.

"Bobbi Harwood?"

"*All* the others are checked out– It's *her*, Jerry, it's definitely her!"

For some reason he hated that. "Great," he said. "I'm on her trail."

"Go get her, tiger," Mel said.

"Right," said Jerry.

# AT JFK . . .

"Foreigners," said the driver of the CBS remote unit truck. "That's what it is; it's foreigners, they don't know shit."

"You can say that again," said the announcer, a guy named Jay Fisher, sitting beside him in the cab. The truck was a huge monster full of equipment, including its own generator, and it could send live pictures direct to the studio in Manhattan, which is what it was going to do as soon as those South American assholes in that South American asshole of an airplane got the hell onto the ground and got this goddam business over with.

The driver said it again: "They don't know shit," he said. "An American, now, he'd come down in prime time, am I right? Make his point when there's somebody around to listen. Look what the hell time it is," he said, and looked at his own watch to see. "Five minutes after fuckin' three o'clock in the morning. Who the hell's up now?"

"You and me," said the announcer.

Inside the plane from Descalzo, circling for its final approach, drama had given way to exhaustion. The air conditioning had failed over northern Louisiana, and most of the passengers were now sprawled out asleep, with their mouths open; just like home. The pilot, the co-pilot, the stewardess, and Pedro himself were all dressed in strange oddments of this and that; for the pilot, it was the fifth complete set of clothing this trip. Fortunately, however, by Mobile, Alabama, Pedro had finally become inured to the processes of landing and taking off, and there had been no unfortunate incidents either there or later in Columbia, South Carolina, the ultimate refueling stop before New York. Perhaps relevant to that, there was also no more gluppe aboard, and Pedro was becoming increasingly sober. If he weren't so weary that he could barely keep his eyelids and gun raised, he would be terrified out of his mind.

Back in the passenger compartment, Edwardo and José *were* terrified out of their minds. They kept staring out the windows at all those lights down below; rows of lights, clusters of lights, masses of lights. At three o'clock in the morning, in

249

a world of pitch-blackness, lights everywhere, white and amber and red. *That* was a civilization, by God!

Back in Quetchyl, the idea of hijacking an airplane to New York and then casually walking away in the confusion had seemed both clever and realistic, but the millions of lights told them, more than anything else, that they were about to face authorities who were less mean than Descalzan authorities only because they were so much smarter. They didn't *need* terror to do their jobs; they had brains instead. And light. And experience. And they'd seen bush leaguers before.

"We'll just walk away," Edwardo whispered, his tongue tripping fuzzily over the consonants.

"Yes yes," José said. He had the window seat, and he was staring down at all those lights.

On the ground, the CBS remote unit deployed itself within the area permitted by the police. Live shots presented a long-distance view of a really rotten landing; *SMASH*, went the DC-3, SMASH, *smash, smash, bap-bap-bap, rattle rattle rattle*, bouncing itself halfway down the runway, every thud making a noise like a television set dropped out a window. Sleepers bit their tongues, and awoke to a world gone mad. Phillips-head screws rained down onto the runway in the plane's wake, small pieces fell off and clanged away, and a lot of mice fell out of the overhead storage racks, wisps of wicker clenched in their teeth.

In the racketing command cabin, the crew flinched from Pedro, but his stomach was utterly empty, and his esophagus muscles were worn to a frazzle, and the worst he could come up with was a burp. Clinging to various metal projections with one hand, and to the madly waving gun with the other, Pedro fouled the air but nothing else, and at last the plane quivered to a halt and silence descended, like the mice.

The pilot, bleary-eyed and as worn as Pedro's esophagus, panted a little and then said, "All right, what now?"

"Everybody off the plane," Pedro said.

The pilot spoke to the control tower, and shortly a lot of FBI men disguised as airport personnel surrounded the plane, and Lupe Naz opened the door, and the passengers all tottered out. The FBI men pointed many fingers toward the nearby terminal building, and the passengers staggered away.

Then the crew and Pedro came out, and a whole *bunch* of FBI men jumped on Pedro, who offered no resistance. He was hustled into the terminal building and into a fairly large room that had been set aside for this scene. The passengers were already in there, milling about and asking for the bathroom, and now an FBI man with an exquisite Castilian accent demanded of Pedro, in Spanish "Jutht what do you thuppothe you're doing?"

Pedro had never heard Castilan Spanish in his life, and all he could do was blink. "I don't speak English," he explained.

Another agent, who had been a Guevara-chaser back before switching to a domestic job, spoke to Pedro in the rotten slurred disgusting Spanish of Descalzo: "Whadaya trina do?"

Now, this was a question Pedro had known he would be asked, but which he could not answer truthfully, not if José and Edwardo were to get away. So Pedro had to tell a lie, and he had spent the last several hours deciding what lie he should tell. It had to be believable. It had to explain why he had gone to all this trouble to hijack an airplane to New York City. And now he gave the answer he'd finally decided on:

"I wanted to go to Radio City Music Hall."

The FBI man looked at him. Except for the whine of passengers asking for the bathroom, there wasn't a sound in the room. Until all at once Lupe Naz, girl stewardess, yelled out, "Stop them! They're his collaborators!"

The FBI men all spun around, and there were José and Edwardo halfway out the door. "Hey!" said the FBI men.

"Bathroom!" Edwardo cried, with gestures. "Men's room! Great urgency!"

"They're part of the gang!" cried Lupe Naz, as several FBI men laid hands on Edwardo and José. "They're all in it together!"

"No no!" cried Edwardo. "I never saw that hijacker before in my life!"

"They were in the men's room together!" cried Lupe Naz. "They are hijackers and deviants!"

Now, FBI men and hijackers have a comprehensible relationship, a simple matter of property rights, but between FBI men and deviants there is only a gulf, an abyss. The idea that these people had been in a DC-3 lavatory together was so repellent to these FBI men that their eyes lost all color, becoming slate gray, like the November sky just before a snowstorm.

Edwardo and José were shouting all manner of denials when they were upstaged by yet another event. Among the passengers in the plane, it will be remembered, were an American doctor on a malnutrition survey for the United Nations, and his Canadian assistant-mistress. The doctor, a man with a wife and three children in Racine, Wisconsin, having noticed that a UPI photographer had slipped into the room and was taking pictures of him consoling his assistant in a not entirely medical manner, now gave a whoop and a holler, flung his assistant-mistress from him, and began to wrestle with the photographer for his camera.

Several of the FBI men turned their attention to this new ridiculousness. The rest kept their attention on Edwardo and José. The remaining passengers milled around, bleating for the bathroom.

Pedro could use a bathroom himself. The door behind him was open, and possibly led to a rest room. Stepping through it, he turned right and walked for some time, and then saw a door with a silhouette of a man on it. Yes?

Yes. Pedro relieved himself, extensively, and then took a moment to wash his face and hands and neck and elbows and feet at the wondrous row of pearly white sinks along one wall. What a bathroom this was! All of the bathrooms in Quetchyl put together didn't have as much equipment as this, nor as varied, nor as clean and shiny. Pedro stayed in the bathroom for quite some time, admiring it, running water, flushing toilets, frowning in perplexity at the urinals—what were *they* for?—and generally having a terrific touristy time. Finally it occurred to him he ought to get back—those FBI men might get angry if he kept them waiting—so he left the men's room and with some difficulty found his way back to the room he'd left, and it was empty.

They'd gone ahead without him.


# IN THE PARKING LOT . . .

Three-fifteen in the morning. Darkness and silence everywhere. In the parking lot of the Holiday Inn along Interstate 80 near Oil City, Pennsylvania, *snick* goes the hood release of Hugh Van Dinast's Jaguar XJ12. Jerry pauses, looks around, hears and sees nothing, and goes to work.

Twelve cylinders, that's a lot of cylinders. It's also a lot of spark plugs. One by one, Jerry removes each spark plug and uses a screwdriver blade to widen the gap. When each plug has been altered sufficiently so it won't spark, it is neatly put back in place. It is not enough that this car not run tomorrow;

it is also necessary that any mechanic called in have a difficult time deciding *why* the car won't run.

Eleven, twelve. So much for that. Next, Jerry uses the same screwdriver to turn the air-flow screw on the carburetor right down tight. There; try driving with *that* mixture.

And another thing. The tools from Angela's station wagon include an icepick; sliding under the Jag with that, Jerry pokes it through the automatic transmission pan. Ochre fluid drips thickly down, and Jerry emerges again, to alter the pressure on the fan belt, so that it won't turn with the engine.

Is that enough? Probably; as it is, the mechanic is going to wonder how the damn thing ever got this far. Jerry closes up the Jag, returns the tools to the station wagon, and goes back up to his room and to bed. His call is in for nine o'clock. He isn't worried; his quarry will still be here.


## AROUND THE CIRCLE . . .

Nearly everyone is asleep. Four in the morning, and nearly everyone sleeps, and why not? It's been a busy day.

In the Bernstein house, Mel and Angela are asleep in one another's arms. Both are smiling, Mel because Angela is in his arms and Angela because Mandy has agreed to stay. In the guest room, Mandy also sleeps and also smiles; this is a *much* better gig than Valerie Woode.

Frank and Floyd McCann are asleep in their separate beds with their separate wives. Frank is smiling in his sleep, because he is dreaming of gold. Floyd is frowning in his sleep, because he is dreaming of blacks.

Augie Corella, asleep beside his plump wife in his expensive house in Red Bank, New Jersey, has no expression on his blocky face at all. He looks like something in a wax museum.

Victor Krassmeier, having informed his wife that he would be staying in town tonight due to the pressure of work, is sleeping with the occupant of the apartment on 65th Street, who figures so prominently in his negative cash-flow. Neither of them is smiling.

Oscar Russell Green and Chuck Harwood are both asleep in Chuck's apartment, and despite the day's setbacks both are smiling, since they blew a whole *lot* of grass after dinner.

253

In Connecticut, Bud Beemiss sleeps fitfully beside his expensive second wife; his dreams are full of lifelines slipping through his fingers.

Felicity Tower's dreams are also full of fingers, among many other things. She never never never remembers her dreams the next day, but they sure do keep her smiling at night.

Awake, but soon to be asleep, is Wally Hintzlebel, who is sitting at the kitchen table with his mom, saying for the thousandth time, "You know I didn't mean it, Mom." Mom, unfortunately, has remembered *every word* that Wally said to her during this morning's argument, and has been more than willing to share her memories with Wally.

Also awake, but also soon to be asleep, are Jeremiah "Bad Death" Jonesburg and Theodora Nice. There was no way Bad Death could keep himself from talking to "Pam Grier" after the funeral, and Theodora hadn't at all minded maintaining the fiction up close, and they are having an evening neither will ever forget. *Ter-rif-fic!*

Also awake, and not likely to sleep for some time, are Edwardo Brazzo and José Caracha. Sitting in adjoining cells, charged with more violations than there are yams in Descalzo, what *really* frosts them is that *Pedro got away.* Unless their belated appeal for political asylum is accepted by a not particularly amiable American government, they will both be back in Descalzo within the week, hanging by their tongues. It's enough to keep anybody awake.

As for Pedro, he is sleeping like a baby. Having wandered around Kennedy Airport for some time, he eventually stumbled on Jerry's cul-de-sac, and in it Jerry's truck, and he is now in the truck, sound asleep on Jerry's coveralls. *None* of which Jerry can be expected to like.

Jerry Manelli and Bobbi Harwood, in beds separated by seven walls and eleven other sleeping bodies, are dreaming of one another. The dreams are tentative, the characters keep getting mixed up with other characters both have known in the past, and nothing really conclusive occurs in any of the dreams, but nevertheless both dreamers are smiling.

Awake on the Holiday Inn dresser in Bobbi's room, prancing and dancing, glittering gold in the dim light gleaming through the gap in the window drapes, stands the Dancing Aztec Priest. To look at him, nobody would think he was at all valuable, and in fact he is not. He's the wrong one, he's made of plaster.

What? That's right, he's a copy, he isn't gold at all, everybody's chasing the wrong statue. *One* of the sixteen statues handed out to the Open Sports Committee is the real one, worth over a million dollars, but not *this* one. This one is maybe worth twenty bucks.

Someone has made a mistake.

# THE
# THIRD PART
# OF THE
# SEARCH

Everybody in New York City wants to be somebody. Young people want to be older and old people want to be younger. Poor people want to be rich and rich people want to be richer. First nighters want to be hip and last nighters want to be hipper.

Blacks want to be equal. Women want to be equal. Puerto Ricans want to be equal without having to learn a new language. Sanitation men want to be equal with the other uniformed services. Jews who claim their middle name is their last name want to be superior, while drunks who hang around Third Avenue and East Houston Street want to be inferior.

*New York* magazine wants to be *The New Yorker*.

Outsiders want to be insiders. Singles at Adams' Apple and Maxwell's Plum want to be doubles, without getting hurt. Drag queens *don't* want to be women; they want to be drag queens.

Cab drivers want to be Bobby Unser, and subway riders want to be sitting down. Architects want to be artists, and artists want to be useful.

Priests want to be relevant. Novelists want to be relevant. Eric Sevareid and David Susskind want to be relevant. Andy Warhol wants to be irrelevant, and is.

High schoolers from Staten Island want to be sharp. High schoolers from Brooklyn want to be cool. High schoolers from Queens want to be funky. High schoolers from Harlem want to be the baddest. And high schoolers from the High School of Music and Art in Manhattan want to be Leonard Bernstein.

Leonard Bernstein wants to be *everybody*.

The Landmarks Commission wants to be effective. The real estate developers want to be 100 percent leveraged. The powerless want to be powerful, and the powerful want to be unobserved.

Wall Street clerks want to be financiers, financiers want to be great lovers, great lovers want to be serious actors, serious actors want to be called to the Coast.

Cops want to be cowboys. Cowboys want to be sophisticates. Sophisticates want to be liberal. Liberals want to be tough-minded. The tough-minded want to be in charge. Those in charge want to be chauffeured, and chauffeurs want to be in the driver's seat. Everybody wants to be in the driver's seat, but nobody is.

Everybody in New York City wants to be somebody. Every now and then, somebody makes it.


## THE HERO . . .

Jerry Manelli wanted to be a tough guy. Growing up in a neighborhood like his, a smart guy learns to be a wise guy, and a wise guy knows how to be a tough guy. Jerry Manelli never wanted anything except to be a tough guy, and a tough guy was what he had always been.

But does a tough guy grin for no reason at all? Does a tough guy hum "In the Mood" and dance with his reflection in the bathroom mirror?

The hell with it; *this* tough guy does.

Jerry's wake-up call was for nine, but he'd been up since eight-thirty, his mind fuzzy and full of confusions. After brushing his teeth with his fingers and putting on yesterday's clothes, he looked out the window and saw below him the tableau in the parking lot; arm-waving girl, shoulder-shrugging mechanic, raped Jaguar, massive tow-truck. And does a tough guy feel guilty when one of his hustles work out?

The phone: "Good morning, Mr. Spaulding. Nine o'clock."

"Thanks," Jerry said, and went away to breakfast.


## THE HEROINE . . .

Bobbi was *furious*. After dragging herself out of bed at seven-thirty this morning—a cold empty bed, too, since she'd so nobly resisted that fellow Jerry last night—and after rushing through a mediocre breakfast, the *car* wouldn't *start*. Nothing at all from it, just nothing. The starter would grind, but the engine simply refused to operate.

At Beacon Auto Transport, back in New York, she'd been told what to do in case anything went wrong with the car. Take it to a garage or call a mechanic, and if the repair would cost less than twenty-five dollars she was authorized to spend the money, get a receipt, and expect reimbursement from the owner on delivery of the car. If it would cost over twenty-five dollars, she was to call the owner, turn him over to the mechanic, and let them work it out together.

"Let it be less than twenty-five dollars," she muttered to herself, as the nice desk clerk phoned for a mechanic, and when the mechanic arrived with his tow-truck she told him the situation at once, finishing, "So if it's *under* twenty-five, it'll be a lot simpler for everybody."

"Uh huh," he said. He had a flowing brown mustache and black hornrim glasses and a dirty white T-shirt stretched over his beer belly, and he didn't seem to much care about anything at all. He sat at the wheel of the Jaguar—he couldn't have looked more out of place in a convent—grinding the starter and gazing mistrustfully at the instruments, and then he shook his head and got out of the car and opened the hood. After poking and prying under there for a while, he said "Start 'er up."

Bobbi slid in at the driver's seat, hope suddenly blossoming inside her, and turned the key in the ignition. *Grind grind grind,* while the mechanic did something or other under the hood. She stopped finally, hating the noise, but he gestured at her to do it some more. She did, but then at last he withdrew his head from under the hood and shook it at her, as much as to say, this-thing'll-never-live-again.

Bobbi was reluctant to leave the wheel. Leaning out, she said, "Do you know what it is?"

"Could be a lot of things." He was wiping his hands on an already filthy orange cloth.

"Well, can you find out which one?"

"Not here," he said. "Have to take it in."

"*Tow* it?"

He shrugged. "Ain't gonna move on its own, lady."

Bobbi got out of the car, abandoning hope. "That's more than twenty-five dollars, isn't it? This is going to cost a *lot,* isn't it?"

"Depends what it turns out to be."

"But more than twenty-five."

"Probably so," he admitted. "The tow's fifteen."

"We'll have to call the owner," Bobbi decided, and she couldn't have hated that knowledge more. The idea of contact with Hugh Van Dinast on *any* subject was distasteful, but to have to tell him that his car had broken down within a day of her taking charge of it was doubly grim.

Still, she never expected the response she got, once Van Dinast had accepted the collect call and she'd told him the situation: *"You* did it!" he screamed. "To get even with me!"

*"What?"*

"What a filthy, sneaking—"

He probably went on like that, but Bobbi listened to no more of it. Instead, she handed the receiver to the mechanic, saying, "Tell him about it."

"Right." But after listening for a second he said, "He's talking to somebody."

"That's all right. Just tell him."

"Okay." Into the receiver he said, "Hello? Hello?" There was a little pause, and he said, "I'm from Coe's Garage, here in Oil City, Pennsylvania." Another pause. "My name's Tucker, what's yours?" Apparently, whatever Van Dinast was saying back there in New York was not sitting too well, because the mechanic raised an eyebrow at Bobbi while saying into the phone, "I'll tell you, pal, I got all the business I need. That Jag of yours can sit in this parking lot till kingdom come for all I care." Another pause. "Just a second." Cupping his hand over the mouthpiece, he said to Bobbi, "He wants to know did you sabotage the car."

"Of course not! Let me have *that* phone!" Snatching it from his willing hand, she shouted into the mouthpiece, "If I *was* going to wreck your stupid car, I'd do it in *California,* you imbecile! I don't want *me* to sit in this parking lot till kingdom come!"

"I'll speak to Mr. Tucker, if you don't mind," Van Dinast said.

"Asshole!" Bobbi slapped the phone back into the mechanic's hand, telling him, "If you want me, I'll be in the bar."

"I don't think it's open yet."

"We'll see about that," Bobbi said, and marched away.

# THE RIVALS . . .

Ginny Demeretta didn't know *what* to think. She'd been an interviewer with Beacon Auto Transport for seven years, and she'd *never* had a day like this one. Working in an operation where on the one hand you have people too rich to drive their own car, and on the other hand hippies and flake-outs with bedrolls, you can expect the job isn't exactly going to be tame, but *never* a day like this. Never. And to think it all had to do with that nice Mrs. Barbara Harwood. Of all the drivers Ginny Demeretta had interviewed in the last seven years, Mrs. Barbara Harwood was the *last* one she'd expect to make trouble.

In the first place, Mrs. Harwood wasn't really poor. She was broke, but as Mike Todd used to point out, that isn't the same thing. In the second place, she was a respectable ongoing member of the middle class. *Harpist* with the New York City Symphony Orchestra! And in the third place, the owner of the car, Mr. Hugh Van Dinast, had phoned yesterday afternoon especially to say how pleased he was with the person chosen to drive his car. Now, a thing like that *never* happens, an owner calling to say he's happy about something. Never.

But that was yesterday. As for today . . .

It started exactly at ten A.M., as Ginny was walking in the door. Mickey, the receptionist and switchboard girl, was nodding and talking on the phone, her head down and shoulders hunched in that inevitable way when the shit is hitting the fan, and when she looked up and saw Ginny a relieved smile covered her face and she said into the phone, "Excuse me, Mr. Van Dinast. Here she is now."

"Oh, shit," Ginny said. But it was too late to duck back out the door.

Mickey was waggling the phone at her, saying, "One of yours, left yesterday. The owner says she racked up the car."

"Racked it up?"

"On purpose."

"Beautiful," Ginny said. "Wait a minute; did you say Van Dinast?"

"Right. The driver's a——"

"Mrs. Harwood." Shaking her head, Ginny said, "There's something wrong here. I'll take it at my desk."

"Better you than me," Mickey said.

Ginny settled herself at her desk, popped a Tum, picked up the phone, pushed the right button, and said, "What appears to be the problem, Mr. Van Dinast?"

"The problem?" His voice was an enraged squeak, with intermitting bass notes. "The problem is, your driver deliberately destroyed my car!"

"Deliberately destroyed, Mr. Van Dinast? If there was an accident of——"

262

"This was no accident! She called with some lame story that the car won't *start* this morning! She has a *mechanic!* She *says* he's a mechanic! She vandalized my car!"

"Mr. Van Dinast, you can't mean that. Why would she do such a thing?"

"Well, she—I presume she's insane, that's why!"

"Mr. Van Dinast, did the mechanic say the car had been vandalized?"

"He's *her* mechanic!"

"Here in New York?"

"In Oil City, Pennsylvania! *Oil City*, Pennsylvania!"

"Then he's hardly her mechanic, Mr. Van Dinast. Who told you she'd vandalized your car?"

"Nobody *had* to tell me! I *know* she did it!"

"Why?"

There was silence on the line; in it, Ginny could hear heavy breathing. "Mr. Van Dinast," she said, "you're making a very serious accusation here. I assume you've called the Oil City, Pennsylvania, police."

"Not yet." And all at once Van Dinast sounded oddly defensive.

Hmmm. Had the son of a bitch thrown a pass at Mrs. Harwood yesterday? Is that why he thought she'd vandalized his car? Getting even. Good Christ, maybe she *did* vandalize it!

"Well, Mr. Van Dinast, I'll certainly look into this, but before you make accusations, I—"

"I'm not making accusations," he said, with astonishing inaccuracy. "I just don't want her to drive the car any more, that's all."

"But what if it turns out she *didn't* vandalize your car?"

"I don't want her to drive it!"

"I have your number, Mr. Van Dinast. Let me check with our driver in Oil City, and I'll get back to you. Do you have the number there?"

He gave it, a Holiday Inn; she *was* traveling first cabin. Ginny called and got Mrs. Harwood's side of the story. The car had been working fine yesterday, it didn't work at all this morning, the mechanic said it could be a lot of things, and when she'd called the owner as per instructions, he'd blown up at her. "Hm," said Ginny. "Listen, Mrs. Harwood. Did he try anything with you yesterday?"

"He got very grabby, if that's what you mean. I fought him off."

"Successfully?"

"Of course!"

"He thinks you're trying to get even with him."

"Getting *away* from him was all I needed."

Ginny sighed. "What a mess. He says he doesn't want you driving the car any more. I don't know *what* we'll do."

"You mean I'm stuck here in Oil City, Pennsylvania?"

"I'll get back to you," Ginny said, and called Van Dinast again, and he was *much* calmer. "I may have been hasty," he said.

"I thought you probably were," Ginny told him.

"Nevertheless," he said, "I can't be sure one way or the other, and I would prefer that . . . she, not drive my car any longer. I'll pay the fee, of course, but I'll arrange to have the car picked up and transported."

Well, she argued with him, she tried to jolly him, she implied her knowledge of his bad behavior of yesterday, but nothing would budge him. Mrs. Harwood was not to drive his car ever again; he would pay the company's fee, and he would make his own further arrangements regarding the car.

So she called Mrs. Harwood back, and broke the news, saying, "I'm sorry, Mrs. Harwood. If you can get a bus back to the city or something, I could probably get you into another car the early part of next week."

"*Back* to the city." She sounded very depressed.

"Sorry," Ginny said. "Give me a call when you get back."

"Sure."

Ginny hung up, and at that point discovered an individual seated in the client's chair at the side of her desk. He flashed an untrustworthy smile with a rancid cigar stuck in the middle of it, and he was wearing a powder-blue shirt with a white collar, a broad powder-blue tie with tiny white windmills all over it, an off-white sports jacket with powder-blue stitching, powder-blue slacks with a white belt, and white patent-leather shoes. Ginny's guess was that he was a pickpocket disguised as the Virgin Mary. "And what can I do for *you?*" she said.

"Information," he said, leering, and placed a palm on the surface of the desk. Through the slightly spaced fingers she could see a touch of green, a bit of currency, a twenty-dollar bill.

Never in her life had Ginny Demeretta ever been offered a bribe. What would anybody bribe her for? She didn't know anything, she didn't have any clout anywhere, and none of her decisions made any difference. Ginny's immediate reaction, therefore, was suspicion; she frowned at the twenty, glowered at its offerer, and said, "What's that for?"

"Like I said. Information." And he made a little go-on-and-take-it gesture with his chin.

"Information. Information? *What* information?"

"About Mrs. Barbara Harwood."

Suspicion deepened. Ginny glanced at the phone, so recently full of the subject of Mrs. Barbara Harwood. What was going on with that woman? If this was a private detective—and on television bribes were *invariably* offered by private detectives—what had that nice lady got herself mixed up in?

"Don't worry," the private detective told her, with a smile that would have made anybody worry. "You can't get in any trouble for this."

"And Mrs. Harwood?"

He looked surprised. "Mrs. Harwood? I'm on her side!"

"Against Van Dinast?"

Was that doubt, briefly on his face? If so, it cleared up at once, replaced by a confident smile as he said, "Absolutely! Against Van Dinast!"

She wasn't sure of him yet; personally, she thought he was a creep. "What do you want to know?"

"Her present location, and her final destination."

"No." She shook her head.

He seemed surprised. The hand covering the twenty nearly lifted. He said, "Why not?"

"Maybe you *aren't* on her side."

"But I am! And I have to get in touch with her, right away."

"Then you don't need to know her final destination."

He didn't like that, but he recovered. With a shrug, he said. "Fine. Present location, that's all I need."

Could that be harmful? This fellow would be able to phone Mrs. Harwood, but he'd never physically reach Oil City before she'd left it. "Okay," Ginny said, and gave him the information, and the twenty-dollar bill disappeared into her desk drawer. She'd been bribed!

And all at once the private detective was on his feet, smile gone, expression anxious, noxious cigar smoke fuzzing his head as he leaned close and harshly whispered, "Tell them nothing! I'll go out the back way!"

"There *isn't* any back way," she said, but he'd already trotted away toward the filing cabinets, and now she saw the two new men who had just walked in, and who were pointing in surprise and anger toward the fleeing private eye.

On television, these two would be plainclothes police. One was white, and the other was black. Both were tall and moderately well-built and in early middle age. Both were

265

dressed rather seedily, and the white was dressed *very* seedily. In fact, his shoes didn't match. Even Columbo has shoes that match.

"Hey!" the black man yelled. He had a speaker's voice, with good projection. He and the other one started down the long office space past the row of interviewers' desks.

Ginny turned, and saw the first one coming back from the dead-end wall, a big insincere smile spreading like a stocking-run across his face. "Well, hello, fellows!" he said. "You're up bright and early."

"Yeah," said the black man. "And we caught us a worm." *Exactly* what he would have said on television. Ginny watched, fascinated.

But now the scene took a turn into some other plot, because the alleged private eye stopped in front of the alleged cops, and smiled at them, and said, "You don't think I'd try to cut you boys out, do you?"

The white had taken a pipe from his pocket, and now he smiled in a calm and amiable way, pointed the pipe at the non-private eye, and said, "My good friend, of *course* that's what you'd try to do. You're too stupid to do anything else."

"Such kidders," said the nonprivate eye, with a big confident grin. "I got the info and I was on my way to the office. Can I give you fellows a lift?"

"You sure can," said the black man, and the three of them walked out of the office together.

Ginny gazed after them, frowning. Should Mrs. Harwood be told? Should *Van Dinast* be told? It was, after all, his car. Who was the villain in this piece, anyway?

Maybe what Beacon Auto Transport ought to do, maybe Beacon Auto Transport ought to mind its own business. "Next!" said Ginny.


# THE SURVIVOR . . .

There are three kinds of hangovers. There are hangovers that are green and wet and slimy, full of queasiness and trembling and the conviction that one has somehow been disemboweled in one's sleep and a recently dead muskrat has been placed where one's stomach used to be. Then there are hangovers that are gray and stony and cold, in which the granite of one's skull has been cracked like the veil of the temple, and the rock of one's brain has been reduced to rubble within, *painful* rubble. And finally there are hangovers that are red and jagged and jolting, lightning bolts shooting in one ear and out the other, more lightning in the elbows and knees, buzzers and electric chairs and whoopee cushions in the stomach, flash bulbs in the eyes and battery acid in the mouth. Those are the three kinds of hangovers, and Pedro had all three of them.

When he staggered out of the Inter-Air truck into the semidarkness of Jerry's cul-de-sac, Pedro had no memory of the preceding day and could only assume that he was still in Quetchyl and that the city had for some reason been hydrogen-bombed during the night. Surely he was the only survivor, if he could in truth be called a survivor.

"Hii," Pedro said, staggering this way and that over the neat white lines Jerry had drawn on the concrete. "Hii hii hii."

Gradually his staggering led him away from the truck, away from the darkness, up the curving ramp and around the wooden fences toward light and day and—

—Kennedy Airport.

"Hu!" said Pedro. With both hands pressed to his forehead, partially to keep it from exploding and partially to shield his eyes, Pedro squinted in the sunlight and stared out at John F. Kennedy International Airport, New York, New York. A yellow taxicab went by. A bus went by. Taxi-bus-car-car-car-van-taxi-taxi-bus-car-bus-car-car-taxi-van-bus-taxi-taxi  went by. Beyond all this sweeping movement swept a broken expanse of intermixed greenery and roadways, fringed by terminal buildings. Sunshine griddled down, turning Pedro's eyes and brain to goat fat.

And bringing memory. Hijack! New York! Gluppe! *Hiiiii*—Pedro staggered backward into the wooden fence and slowly slid down it till he was seated on the concrete. *He* was the one who was supposed to be arrested, and *José and Edwardo* were supposed to get the money and rescue him. Those job assignments made sense; Pedro would be very good at being arrested, and José and Edwardo would be very good as rescuers. The other way around made no sense, it was hopeless.

"Hey, brother. What's the problem?"

Pedro was still too befuddled and miserable even to be surprised at having understood the question, which had been spoken in Spanish. Looking, squinting under his protective awning of hands, he saw a smiling round olive face fronted by a bushy black mustache. The fellow was perhaps thirty, short and slender, in open-necked white shirt and black trousers, and a laminated card pinned to his shirt pocket identified him as an employee of Air Canada. He had been on his way to the employee bus stop when he'd noticed Pedro sitting here, and now he said, "You need help or anything?"

"I drank too much," Pedro told him. His throat hurt when he talked.

His new friend laughed, the way people always do when faced with this particular kind of misery. "Hung over, huh?" Then, with a little frown, he said, "Where you from, anyway?"

"Descalzo."

"Never heard of it. That the way they dress there?"

Pedro looked down at himself, slowly aware that his clothing consisted of faded dungarees raggedly cut off at the knee, and a kind of scoop-necked white peasant blouse with puffy long sleeves. The dungarees, which were too big in the torso, were cinched in around his waist with a white plastic belt, and on his feet were red four-inch wedges. "Oh," he said. "No, I got these on the plane."

"That must have been a hell of a flight," said the fellow. "Why don't you go get a cup of coffee?"

"I have no dollars," Pedro said. "I don't even have peserinas."

"You been rolled?" A resident here for nearly eight years, he had the true New Yorker's reaction of disinterested sympathy: "That's tough. You know anybody in town?"

Which made Pedro squint up at him all over again, struck by a belated realization. "You speak Spanish!"

"What do you think *you* speak? Eskimo?"

"But this is New York!"

"You bet. You know anybody here?"

"I need—" Pedro struggled with a hostile environment of concrete and wood, trying to get up on his feet. "I need to find—Huh!"

The fellow laughed, saying, "You need help, that's what you need. Here." And, grabbing an arm, he hauled Pedro to his feet. "There you are."

The world dipped and swayed. The world spun and twirled. In short, the world did the Hustle. Clinging to the wooden fence, Pedro managed to complete his sentence: "I need to find the Museum of the Arts of the Americas."

"You're putting me on."

"Do you know where it is?"

"I don't even know *if* it is."

"Oh." Pedro nodded, a move he immediately regretted. Groaning, he clutched his forehead.

"A museum won't help you," the fellow said. "Let me get you a cup of coffee. My name's Edgar, by the way."

"Pedro," admitted Pedro.

"Come on with me," Edgar said.

So Pedro went with him, having nothing else to do, and his new friend led him across alternate swatches of sod and concrete until they suddenly stopped for no reason at all somewhere in the middle of the grid. "Be here in a minute," Edgar said.

Pedro had no idea what would be here in a minute, nor did he care. Walking in these ridiculous red shoes would have been difficult at the best of times, and for Pedro this was one of the worst of times. That they were no longer walking was success enough for him. Traffic continued to curve by on a couple of roadways, several million cars were parked in neat clusters here and over there, the sun glared down like the eye of a disapproving god, and a bus angled out of nowhere to cough to a stop at Pedro's red feet.

"Come on," said Edgar.

Pedro got on the bus with him. Edgar said a few words to the bus driver in English, and the driver glanced without interest at Pedro and nodded. Then he glanced again at Pedro, looking him up and down, and raised an eyebrow at Edgar, who laughed and said something else in English. He and the driver chuckled together, and then Edgar led Pedro to a nearby seat, and the bus jolted forward once more.

This was one of several bus lines connecting the spread-out parts of Kennedy Airport, this one being a free service exclusively for airport employees. A dozen or so people were aboard now, most of them reading newspapers, and when a man in white coveralls like Jerry's got off at United leaving *El Diario* behind Edgar took the paper off the seat and began to read. Beside him, Pedro rested in the cushioned seat and watched dull-eyed as more and more and more airport went by.

"Huh!" said Edgar.

Pedro turned his poor head and saw Edgar staring at him in wild surmise. "What?" said Pedro.

"Descalzo, huh?" And Edgar pushed the newspaper toward Pedro, folded to one particular story. "Take a look at that."

Pedro tried, he really did, but his eyes refused to cooperate. They showed him two overlapping newspapers, with all the words fuzzy. He could see it was in Spanish, and he could see

269

there was a murky photograph of an airplane, but that was about it. "Oh," he said, because staring at the paper was making him feel sick. "I can't," he said, and closed his eyes. That, however, was a mistake; quickly he popped them open again.

"I'll tell you what it says," Edgar offered.

"Thank you."

"It says three men hijacked an airplane to here from Descalzo last night. It says two of the men are in custody but the third one got away."

"Oh," said Pedro.

"It says the police are looking for him."

"Oh," said Pedro. Fatalistically he said, "They're going to hang me by my tongue."

"The *police?*"

"In Descalzo."

Edgar gave him a keen look. "It's political, huh?"

Pedro could say yes, or he could say no. If he said no, he'd have to explain what it was other than political. If he said yes, the conversation would be over. "Yes," he said.

Hispanics have a long tradition of defiance against authority. Come to that, the Irish and Italians and Jews also have a long tradition of defiance against authority. Thinking it over, *everybody* has a long tradition of defiance against authority. (Except the Germans, of course.) Therefore, it was only natural that Edgar would smile encouragingly at Pedro, pat his dungaree-fringed knee, and say, "Don't worry. We'll take care of you."

"You will?" And Pedro, virtually for the first time in his adult life, found himself smiling.


# THE CASTAWAY . . .

Since Bobbi had already given up her room, she'd been taking all these phone calls at the Holiday Inn desk, and after the second conversation with the girl from Beacon Auto Transporters, she spent a minute leaning against that desk, brooding. It wasn't fair, that's all. Denied that terrific car, just after she'd gotten it. Falsely accused. And forced now to turn around and go *back to New York,* probably spend the whole weekend there before she could get another car to the Coast.

The desk clerk, a neat and friendly young man in a 1957 haircut and a yellow blazer, came over and said, "Anything wrong?"

"Hardly at all," Bobbi told him. "What time did you say the bar opened?"

"Not till twelve noon. Sorry, it's the law."

"I'll never make it," Bobbi told him, and went away toward the restaurant, to have another cup of coffee and try to figure out what to do next.

Her pal from last night was in there now, surrounded by several breakfasts; sunny-side-up eggs on one plate, Canadian bacon on another, a stack of pancakes on a third, several slices of toast on a fourth, pats of butter and little containers of jelly on a fifth. Plus coffee, plus orange juice, plus a glass of water. Stopping by his table, Bobbi said, "When do you expect them to arrive?"

He looked up, a happy smile on his face. "Hey, there. When do I expect who?"

She gestured at all the food. "The Boy Scout troop."

"Oh." Grinning, he said, "I ordered this stuff for you. Sit down."

"I already had breakfast," she said, sitting across from him. "But I will take a cup of coffee."

"Fine." He waved his fork at the waitress, who was already on her way, empty cup in one hand and Pyrex coffeepot in the other.

Bobbi accepted her coffee, asked for Sweet and Low, got it, stirred, and said no, thanks to Jerry's offer of pancakes, toast, a piece of bacon, one of his eggs. "No, really, I'm fine."

"I thought you were going to be on the road by now," he said.

"So did I."

"Trouble?"

So she told her story, with appropriate expressions of surprise and sympathy from him, and as she was finishing the mechanic came in and said, "Could I talk to you for a minute, miss?"

"Pull up a chair," Jerry told hm.

"He's the mechanic," Bobbi explained.

The mechanic, having pulled up a chair, rested his elbows on the table and turned a worried frown toward Bobbi. "The owner called again," he said.

"He did, huh?"

"I'm supposed to tow the car in, look it over, let him know what the problem is."

"Fine," she said.

"But I'm not supposed to let you drive it any more."

"I already know about that."

"So what do I do with your luggage?"

"Oh." Depression was settling over Bobbi like a stationary low. "I guess they better come in here for now."

"Okay." The mechanic made as if to go, but then hesitated, frowning again at Bobbi. "There is something else," he said.

"Oh, I hope not."

"About this thing of the car being vandalized."

"Oh, *that*." Depression gave way briefly to anger.

"The owner wanted me to let him know if it looked like anything had been done to the car on purpose."

"He really stinks," she said. "He really does."

Jerry, who'd been watching and listening to all this, now said, "The owner thinks somebody screwed up the car on purpose?"

"He thinks I did," Bobbi told him.

"The fact is," the mechanic said, "I looked it over some, and I think maybe something really was done to it."

Bobbi stared at him. "That's impossible!"

"Transmission fluid on the ground," said the mechanic. "Looks like the pan was poked with an icepick or something. And your fuel mixture looks to me like it's screwed down so you wouldn't get any air at all. You didn't drive *in* here like that."

Bobbi said, "Do *you* think I wrecked his car?"

"No, I don't," said the mechanic. "But I think maybe somebody did. And if it was you, I wouldn't blame you. If you'll pardon my saying so, I think that guy's a prick."

"You're excused," Bobbi told him. "But I really didn't do it, you know. That car was supposed to take me to California. Besides, I don't even know what those things are that you said. I wouldn't know *how* to wreck a car."

"No, thanks," the mechanic told the waitress. "No coffee for me." To Bobbi he said, "The thing is, if I tell him what happened to the car, he'll blame you and he'll maybe make trouble for you."

"Oh, God. What a mess. And who would *do* such a thing?"

The mechanic shrugged. "Fancy car," he said. "New York plates. Somebody in a bad mood, maybe."

"I sure hope they feel better today," Bobbi said.

Jerry said to the mechanic, "Listen, you know she didn't do it. So why not cover, tell him it was just an ordinary breakdown?"

"Maybe," the mechanic said. "If there aren't any parts screwed up. That's not like some Chevy or VW, you know. We don't have Jaguar parts laying around this part of the country."

"But if you can," Jerry said.

The mechanic shrugged. "If I can cover without getting my own ass in a sling," he said. Then he ducked his head at Bobbi, saying, "Pardon the expression."

"Be my guest."

"Anyway," the mechanic said, getting to his feet, "if I *do* have to report it, I got a cousin on the state troopers, I'll let him know the situation. But probably you'd be better off if you weren't around here any more."

"Thanks," she said.

"I'll get your stuff."

"Thanks."

He went away, and Jerry said, "When he comes back, slip him a thank-you ten bucks."

"You think so?"

"I know so. What are you gonna do now?"

"Christ knows," she said. "Get back to New York somehow, I suppose."

"I'll give you a lift," he said.

She looked at him in surprise. "I thought you were heading west."

"I got what I came out after," he said. "Now I'm going back. Come on along."

She frowned at him, unsure. Wasn't she being hustled into some sort of relationship? It was all too fast, and far too soon; she'd had barely a day of independence, and here's some brand-new guy on the doorstep.

Correctly interpreting her frown, he grinned at her and spread his hands, saying, "No strings."

"I don't know," she said, and at that point the desk clerk in the yellow blazer appeared, saying, "Another phone call for you, Mrs. Harwood."

"Ah!" Getting to her feet, she said, "Maybe he changed his mind! Maybe he'll let me drive it after all!" And it was only natural she should misread the look of annoyance that crossed Jerry's face.

But it wasn't Van Dinast on the phone, it was goddam Chuck. "Bobbi," he said, "I miss you terribly."

"Oh, for God's sake. Chuck, forget it."

"I don't want to live without you, Bobbi. You're too important to me."

"That's a lot of bullshit, Chuck, and you know it. How on *earth* did you find out where I was?"

"I'll find you at the ends of the earth, Bobbi. Doesn't that prove how much I need you?" But male voices were speaking somewhere in the background.

"Where are you?" she said. "Who's there? What are those voices?"

"Voices? There aren't any voices," he said, and the conversation behind him abruptly cut off. "There's just you and me, Bobbi, in the whole world, that's all that matters."

He had never spoken like that in his life before. Never. Something was screwy, though she had no idea what. "Chuck," she said, "I'm sorry, but I haven't changed my mind. We're through, that's all. Good-by."

"Wait! Bobbi, stay there, I'll fly right out, I'll be there this afternoon. Wait for me, Bobbi!"

"Not on your life," she said.

"Wait for me! I'm coming out anyway, *please* don't leave without at least seeing me, talking with me. Give me that much, *please*. You have to!"

"Forget it, Chuck. I'm leaving right now."

"Don't! I'm on my way, I'll be there just as soon as I can!"

"Don't you dare!" But he'd hung up. He'd hung up, and he was actually going to come chasing out across the world after her, and none of it made any *sense*. That wasn't his style, to act like that; his style was to find out where she was supposed to arrive in California, and be there ahead of her, smirking and looking superior.

And who were those people talking in the background? And *how* had he found her?

Good Lord; was he in league with Van Dinast?

Bobbi marched back to the restaurant, where her two suitcases now stood next to Jerry's chair, with the harp looming in its black case on the other side. He grinned a welcome when she sat down, saying, "I took care of the mechanic."

"Fine," she said. "And now you can take care of me. I'll go back to New York with you, if the offer still holds."

He smiled like Christmas morning. "Glad to have you," he said.

# THE PROFESSIONAL . . .

"This is a fine office you got here, Mel," Frank said.

"Thanks," Mel said. He was grumpy, and he didn't care who knew it. He didn't like these guys cluttering up the Zachary George Literary Agency office; they didn't look right.

It had been Angela's idea to switch the command post from their house to his office, since she and Mandy intended to do a lot of intensive spring-cleaning today, but when Mel had agreed all he'd expected was maybe a phone call or two from Jerry. Instead of which, here were Frank and Floyd hanging around for no reason at all, using up his phone and poking into things that didn't concern them and getting Ralphi the receptionist all upset.

For instance. Floyd was out there right now in Ralphi's office, sitting on the sofa with his feet up on the coffee table, trying his miserable chit-chat on Ralphi, and Mel could tell from the sound of her typing that she didn't like it one bit. Also, Frank was wandering around like he was planning to buy the place, opening file cabinets and smelling the plastic ferns and rubbing his hand over the wallpaper. Who *cared* if he thought it was a fine office?

But the worst problem was Floyd. If Ralphi got sore enough —and she hadn't liked Mel being out all yesterday, after leaving early the day before—she might just up and quit, and then what? Because if Ralphi quit she would definitely take Ethelred Marx with her, her zonked boyfriend next door reading the manuscripts and writing the letters, and if *that* happened Mel would find himself back doing his own reading. The very thought made his head throb and his stomach roll over.

And finally enough was enough. Rising from his desk, Mel marched to the connecting door, ignored Ralphi's glower, and said, "Floyd, come in here a minute. I want to talk to you about your *wife*."

Floyd looked immediately outraged. Jumping up, knocking half the magazines off the coffee table and not picking them up, he stormed into the inner office, slammed the connecting door, and said, "Goddam it, Mel, wha'd you do *that* for? I was just making time with that girl!"

275

"You were making a horse's ass of yourself with that girl," Mel told him.

"Horse's ass yourself! She goes for me!"

"She doesn't go for you, you chowderhead, she goes for an insane spaced-out poet named Ethelred Marx that she's *living* with."

"Living with, huh?" Speculation glinted in Floyd's eye. "Not married, huh? But living with the guy. I *knew* she put out."

"I married into a lot of wrong families," Mel said. "Frank, get outa that filing cabinet!"

Frank looked vaguely surprised. "What's the matter with *you?*"

Floyd, having settled onto the sofa, said, "What about this guy she's living with? Is *he* married? Maybe she likes married men."

Pointing a finger at Floyd's nose, Mel said, "You say one more word *to* or about that girl, I'll call Barbara."

"You wouldn't!"

Frank, still poking in the filing cabinet, said, "Is that what's wrong? Floyd, you been pestering that girl?"

"What pester? A couple of jokes, that's all."

"You were the only one laughing," Mel said.

Frank said to his brother, "Lay off, Floyd." And just as Mel was about to thank him for the assist, he spoiled it all by grinning and winking at Mel, saying, "You got a little something going there, eh, Mel?"

"Oh!" said Floyd. "Jeez, Mel, why didn't you say so? I wouldn't try to beat your time, pal."

"Listen," Mel said. "You clowns may not believe this, but a woman is more than a sex object."

"Is that right?" said Frank, and went back to examining the contents of the filing cabinet.

"For instance," said Floyd.

"For instance," Mel told him, *"that* one is a *receptionist!* And a goddam good one. And at the salary I pay, it's not easy to find a good receptionist. Also her boyfriend is a reader for me, and *he's* good, and if she quits and he quits I'll never be able to replace either of them, and especially him. So lay off!"

"Okay okay," said Floyd. "What's the big deal?"

Then Frank said, "Hey, listen to this! 'Her hand unzipped his trousers, and what she found inside brought a smile to her moist mouth. "Don't worry, Doctor," she said. "I don't bite." ' "

Floyd said, "What's *that?*"

276

*That* was a manuscript in a box that Frank had found in a file drawer. It was, in fact, as Mel immediately realized, his own manuscript, *The Neurotic and the Profane*, his novel about the girl who kidnaps a psychiatrist to force him to cure her nymphomaniac twin sister. "Stop!" he yelled, flinging out both arms in Frank's direction. "Put that away, right now!"

But it was too late. Floyd was approaching Frank, saying, "What is that thing?"

"I dunno," said Frank. "Some kind of fuck book."

"Who wrote it? Lemme see it."

Mel shouted, "Put it *away!*"

Not a chance. Frank was turning it this way and that, was finding the title page, was reading it aloud: *"The Neurotic and the Profane, by Mel Byrne."* He frowned at the title page, frowned at Mel, frowned at the title page. "Mel Byrne. Mel Bernstein. Mel Byrne." He frowned at Mel. *"You* wrote this."

"No, I didn't."

"Sure you did. You're writing a fuck book!"

Floyd, who had grabbed a chunk of manuscript, shouted, "Listen to this part!"

"Not out loud!" Mel screamed.

Frank said, "You're writing a book. What's to be ashamed of?"

"It isn't finished," Mel told him. "I'm embarrassed, all right? I didn't want anybody to know until it was done."

"Jesus," Floyd said. "This is raunchy stuff."

Mel pointed a trembling finger. "If either of you bastards tell anybody—Anybody."

"Not a word," Frank promised.

"Not your wives, not Angela, not *anybody.*"

"Angela doesn't even know?"

*"Nobody* knows," Mel said, and the buzzer rang. He picked up the phone: "Yeah? Yeah?"

Ralphi's cold voice said, "Somebody named Jerry calling you."

"Oh. Okay. Listen, Ralphi, I'm sorry about the problem before. It's all over now, guaranteed." (He could say that because Frank and Floyd were immersed in different parts of the manuscript and not listening to a word he said.)

"That's perfectly all right," she said, and hung up.

*I'll give her the day off*, Mel thought. *No, I'll give her tomorrow off, and take tomorrow off myself.* And he pushed the other button and said, "Hello?"

Jerry's voice said, "I'm on the way back."

Mel clutched the receiver. "You got it?"

"Not yet. The girl's coming with me."

"You're bringing her back to the city?"

"Sure."

"Not all the way, Jerry."

"Listen, Jerry," Mel said. "Get the statue along the road somewhere and ditch her. You bring her all the way back, she'll blow the whistle on us before we unload the thing. We don't know what friends she has, we don't know anything about her."

"Whadaya mean, Mel? Just leave her beside the road?"

"She'll be okay, Jerry. She's got some money, she's a grown-up person, she doesn't need anybody to take care of her. Besides, you can't keep her with you *after* you get it or she might catch on, and you don't want to wait till you get her all the way to the city, because then maybe you can't get it at all. So grab it on the way, ditch her, and come on back."

"Jeez, Mel—"

Mel said, "What's the matter wih you, Jerry? You're usually smarter than everybody. *Think* about it, here's nothing else to do."

A pause, a silence, a hesitation; what sounded to Mel suspiciously like a sigh, and then Jerry's voice saying, "Okay, Mel, I guess you're right."

"Of course I'm right. You *know* that."

/ "Anyway, we're leaving now. The way I figure, we should hit the city right in the middle of rush hour."

"By yourself. With the statue."

"Yeah."

"We'll be waiting," Mel told him, and hung up, turning to the others to give them the news.

Not likely. Both of them were on the sofa, each with a chunk of Mel's manuscript, and the intensity with which they were reading suggested that maybe he did have a best seller there after all.

Mel sighed. Well, at least it was keeping them out of trouble.


# THE TRAVELERS . . .

Mel was right, of course. Jerry knew that, he'd known it

before he made the call. His only choice was get the statue as quickly as possible, skip out on the girl, and hotfoot back to New York. That was the idea, wasn't it? Always had been, still was. Like, what was the alternative?

That's right; there isn't any alternative.

Leaving the phone booth, Jerry walked back to the restaurant and found her touching up her lipstick. Yet another cup of coffee had been poured at his place. "Good Christ," he said. *"More* coffee."

"I told her I didn't think you wanted it."

"They don't push the coffee like that in New York."

Bobbi looked sour. "They don't give you *anything* in New York."

"They don't have to. You ready?"

She was. He'd already paid the check, so he grabbed her suitcases while she pushed the harp, and they walked out together to Angela's station wagon in the parking lot. Which bag had the golden statue in it? He hefted the things as though he'd be able to tell by the weight.

"Well, it isn't a Jaguar," he said, when they reached the car, "but it'll take you the same places."

She shook her head. "No it won't. The Jaguar would have taken me to California."

"Sorry," he said, grinning at her. "That's a little off my route."

"I know."

He stashed the luggage, they got into the car, and he headed for route 80.

A funny thing happened—or almost happened—when they got to the interchange. Jerry saw the sign beside the road, saying *Junction 80* and *West* with an arrow to the right, *East* with an arrow straight ahead. And it suddenly came over him to get on *80 West* instead of *East*, and line out for California. Tell the girl the truth about the statue, call the guys later on when they stopped for lunch, and then just head out to see the world. Floyd could take over the Inter-Air route, at least for a while, and Mel could arrange for the sale of the statue back in New York, with Jerry to make delivery when and where the buyer wanted. So what if the world wasn't New York? He could go *look* at it, couldn't he? And go back to the city any time he got bored.

All of this flashed through his mind, as a complete and detailed plan, in the blink of an eye. Then he turned to look at Bobbi's profile, and the whole thing vanished, like breath off a window.

In the first place, he didn't even know this girl. They weren't shacked up together or anything, and even though he was pretty sure she liked him that wasn't any guarantee she wanted to hop in the rack with him.

In the second place, *it was her statue.* If he told her the truth, why would she have to split with him, or anybody else? Then he'd have to take it away from her by force, which he didn't want, and if he did she'd have a perfect bitch to the cops, and he wasn't all that sure she couldn't find him and identify him later on.

Then there were other things. Her expression, for instance; she was depressed and angry, and that gave her a frowning, unfriendly expression that just didn't invite the sharing of adventures or telling of secrets. And she was married, after all, which meant the odds were still that she'd go back to her husband. Also, how tied up did he want to get with a woman who threw all your clothes out the window when she got sore? Then, there was a memory of the Harwood kitchen; even *Angela* wasn't that big a slob.

On the other hand, she was fun to talk with, she was good-looking, she was a good Hustler, she was a New Yorker, she seemed bright and sharp, and he had the idea she liked him.

Not enough. *80 East.*


# THE PRODIGAL . . .

"Would you like some more coffee, Wally?"

"No, thanks, Mom. I'm full. *Boy,* that was sure some breakfast."

Wally and his mom smiled at one another, full of breakfast and camaraderie. "I'm *glad* to be back, Mom," Wally said, and he meant every word of it.

"And I'm glad to have you back, Wally."

They'd talked themselves out over the long night, and now they were just where they'd been before all this foolishness got started. Wally had told her everything—well, almost everything. He'd left out a few things that might have upset her; the sex act he'd performed with Angela Bernstein, for instance, and one or two other items. But other than those elisions, made exclusively for Mom's own good, Wally had told her everything. How he'd been in a house in Queens, peddling pools, when he'd happened to overhear the conversation about the million-dollar statue. How that conversation had driven him temporarily mad, and he'd gone running around like a crazy person trying to find the million-dollar statue for himself. (Just as though he didn't already have everything he wanted and needed right here in Valley Stream, with a fine job and the world's best mom.) How he'd even gone so far as to become a partner with one of the crooks, who had then abandoned him way over in New Jersey. And how being alone and friendless in New Jersey, surrounded by flashy people, jet-setters, and movie stars, all of whom cared nothing and less than nothing about Wally Hintzlebel, had suddenly brought him back to his senses.

And all at once the compulsion within him had just faded away, like smoke on a snowy mountain after a fire. All the urgency, all the frenzy, all the electric trembling, the nervous passionate craving to *be*, to *do*, to *become!* Gotta hustle, gotta *dance!* Gone, all gone, the battle over, the warm blanket of contentment descending once more, the Mason jars on the high dark shelf reconstructing themselves, imploding back to wholeness, trick photography, the film run backward. "I suddenly understood," as Wally had told his mother last night, "that money wouldn't bring happiness."

And so he'd made his slow difficult way home—hitchhiking, catching buses and subways and taxicabs—arriving late last night to make a clean breast of it with his mom (almost a clean breast), and ask her to forgive him and take him back. And after a good long talk, a long talk, of course she *had* taken him back, and they were best friends again, just like before.

And now Wally, just like any other day, had eaten the wonderful breakfast his mom had made for him, and was kissing her on the cheek, and was going out to sell swimming pools to the grandchildren of penniless immigrants. And he was content, all crazy thoughts of the Dancing Aztec Priest swept away out of his head.

But if all that is true, why is he still in our story?


# THE POSSE . . .

If politics makes strange bedfellows, greed makes strange

fellow travelers. College professor Chuck Harwood, off to the wilds of Pennsylvania in pursuit of his wandering wife, traveled in company with financier Victor Krassmeier, thug August Corella, activist Oscar Russell Green, and publicist Bud Beemiss. All they needed was the wife of Bath.

Their chartered plane brought the five men from New York to Greater Pittsburgh Airport in less than an hour and a half, where they transferred to a bronze Oldsmobile Delta 88, the largest vehicle Pittsburgh Hertz could come up with on such short notice. They reached the Holiday Inn near Oil City an hour and a half later, and Oscar said, "Go ahead, Chuck. We'll wait out here."

"Why?" Chuck asked. "Let's all go in together."

"For a husband-wife reunion? Chuck, before you get that statue you're going to have to make friends with Bobbi."

"Oh, yes. I suppose you're right." Chuck stepped out onto the blacktop. "I'll, uh——" he said. "I'll just be a minute."

Oscar said, "You take your time, Chuck. You want her back, don't you? I mean, besides the statue."

"Oh, of course," Chuck said. "But she'll come back anyway, you know. Sooner or later."

"Still," Oscar told him, speaking out of the experience of three marriages, "you take it slow and easy with that girl. We'll wait right here."

"All right." Chuck drifted away toward the entrance.

Now the others all got out of the car and stood in the sunshine. They were still all stretching and scratching when Chuck *did* come back out, barely a minute later, looking vague and disoriented. "She didn't wait," he announced. "The fellow in there says she left hours ago. She didn't wait at *all*, she went away right after I talked to her."

"Terrific," Corella said. "You got no control over your wife at all, do you?"

"Control?" Chuck seemed ignorant of the word. "She is an adult human being, after all."

"Bullshit."

Oscar said, "So what do we do now? Chase her all the way to California?"

Corella said to Chuck, "What's she driving?"

"I have no idea."

Corella gave him a sour look. "Fuckin' babes in the woods," he decided. "You all wait here, I'll be right back." And he marched away, smoothing down his off-white jacket and powder-blue slacks, both of which had become very wrinkled on the trip.

The others continued to mill around beside the bronze Oldsmobile until Corella came back out, smiling in the sunlight and looking very pleased with himself. "Good thing I checked," he said. "She isn't on her way to California at all. She's headed back to New York."

Everybody said, "New York!" Chuck said, "I knew she'd come back to me."

Corella sneered at him. "Oh, yeah? Your name wouldn't be Jerry Spaulding, would it?"

"Jerry what?"

So Corella told them the story the desk clerk had told him, about the Jaguar breaking down and being towed away for repairs, about Bobbi Harwood engaging in any number of phone calls, and about Bobbi at last accepting a ride with a gentleman named Jerry Spaulding who was on his way to New York. The lubrication of a ten-dollar bill had oiled Corella's way to a viewing of Jerry Spaulding's registration card, from which Corella had copied the license plate number. According to the desk clerk, the car was a dark-green station wagon, possibly a Ford.

Krassmeier said, "In other words, we should fly back to New York and get there before she does."

"Wait a minute," Oscar said. "This fellow's name is Jerry Spaulding?"

"Why?" said Corella. "You know him?"

"The guy leading the other bunch. Manelli. Isn't *his* first name Jerry?"

Everybody looked at everybody else. "Son of a bitch," Corella said.

"He's got the statue!" Chuck cried.

"And your wife," Bud reminded him.

"He can't sell my wife," Chuck said. "Back in the car! We've got to catch them!"


# THE GOOD FRIENDS . . .

From the top of the hill they could look northward over steep slopes of pine forest, darkly green, toward higher mountains seeming violet and purple beneath the blue sky. The twin pale lines of route 80 climbed into sight to their left, sliced through a fold in the hills, then lifted over a ridge on the right, dropping out of sight toward New York. A few dynamite scars from the leveling process were still visible as red-earth-white-stone scabs against the prevailing dark green. A few trucks lumbered along the highway, emitting little black puffs of diesel smoke. A white Porsche scampered among them, eastbound, and disappeared over the rise. Far to the north small cottony white clouds were stationary in the sky. No highway noise reached this hilltop, but down the slope birds were calling and responding.

"It's beautiful here," Bobbi said. "Truly beautiful."

"Sure is," Jerry said, but she could hear in his voice that he wasn't really interested. He was only being companionable.

Turning away from the view, to where he was sitting amid the remnants of their picnic lunch, she said, "You really are a city boy, aren't you?"

"Never said I was anything else. Comere, have another Bloody Mary."

"Another? I've already had two."

"We gotta use up these ice cubes," he said.

So she laughed, and sat down beside him, and had another Bloody Mary.

They had driven more than two hours across Pennsylvania, into the rising sun, while Bobbi talked about her marriage, and about the times she and Chuck had lived in Chad and Guatemala, and what it was like to work in a symphony orchestra, and what she planned to do in California, and it wasn't until much later that she would realize Jerry had told her almost nothing about himself. Every time she'd slowed in her autobiography he'd asked another question, drawing another chapter.

Until, simultaneously, both had discovered they were hungry. Leaving route 80 near State College, they'd found a grocery store to provide bread and cheese and cold cuts and cantaloupe and tomato juice and plastic cups, plates, utensils. A state liquor store had furnished the vodka, and a gas station's dispensing machine had given them a bag containing enough ice cubes for an opening night party. Then they'd driven nearly another hour on route 80 before finding a picnic spot they could approve; a place where the car could be pulled some distance off the road, where there were no nearby fences to clamber over, and where a high but gradual slope on their side of the road suggested they'd be able to climb easily away from the influence of the highway. They didn't know they were in Bald Eagle State Forest, and that was a pity; they would have liked the name.

284

As for sex. Well, yes, as for sex, there hadn't been any, but on the other hand it had been very much on Bobbi's mind. A distraction, in fact. Last night, there had been a certain self-satisfaction in knowing she *could* have taken this fellow to bed, and probably would have enjoyed it at the moment, but that she was too smart and independent and *individual* to leap into that sort of messy mistake. Trailing off toward sleep, she had mused on her ten years of marriage, ten years of fidelity to one man (except for one confused, inept, barely remembered episode while a drunken houseguest on the Jersey shore), and it had seemed to her then that a return to *exciting* sex would soon prove to be one of the more important fringe benefits of her decision to leave Chuck. But there wasn't any hurry. A new and different sex life would definitely be coming her way, when she was ready for it; and in the meantime anticipation was satisfaction enough.

So much for last night. Today, the young man she'd rejected forever was somehow still in the foreground. He was no longer quite the same bar pickup, casual dance partner, thanks-but-no-thanks. He had become a personality, an individual she had to respond to in an individual way. And today the thought of sex was *very* insistent.

Which could hardly be called his fault. He hadn't come on strong, he hadn't been suggestive or pushy, he hadn't made any sort of blatant sexual suggestion at all. On the other hand, his ease and self-confidence and rather challenging smile were all implicitly sexual. His *words* were no more than questions expressing an interest in her history and opinions, but his *manner* insistently said *You'll be glad we did.*

And would she be glad, if in time they did? She wasn't sure of this man Jerry. He couldn't have been more of a contrast with Chuck, which on the surface was a mark in his favor, but did she really want to make some sort of crosscultural leap? Jerry seemed bright, but he was hardly an intellectual. Whatever he did for a living—some sort of salesman, she guessed—he was no faculty man. His friends, his interests, his life-style, would all be far removed from the life of the mind; despite occasional humid magazine articles about hard-hats being terrific lovers, Bobbi doubted there was ever much future for a couple who had nothing in common except heterosexuality.

On the other hand, Jerry's self-confident silence contrasted rather markedly with the loud insecurity of Hugh Van Dinast. If Jerry was totally unlike Chuck, Van Dinast was rather uncomfortably similar to Chuck, and undoubtedly even less

285

satisfactory as a lover. (Chuck's failure was not in his being mindless of her needs. Quite the reverse; he was *so* mindful of her needs, her desires, her whims, her moods, and her responses that everything invariably deteriorated into insecurity and mechanization. She hadn't experienced a good spontaneous *fuck* in seven or eight years.)

In the meantime, while her mind was full of sexual speculation their conversation could not have been more sexless. The tension thus created would have to be dealt with sooner or later, and one way to ease the pressure would be to bring sex, however obliquely, into the conversation, which Bobbi did when Jerry handed her the new Bloody Mary: "Trying to get me drunk, eh?" (A negative statement, full of layers of class assumption, an effort to dismiss him by defining him as sexually graceless.)

But he looked at her with only the slightest trace of a smile and said, "Did you ever screw while drunk?"

The question startled her—in an earlier day, she would have acknowledged that it had shocked her—and she automatically gave a truthful answer: "Yes, of course. Hasn't everybody?"

"How was it?"

He wasn't smiling at all now, but she risked a tiny smile of her own, saying, "One hardly remembers."

His expression changed, and for the first time in her life she truly understood the phrase "a cocky grin." "I like to be remembered," he said.

She couldn't help mocking him. "Ho ho," she said, "you sure do talk a good fight."

"Right," he said. He took the Bloody Mary glass out of her hand, threw it away into the view, and drew her close.

(Novelists, when their characters drive cars, never feel compelled to describe precisely what the physical actions are of hands, feet, eyes, knees, elbows. Yet many of these same novelists, when their characters copulate, get into such detailed physical description you'd think they were writing an exercise book. We all know the interrelation between the right ankle and the accelerator when driving a car, and we needn't be told. In sex, we all know about knees, thighs, fingers, the softness at the side of the throat, here-let-me-help, how's-that, *mf, mf, mf, mf*. And if you don't know it, you shouldn't read dirty books, anyway; they'll only give you the wrong idea.)

286

# THE HOUSEGUEST . . .

Pedro had never seen so much.

He had never seen so much *anything.* So much city, for instance; Edgar had transferred him from the airport bus to an automobile that was apparently *Edgar's own vehicle,* a pink and white Mercury barely six years old with all its seats still in it, and had then driven him endlessly through cityscape after cityscape—could this *all* be New York—all the way across Queens to Jackson Heights. And when Pedro commented on the vastness of what he had seen, Edgar laughed and said, "This isn't anything! All you saw so far is one part of Queens! There's four other boroughs!"

Remarks like that grazed off Pedro's forehead and fell—incomprehensible and dead—to the floor at his feet.

Another thing he had never seen so much of was people. Probably more living human beings, complete with heads and arms and feet and clothing, had passed before his eyes so far today than there were in all of Descalzo put together, counting Quetchyl and Rosie and the countryside and the mountains *and* the inbred Moogli people that lived in Elephant Fart Swamp. (Many of them, in fact, the people walking along the New York sidewalks, looked something like Mooglis.)

Also cars; never saw so many of them, and not one of them an Army tank or an Army jeep or an Army two-ply truck. Not *one.* (Also, the few police he saw en route were virtually naked, with nothing more than a little pistol holstered at their sides. Where were their sten guns, their bren guns, their BARs? What a lawless city this must be, with such unarmed police.)

Then when he got to Edgar's home, a neat small house with a full roof, one of a long line of similar neat small houses with full roofs up and down both sides of the street, he realized he'd never seen so much housing for so few people. Edgar turned out to have a fat jolly wife and three fat jolly young children, and they had *half* of this entire house all to themselves. Only one other family lived in the house, in the downstairs half. And just as Pedro was getting over the impact of Edgar's kitchen and bathroom, he was asked to believe that the downstairs family didn't share these plumbing wonders but *had their own!* Was that at all believable? Pedro watched closely, but so long as he was there nobody from downstairs ever came up to boil a chicken or take a shit. Incredible.

Then there was the food. Edgar's wife Rita started bringing out food, from the pantry and the refrigerator and out of closets and from behind the sofa and from under the bed and God knows where all. *Such food!* Mountains, mountains, mountains. Lakes, lakes, lakes. Pedro had never seen so much food, and shortly afterward he had never eaten so much food.

Food may not cure a hangover, of course, but who cares? A full belly is its own reward.

While Pedro had been scoffing down, shoving it in with both hands and only pausing to chew the bigger pieces, Edgar had been giving Rita a slightly romanticized explanation of Pedro's presence in this part of the world. It seemed that Pedro and José and Edwardo were three members of the pro-Democratic, anti-American revolutionary movement down in Descalzo, who had come north to try to present their case to the United Nations. Edwardo and José were now in the hands of the United States government, but Pedro would spearhead the effort to gain them asylum as political refugees. Pedro had a mysterious contact at a place called the Museum of the Arts of the Americas, who would provide funds and legal assistance in the struggle. So, after lunch, Pedro would seek out this Museum of the Arts of the Americas, and set in motion the rescue of his friends.

"But first he'll have a nap," Rita said. "He looks exhausted. You could use a nap, couldn't you, Pedro?"

"Pedro doesn't have time to nap," Edgar announced. "He wants to get *moving*. Don't you, Pedro?" And he looked at Pedro, who at that moment was in the middle of a huge rhinoceros yawn, showing a mouth full of chicken and tomatoes and cheese and pastrami with mustard and Sara Lee cheese danish and maybe one little remnant of Hostess Twinkie. "Well," Edgar decided, "maybe you *could* use a little nap."

"And a screwdriver," Rita said. "Would you like a screwdriver, Pedro?"

Pedro looked himself over for loose screws. "For what?"

"It's a drink," Edgar told him. "Vodka and orange juice?"

"Oh. What's vodka?"

"Something to drink," Rita said. "With alcohol in it."

288

"Like gluppe?"

Edgar and Rita both looked blank; neither had ever heard of gluppe.

Pedro said, "Does it make you drunk?"

"If you drink too much of it," Rita said.

Pedro nodded. "Gluppe," he said. "I'll take one."

# THE RAT . . .

When he was sure she was really asleep, Jerry carefully slid his left arm out from under Bobbi's shoulder and sat up.

The world remained beautiful. High sun in bright blue sky, dark green forest, paler green glades and meadows, this sweet-scented secluded hilltop, the science fiction river of route 80 down below, the songs of birds, the aromas of grass and flowers, the splendid beauty of the naked girl sleeping in the sunlight. Time to steal her statue and get the hell out of here.

(All other thoughts must be ignored. Alternate plans made no sense. *Yes*, she was a terrific person to have sex with, and also to dance with and talk with and drive in a car with. Which wasn't enough, and everybody knows it.)

At least he could cover her, so she would get neither a burn nor a chill. Spreading her clothing over the warm hills and valleys of her body, he noted again the small pleasure lines at the corner of her sleeping smile, where the lightly tanned skin creased at the curve of lip. He'd like to kiss her there, but she might wake, so he simply spread her skirt and sweater and swiftly backed away.

Down the slope, very fast, to the station wagon. Her suitcases and harp were in the back. He removed the two bags, opened one, and found the statue right away. (Her clothing fluttered through his fingers.) The creature glistened like radiation in the sunlight, its evil little green eyes staring at him as though they were brothers. "It wasn't gonna work out," he told the little bastard. "She's some sort of symphony musician, married to a college professor, all that shit. She'd look down her nose at me."

The green eyes kept looking at him, so he put the fucking statue under a blanket on the rear seat. Then he carried the suitcases partway up the slope leaving them where they couldn't be seen from the highway but where she would have to find them on her way down. Then back to the car, to wrestle the damn harp out. *She* managed to carry the thing around like it was a roller skate, but with Jerry the harp would not cooperate. The shape of the thing was all wrong, and there wasn't any sensible way to get hold of it, and the wheels kept hooking into different parts of the interior of the car.

But he did finally get it out, a great tall gawky black triangle crammed with disapproval, and of course the wheels had no interest at *all* in rolling on grass. Struggle struggle struggle, half-dragging and half-carrying it all the way up to the suitcases and leaning it against a tree there, where it slanted like a weeping nun.

Down to the car again, with one last look up the slope to that spot where she slept, invisible from here. If she sat up now, if she saw him—

She didn't. He started the engine, waited for a tractor-trailer to go by, and headed out onto the highway. In no time at all he was doing eighty on 80. Next stop New York.

Well? Something the matter with *you?*

# THE LATE ENTRY . . .

Six members of the Open Sports Committee—David Fayley, Kenny Spang, Felicity Tower, Ben Cohen, F. Xavier White, and Wylie Cheshire—sat in the living room of David and Kenny's apartment and told one another stories about statues. And the more they talked, the more it seemed to them that something funny was going on.

This meeting had been prompted by a phone call Wylie Cheshire had made to Ben Cohen this morning. After the two of them had compared notes—Wylie's statue smashed on Wylie's head, Ben's statue stolen from Ben's boat—they'd made some more phone calls, and not the least interesting discovery they'd made was that several committee members seemed to have disappeared. Among those still available, these six had gathered here to try to figure out what was going on, but they weren't having much success. "Our trouble is," Ben Cohen said at one point, "we're coming into this too late. We don't know what it's all about."

Felicity unexpectedly said, "I do know something about the statue."

They all looked at her. Wylie Cheshire shifted his football player's bulk on one of the little living room chairs (David Fayley winced), and said, "Well, let us in on it."

"I saw a copy," she told them, "in the Museum of the Arts of the Americas. I took one of my classes there, from Liberation High. Some of the children have Hispanic parents on one or both sides, and of course it's vital to reconnect the children with some sense of their heri—"

"That's fine, that's fine," Ben Cohen said. "But what about the statue?"

"They have copies of some items in the museum," Felicity said, "because the originals are still in their native land. And I distinctly remember seeing a copy of the Dancing Aztec Priest there, with a notice giving information about the original."

Kenny Spang said, "We probably ought to look into that."

"I'll go down there, if you like," Felicity offered.

They would like. As for the others, they would continue to search for Oscar, and Chuck, and Bud, and Mandy, and everybody else. And try to figure out what was going on.

# THE RECIDIVIST . . .

Jerry's argument with himself was only half vocal. Every time his interior monologue came up with some other damn stupid pointless argument he invariably replied to it out loud: "How do *I* know she likes me?" he yelled at one point. "She doesn't even *know* me!" And a little later he announced to the empty car, "No, I *don't* have to give a damn what the other guys think, and that isn't the point, anyway." And somewhat farther east he slapped an angry palm against the steering wheel and shouted, "I *know* I'm as good as she is. *She's* the one, with the goddam symphony orchestra and her goddam college teacher husband!" And a bit after that: "All right, all *right*, so what if nobody said anything about permanent? And if it isn't permanent, then what's the fuss all about?" And right on the heels of that one: "Bullshit! I hardly know her! Okay, she's fine, she's all right, there's

291

nothing wrong with her, some other time I could go for her, it's just too bad we met this way, all right?"

*No U-turn* said the small black-on-white sign marking the little dirt road that crossed over the central grass strip to the westbound lanes. "GODDAM IT TO *HELL* AND BACK!" Jerry screamed, punching the steering wheel and the seat and his own leg, and he made the U-turn, anyway, despite the sign and despite everything else, and headed west as fast as the goddam drag-ass station wagon would carry him.

Maybe she was still asleep, and she'd never know he was even gone.

Maybe she woke up and hitched a ride already, and he'd never see her again. (Get herself murdered by some passing maniac?)

But when he got there she was on the other side of the road, wheeling the harp along through the grass (how did she *do* that?), the suitcases already side by side on the gravel shoulder. Jerry didn't waste time looking for any more *No U-turns*. He made a no-u-turn of his own, across the lumpy greensward, squealing to a stop at her feet, jumping out with a combined expression of relieved smile and repentant frown, saying forcefully, "Listen."

She pointed a finger at him. Her face was as hard as granite. "Where's the statue?" she said.


# THE INTERROGATOR . . .

Which wasn't even the main question. The main question, of course, was *Why?* Everything else Bobbi already understood, and had understood almost from the instant she'd awakened, alone and stiff, on that sunny slope. Only in the immediate dislocation of coming to consciousness naked on the open ground in the sunlight were there any other questions in her mind: *Where am I? Where's Jerry? What's happening?*

Well, all of *those* questions answered themselves almost at once. As they say in the detective novels, everything fell into place. Of *course* their meeting last night had not been accidental; a young man from New York, traveling alone, having dinner in a place that was usually closed by that hour. And of *course* he'd vandalized the Jaguar himself, in order to get her into his own car.

292

But why? Just for a quickie in the grass? That made no sense at all, but what other reason was there? Hurriedly dressing, taking it for granted the son of a bitch had stolen her luggage—all of her clothing, all of her possessions, her harp—she was both relieved and bewildered to see her bag still here where she'd left it, with its cash and its credit cards and everything else still inside. Touching up her face and hair, checking her progress with the mirror in her compact she was astounded to discover tears on her cheeks. She was *crying* over the bastard?

No, over the betrayal. The leavings of their picnic lunch were about her, the crumpled papers, the nearly empty tomato juice jar, the melting ice cubes in their plastic bag. Giulietta Masina near the finish of *Nights of Cabiria*, when the guy runs away with her purse. God*dam* it! Why had he done such a miserable thing?

Partway down the slope she came across the harp and the suitcases, side by side. At that point his motivation utterly bewildered her, and it was due to her perplexity that she opened both bags and discovered the loss of the Other Oscar.

So the only question left to ask was *Why?*; but she didn't start with that one. She started with an irrelevant question, "Where's the statue?" (when of course it had just been delivered to a confederate somewhere) because she wanted to hear him lie. Get the first bunch of lies out of the way, and then keep at him until she got the truth. Flag down another driver if necessary, bring in the police if necessary, but get the truth. After the lies.

(It never occurred to her he might have returned to do her harm, or to murder her. *That* opportunity had come when they were isolated and alone—and when she was helplessly asleep—and if he hadn't done it then, he never would. No, he was here to lie her out of suspicion.)

"It's in the car," he said. "On the back seat, under a blanket."

"What?" That was certainly a lie—he wouldn't have come back without getting rid of the evidence—but it was the *wrong* lie. It was a lie that admitted the theft, and what was the point in that?

Determined to get beyond bewilderment and obfuscation at *once*, Bobbi marched to the car, yanked open a rear door, flipped the blanket on the back seat out of the way, and found herself staring at the naked yellow ass of the Dancing Aztec Priest.

"Well, shit," she said.

"Listen," he said, less forcefully than before. "Let me tell you what happened, all right?"

Now there'd be some lies. Folding her arms, leaning against the side of the car, glaring at his face in the clear sunlight, she said, "Go right ahead."

"In the first place," he said, "that wasn't any accidental meeting last night. I followed you from New York."

She took a deep breath. "You son of a bitch," she said, "you're trying to confuse me."

"I'm trying to tell you the truth."

"That's what's confusing me. Go ahead, let's hear some more of it."

"Okay." He looked pained and uncomfortable. "I didn't know you, okay? All I knew about you, you were some half-ass broad throws her husband's clothes out the window and takes off."

"What? Wait a minute, are you a friend of *Chuck's?*" No, not a friend. "Did he *hire* you?" A private detective, sent out by Chuck to get the Other Oscar. Was Chuck that crazy?

"You mean your husband?" Jerry shook his head. "*He* doesn't have anything to do with it. I met him once, that's all, and you were right, you shouldn't stick with him. But the thing is, I didn't know *you*, you know what I mean? So I figured you're this nothing broad, I'll just dance you around a little, cop the statue, and take off. Like, if I'd come up to your room last night, that's the way it would of been. No fuss, no trouble, you'd still have the Jag this morning, on your way to sunny Cal."

"So you admit you vandalized that car."

He shrugged, with the hint of an unrepentant grin. "Sure. I couldn't keep chasing any Jag forever with that beat-up clunker of mine. That's my sister's car, by the way, the cops towed mine away yesterday when you went into the building where your orchestra is."

"Orchestra? How long have you been *following* me?"

"That's where I picked you up," he said. "I was looking for you for a while before that."

Now she narrowed her eyes, peering at him more closely and more suspiciously. "Have I *seen* you someplace before?"

"Well, a couple of times," he admitted. "The first time was when you left your place, after you threw the clothes out the window. I was down by the street door, trying to get in."

She had no memory of anyone there when she'd stormed out; she'd been pretty singleminded at that point. "Where else?"

"We went up in the elevator together, when you went to the auto transport place."

"Right!" She pointed a finger at him, as though she'd finally trapped him in some clumsy falsehood. *"That's* where I saw you! So what in hell is it all about? What are you *doing* all this for?"

"To get the statue," he said.

"The statue? The Other Oscar? But what *for? Why?"*

"Because it's real gold," he said. "And the eyes are real emeralds, and it's worth a million dollars."


# THE COUNTRY COUSIN . . .

Pedro couldn't sleep. He had eaten, he had drunk vodka, he had showered, he had entered this clean bed with the cool sheets, and now he couldn't sleep. He lay here, and lay here, and lay here, and finally enough was enough. Up he got, dressed himself in the neat clean clothing Edgar had loaned him, and left the bedroom.

Rita was watching a soap opera on television when Pedro came out. (Television!) Looking up, she said, "Can't sleep?"

"I got to go to the museum."

"I understand. Your comrades need you."

"Yeah," said Pedro.

"Let me make you a cup of coffee before you go," she said, getting to her feet. "Edgar had to go to his class."

Pedro followed her to the kitchen. "His class? He still goes to school?"

"Part-time at Long Island University," she said proudly. "He's going to be an accountant some day."

Pedro sat at the kitchen table. "What's an accountant?"

"A man who counts money."

"Sounds like a good job."

She laughed. "It is."

But why would anybody have to go to college to learn how to count money? If Edgar was still a schoolboy at his age, he couldn't be much of a man. Pedro look at his host's plump, friendly wife, and said, "You like to fuck?"

She knew country boys. She gave him an easy smile and said, "Only with my husband. He's very terrific."

"Okay," Pedro said, and when she'd made the coffee they

295

sat at the table together and drank it, while she described to him how to travel on the subway to the Museum of the Arts of the Americas, which according to the phone book was on 53rd Street in Manhattan, near Fifth Avenue. First she described it all to him, and then she wrote it all down, in large block letters that he could read. Then she also wrote down their telephone number (they had their own telephone!) so he could let them know what happened, and after that she gave him a couple of subway tokens (with instructions for their use), and two five-dollar bills, a loan he could repay once he'd rescued his companions. And at last she gave him a kiss on the cheek, and told him, "You've a very brave man."

"Okay," said Pedro, and left, and walked across a buzzing, cluttered, bewildering, overpopulated, deafening, and utterly alien dream landscape to the subway entrance. The only comforting touch was that posters and billboards along the way did some of their advertising in Spanish. That made it a little more like the real world.

The subway, on the other hand, wasn't like any world at all, and having a lot of instructions posted in Spanish didn't begin to help. Pedro managed to put his token in the slot and make his way through the turnstile, but after that he just stood there, stunned, unable to move in any direction. Vodka and ignorance had carried him this far, but now he could go no farther.

He couldn't even run when he saw the cop coming. He stood there, and the cop arrived, and the cop said something. Pedro stared at him. Then the cop said, in Spanish, "You don't speak English?"

Pedro shook his head.

"You speak Spanish, don't you?" (This cop was one of the results of the New York Police Department's campaign to find policemen who are at least fairly fluent in Spanish. New York City, since the Second World War, has become a bilingual city, with one third of its population Hispanic. Subway notices are in both English and Spanish. *El Diario* is a major newspaper. Every public school report card is bilingual, and there are now *two* local Spanish-language television stations; the girls on Spanish-language soap operas are prettier, but more volatile.)

Pedro nodded. "I speak Spanish," he agreed.

The cop said, "Where you headed?"

Pedro couldn't remember. He jerked his arm up and shoved Rita's instructions toward the cop, who read them, nodded, and said, "You want the F train to the city. Go over that way." And he gave Pedro careful directions.

Once Pedro was moving again, things got better. He went to the concrete platform the cop had pointed out, and after a while an *incredibly* loud train came shrieking and screaming into the station, and when it stopped the doors all opened without anybody's assistance, and Pedro stepped aboard. Behind him, the door slid shut again, still without the aid of a human hand.

There were available seats, but as Pedro headed for one the subway jerked forward and Pedro found himself sitting on the floor instead. Two male passengers, both laughing, approached him from opposite directions, helped him up, brushed him off, and sat him down on a seat. Then they chuckled comments to one another, moved away in opposite directions, and left Pedro sitting there, clutching his seat with both hands.

*Roar roar roar roar roar* went the train, past stations without stopping, and when it did stop the signs said *Queens Plaza. Fwip,* opened the doors, and *fwip,* they closed again, and the train hurtled on.

It was several stops before Rockefeller Center, and Pedro was so benumbed by then that he nearly missed it. The words on the platform signs slowly sank into his culture-shocked brain, and when finally he realized he was *here* he pitched himself willy-nilly through the snicking doors and would have fallen if he hadn't run into a blue-and-orange trash barrel.

Sixth Avenue, when he climbed up to it, was— Well, there just wasn't any point trying to absorb anything any more. Pedro found a Spanish-speaking citizen on his fourth attempt and was given directions to 53rd Street. He walked, paying little attention to the traffic until a horn-blaring truck nearly drop-kicked him over the American Metal Climax Building. After that, he moved so cautiously that other pedestrians kept hitting him with elbows, shoulders, purses, attaché cases, shopping bags, rolled-up newspapers, and small children. He persevered, however, found 53rd Street, turned left, and came eventually to a gray stone building with its name chiseled into the stone over the massive doorway:

MVSEVM OF THE ARTS OF THE AMERICAS.

What would Pedro find in here?

Confusion compounded. There was a charge for admission, which he couldn't understand. Neither the woman at the desk near the entrance, nor the uniformed private guard standing behind her, could speak a word of the language Pedro shared with most of the artisans whose work was on display in this building, but eventually a janitor was found who could speak Spanish and who helped Pedro pay the buck-fifty. But when Pedro asked whom he should see about the payment for the Dancing Aztec Priest, the janitor got the wrong handle on the question, and it came out as, "He wants to see our copy of the Dancing Aztec Priest."

Directions were given by the woman at the desk, via the janitor, and off Pedro went through the cool empty rooms filled with swag. But when he reached the right spot there was nothing there but a fake copy of the Priest, capering on a green marble pedestal. And not a very good copy, either; José's were a lot better than that.

As Pedro stood there, trying to figure out what to do next, a brown-skinned girl approached, took pen and notebook from her shoulder bag, and began to copy the information on a notice (English only) attached to the front of the Priest's pedestal. Pedro, pessimistic but not knowing what else to do, said to her, "Do you speak Spanish?"

"Yes, I do," she said, turning a helpful face toward him. "I'm a teacher, you see, and many of my students have one or more Hispanic parents. I must communicate with them in the language they speak at home, if I'm to be really useful to them in any way. Can I help you?"

Pedro gestured at the imitation Priest. "I want to know where I can get my money for the Priest," he said.

The girl frowned at him; she hadn't understood. "I'm sorry?"

Pedro looked at her. She was beautiful. She was like a movie star in the movies. She was the tallest, thinnest, cleanest, brownest, most incredibly beautiful and lust-making woman he had ever seen. He said to her, "You like to fuck?"

*That* she understood. "Yes," she said. Putting pen and notebook away in her shoulder bag, she grabbed Pedro by his thick-fingered hand. "My name's Felicity," she said. "Come along, we'll take a cab to my place."

# THE FELLOWSHIP . . .

"You're driving too slowly!" Krassmeier insisted, and pounded the seat back next to Corella's ear, a sight that would have done the long-suffering chauffeur Ralph a world of good to see. Let *Corella* find out what it was like to have the goddam seat back pounded next to your goddam ear. Let *him* see how much he liked it.

He didn't like it at all. "Cut out that pounding!" he yelled. "I'm *not* driving too slow! You wanna get stopped by a cop, waste half an hour getting a ticket? I'm doing a steady sixty-four!"

The bronze Oldsmobile, filled with Corella and Oscar Russell Green in front and Krassmeier, Bud Beemiss, and Chuck Harwood in back, was not in fact going too slowly. If anything, it was going a bit too fast. Had they being doing a steady sixty-*one* for the last four hours, they would not have zoomed past Jerry and Bobbi's picnic spot before Bobbi reached the side of the highway with her first suitcase. As it was, she'd just been awakening on her hilltop when they'd driven past, and was out of their sight.

Not only that, they'd also seen the station wagon, though they didn't know it. In the first place, "Jerry Spaulding" had put a false license number on that motel registration card to go with his false last name, so Corella and party were now looking for a license plate that probably didn't exist at all on this road. And in the second place, they'd had no reason to pay attention to the dark-green station wagon when they'd seen it, because it had been going hell for leather the other way.

The five men had been cramped together in this car a long long time, and they were all getting irritable. They were also hungry, and every one of them was in increasingly desperate need of a men's room. With the atmosphere also poisoned by the mingled smokes of Corella's cigar, Chuck Harwood's pipe, and Krassmeier's cigarettes, it was not a happy vehicle.

And now Chuck, in the back seat with Krassmeier and Bud Beemiss, twisted around to look out the rear window—elbowing Bud pretty badly in the process—and mildly said, "Here comes somebody who isn't as afraid of the police as you are, Corella."

Corella glared at the rear-view mirror. A dark automobile was coming lickety-split in the left lane. "Let *him* get picked up," Corella groused. And he doggedly maintained his sixty-four as the other car rapidly overtook them, passing on their left.

"There she is!" Bud suddenly yelled, and in waving his

arms around he gave both Krassmeier and Chuck a mean flurry of elbows.

"Stop that!" Krassmeier slapped at Bud's waving arms.

"There she *is!*" Bud insisted, and now everybody looked to the left, at the dark-green station wagon passing them, and *that was Bobbi in the passenger seat!*

"That's her!" Oscar shouted, up front beside Corella, and he thumped his fist onto Corella's leg.

The station wagon was ahead, was moving away. "Stop *hitting* me!" Corella yelled, but everybody else was yelling louder:

"Stop her!"

"Catch them!"

"Run them off the road!"

"Hustle, man, hustle!"

*Gotta* hustle.

# THE FAST FRIENDS . . .

Flashback:

Jerry told her the rest of the story as they sat together in the car, parked by the side of the road. "I have a little independent trucking outfit at Kennedy," he started, and told her about the Spanish alphabet, the box marked *A*, the box marked *E*, the million-dollar statue, the dispersal of the sixteen candidates, the several searchers, the gradual winnowing of the prospects, and the ultimate discovery that hers indeed was The One. She listened, wide-eyed, not interrupting, and at the finish she gazed with awe at the golden behind of the statue on the back seat. "A million dollars," she said.

"Maybe more."

She frowned at him. "Then why come back?"

He became immediately uncomfortable. Drumming his fingertips on the steering wheel, looking past her left ear and then her right ear, he said, "Well— I just did, that's all."

"Why?"

"How do I know? I mean, why not? Can't leave you out here. Somebody come along and sex-crime ya, something."

"You got away with it," she pointed out, "and then you turned around and came back. After all, the statue *is* mine."

"Yeah, I know." And he looked glum, as though he too realized he'd behaved with less than brilliance.

"Do you expect me just to *give* it to you?"

"I don't know, lady." Irritation was popping to his surface like bubbles on fudge. "I come back, all right? We'll work it out later. So now we'll go to New York." And, under her level gaze, he started the engine, jammed it into gear, and kicked the station wagon out onto the highway.

Flash forward:

"I'll give you the statue," she said.

He showed her a sudden frown. "You'll what?"

"Well, not exactly give," she said. "I tell you what I'll do. You're supposed to split with your brothers-in-law, right?"

"Right."

"So you can share your part with me."

"That's an eighth," he told her. "You want an eighth, instead of the whole thing? A hundred grand instead of a million?"

"Sure."

"Why?"

"They're both unreal. A hundred grand, a million. What difference does it make?"

His look at her this time was keen and unbelieving. "Come on, kid," he said. "You know better than that."

"Maybe."

"So what's the idea? Why you being so good to me?"

"Because I think you're in love with me," she said.

He laughed, trying to hide how much he was pleased. "In love with you! I don't even know you!"

"Maybe once you get to know me you won't love me any more," she said, "but right now I think you do."

"Is that right? *I'm* in love with *you*, huh?" He steered out and around a slowpoke bronze Oldsmobile; he himself was doing ninety-three. "And what about *you?*"

"Maybe once I get to know you I won't care for you at all," she said.

"And in the meantime?"

"I think you're terrific, if you want the truth."

"Is that love?"

She frowned. "Love is such a big word."

"You don't mind hitting *me* on the head with it," he said.

She grinned at him, and he grinned back, and she said, "You know what I'd like to do?"

"Me, too," he said. "There's some woods over there." And

301

he put on his right directional, to let that bronze Oldsmobile behind him know he was going to pull off the road and come to a stop.

## THE OMNISCIENT VIEWPOINT . . .

The hawk was looking for a nice plump rabbit, or maybe a good juicy field mouse. Hanging in the middle of the sky, just to the south of route 80 in eastern Union County, Pennsylvania, the hawk held its wings outspread, catching the updrafts, watching the ground for movement.

Movement ensued. A dark-green Ford station wagon slowed and left the concrete of the highway and came to a stop off the road, just at the edge of the field the hawk was studying. The front doors opened and Jerry and Bobbi emerged, just as a bronze Oldsmobile squealed to an angry shuddering stop, angled across the front of the Ford, the two vehicles almost touching. All four of the Oldsmobile's doors opened; Corella leaped out of the left front, Oscar leaped out of the right front, Krassmeier lunged out of the left rear, and nobody emerged from the right rear because, after opening a mere three inches, that door of the Oldsmobile stuck the left corner of the Ford's front bumper. Therefore, as Oscar and Krassmeier and Corella all ran toward Jerry and Bobbi and the Ford, first Bud and then Chuck crawled out the left rear doorway of the Oldsmobile.

Meantime, Bobbi shrieked and Jerry jumped back into the Ford, yelling, "In the car! In the car!" But Bobbi didn't get into the car; she stood gaping instead. Not that it made any difference, since Jerry had taken the key from the ignition and didn't have time to reinsert it before Corella and Krassmeier were all over him, grabbing at him, trying to pull him out of the car. He punched Corella on the nose and kicked Krassmeier in the belly, but by then Bud and Chuck had arrived, and he couldn't fight off all four of them.

The hawk watched all this with fascination.

Oscar tried to grab Bobbi in a bear hug, but she didn't *want* to be grabbed in a bear hug, so she kicked him hard on the shin. "Ow–" Oscar said, and clutched his shin, and went hopping around in an off-balance circle, grimacing and saying several more Ows. And Bobbi yanked open the rear door of the Ford, grabbed the Dancing Aztec Priest by the upraised leg, and went running out across the field, waving the golden statue in the air over her head.

The hawk didn't know *what* to make of that.

The four men who'd been struggling with Jerry all noticed the saffron flash of the departing Priest, and at once gave off from kicking and punching and butting and pulling and pushing, to run instead, shouting Hi and Stop and Come *back!* Jerry himself ran after them all, yelling, "Bobbi, keep running!"

The hawk moved its wings, circled to a higher plateau, and went on watching.

Jerry tripped Krassmeier, who fell down in a muddy place.

Chuck caught up with Bobbi, but she ducked away from his flailing arms, kicked him on the kneecap, called him a couple of unladylike things, and found herself tackled by Corella, who had run into her like a charging bull. "Yi!" she cried, flinging her arms up, and the Dancing Aztec Priest sailed up into the air, head over heels, ass over teakettle, glinting aureate in the sunshine, arcing through the lazy air, and landing in the outstretched arms of Bud Beemiss, who clutched the creature to his chest, reversed direction, and ran smack into the left fist of Jerry.

Bobbi, in separating herself from Corella, inadvertently kneed him in the nose and he began to bleed all over his off-white sports jacket and his powder-blue tie with tiny white windmills all over it. He already had grass stains and mud smears all over his powder-blue slacks and his white patent-leather shoes.

Jerry had the statue, in the middle of the field. To his left, Krassmeier was attempting to get back on his feet. Behind him, Bud was sitting on the ground, holding his nose with both hands, while farther back Corella was sitting on the ground holding his nose with one hand and his side with the other, and Bobbi was trying to find her other shoe. Chuck was limping hurriedly after Jerry from the rear, and Oscar was limping hurriedly after him from the front.

Jerry ran at Oscar, dodged to Oscar's left, ran around Oscar on Oscar's right, and was tripped up by Krassmeier's straining outflung arm. Jerry did a somersault on the ground, wound up on his back, and Oscar fell on him. Bobbi found her other shoe and hit Corella on the top of the head with it.

The hawk closed one eye, cocked its head to one side, and viewed the action one-eyed. It made no better sense that way.

Jerry and Oscar rolled over and over, tripping up Chuck, who fell on both of them. Krassmeier made another attempt to get to his feet. Bud got to *his* feet and ran over to fall on the pile of Oscar and Chuck and Jerry and the statue. Bobbi rapped Corella once more on the head with her other shoe, and ran over to rap Krassmeier on *his* head with her other shoe. Corella sat on the ground and tried to hold five of his parts simultaneously. Krassmeier tripped up Bobbi, whose skirt wound up around her waist, which enraged her so much she jumped up and kicked him in the side with her shod foot.

Jerry and Oscar and Chuck and Bud rolled around and around in the field, and all at once the statue squirted out from the middle of them. Bobbi grabbed it, threw her other shoe at Krassmeier, and ran for the cars. Jerry tripped *everybody*.

Bobbi was getting away. Corella and Krassmeier were both staggering around at the far end of the field, and Jerry was trying to hold onto Bud *and* Chuck *and* Oscar.

Bobbi was almost to the cars. The six men straggled out behind her, puffing after her but not getting anywhere. Then her shoeless foot landed on a sharp rock, she let out a shriek, her forward momentum threw her off-balance, she flung her arms out to break her fall, and once again the Dancing Aztec Priest was airborne.

The hawk slid diagonally down the sky, watching the progress of this unlikely flying creature. The statue rose, it rose, on a long gradual trajectory. It soared out over the hood of the Ford station wagon, it angled swiftly down, it suddenly rushed, it crashed to the concrete directly in the path of a giant tractor-trailer coming along at seventy-seven miles an hour, and eight rushing huge tires sequentially smashed it down into a million jaundiced pieces on the highway.

The seven bedraggled, panting people lined up on the verge, gazing at the golden shards. White plaster dust dimmed the gilt. Another hightailing truck roared by, and the remains became less visible. Already the pieces were hard to see.

"After all that," Bobbie said.

"It's the wrong one," Krassmeier said.

"The wrong one," Chuck said.

"It isn't gold," Oscar said.

"Back to New York," Jerry said.

"Back to New York!" Bud and Corella said.

"Back to New York!" Krassmeier and Chuck and Oscar said.

"Back to New York! Hustle!"

Into the cars they clambered and peeled away, Jerry and Bobbi first in the Ford station wagon, the other five immediately after. The wind of their passage raised a bit of plaster dust, which soon dispersed.

The hawk rested on the air currents a minute longer, but nothing else occurred. As for that field, all those people had pretty well loused it up as a hunting spot. Any rabbit or mouse that *might* have been in that territory would be miles from here by now.

*"Caw!"* said the hawk, which translates as "Assholes!" His wings beating, he headed south.


# THE RABBLE . . .

*Everybody* was there.

Well, not exactly everybody. Swimming pool salesman Wally Hintzlebel wasn't there, because he hadn't been invited; in fact, he was at home right now, in his kitchen, playing canasta with his mother. And nobody had been able to find Jenny Kendall or Eddie Ross, who at this moment were sharing hamburgers over a wood fire beside a New Hampshire stream. And neither Felicity Tower nor Pedro Ninni was present; both were uptown, exhausted, but gradually rebuilding their strength and beginning once again to eye one another. And José Caracha and Edwardo Brazzo were seated at a wooden table in an underfurnished room downtown, filling out forms for the State Department, Customs, Immigration & Naturalization, FBI, CIA, the Public Health Service, the Foreign Assets Control division of the Treasury Department, Secret Service, the New York City Police Department, and the New York State Parole Board. (They had writer's cramp.)

Which is seven people who weren't there. But nineteen people *were* there, and that's a lot of people. Particularly to all be crowded into David and Kenny's living room, which wasn't that big to begin with.

Here's who was there: Victor Krassmeier, and his associate August Corella. Jerry Manelli and the other three members of Inter-Air Forwarding, being Mel Bernstein, Frank McCann, and Floyd McCann. And thirteen members of the Open

Sports Committee: F. Xavier White, Mandy Addleford, Ben Cohen, Mrs. Dorothy Moorwood, Oscar Russell Green, Chuck and Bobbi Harwood, Bud Beemiss, Wylie Cheshire, David Fayley, Kenny Spang, Leroy Pinkham, and Marshall "Buh-buh" Thumble.

It was nine o'clock at night, and they'd all been here for nearly an hour, and so far nothing had been accomplished except a lot of belated discoveries and realizations, some of them positive and some of them less so. Members of the Open Sports Committee kept pointing at members of the Inter-Air Forwarding group and saying, "You!" Ben Cohen and Wylie Cheshire, for instance, both pointed like that at Mel, and both seemed prepared to settle personal grudges with Mel right here and now. Leroy and Buhbuh, they had the same feeling about Frank and Floyd, but F. Xavier remembered Frank and Floyd with fond humor. And David Fayley and Kenny Spang were absolutely *ecstatic* when they recognized Jerry and realized what they meant. "You little goose," Kenny said to David, "did you really think I'd—" "Oh, Kenny!" David cried. "I was so afraid!"

The main problem in getting the meeting under way was that everybody wanted to run it. Oscar wanted to run it, but so did football lineman Wylie Cheshire. So did Bud Beemiss, and so did Chuck Harwood. Krassmeier took it for granted *he'd* run the meeting, and Corella tried to take over by intimidation.

Corella finally won. What he did, he went to the kitchen and found a package of four light bulbs. He brought these back to the living room, stood on a chair, and threw one of the light bulbs against the wall. It made that satisfactory HO gauge explosion that light bulbs do, and there was a shocked and bewildered silence. Into it, Corella attempted to insert himself, saying loudly, "Okay now, let's get organized!"

Which resulted in eleven people all simultaneously having something to say. So Corella threw another light bulb against the wall, was rewarded with another *pop*, and silence returned. Except that this time it was Kenny Spang who inserted himself into it, crying, "Jee-ziz *Christ!* What are you *doing?*"

Corella glowered. If you asked *him*, that bird was a fruit. "Getting a little peace and quiet," he said, and held up a third light bulb. "And this one," he said, "I throw at the next big mouth that opens up. *Now* let's get organized."

There was some mutinous rumbling, and much shuffling of

feet, but no big mouths opened up, and Corella went on: "The situation is," he said, "there was sixteen statues. *Definitely* one of them is real, but we all missed it the first time through. Now, a lot of them are for sure not it, because they've been busted up, so it's gotta be one of the ones left over. Any of you people got a list of the Open Sports Committee?"

Bud Beemiss did. He handed it to Corella, who used it to run down the fate of every statue, and when he was done the mystery was deeper than ever:

Oscar Russell Green—broken in three places.
Chuck and Bobbi Harwood—both smashed.
Bud Beemiss—smashed.
Wylie Cheshire—smashed (Wylie winced, and touched his head).
F. Xavier White—head broken off.
Mandy Addleford—finger broken off.
Ben Cohen—chipped, and then paint rubbed off.
Mrs. Dorothy Moorwood—smashed.
David Fayley and Kenny Spang—both heads broken off.
Jenny Kendall and Eddie Ross—both smashed.
Leroy Pinkham—head broken off.
Marshall Thumble—head broken off.
Felicity Tower—finger broken off.

"Well, goddam it," Corella said.

And Krassmeier snapped. "Goddam *you!*" he screamed at Corella. "It's another of your failures, Corella, the statue never left South America! You've cost me thousands, you've ruined my clothing and my digestion, you BAAASTAARRRD!!" And he flung himself at Corella, knocking him off the chair, knocking them both off their feet, punching and kicking and biting and gouging while Corella thrashed around and yelled, *"Help! Help! Help!"*

The others finally did get them separated and quieted down, and in the depressed silence that followed Mel Bernstein suddenly said, "Hey! Where's Jerry? Jerry?"

Which caused everyone else to look around, which caused Chuck Harwood to say, "Where's Bobbi? Where's my wife?"

People called, "Bobbi? Bobbi?" Other people called, "Jerry? Jerry?" Other people walked through the Fayley-Spang apartment, opening doors and rucking up the rugs, but they didn't find anybody. Jerry and Bobbi were both gone.

# THE WINNERS . . .

The old man was on his hands and knees on the front lawn, a mixing bowl beside him, a tablespoon in his left hand, and a flashlight in his right. Jerry said, "What's up, Pop?"

"Looking for worms."

"You're collecting worms?"

"Thought I'd take up fishing," the old man said. He looked up, and shined an appreciative flashlight on Bobbi. "Well, look at that."

"Bobbi Harwood," Jerry said, and explained to her, "This is my father."

"Hello," Bobbi said. "Don't get up."

Gratefully, the old man sank back to his knees. "Your mother's inside."

"Right. Have fun with the worms, Pop."

"Fish," said the old man.

"Nice to meet you," Bobbi said, and Jerry took her around the house and in through the back door to the kitchen, where his mother was tasting the latest spaghetti sauce. "Hiya, Mom," Jerry said. "How is it?"

"Not so hot," she said, and dropped the ladle back in the pot.

Not so hot? Since there were about fourteen ways to take that—so-so, heat, spicy—Jerry dropped the subject and said, "Mom, this is Bobbi Harwood, a new friend of mine."

His mother frowned at the girl. "Bobbi?"

"Barbara," she said. "It's a nickname."

"How are you, Barbara?"

"Wonderful," Bobbi said, "This has been the most different day of my life."

Mrs. Manelli looked keenly at their faces. "Oh ho," she said. "So this one's special."

Jerry laughed and said, "The perfect spaghetti sauce, Mom."

Bobbi said, "What?"

Mrs. Manelli said, "You're hungry?"

"Starving," Jerry told her. "The last thing we had was lunch, way out in Pennsylvania."

"Go wash," she said. "Dinner in fifteen minutes."

So they went up the outside staircase to Jerry's apartment, and he let her use the bathroom first. Waiting, he stood by his front room window, whistling as he looked down at the dot of flashlight on the lawn below.

What a day. First he had a statue worth a million dollars, and then it wasn't worth anything. First he was ditching this girl, and now he was bringing her home. Everything was changing, inside and out.

Back at the Fayley-Spang apartment, while Corella was leading the recap of what had happened to all the statues (and Jerry already *knew* they'd all been dealt with), he had walked over to Bobbi, sitting there alone on one of the delicate chairs against the wall, and he'd said, "You know, I just worked it out. There's nineteen of us here, plus three more in your committee, so that's a twenty-two way split even if we *do* find the damn thing."

That had made her laugh. "What's one twenty-second of a million dollars?"

He'd already worked it out: "Forty-five thousand. And I'll tell you, Bobbi, I don't know if that statue ever came up from South America or not, but I do know I don't need to run around with twenty chowderheads to hustle forty-five grand. *That* much I can pick up on the street."

"So what are you going to do?"

"I'm going home," he'd told her. "Wanna come along?" And she had said, "No."

"No?"

"No." But then she had grinned and said, "But I'll let you drive me to California."

He had hesitated. "Leave New York?"

"We can always come back. But right now you owe me a trip to California."

"Then I better pay off," he'd said.

So here they were, and tomorrow they'd call Beacon and get another car, and who knew what would happen after that? Something different, that's all. Let the hustles run without him for a while. A guy was crazy to spend all his life hustling a dollar, anyway. Where'd it get you? What you wanted was a person, and something to laugh about.

It was a weird thing, but the search for the Dancing Aztec Priest was what had changed him around like this, starting with the revelation he'd had when he'd first seen the fags' living room. *There were other ways to live.* You could do something else, if you wanted. And if you had a reason. Like Bobbi Harwood, for instance, that was a reason.

When Bobbi came out, shiny-faced, he grinned at her and kissed her and then went into the bathroom while Bobbi went back downstairs to the kitchen, where she found Jerry's mother dropping a fistful of spaghettini into boiling water. Shutting the door behind herself, Bobbi said, "Is there anything I can do?"

"One thing."

"Yes?"

"Never, as long as you live, call me Mother Manelli. In the meantime, sit down at the table there, tell me about yourself. You Catholic?"

"No, I'm not," Bobbi said. "Does it matter?"

"Barbara," Mrs. Manelli said, "from what I can see the last few years, the *Church* isn't Catholic any more. You a New Yorker?"

Bobbi hesitated, and felt a sudden rush of elation and discovery. "Yes," she said, and grinned broadly, and said, "Originally from Maryland." And went on to give her life history to this round red woman who smelled like a tomato, while at the same time she was still trying inwardly to explain her recent history to herself.

What a day. When it had started she'd been on her way to California, alone, in a snazzy Jaguar, running away from her husband. Now she was in New York, without the snazzy Jaguar but *with* some sort of strange new man, who had at first stolen from her and then returned to her a statue that had at first been worthless, then worth a million dollars, then worthless again. And then she'd seen her husband Chuck in a roomful of strangers, and *he* had become a stranger. A shabby seedy down-at-the-heels stranger whose shoes didn't match, and whose haircut was too long and uneven, and whose facial expression was too wishy-washy and self-centered.

Things were shifting very fast. All her life Bobbi had thought about what would happen *ultimately*, would things work out *in the long run*, would everything be all right *from now on*. She and Chuck had spent ten years battling unsuccessfully for a permanent truce. And suddenly none of that mattered. She wasn't sure whether the run would be long or short, and she didn't care. She knew what was happening today, and she knew what would happen tomorrow, and she could make some guesses for maybe a week into the future. Who needed more than that?

When Jerry came downstairs, he and Bobbi grinned at one another, and Mrs. Manelli nodded and said, "That's one of the things they can't fake on television."

310

Jerry frowned at her. "What's that?"

"That look between two people." Draining the spaghettini, she said, "Jerry, go ask your father would he like a little something."

"I will," Bobbi said, and bounded up and out of the room.

Jerry, watching his mother watch Bobbi depart, said, "She's okay, Mom."

"She bounces a lot." Mrs. Manelli brought the bowl of spaghettini to the table. "One of my daughters married an Irish and the other one married a Jew. What's this you brought home?"

"I don't know for sure. I think she's a Wasp."

"Good," said Mrs. Manelli. "This place has been needing some class. And *you*," she said, turning and pointing at her entering husband, "you get out of here with those worms."

# SIX
# MONTHS
# AFTER THE
# SEARCH

The Inter-Air Forwarding truck came to a stop at Southern Air Freight and Floyd hopped out, wearing his white coveralls and aviator's sunglasses and carrying his clipboard. "Hello, Hiram," he said to the guard. His breath frosted in the crisp December air.

"How you doing, Floyd?"

"Not too bad. Got a couple pickups here," Floyd said, and cast an eye over the nearby stacks of cargo.

"How's your partner Jerry?"

"Still out at the West Coast office," Floyd said. A sack of registered mail from Brazil struck his fancy. "There it is."

Hiram helped him carry the mail sack and a wooden crate marked FRAGILE over to the truck. "Thanks," Floyd said. "See you around, Hiram."

"Have a nice day," Hiram said.


But where's the statue?


Frank McCann and August Corella and Chuck Harwood, an unlikely trio, were together in Chuck's apartment, where they had spent a lot of time in the last six months. "It doesn't make sense," Frank said, for about the millionth time. "None of it makes sense."

"There's an answer to it," Corella told him, and ran distracted fingers through his oily hair. "*Somewhere* there's an answer to it." Turning his embittered expression on Chuck, he said, "*You're* a goddam college professor, why don't you figure the goddam thing out?"

Chuck never bothered to answer jibes like that. As usual, he merely sighed and went on studying the list of Open Sports Committee members, with the record of what had happened to each of the sixteen statues.

Corella kept prodding. "There's only the three of us left," he said. "Everybody else quit, so when we find it it's *ours*. A million dollars, split three ways!"

"We know," Frank said. "But it just doesn't make sense."

"Somewhere," Corella said. "Somewhere."

314

Pedro, naked, thinner, and yet healthier-looking than when he'd first arrived in the United States, tiptoed into the living room, his arms full of clothing. But he was only halfway to the door when Felicity, also naked, came giggling and jiggling after him, to grab him by a part that couldn't refuse and lead him back to the bedroom.

"Mother of Mercy," moaned Pedro, "is this the end of Pedro?"


"Yes, Mr. Susskind," said Edwardo Brazzo, "the people of my brave little country have put up with the dictator Malagua long enough. With the kind help of the American people"—he gestured gracefully toward the TV camera—"we will raise sufficient money, José here and I, to purchase the armaments we need to *liberate* our poor tortured nation!"

"That's very interesting," said David Susskind.


But where's the goddam statue?


Mel came whistling down the stairs to find Mandy at the dining room table, reading the galleys of *The Neurotic and the Profane.* "Mm *mm*," she said, looking up with a roguish glint in her eye. "This a *dirty* book!"

"That's what the public wants!" Mel told her cheerfully, and went out to the kitchen to smack Angela on the bottom, kiss her on the lips, and have a cup of coffee. "Terrific day!" he announced.

"Every day is, with you, lover," Angela said, and nuzzled his neck.

"Got to get to those galleys, though," Mel said. "I'm not sure Mandy should be reading that sort of thing."

"Why not? She's free, black, and twenty-one."

Mel frowned over that one, but then he let it go. Why break in on the sunshine of his existence?

The encouragement he'd received from Frank and Floyd, during that long day of reading and comments and criticism back in June, had pushed Mel over the top on the book, and damn if the first publisher he'd sent it to hadn't bought the thing! A September publication was anticipated, biggest thing on the publisher's fall list. Already Mel's coast-to-coast publicity tour was being set up, and if the book did as well as expected he'd just about be able to retire on the movie money alone. (The movie sale was already made, but escalator clauses would give him extra payments if the book made it to, and stayed on, *The New York Times* best-seller list.)

Angela said, "We got a postcard from Jerry and Bobbi yesterday."

"Oh? Where are they now?"

"New Orleans."


Yeah, yeah. But how about the golden statue?


In far-off Descalzo, in the capital city of Quetchyl (pronounced *Clutch*), in the dim adobe main corridor, curator Hector Ovella paused before the niche containing the Dancing Aztec Priest. Three children were making fun of it, as usual; giggling at it, prancing before it, trying to imitate its stance.

It looked so real. The finest example of José Caracha's art. And it gave just as much enjoyment to these disrespectful brats as had its predecessor. What do children care whether their plaything is gold or gilt, the original or the copy, priceless or valueless? In any event, the true original Priest long ago was flesh, and long since dead, that flesh ages ago converted to yams by the wonder of the natural order. And we eat the yams, and we are *all* the Dancing Aztec Priest.

Would Edwardo return, with Hector's share of the money? Hector sighed. He asked himself, if the situation were reversed, if *he* were in New York and Edwardo Brazzo were awaiting him here in Quetchyl, would *he* return?

How long before the museum in New York would announce its acquisition? Hector sighed again, and passed through the capering children, on toward his office. A jug of gluppe was there, under the desk.

Hector's tongue ached.


But the *real* statue. Where *is* it?


It stood in the dark, silent, alone, cold to the touch, half-hidden among shoes and forgotten tennis rackets and the skirts of raincoats. The true gold of the body had been covered with gold paint, to make it look like an imitation of itself, but the emerald eyes had been left alone, and even

316

in the blackness of the closet they glittered with malevolence.

Whenever Wally opened that closet, he glanced down at the corner where the statue danced, and smiled a secret smile. "Coming, Mom!" he would cry, but then he would smile again at the statue, because he could *leave any time he wanted.*

In his dreams sometimes he had already left, was in Paris or Hawaii or Rio, had money and rich clothing and charm and beautiful women. Guitar music played around him, fountains under green and rose lights splashed in the background, he had everything he wanted. But in other dreams he performed again the sequence of acts that had brought the original, the real, the golden, the million-dollar Dancing Aztec Priest here, to this closet, ready to release him at an instant's notice. In his dream:

Mel Bernstein drops Ben Cohen's worthless statue into Wally's lap and walks off. Wally carries it to his car, runs with it to his car because a vague plan has entered his mind; he will join with Mel Bernstein, will stay with that group until the real statue is found, will switch this one with the real one and make his getaway. Into his canvas bag goes the Cohen statue, and back to Mel Wally goes, and makes their pact. And carries the Cohen statue into the Moorwood house, and *finds the right one!* At once! The creature grins at him, there in that house full of dancing, laughing, drinking, eating, fucking, running, swimming, *living* people, the creature prances for Wally alone. And Wally tosses out the Cohen statue in the bag to Mel Bernstein, who runs away. Leaving Wally with the statue. Alone, with the statue. Alone.

At first he's terrified he'll be discovered, but as he moves through the house, clutching the golden figure to his chest, he realizes these people can't see him. He's invisible. *With* the statue, he's still invisible, these swirling partygoers can't see him, never will see him. And home he runs, like a cockroach scrambling when a light is turned on. Home. Safe. Until he's ready.

That was the dream, and every time he had it Wally woke up trembling and perspiring, then almost fainting with relief to find the familiar four walls of his own room about him. And the Dancing Aztec Priest still in its corner of the closet. His passport. His escape. As soon as he was ready.

Any time he opened the closet door, for whatever reason, he always paused and looked obliquely downward, his glinting eyes and the glinting eyes of the Dancing Aztec Priest striking green fire together. Any time he wanted. It was all there waiting for him, any time he wanted.

"Coming, Mom!"

The green eyes glittered, and Wally closed the door.

Jerry opened the door of their room at the Royal Orleans Hotel and said, "How ya doin, baby?"

"Fine," Bobbi said. "Sending postca—*mf.*"

So they kissed awhile, and then she finished the sentence: "Sending postcards to some people in the orchestra."

"Terrific. How'd you like to spend Christmas with snow?"

"Sure. Where?"

"Winnipeg."

"Winnipeg!"

"That's up in Canada."

"I know where it is," she said. "But Winnipeg? Why?"

"Why not? Christmas in Canada. Beacon has a car going there, ready to leave Thursday. I just got my dividend check from Floyd, so we can take off any time we're ready. And the great thing is, they got another car in Duluth, third of January, coming back down here! So we can have Christmas up in the north country and then get back here for the Mardi Gras. How about it?"

"I think it's wonderful," Bobbi said. "But what about you?"

"Me? It's my idea, isn't it?"

"When do you want to go back to New York?"

He shrugged. "April, May, something like that. Wait'll the warm weather."

She still didn't quite understand what his trucking business was all about, and in another indirect attempt to learn more she said, "But can you stay away from the business that long?"

"Floyd's doing fine without me, he said carelessly. "In fact, when we get back to the city I think maybe I'll sell Floyd the whole outfit. I was getting bored with it, anyway."

"What'll you do instead?"

"I don't know," he said, shrugging again. "There's always some hustle around, if you look for it. We'll work something out together, okay?"

She seemed to grin a lot these days. "Okay," she said.

"Where you want to eat tonight?"

"With you," she said.

Everybody in New York City wants something.

Every once in a while, somebody gets everything he wants.